I0831350

VAMPIRE DEBT

VAMPIRE TOWERS

KELLY ST. CLARE

Vampire Debt
by Kelly St. Clare

Edited by Hot Tree Editing
Cover design by Covers by Christian

VAMPIRE DEBT

ABOUT THE AUTHOR

When Kelly is not reading or writing, she is lost in her latest reverie. Books have always been magical and mysterious to her. One day she decided to unravel this mystery and began writing.

Her works include *The Tainted Accords, Pirates of Felicity, and The Darkest Drae.*

Kelly resides in New Zealand with her ginger-haired husband, a great group of friends, and whatever animals she can add to her horde.

Join her newsletter tribe for sneak peeks, release news, and disjointed musings at kellystclare.com/free-gifts/

"A gem cannot be polished without friction."
- Lucius Annaeus Seneca

1

Attending my grandmother's funeral would seal my fate.

Behind the podium, I looked out at the gathered social leeches looking to get close to me without delay. Becoming the seventh richest person in the world had that effect.

They were human and, therefore, the least of my numerous concerns.

Numb denial warred with soul-aching fury and the cold knowledge that *vampires* were listening right now. Kyros would take my grandmother's funeral from me over my damn dead body.

My grandmother had loved lavender, so we were at the lavender fields of Bluff City's botanical gardens—much to the disgust of several of the wealthy attendees who appeared to think they'd melt with exposure to a public venue.

Why was my grandmother gone when these people were alive?

She'd upped and left forever. Her body rested in a white coffin to my right covered in lavender and pictures of her.

What am I doing here?

Standing beside me, Tommy cleared her throat and squeezed my hand. I took her hint, dropping my gaze to the speech I'd written, feeling my glasses slip down my nose.

"Agatha Le Spyre was my grandmother. She was my parent from age nine. She was—" *Oh, god.* A lump rose up my throat.

I hadn't cried since nine years old and I wasn't about to in front of these fuckers!

Tommy squeezed my sweating hand again, and I took a steadying breath.

"... She could whip a fly off a horse's back with her tongue and wit. Yet her kindness, her ethics, and her *wisdom* were undeniable. I'm not going to stand here and say she was a quiet, peaceful sort of woman. If you knew her, you wouldn't believe that."

Several people laughed.

The laughter from those in the front row—her *genuine* friends and long-held employees—I could accept. The people chuckling beyond that made me want to tear this speech, followed by their faces, into a million pieces.

"—but the truth she pursued was a quiet thing," I whispered.

"You got this, lovely," Tommy whispered.

Her sympathy nearly undid me. I blinked several times.

I wanted these fake bastards to fuck off. I never wanted to see them again. My hands shook for an entirely different reason, and I drew free of Tommy's hold to clutch the paper with both hands.

It's nearly over.

I tried again. "My grandmother inspired me. I hope to be half the person she was."

A choked cry from the crowd drew my attention. My hands clawed, the paper crinkled in protest.

Harriet Gregorian sat in the third row back crying her eyes out.

As I watched, she sobbed, clutching her manufactured chest.

Nope.

I screwed up the paper containing my speech.

"Uh, Basil?" Tommy hushed.

"I'm going off script," I told her.

She didn't need to be told twice. My ex-bestie backed the fuck up.

I rounded the podium.

These were the people who scrambled for any foothold against my family estate, tearing down others to get there. Or worse, kissing our asses for as long as I could recall. Not everyone, but most. It was a mistake to let them come.

"What the hell are you all doing here?" I demanded.

Harriet's tears switched off faster than a power outage. A small smirk curved her lips.

The guests turned to each other. Most in shock, some displayed pity for my *mourning breakdown*.

I'd show them a breakdown.

"I don't even recognise most of you." I hurled at those in the second row and beyond, fists balled on my hips. "You want to know something about Agatha Le Spyre? She hated your damn guts. She thought you were trash. Tony Freg? She told me once that your head was stuck so far up your ass, it was a miracle you didn't see the world through brown-tinted glasses."

Tony spluttered for a moment, then stood abruptly, clicking his fingers at his family before storming out.

I pulled up short.

What a great idea, Tony.

Clapping my hands loudly, I shouted, "Everyone beyond the front row, leave. *Right now.* You motherfucking leeches."

No one moved, gaping.

Oh? You don't believe me?

Turning, I picked up a vase of flowers off my grandmother's coffin and whirled.

A hand gripped my wrist.

"You heard her," Tommy called loudly, jerking her head. "Everyone but the front row out. Agatha wouldn't want you here."

The rich bastards left in a trickle. If they expected me to run after them and throw myself at their feet, they'd be sorely disappointed.

It'd be a cold day in hell when that happened.

Tommy released my wrist.

"Why'd you stop me?" I grumbled. That vase was heading straight for Harriet's face.

"Because that's the vase of flowers I brought," she replied, snatching the vase and replacing it on my grandmother's coffin.

Fair enough.

Straightening my blazer, I circled my head in an attempt to loosen the tension in my neck. Not happening.

Dropping my chin, my gaze landed on those in the front row—not a single one of them under sixty-five.

Sir Olythieu's lips twitched.

Mrs Syrre choked on a snort.

My mouth curved.

A whoop went up. Mr Dithis and Lady Treena held each other up.

Laughter bubbled up my throat.

Tommy's father, Mr Tetley, clutched his stomach, tears rolling down his face—tears I suspected weren't purely from mirth.

I supported myself on my grandmother's coffin as I doubled over, gasping for air between soul-shaking bouts of laughter.

"That was fucking perfect," Mr Hothen howled.

Dame Burke wasn't amused. "Those cunts. Closing in on Basilia like that." Being from Australia, *cunt* was her favourite word—to the constant horror of strangers within listening distance.

Sir Olythieu, owner of *Bluff City Bank*, used his cane to push to his feet. "They tried. Our Basilia told them where to go."

"Best funeral ever," Lady Treena said, raising her token glass of champagne in salute.

Fred, my grandmother's butler, approached at a staid pace. The familiar grey-haired man had never lost his military training. He'd read stories to me as a child and always protected my family.

He wasn't laughing.

My smile faded as Fred took my hand and kissed it, his brush moustache itching the skin there. The last time he blurred professional lines like this was twelve years ago when my parents died.

He met my gaze, brown eyes filled with unshed tears, and I tensed as the burning behind my eyes surged anew.

Not today. Not here.

"Your grandmother would have loved that," Fred murmured, squeezing my hand. "She adored you so much, Miss Le Spyre. Everything she did was for you."

And there it was—the moment I'd been waiting for.

He'd just said my real name aloud.

For a month, I'd been *Miss Tetley*. And for good reason.

Unaware of what he'd just done, Fred tugged me into his arms. I went, resting my head against his familiar chest, inhaling his soap smell. Part of me had held out hope Kyros wouldn't discover the truth via the guards who followed me everywhere. That hope disintegrated as I swayed gently in the butler's wiry embrace.

"I'm sorry I had to discuss funeral plans via email," I murmured.

"I understand why you had to."

I drew away. *You do?*

"Talking about death aloud can be difficult." Fred continued, deflating my hope all over again. "Makes things more real somehow."

"Right," I replied softly, nodding to mask my crushing disappointment.

He held me at arm's length. "Are you coming back to the estate after the burial?"

I'd run from the estate a month ago, and ironically there was no place I'd rather be right now. "I can't come yet, Fred," I answered. "It's too painful."

Not a total lie.

I wasn't sure I could bear to see her suite—the place she died. I'd have to walk through the halls, the kitchen, and the lavender tiers where we'd shared so many beautiful memories that seemed so impersonal and cold now she wasn't here to share more with me.

Really, my return to the estate depended on how Kyros intended to use my fortune when my guards reported back after the funeral. Maybe they were on the phone to him right now. While most of my regular crew hung around the perimeter of the botanical gardens on constant lookout for the Tonyi triplets, Laurel hadn't budged when I'd requested she also linger out of earshot.

Fred's eyes misted. "Of course, Miss Le Spyre. I hope to see you at the estate very soon."

"In the meantime, could you please make sure everything is cared for?"

Fred swallowed hard, his voice hoarse when he said, "You don't even need to ask."

Throat constricting, I turned back to my grandmother's coffin, feeling his grip on me fall away.

Her coffin was white with silver handles and covered in lavender. None of the trimmings changed that my last family member was now contained in a wooden box.

How can that be right?

I'd forced myself to look upon her embalmed body before the casket was sealed. She'd been a virtual stranger to me with her eyes closed. Whoever saw people with their eyes closed like that? It wasn't a thought I'd had before that moment, but something that unsettled me greatly until I peeked under the silk blanket covering her legs and spotted her wrinkled hands.

Her hands, I *knew*.

My grandmother *was* in the casket.

She was dead.

I squeezed my eyes shut, the powerful scent of lavender invading my senses.

The remaining guests squeezed my shoulders, whispering their hollow goodbyes to a person they'd loved. Some joked, some cried, and some said nothing at all.

Yet there was no artifice during my grandmother's farewell, and that felt like the first right thing to happen in a long time.

Agatha Le Spyre had deserved no less.

"Basil, the hearse is waiting." Tommy's soft voice drifted to me.

My forevermore love, Grandmother.

"I'm ready," I said around the lump in my throat.

A leaden weight dragged me down as six of us slid her coffin into the funeral car, and as the few guests ambled away to find their chauffeurs, my heart began to pound. It took my palms slickening to identify the cause.

I'd learned to compartmentalise the natural fear Vissimo induced in humans after a month in *Kyros Sky*. My body reacted, but unless the vampire was unmuted, I could generally think and act through the fear.

"I can follow behind the hearse if you'd like to ride with your grandmother," Laurel said from behind me.

I faced the Indebted, dread filling me despite knowing this route was inevitable.

She knew who I was—who I *really* was. Not Basilia Tetley, born and raised in Orange. Basilia Le Spyre, the new head of a hundred-and-fourteen-billion-dollar estate—at the last count.

"I know you can't keep things from him." I squared my shoulders. After swapping blood with Kyros three times, I wasn't sure I could either. But Laurel was in debt, a slave, to pay off her father's crimes, and Kyros was her master.

Laurel's blue eyes burned brighter than usual, a rare lapse in control.

"I can keep this between us," she stated, muting her gaze again.

My mouth dried. "That can't be without consequences."

Her lips pressed together.

Yep, called it.

"I appreciate your loyalty, Laurel," I said, my eyes trailing toward the hearse. "I won't risk adding to your burden. This is my shitshow, not yours."

I stepped in the direction of the funeral car.

"Are you aware of what Kyros will do if he discovers who you really are, Miss Le Spyre? Are you aware of what it would mean for *Ingenium*?"

Hearing my real name on a Vissimo's lips was... foreign. My heart hammered at the thought of standing before Kyros when he learned the truth. And yet part of me just didn't care. My grandmother was *dead*.

I halted, my gaze darting where Tommy lingered just out of listening distance. She watched us with keen eyes.

"A fair idea," I answered quietly. *He'll drain me until I'm dry*—whether for my money, assets, or connections.

Maybe he'd literally drain me dry.

Hell, if I had a family and their lives were under threat, I'd use Kyros to help save them in a heartbeat. I understood why he'd fuck me over even if I hated him for it.

But perhaps I shouldn't be so quick to dismiss Laurel's help. I was so far out of my depth, I didn't know up from down.

She spoke again. "I'll follow you to the cemetery so you can ride with your grandmother, Miss Tetley. And you can count on my discretion."

2

My ears popped as the elevator shot down from Level 61 where I slept to Level 44 where I worked.

Live Right Realty was the human face of Kyros's operations. He controlled the realty, rental, and leasing industry for Clan Sundulus in the game.

Once a human knew the secrets of this vampire tower, there was no going back. But I was still *Miss Tetley*, thanks to Laurel. That meant I wasn't being taken advantage of because of who I was.

Yet.

It *did* present an entirely different set of problems that my grief-numbed mind didn't want to work through.

For instance, when I'd agreed to the second blood exchange, it wasn't in the knowledge that Kyros would then feel my location for the rest of my life. *Anywhere* in the world. Anger thrummed deep in my stomach as Kyros's dishonesty hit me for the umpteenth time in the last week.

I couldn't run. He'd always find me.

That meant that without good reason, I couldn't return to the estate as Miss Tetley either.

Kyros lied and placed me in a cage I'd never be free of. With my grandmother's death, I hadn't processed just how much that had fucked my life. At all.

Ding!

I glared at the elevator as the doors slid open, smoothing my loose white tee, tucked into high-waisted, straight-leg trousers—also white. I really needed to get my own fucking clothes. *Stat.*

Head down, I beelined for my office.

"Miss Tetley?"

Nearly made it to the corner today. *Dammit.*

Angelica, Kyros's matchmaking aunt, was about to request I take the day off. *Again*. She'd done it every day since my grandmother died. Each day I'd replied that I wanted to work.

The truth.

Stewing in grief alone in my hotel room here? *No, thanks.*

Wearily, I glanced at the reception desk.

Angelica wasn't alone.

Kyros straightened from where he'd leant on the desk. His meadow-green gaze scanned me from head to toe, returning to my face where they stayed.

So many conflicting emotions assaulted me at once that I closed my eyes. *Lust, hurt, anger, loathing, bitterness, yearning.* Each of them fought for first spot, and I reached a hand to my head, dizziness assaulting me.

"Miss Tetley," Angelica repeated.

Stilling, I didn't bother looking at Kyros again. He'd seriously fucked up. So many times I'd lost count.

"Angelica," I replied calmly. "I'm staying at work. Please stop asking me the same question every day. If I want to be elsewhere, I will tell you."

She cut off, halfway through the inevitable request for me to take time to grieve.

"Is that all?" I said bluntly.

For the last month, Angelica had done nothing but manipulate Kyros and I into each other's company.

I'd told her I didn't like games.

She'd continued to play them.

My goodwill was officially expired.

"We're worried about you," she said, casting a look at her hulking nephew.

The other half of the *we* couldn't speak for himself?

She rounded the desk, standing between us. "We just wanted to say that we're sorry about the passing of your grandmother. It was a heart attack?"

And there it was.

Every Vissimo in this tower found out my grandmother's death as I did—their sensitive hearing made it hard to keep secrets within the confines of *Kyros Sky*.

Yet only the Indebted came to speak their condolences.

My voice was ice. "A heart attack, yes."

I wouldn't look at him. Because he'd see everything in my eyes. He'd see how much I still craved his touch. How much I didn't want him to touch me at all. How much pain I was in.

The third blood exchange hadn't solved the tension between us one bit. The draw to him was an itch under my skin. Now, Kyros occupied my mind *at all times*; however, his presence made things exponentially worse. The urge to go to him. To feel him. To have his hands on my body somewhere. *Anywhere*.

Nearly overwhelming, and a headache I couldn't take.

Especially when I hadn't seen hide nor hair of him since the thrall of our unplanned third blood exchange ended. For a month, I couldn't get him off my fucking back. Since I last drank his blood in a basement, surrounded by his enemies, petrol, and in a pool of blood. Not a damn peep.

"You have our sincere condolences," Angelica said, dipping her head.

I snorted. "Cool. Thanks. That it?"

"We need to discuss the developments between us."

Oh, he *could* speak?

His eyes bored into the side of my face. "We sure do," I said sweetly. "Is now convenient for you?"

A wise man wouldn't have answered.

"It is," he replied, face impassive.

The wave of conflicting emotions slammed into me anew, and my head spun.

What the hell was going on?

"That's a shame," I murmured, turning away as I blinked through the dizziness assaulting me. "Any time in the last week would have been convenient for *me*. Now, I'm all booked up."

He hadn't texted.

He hadn't visited.

He hadn't sent so much as a minion to check on me.

No flowers. No apologies. No fucks given.

Message received.

"Don't turn your back on me." His snarl filled the space.

My heart leapt at the sound, sputtering in fear.

"How *rude*." I bowed low as I backed down the hall to my office. "This is how you prefer people to leave your royal presence, right?"

Angelica edged from between us, her downcast gaze turned in Kyros's direction.

The vampire placed a hand in his trouser pocket, face hardening in the first sign of emotion he'd displayed. I recognised the gesture for the brittle hold on his alpha temper that it was.

My laugh was just as brittle.

Nearly at my office, perhaps the wisest thing to do would have been to remain mute.

I spun to enter the room, saying, "What a fucking joke."

He was just *there*.

Kyros spun me so fast my knees buckled. Only his grip on my arms held me upright.

"What's a fucking joke?" he hissed.

You.

This.

Everything.

Life.

Angelica's voice was a mere whisper. "Sir, consider taking care. She's human."

Clever phrasing. A direct order could inspire a new tantrum from the crown prince. Usually, I understood that Kyros strove constantly for control over his alpha nature. He hated being victim to his own possessiveness.

Right now?

I tried to shake his hold. He let go, and I placed both hands on his chest, shoving as hard as I could.

"Just leave," I shouted up into his face.

He wanted to go. I could see it. Since we'd met, part of him never wanted to be around me, and it was no different now.

The sentiment was entirely returned.

"Let me guess?" I panted from the heat of our bodies touching. "You need something? *That's* why you're here."

I shoved him again to zero effect.

"Stop," he ordered, capturing my wrists.

I tried to pull away. His grip didn't alter, and panic found me.

"Let me go." I kicked out, barely recognising my voice.

"You can't run away from this, Basilia," Kyros said, his eyes dimming.

I can. I will.

"Why not?" I spat at him. "You want to."

He didn't deny it. I could take solace in that. We were as miserable and trapped as each other.

My head tipped back as I laughed—my usual throaty sound warped to bitterness. Because the third blood exchange we'd completed was important for a whole other reason. Yet another thing I hadn't paused to decipher since my grandmother's death.

If Kyros and I weren't mates, we'd feel nothing for each other. No itch under the skin. No drive to touch each other.

My laughter swelled. "Your true mate is a fucking human."

Now I'd said the words aloud, I realised that was about the most hilarious thing in my life.

"*Stop*," Kyros rumbled, shaking me hard enough to rattle my teeth.

To no effect. My laughter continued.

He bowed his head, holding my wrists tight as I whooped at the shitshow of my life. No friends under the age of sixty. No family. No fucking chance.

Kyros swayed in rhythm to my vicious efforts to be free, his head still bowed, and his expression serene.

No one was more disappointed than I when my manic laughter wouldn't go the distance against Kyros's meditative state.

"Please let me go," I whispered, wrung out. *Free me.*

The Vissimo game master didn't obey. *Surprise, surprise.* Lifting his head, he tugged me against him instead.

"Don't you dare," I snapped.

His arms tightened. "I'm here now, Basilia."

I didn't need him *now*. Even with his bullshit fucking lie about the second exchange, I might have accepted his support a week ago. Now, I refused to *need* anything from a Vissimo.

The funniest thing of all? Only blood bullshit was making me want this contact or his arms around me. The itch under my skin, the drive to touch him. None of that was *real*. Not like my friendship with Tommy had been real.

Not like the burning truth of my grandmother's love.

I didn't relax in his embrace, and eventually, Kyros let go.

Round two to Basi.

"Why are you here?" I flung at him.

"My sisters told me about the conversation you had with them during the thrall."

"About you being able to feel where I am for the rest of my life?" I asked in a dangerous voice.

He searched my face. "Yes. That."

"Is that why you took a week to talk to me? I pegged you for an asshole, not a scared asshole."

His jaw ticked. "I had things to attend to."

Ingenium. "I hope the game goes fruitfully."

I got why he had to play, but their game hurt people. *Me.* Tommy. The citizens of Bluff City. The clans compelled human liaisons who likely lived in daily fear.

... *Rhys*, whose funeral I'd missed while in the injured haze of my third thrall. Not that I would have attended anyway, being partially responsible for his death.

Kyros's nostrils flared, but his voice remained steady. "It is. Thanks to the property you secured in Black... amongst other things."

I didn't need the pointed look accompanying his words.

Sundulus bluffed Clan Fyrlia into entering a massive development deal for re-zoned agricultural land. The subdivision developer was a heroin addict—something I'd picked up on—and they expected the deal to fall through.

Whatever. I didn't have two fucks to rub together where *Ingenium* was concerned. What I *was* concerned with were the Tonyi triplets.

When Clan Fyrlia attacked me ten days ago, they had specific knowledge of the weak spots in my route. Which meant...

"There's another matter we need to discuss," I told him. "Someone in this tower is a—"

He blurred, covering my mouth with his behemoth hand. And *Zeus's left nut*, I tried not to acknowledge how perfect his warm, calloused hand felt against my mouth and skin. How did a crown prince even have callouses?

And why couldn't I hate him in peace?

I *hated* it. I hated him.

Whipping out his phone, Kyros typed a message.

I've been interviewing suspects all week

I sniffed in disdain and grabbed his phone.

One week and you haven't found them yet?

His lips twitched.

You could do better?

Ice filled me as I typed a final message.

I was a teen girl far more recently than you. YES.

Kyros scowled.

Fool. It was a compliment—teen girls were fucking smart at this shit.

He considered me, and I refused to break away first. In addition to what Fyrlia put me through, five Indebted were now dead and another barely recovered because of the spy in Kyros's ranks.

The vampire dipped his head. "Come."

Did he have to use that word in particular? "I have work to do."

I'd planned on visiting three properties in three different suburbs to hedge my bets on which colour we'd land on at the midnight roll. It made sense to spread my time amongst the suburbs, so then I could hone in on the owners I'd warmed up. I'd secured six houses for *Live Right* already—all of them on the clan's trouble list.

"Not today," the vampire answered, taking my hand and all-but dragging me back to reception. "Angelica, clear Miss Tetley's day."

But diving into the personal lives of my growing clientele meant I wasn't required to think about my own.

"Yes, sir," she replied from behind.

Kyros glanced toward the stairs to the left of reception as we exited the wide hall.

"No," I growled.

If he took the stairs, I'd need to be in his arms.

His gaze narrowed an instant before he pounced, swinging me into his arms.

I shrieked as he *ran*, flinging my arms up to loop them around his neck.

Hmm, actually.

I squeezed tighter and tighter, only stopping when Kyros paused less than a minute later by his office desk on Level 65.

"You wouldn't be trying to strangle me, would you, Miss Tetley?" he murmured, punching in his stupidly long password.

"Yes," I answered, loosening my grip.

I'd only tried it on the off chance it would work, but only fire and beheading and irreversible damage to the heart killed them. Even then, the thought of killing Kyros was abhorrent because of the bond.

He pursed his lips.

Another burst of speed and I was bouncing on the massive bed in his minimalist, devoid-of-warmth excuse for a Batman lair.

"I thought you wanted to have a serious discussion with me," I bit out as he closed the door. "How can you even *think* that I'd sleep with you after all the lies and stunts you've pulled?"

His green eyes darkened over crooked lips. "This room is soundproof."

Forgot about that.

Dammit.

"Right." I could have told the jackass there was a soundproof hot water cupboard on Level 44.

Avoiding his intense stare, my gaze snagged on the pinecone I'd gifted him for saving my life.

He'd put the Pinterest-induced embarrassment on top of his drawers.

One more regret. I wish I'd never given it to him.

I bounded off the bed and walked to the circle sofa but stopped halfway, staring at the furniture.

Me straddling him.

Him straddling me.

Blood pouring down my throat.

Pure heat surged within me—so white-hot I had to bite down on my whimper.

Shit.

The sexual tension after the third exchange was definitely stronger. The itch was almost a burn. Panic flooded me as the trapped feeling returned, only to be battled by a fierce longing and aching sadness.

I lifted a hand to my temple again.

My brain was on the fritz.

"We've exchanged blood three times," I whispered, glancing at the circle sofa in longing. Because it really was the most comfortable place to sit in his lair. "After the second swap, you could feel my location. What can you do to me now?"

I didn't plead for him to tell me straight. I didn't use one of my two remaining *honesty* questions. Honesty meant fuck all to this vampire. If the answer adversely affected the game and thus his family, he'd lie without batting an eyelid.

Kyros strode to the kitchenette on the opposite wall. There, he opened the small fridge and extracted a bag of red liquid.

My eyes widened on the plastic pouch.

Oh. My. God.

He poured the *blood* into a tall glass and tossed the drained bag into the bin under the sink.

Kyros's eyes locked on mine as he sipped.

Meanwhile, I was just relieved not to feel jealous over him drinking another person's blood. Thank fuck for small mercies.

He knocked back the contents of the glass as I decided whether the sight bothered me or not. After, Kyros ran his tongue over his teeth, removing traces of some unaware human.

Don't be turned on. It's weird.

"The third exchange changed things, yes," he answered.

"Did it get rid of the location thing?" I blurted, mentally crossing my fingers.

Kyros scowled. "Developments between us aren't erased, merely added to."

Fucking great.

I plonked down on the sofa at last, eyeing the blasted décor pinecone again.

Nope. Couldn't handle it being here.

I'd take the pinecone when I left.

"Tell me what new hold you have over me then," I said wearily, the hairs on the back of my neck rising with Kyros's position behind me.

"I thought you'd have noticed by now. I certainly have. But you've been... occupied."

Understatement of the century. "*Just fucking tell—*"

"We can feel each other's emotions."

What?

Pivoting on the sofa, I fixed on his face, waiting for the punchline.

"*Disbelief*," he said, arching a brow. "It's no joke, Miss Tetley. I may omit the truth on occasion, but I wouldn't joke about what we share."

Share? How was me losing every scrap of my life while he continued happy as Larry *sharing*?

"*Loathing. Loss*," he said quietly.

The mess of emotions I'd felt since the thrall ended was because I was feeling his emotions too.

My human mind wanted to baulk at that. Because *WTF*?

And yet, hadn't the swirl of emotions left me dizzy several times? When had that ever happened? How could a person be dizzy from *feeling* too much?

Shit, shit, shit.

His next word rang in my ears. "*Acceptance*."

I knew better than to question what could and could not be when it came to Vissimo. As Angelica once aptly said, *a mouse looking at a human would think they possessed magic.*

"How does it work? You can't hear my actual thoughts, right?" If so, I was screwed.

"That doesn't occur on this exchange, no."

I scoffed. "A fourth exchange? That's not happening. It may not have been your fault we swapped blood a third time, but that's where this circus ends."

"You're my true mate," he growled.

Cue eye-roll. "Yeah, and you look as thrilled about that as I am."

"Having you as a mate is my honour." He executed a small bow.

Colour me surprised his spine could bend like that.

"Save it, Kyros. I don't need to feel your emotions to know that's a lie."

He leaned against the bench—dressed in my favourite air-force blue suit.

Forcing away the itch to eliminate the space between us while throwing off my clothing, I asked, "Why are you offering so much information all of a sudden?"

"You deserve it. You're my mate."

I did my best to control my reaction to his words. Beneath my sarcastic mental snort was another emotion.

"Concealment?" I announced after a beat. "You're lying. You don't think I deserve the truth."

His disagreement to *that* was strong.

I shook my head, trying again. "I deserve the truth, but that isn't why you're telling me."

Shit.

Feeling his emotions could come in handy. *Really* handy.

He pushed off the bench. "To reiterate, I can't hear your thoughts. Only your emotion. Which is often hard to decipher unless the emotion is strong."

There was something he wasn't saying. That could join the slew of other *omissions* he'd made.

"*Relief, Suspicion,*" Kyros stated, amusement plain in his voice.

"I don't suppose this new development is affected by distance?"

"It is not."

I flopped back on the sofa, covering my face with both hands. "Why us?" I wasn't selfish enough to say why me. Not when he was so miserable about this too. The third exchange was forced on both of us.

Kyros wasn't amused anymore. "Who can say, Miss Tetley?"

An odd flash punctuated his comment. The emotion was gone before I could peg it. I had a personal lie detector for the eldest son of Clan Sundulus, and I'd practice this new ability whenever possible.

Swinging my legs down, I glanced at the pinecone again. "Is that everything I need to know about the third exchange?"

"The urges have intensified, we feel each other's emotion, and we are true mates. Yes."

Oh, was that all? Call me Overreacting Olive.

The sparkles I'd hot glued onto the pinecone caught the light streaming in through the ceiling-to-floor windows. I'd given the pinecone to Kyros in a weak moment—during the thrall, and just before Tommy came to tell me the terrible news about my grandmother.

My pinecones were for people who weren't narcissistic owners of towers and slaves.

I stood and lunged toward the dresser.

Kyros captured my wrists in one hand.

"That's cheating," I said, teeth clenched. Using his vampire speed wasn't allowed.

"Don't touch my pinecone," he said calmly.

"You're not allowed it anymore."

His eyes searched mine. "You gifted it to me for saving your life. Has that changed?"

"Just about everything else has."

"You knew I'd omitted the long-term consequence of the second blood exchange *prior* to gifting it."

I yanked, and he released my wrists. I nearly groaned at the sliding contact.

Jesus.

Hands on hips, I pinned him with my grandmother's quelling glare. "Other things have changed. I was in the thrall when I gave it to you."

"Tell me what has changed," he rushed in a low voice.

My fucking grandmother is dead, you callous bastard.

Kyros knew what had happened, but he couldn't know what that felt like because I hadn't *allowed* myself to feel everything since Tommy gave me the news.

He wanted to know what had *changed*?

Fine.

Holding his gaze, I thought of my grandmother lying in her open coffin looking like a stranger with her eyes closed. I thought of my fear that Laurel would report my real identity after the funeral; that my terror over that had overshadowed the grief that *should* have been my sole focus. I thought of the five Indebted who were no longer here, of hurting Tommy, and of my grandmother's friends who'd lost a part of themselves too.

Kyros's lips parted.

I thought of how I'd crawled to him across the ground of that basement, blood pouring from my stomach, unable to feel anything but white-hot fire roaring between us.

Kyros's eyes blazed. His breath hitched.

I was so alone.

Sinking.

I wanted to sink.

Why couldn't I sink?

When he reached for me, I stumbled away, shutting down the chasm I'd opened. Losing my parents made me pretty adept at slamming the door shut when needed.

"That's what changed," I whispered when I could trust my voice. "So keep the fucking pinecone. There are one hundred and twenty more in circulation anyway."

A tendril that wasn't mine panged in the centre of my chest.

Ignoring his hurt, I strode to the door.

"We're yet to discuss the spy in our midst," he called quietly.

We didn't have a midst.

Hand on the doorknob, I cocked my head to look at the vampire. "Is it fair to say that someone close to me is the most likely candidate?"

"You know what our hearing is like. But in my experience, spies work themselves into profitable positions."

"If they're close to me, I'll get back to you with the name in a week."

Kyros regarded me with surprise. "Is that so?"

I lifted a shoulder. "I grew up amongst wolves, Kyros. Watch and learn."

3

Sitting in the back, I leaned forward between the front seats. "Could you take the next right, Loz?"

Since the attack, Kyros hadn't allowed me to resume driving lessons. *Whatever*. It was hard to care about the driver's licence thing when my grandmother was buried in the ground.

Laurel checked the clock.

"I'll just be a minute," I assured her. The funeral service didn't start for half an hour.

After the argument with Kyros, I wasn't ready to feel the ache of another funeral so soon, but I owed it to the Vissimo who'd died saving my life to attend.

Laurel turned the car right without further comment.

"Just up here on the left," I instructed.

Josie, the Indebted who'd unfortunately introduced me to Pinterest in my second thrall, studied the orange roof. "Where are we? The roll put us on Green, didn't it?"

"Yeah. This is Mrs Gaughton's."

I waited for Josie to clamber out so I could slide from the vehicle. They no longer let me sit anywhere but the middle—Kyros's orders, I assumed.

It was now the norm for three Vissimo to sit behind me, one to sit on either side, and two to sit in front. I had a cage of fanged females.

A cage I was okay with after my run-in with Clan Fyrlia.

"I want to check on something," I told them before setting off up the steep driveway.

I stopped in front of a nearly lifeless lavender bush halfway to the front door.

Shoot.

"I said it was drought resistant, not drought *invincible.*" I specifically told Mrs Gaughton she should water the bush when the dirt was dry to the first knuckle.

"Has anyone got a bottle of water?" I said at normal volume, knowing my crew would hear.

Josie joined me, passing over a bottle.

I twisted off the cap, soaking the soil in a circle around the base of the dilapidated bush.

After that, I removed the dead heads, surprised Mrs Gaughton's curtain wasn't already twitching in response to my presence. Oh, but it was Sunday. She'd be at her *extended lunch*. Which was old-person code for getting plastered every weekend.

I slid back into the SUV. "All done."

The surrounding women exchanged glances, except Laurel, who simply looked at me in the rear-view mirror. She was at Grandmother's funeral. She could probably guess why lavender was important to me.

"Did you guys end up telling Lalitta about the service?" I asked.

The temperature in the SUV plummeted.

"Yes." Kelsea sniffed. She'd healed completely from near death in one week. Guess that told me all I needed to know about the healing properties of Vissimo blood. Their saliva worked on others too. At least, Kyros helped my stomach wound close with some serious licking in the basement.

"Kelsea," Laurel said low. The word, delivered in a calm tone of voice, was nevertheless an order.

I darted looks at them. "I'd never tell on you guys. Of my own volition." *Huh*, guess my ability to store secrets was as impaired as their own. Kyros could compel me at any time. Actually, any vampire could—but it was considered rude because I already shared a tie with another.

"I know, Miss Tetley," Laurel answered. "But Indebted who don't take care to always uphold the rules of servitude do not last long in our world."

Kelsea hung her head. "Sorry, Laurel."

"Always keep your guard up," replied the older vampire—who by now I'd gleaned was the Indebted's unofficial leader—of those in Kyros's tower at least.

At two-hundred-and-eighty-years-old, her status amongst them could be an age thing, yet Laurel had something more to her, a staidness that reminded me so much of my grandmother's unshakeable dignity. When she spoke, everyone listened, regardless of her position in their society.

I noticed our surroundings for the first time. "Where's the ceremony?"

"We bury our dead in the forest," Josie answered. "We can't afford graves unless we go into more debt."

Those in the SUV quietened, accentuating my harsh breaths. That was so fucking wrong. The Indebted died working for the clans because they *had* to in order to rejoin society one day. And they weren't given money to bury their comrades?

I had no words. Only disgust.

"It's okay, Miss Tetley," Kelsea said, picking up my hand. "We can feel how upset you are. That means more than you know."

Meeting her gaze, I nodded, squeezing her hand tightly.

We pulled up into the *botanical gardens* of Orange. The term was a running joke amongst locals. The closest thing people found to plants here were the tin-foil wrappings of old joints. Cigarette stubs littered the ground between broken bottles and junk food wrappings.

This patch of trees in the butthole of Bluff City was a place for druggies, drunks, and the desperate.

My stomach lurched with the wrongness of the situation as I

walked behind Laurel into the dense bush bordering the parking lot. "Will the others be here soon?"

We were the only ones here.

"Most came on foot. We don't have cars."

Good one, Basi. Keep rubbing in that they don't have money.

"Thank you for coming so soon after your grandmother's death," Laurel said, dropping back beside me. "This can't be comfortable for you."

I studied the vampire who carried the burden of much more pain than she showed. "Some discomfort should be felt."

She caught my gaze, her expression unfathomable.

We wound deeper into the trees, and my eyes widened as my heart began to splutter and kick. Vissimo were dotted throughout the small forest. *Everywhere.* Super hearing probably negated the need to crowd around the speaker or bodies, but I was grateful they'd spread out. My palms were slick with sweat, but the crowd was manageable to be around.

There had to be more than one hundred and twenty Indebted here—the number Kyros housed. I quickly counted those in sight. *Well* over one hundred in attendance. Four times that amount at least, and I had no idea how far the vampires had spread out through the trees.

I murmured as quietly as possible, ignoring the shake in my voice. "How many are being buried today?"

"Twelve," Kelsea replied.

Five belonged to us.

Indebted from Clan Fyrlia were here? Seven of the bodies belonged to their side. My brows shot up. Laurel had explained that the Indebted didn't separate themselves by clan. I guess that meant *at all.* But *shit,* these guys had killed five of their brethren.

Laurel cut me a hasty look. "I should have warned you. I can take you back to the tower—"

I held up my trembling hand, heart twisting as I thought of the times my grandmother had done the same. "Not necessary. There aren't any sides. I get it. They had their orders, and you had yours."

I couldn't fathom that the opposing Indebted weren't at each other's throats though. That was crazy forgiveness right there.

A hushed murmur rustled through the ranks at my comment.

Good or bad? *No idea.* I swallowed back as much of the automatic fear response as possible, focusing on the proceedings.

"We'll wait here," Josie whispered.

"'Kay." I stepped back beside her, surrounded by my crew.

A sinister growl slipped through the air, cutting off abruptly as Lalitta, Kyros's second youngest sister, strode into the clearing. Dressed to the nines with 1950s flare, she altered her direction when she spotted me. She smiled, unwinding the scarf from around her wide hat before removing her cat-eye glasses with flourish.

"Lalitta," I greeted in a low voice, hoping to convey the urge for her to stop being so fucking flamboyant.

She kissed me on both cheeks. "Basilia, sweet thing. How are you?"

Subtlety was a no-go. "Good. But you're gonna have to shut up. The funeral is starting."

The princess blanched, removing her hat. Her hair was perfect underneath. How the hell did she manage that?

"So sorry," she called. "Do continue."

Laurel was alone in appearing serene after the casual order. The princess was the sweetest of Kyros's sisters. But she'd just established her position amongst those gathered with one word. Sometimes, forgetting her alpha status was too easy.

I cut a second look at her as Laurel started speaking.

The princess's eyes were fixed straight ahead. *But there!* She darted a look to the trees and back. *Yep,* Lalitta was aware of Clan Fyrlia's presence alright. And she still strode into the midst of Fyrlia's fighting force, who could have orders to kill her. For all she'd known, this could turn into a blood bath.

Respect.

I took her hand, and her shoulders eased as I applied pressure, but she didn't glance my way.

"... Twelve have departed our ranks," Laurel was saying. "Too soon. For reasons and causes which are not our own."

Oh, shit. She was going there with Lalitta in tow?

"—but as always, *we* come together in peace after," she continued, her voice swelling. "We owe it to those we put to rest today. *Twelve* of our brothers and sisters. For as surely as we're not connected by blood, we are each other's only family as the centuries pass. We bury them with love. We remember them as *Vissimo*. As is our way, none shall leave this forest until only understanding and respect remains in their heart."

My palms grew slick with sweat as the emotion of the surrounding Vissimo soared.

Did Laurel usually handle the eulogy?

The Fyrlia Indebted deferred to her authority, clearly, but I was willing to bet the vampire had offered to take this particular service after Lalitta's request to be here.

I really hoped Laurel hadn't gotten herself into trouble with that move.

The row of Vissimo at her back stood aside, and I trained my gaze on the twelve blanket-wrapped corpses in the gap.

To hear twelve were dead and to *see* twelve were dead...

I breathed thinly as a high-pitched whine rang in my ears.

"Where are the coffins?" Lalitta asked.

I clamped down on her hand but stopped at the glittering quality in Laurel's eyes. Understanding coursed through me. That's why she'd agreed to the princess being here.

This moment could be crucial to the future rights of the Indebted.

"They can't afford coffins," I replied, not bothering to lower my voice.

"What? Not at *all*?"

"How are they meant to pay for them?" I said, frowning at the painfully beautiful royal. "They're forced to bury their dead in the asshole of Bluff City in blankets because the only way to afford a coffin would be to enslave themselves for longer. Would you want your family buried here, Lalitta? What if it was Francesca, Neelan, or Lionel in those blankets?"

The princess swallowed hard, blood welling in her eyes. "I'll pay for coffins."

"*You think they want you to cover the bill?*" I asked. I felt like ten kinds of butthole for being so relentless, but I wouldn't have bothered if someone like Rory was here instead of her, so it was kind of a compliment.

The princess bowed her head. "No."

I dropped her hand. "No, so don't offend these Vissimo by offering."

"*Vissimo.*" The word was passed around, alarm or surprise tinging the word.

Yeah, I'd decided not to use the word Indebted aloud any longer. Which was probably a massive faux pas.

I spoke louder. "I apologise, Laurel. Please continue."

Laurel bowed low to me, and a second jerking ripple ran through the ranks.

Ugh. I didn't like it when she bowed. That was the second time.

The reverence didn't sit well with me because I wasn't sure whether the gesture meant something more to vampires. If a human friend bowed to me, I'd assume they were drunk.

The vampires closest to Laurel lowered the twelve bodies into one large grave. A mass grave. The thought made me nauseous. Then again, these people weren't dying nameless. They were being buried alongside their brethren, their comrades. Wherever they ended up, they'd have good company.

I wished my grandmother had someone with her in the ground instead of being alone in that white box with silver handles.

I closed my eyes, heart thumping as I clenched my fists.

"Are you remembering your grandmother, Miss Tetley?" Kelsea said.

Opening my eyes, I scanned her blood-streaked face. "Just wondering why good people die when so many douchebuckets are alive."

She wiped her face. "It's shit, huh?"

Lalitta dug in her bag and pulled out a packet of tissues. She glanced at me, and when I nodded, she reached around me, handing the tissues to Kelsea.

"Have I thanked you for saving me yet?" I said to cover Kelsea's wariness as she took the tissues.

Her breath caught on a small laugh. "Only a million times."

I'd think of a way to pay that debt someday.

There weren't more speeches. Everyone paid their respects at the mass grave, some taking far longer than others, and then—without ceremony—the Indebted blurred away through the trees.

Back to slavery.

So fucking wrong. They should be given time to mourn.

I started out of the forest beside Lalitta, my crew trailing behind.

"Would you spend the rest of the afternoon with me, Miss Tetley?" The princess blurted when we reached the parking lot.

Whoa. Way to blindside a gal.

"Uh, thanks for the offer. Why?"

Lalitta wrinkled her cute button nose. "My siblings are on at me to do it."

Well, she was honest at least—couldn't say the same for Gerome. Or Rory. Or *Kyros.* Probably not Francesca, Neelan, or Pantsuit either. Lionel if the mood suited him perhaps. Meanwhile, Deirdre was *too* honest.

"They want you to screw with me to fuck with Kyros." I bit back on a groan.

Her brow cleared. "Oh, you know. Great."

Wait. "I'm not cool with that. Me and Kyros aren't in the mood for bullshit."

Lalitta stopped in front of her vehicle. The paint-chipped pick-up truck momentarily derailed my train of thought.

Did not see that coming.

"You're wrong about my eldest brother," she said, smiling.

Seemed like I was always wrong these days. "Wrong in what way?"

"My brother feels as trapped as you do. He's unsure how to reach you through his bindings."

More like unsure if he wants to reach at all.

"I don't want him reaching for me. That's all anyone has to know, including him."

She dipped her head. "As you say."

My eyes narrowed. That sounded a whole heap like when I said *I hear you*—aka *I'm listening but don't accept what is being said.*

"Regardless, my siblings are relentless in persuading me to steal you away. I don't intend to be unkind to you like Rory and Gerome, but it would mean a lot if you could pretend I was horrible after. Just to get them off my back."

I groaned, looking skyward. "You're fucking me."

"Is that a yes?"

Saying no to her was the equivalent of kicking a puppy. "Depends. What's on the cards."

"Movie?"

Okay, she had my attention. "Popcorn? I'm not watching anything sad or scary. Or romcoms. Hate that shit—apart from the Rebel Wilson one. But that's kind of a romcom for people who hate romcoms, you know? Wait, I'll watch anything with Jason Mamoa in it. That's all I'm in the mood for. A Jason Mamoa film."

Her brows crept up. "... We'll figure something out. Remember, I need you to tell everyone you had a really frightful time."

Really frightful time.

I snorted.

She could sing "A Spoonful of Sugar," and I'd believe she was Mary Poppins. Her plan was doomed to fail even if I held up my end of the bargain. "Sure, Lalitta. Take me to see Jason."

Jerking awake, I rolled in bed, fumbling for the screaming thing.

I cradled it in my hands, eyes shut.

"*Miss Tetley?*" a voice asked.

The shrill ringing that woke me had disappeared. *Magic.* "Invisibility cloak."

Faint laughter erupted.

"*I'll give you a moment to wake up.*"

I rubbed a hand over my eyes. "Daylight savings."

More faint laughter.

People were listening. Wait. *Oh my god.* I was in bed and holding my phone—aptly named Beast.

How…?

Blinking, I stared at the phone clutched in my hands before pressing Beast to my ear.

Who was I speaking to? "Angelica?"

"Yes, Miss Tetley. I apologise for the early call."

What *was* the time? I squinted at the offending blue light of my alarm clock.

"Shit, Angie. It's 2:00 a.m.!"

"I apologised for that."

I flopped on my back, bouncing with the mattress. "Your apology was good for a *7:00 a.m.* call. 2:00 a.m., and I'm gonna need more than that." Fucking vampires.

"Like what?"

"Get creative. You should be up to the task." She was with her matchmaking efforts.

She hummed. "I'll keep it in mind. Could you come up to Level 66?"

I groaned. "Humans sleep during the night."

"You told me once that you were a night owl."

"Your ability to selectively listen is incredible."

"One of our team leaders had an idea. We need to discuss it with you before presenting the idea to King Julius for approval at 3:30 a.m. It's important."

They thought it was important. All because two kings couldn't agree who'd knocked up a queen one hundred and fifty years ago. I found it hard to get worked up over that.

"You can't ask me over the phone?" I tried once more.

Silence.

Grumbling, I shuffled off the bed. "For the record, I'm *not* okay with this."

I hung up, glancing down at the fluffy rabbit onesie I'd purchased yesterday and worn to bed.

The movie date with Lalitta had morphed into a late-night shopping trip. After my money woes and the run-in with Clint, I ironically had nearly seventy thousand dollars from house commissions—the house in Black had bumped me up big time. I supposed it was extra ironic that I considered that a huge amount of money now, what with being in possession of a multi-billion-dollar estate.

I hadn't dared to buy anything—except materials for the décor pinecones—since screwing up so grandly during my first week. But the urge to no longer feel like a white-and-royal-blue wearing trophy wife had spurred me to flush several thousand dollars down the drain. The trip yielded a rack of clothing in every colour *but* white and royal blue.

And a rabbit onesie.

Oh well. I wasn't changing for anyone, let alone those bastards.

Swiping my card key off the bedside table, I set off for Level 66.

Beast was flashing red. He was either about to explode, die, or he had something to tell me.

I read the message from Tommy as I stepped onto the elevator:

How are you doing after the funeral?

After the funeral.

Her wording was intentional, a reminder about the fresh parameters of our tattered friendship. Losing Tommy would be one of the worst fuck-ups of my life—something I'd regret forever. I'd known that *before* cutting the ties between us. Except I was beginning to realise, I may not survive this storm without her.

When I lost my parents, I was surrounded by love and had the blissful resilience of youth on my side. I'd now lost my grandmother, and my appetite had faded to null again. The most substantial meal I'd had was popcorn at the movies last night.

I wasn't coping.

The elevator shot up as I typed out a vague reply that would pass through the security measures—otherwise known as Kyros's possessiveness—on Beast.

Getting by, thanks <3
How are you and your dad doing? <3 <3

Ding!

I hit Send and stepped off the lift, opened Snake as I weaved between the monitors and frantically typing Vissimo toward the glass room I'd once seen Kyros leave.

The top level of the tower was circular. Glass rooms occupied the outer perimeter while standing desks and monitors filled the rest of the floor space in uniform rows. The only break in pattern was a huge glass tube currently out of sight. That's where the dice roll was streamed each night.

I circled the snake around on the screen to collect another brick.

Yesss!

Fernando, one of the Indebted, said he'd reached a high score of 2300. I hadn't come within an eighth of that yet. I really did have a long way to go before I could call myself Snake Master.

Beast flew from my hand as I bounced off a Vissimo. The archaic phone slid across the ground.

Game over.

The female vampire gasped, blurring to pick up the phone.

"Miss Tetley, I didn't see you," the vampire rushed to say, bowing three times before I could blink once.

Taking the phone, I clicked the middle green button. The screen flared to life. Beast was still in working order. Thus, Snake could still be played.

"Don't worry about it," I replied. "I walk into people, too, sometimes—and nothing can kill phones from the 90s." Or whenever this hunk of crap was from.

Relief flooded her face. "Thank you."

Jesus. She needed a holiday.

I tucked Beast away in a front pocket of my rabbit onesie and sidestepped the drop-dead gorgeous woman.

"Is she wearing a rabbit onesuit?"

"They're called onesies, idiot."

Great. I'd found them. Their voices floating out of the glass room.

"I think it's adorable."

"I wouldn't be caught dead in that."

The sooner I could hear about this *plan*, the sooner I could get back to bed. To play Snake.

I eyed the nine royal children of Clan Sundulus and Angelica standing inside one of the glass offices. Easing between more furiously typing Vissimo, I ignored the screen of flashing colour blocks that represented Bluff City, entering the meeting room.

Lalitta blurred to my side, pulling up the hood of my onesie. "It has ears too."

Uh?

I peered at her. We'd been together when I bought it. We'd left the action movie early when Lalitta became too engrossed in the film. Let's just say her eyes lit up and shone two laser points on to the movie screen.

I grinned, and she rounded her eyes slightly.

Yeah, yeah. I remembered. I was *terrified*.

"What's that about?" Neelan asked, peering between us. Whether he intended to flex his muscles as he spoke or they just tended to ripple, I couldn't decide.

"Miss Tetley and I spent some time together yesterday," Lalitta said, baring her teeth. "If you *must* know."

Yep. Kyros looked super worried. Not. A quick search of his emotion platter confirmed his utter lack of concern.

But as though jolted, his face turned thunderous. "Where did you take her, Lalitta?"

She shrugged a shoulder. "That's between me and *Basilia*."

I'd let her call me that this once. Because I was terrified.

She continued, smirking. "I didn't hurt her too much."

Kyros stalked slowly to the long table occupying most of the rectangle space. "Lalitta—"

I stared at him, a wrinkle between my brows.

He wasn't feeling one *jot* of anger toward her. All I could detect was fondness.

"Right on, little sis." Gerome held up his hand. Lalitta slapped her palm against his, grinning wolfishly.

She strutted to her seat and plonked down, beaming.

My mouth bobbed.

They knew she'd done absolutely nothing to me and were pretending for her sake? Mostly dislike them, I may, but that was freakin' adorable.

I pushed my floppy bunny ears back.

Rory blurred to my side and yanked the hood up again. "If you're going to wear that, commit to the whole look. Plus, the hood covers your hair."

I shooed him away, glaring. "My hair looks that way because I just woke up."

"If you say so."

I squinted at his hairline. "At least I don't have grey hairs yet, old man."

He inhaled sharply and whirled away, pulling out his phone to get the camera up.

Pantsuit snorted and I shot her a wry look. Rory was Vain with a capital V.

"Does the one suit have a tail?" Neelan sneered.

I stomped my foot. "I didn't come up here to be quizzed about my onesie. It gets cold in my room and this is warm."

"Aw, she stomps her foot. Just like Thumper in *Bambi*."

I eyed Gerome. "You've seen *Bambi*?"

His mouth snapped shut with an audible click.

Francesca folded her arms. "How come *she* can stomp her foot, but I always get yelled at for it?"

Because you're a brat.

I placed my hands on my knees, smiling at her as I would a three-year-old. "I shouldn't have done that. It's a naughty, naughty habit."

Francesca snarled, bursting to her feet.

"It's embarrassing that you'd elect to wear that," Deirdre stated from where she sat, hands clasped behind her head. "You're a grown woman but look like a child."

My lips twitched. "Thanks for weighing in, Deirdre."

She dipped her head regally.

"It *does* have a tail," Neelan announced. He was behind me? "A little, furry tail."

A hand tugged the back of my suit.

I jumped. "Let go!"

He followed me in circles until I had the sense to stay still.

There were only a few sane people in the room, and holding myself rigid, I addressed one of them. "Why am I here, Angelica?"

"Please take a seat, Miss Tetley."

There went my hope for a quick yes-or-no wrap-up.

Lionel walked to the seat at the head of the table, drawing out the chair for me.

The seat was directly opposite Kyros's.

Lionel's wide smile faded as I took the seat next to Safina, a position that would best shield me from Kyros's view.

"Spit it out." I sighed.

"In your time at Live Right, you have secured six houses," *he* said.

The table was a much nicer place to look than to where Kyros loomed. I tuned into his emotions. *Determination*... maybe? Something fluttery sat beneath it though.

Hold the phone.

That wasn't pride...

Kyros was proud of *me*? Or himself?

Probably himself.

"That's an unusually high success rate," he continued after a beat.

Oh my god. He was proud of me. Go figure.

He added, "More unusual when you consider you were delegated our troublesome properties."

As punishment for a little misunderstanding with the law. I slid my hood down and glared at Safina when she whipped it back up. Pantsuit was meant to be the kickass reasonable one.

Dammit though. Still respected the shit out of her.

Francesca snickered, and Gerome whipped out his phone to take a picture.

Scrap that. Every single one of Kyros's siblings was a piece of shit.

"Miss Tetley," Kyros said in a delicious, *toe-curlingly* deep voice.

I straightened at the oily quality behind his words.

What was that feeling? I'd felt it yesterday when we'd spoke too.

Giving up, I peered down the table at the crown prince of Clan Sundulus.

His meadow-green eyes locked on mine like I was north and he was a compass. "We have gathered the difference is due to you being human."

I pressed my lips together at his serious expression.

He paused. "What's so funny?"

Shoot. "You guys are only just figuring that out?" I shook my head. "Of course that's the difference."

Nine scowls trained on me, plus Angelica's amused crook of the lips. Kyros was too smart to only be figuring this out now. *What?* He thought I was too stupid to put two and two together and decided to ease me in?

Oh, brother.

Kyros steepled his hands. "Every other day—during Clan Fyrlia's turn—instead of outside appointments, you will train my realtors in human behaviour."

Was he *high*?

"You want me to what now?" I blurted, brows climbing.

My response confused him.

"No," I said, standing. "Not happening."

A leaden quiet took hold of the room and plunged it into icy water.

Kyros's confusion slid directly to deep irritation. Fury exploded, followed by intense focus.

Was that him trying to control his alpha temper? Or was he trying to gauge my mood?

My head spun from the emotional influx and I drew in a steadying breath.

"Is that all?" I darted a look toward the door.

Safina leaned back after a swift look at Kyros. "Can we ask why you're saying no, Miss Tetley?"

Because I'm not teaching you to get better at taking advantage of the humans in this city.

"I'm not here by choice. You're acting like I give a single fuck about how this game pans out."

"Kyros is your true mate," Francesca said incredulously.

Vissimo were going to kill me one day. I didn't care that my blood told me Kyros was my mate. Or true mate. Or whatever the correct term was. That meant zilch to me.

Neelan pushed off the glass wall next to Gerome. "You'd stand for that disobedience from your staff, big bro?"

Kyros unfolded to his full height. "My *true mate*, Neelan."

Frustration. Wrath. Confusion. And something warm I didn't want to look too closely at. Hold on, there was that ugly oily quality again. Like a throbbing.

What the hell *was* that?

Kyros moved around the table at an ambling pace I didn't trust for one millisecond. "Basilia, are you allowing your decision to be dictated by what's happening between us?"

I crossed my arms, ignoring the rabbit ear flopping over my left eye. "I don't work any other way. If someone lies to me or treats me like crap, you better believe I won't lift a finger to help them."

"You secure houses for us."

"So I can spend a few hours outside this asylum."

"Might want to rein it in, Basil," Gerome hushed, eyeing his brother.

Yeah, the last bit got to him for sure. Kyros didn't like me displaying distaste for his blood or the homing beacon development after the second thrall. He didn't like me insulting his tower either.

Boohoo.

I eased from between the table and chair as Kyros stopped behind me. He didn't have a waistcoat on to match the form-fitting black jacket and trousers tonight, but the tie remained. I closed my eyes to shut out the sight of the vampire, doing my best to control the fierce awareness of how much I wanted to *touch* him.

The bond wanted me to rip off his clothes, shove him down on the table, and ride him until the sun rose. The itch under my skin burned to be satisfied.

"There doesn't have to be hate between us, Miss Tetley."

Lust. Frustration. Oily throbbing.

I scoffed, opening my eyes. "Really?"

"I'd rather have your willingness in this."

"I'd rather a lot of things, too, Kyros. What we'd *rather* doesn't always pan out." I stepped around him.

Distance was a very, very smart idea.

"Give me one good reason why you're refusing me? Something that isn't related to how things stand between us," he added when I opened my mouth.

Kyros folded his arms across the wide expanse of his firm chest.

They were talking to the *wrong* Basi. It was 2:30 a.m., not to mention anything else from the last week or beyond.

"*Because you're all fucking monsters*," I shouted, my hands balling. "The only ones who aren't are the people you keep shoved down on the lower levels."

I was about to detonate, and I really didn't want to do that.

Kyros stepped closer. "Miss Tetley—"

Oily throbbing.

I held up a hand. "Tell me, Kyros. Why do you feel that way each time you say my name?"

Shock. Fear.

What a surprise. Kyros was hiding more bullshit.

"Something big, huh?" I said sarcastically. "Nothing new then."

He turned away, and I took the opportunity to stride to the door.

His siblings watched in silence, eyes darting between us. Deirdre alone appeared bored by the proceedings.

"No is your final answer?" Kyros said in an even tone, still facing away.

I studied his back. "Sure is."

"Then this conversation is over," he stated.

Finally.

Pulling out Beast, I clicked my way back into Snake, noting the phone's depleted battery.

Tonight seemed like the perfect fucking time to set that high score.

4

I dodged another sloppy missile thrown by the upstanding Bluff City citizen, Mr Triffz.

"Get the fuck off my property, you barrel-scraping hooker," he bellowed.

Age showed in the fragility of his roar, but in the two minutes I'd known Mr Triffz, I'd realised he was anything but frail.

"I'm leaving!" I shouted back, dodging another missile as *slop*, from the throws he'd landed, slid from my hair.

He shook his cane in the air, reaching for the bucket by his feet. "Down with Live Right. You can't put me in a home!"

If this was happening to anyone else, I'd be in stitches. Which, when I dived into the car a moment later, was what I discovered my crew doing.

Laurel hit the acceleration as soon as I was in.

Their laughter rang in my ears as I groaned at my *new* black jeans and sheer white blouse combo. *Ruined.* I might be able to salvage the jeans and white bra, but the blouse was a goner.

"He's crazy," I snapped, plucking the blouse away from my chest.

Josie clutched her stomach. "I've never seen a human run so fast in six-inch heels."

Yeah, yeah. Laugh it up.

"Is it safe for you to be driving?" I asked Laurel. The SUV swerved all over the road. Blood streaked the vampire's face. Crying with laughter never looked so messed up.

She gasped for breath. "Didn't want to risk getting compost on the car."

"That's what this is?" No wonder it smelled so bad. Perhaps I should just be thankful the slop wasn't his shit.

From the middle seat, I stared through the windscreen, recounting the last ten minutes of my life. "It's safe to say, Live Right won't secure that house anytime soon." A house in Pink would always be owned by a human. There was *some* comfort in that, even if he was a compost-throwing sonofabitch.

I leaned forward. "Hey, can we—?"

"Nearly there," Laurel answered.

She pulled over outside Mrs Gaughton's less than a minute later, and I gave up the battle of keeping my white bra from damage. It was over.

Mr Triffz had won.

This round.

Certain the lavender bush would have guzzled the water I gave it three days ago, I reached into my *Elegance* pack and pulled out the bottle of water I'd brought along.

I'd barely taken a step when the front curtain twitched and a flash of garish red lipstick appeared in the gap.

The window opened a crack. "Basilia? That you?"

"Sure is, Mrs Gaughton. Just here to water your lavender bush. I stopped by the other day and it was looking sad."

The front door swung wide. "You came around? Why didn't you knock?"

Because knocking wasn't necessary when it came to Mrs Gaughton. I wonder if she had a rocking chair right at the front next to the window. "It was Sunday. I assumed you were at your extended lunch."

There was no reply, but a beat later, the entrance was yanked open. The mid-sixties woman barrelled down the driveway.

"I forgive you," she scolded, slightly out of breath. "And I told you to call me Mrs Hannah."

"I apologise, Mrs Hannah."

"Don't apologise." Her voice unfurled like a whip. "Just do it right next time."

Yikes.

Laughter bubbled up my throat, accompanied by a sadness that was no mystery.

She took me in. Her red lipstick had leaked into a few of the wrinkles around her mouth, and the sight drew a smile to my lips.

"You roll in something before coming here?" She blinked as though seeing me for the first time.

Grimacing, I stared down the length of my splattered body. "Went to meet a client who thought I wanted to put him in a home."

Mrs Gaughton patted my arm. "Can't win 'em all, dear."

Ain't that the truth. Hell, I'd just like to win one round at this point.

I unscrewed the cap, leaning forward to feel the ground around the lavender bush.

"Wondered why it hadn't died," she muttered, glaring at the plant.

Say what? "I thought you wanted it alive? You asked me for tips."

She hugged herself. "I do. I want it to flourish like Betty Neesin's."

Was she sure? Sounded like she had a personal vendetta against the poor bush.

"Not that I don't appreciate it, but why are you watering an old lady's plant?" she asked after a beat. "Are your messed-up body chemicals affecting your brain? I see those ads about mental health on the TV."

Lawdy.

"There's a lot wrong with my body chemicals," I told her, lopping a smile her way. *Especially my sex hormones.* "But no. Just thought I'd help out."

I became entirely focused on watering the lavender, emptying the entire bottle in the soil around it before plucking out a couple of tiny weeds. I squeezed out my top so some of the compost juice dripped around the bush.

Ha! Take that, you old jerk.

When I straightened, two keen eyes fixed on my face.

I peered down immediately, screwing the lid back on the bottle. "My grandmother died."

A weathered hand reached out and gripped my forearm.

"Oh, *Basilia*. Your grandmother who loved lavender?" Her voice warbled.

I nodded, glancing at the half-alive bush—a weak shadow of the estate's lavender tiers.

"I'm so sorry, Basilia. You meant a lot to her, so I know she meant a lot to you."

"How do you know that?" I whispered, clutching her forearm in return.

She smiled, displaying dentures smeared with red lipstick. "Because young women don't become like you without someone's devotion."

My heart squeezed and the pain of it spliced through me.

"Won't you come in for a cheese and onion toastie and peppermint tea? I stocked up on supplies in case you returned."

She had? For a stranger?

I loved this woman.

"I don't want to traipse compost sludge through your house, but how about I return in a few days for lunch and to check on the lavender bush again?"

Mrs Hannah glared at the plant once more.

What was her deal?

The older woman sighed heavily and faced me, mouth setting. "Between us both, we'll have the entire garden blooming."

Something was up, but it wasn't any of my business. "Sounds good to me."

Really, *really* good, actually.

Smiling to myself, I slid back into the middle seat of the SUV. None of the vampires said a word.

Mr Triffz was my last appointment of the day, and I'd already secured a house in Pink earlier that afternoon, a referral from Vernon Yersaw, my first success—I really was getting a rep for giving people far more money for their property than anyone else. Usually, I'd race back to see how much commission I earned through the house purchase. Now, I had so much money, I didn't know the exact billion-dollar amount after my absence.

"I don't want to go back just yet," I announced.

Kelsea slid me a twinkling look. "You don't want to wash all that crap off?"

"There is that..." I peered through the windscreen. "Are we near Traitor's Lane?"

Laurel zipped through Orange toward the freeway. "We are."

"Let's go that way."

She caught my gaze in the rear-view mirror, her Indebted cloak descending. "What's out there?"

"Guess you'll have to find out."

"No, really. I need to know for security reasons."

My smirk slid away. "A little waterfall." Owned by the ill-tempered Lygons, if she wanted to get *technical* about things. Growing up, everyone snuck in there to swim.

Josie snorted. "Laurel was playing you, Miss Tetley."

Dammit.

I folded my arms, dislodging more grime. "Fyrlia kidnapped me once. The triplets are after me for *real* now. And they're fucking psychos. If Laurel asks me a security question, I'm always going to answer."

"Which is exactly the right thing to do," Jillian piped up from the row behind. She was the youngest of my crew at forty-nine and tended to remain mute unless there was a chance to prove herself.

"Just here," I said, leaning forward to point. "We'll walk the rest of the way."

Laurel's gaze flicked up. "This is legal, right?"

I chh'd. "Course. Come on!"

Grinning, I led the seven Indebted along the quaint back road that formed the border between Orange and the estates. To my left, opulent wealth. To my right, behind a wall of trees, sat moulded walls, cracked paint, and missing roof tiles.

Stopping to remove my heels, I ducked through the treeline, waving them after me.

"Miss Tetley, the sign says No Trespassing," Josie murmured.

"Hmm, what?"

I picked up the pace, and in no time stood upon jutting boulders, staring across a few metres to the clear water below.

Whoa. Higher than I recalled.

"*Oh,*" Kelsea gasped, her blue eyes popping at the sight of the waterfall. Water erupted an arm-length down from our position atop the rockface, pounding into the pool.

"Have you seen a waterfall before?" I asked her.

"Only in pictures. I was born into servitude."

I gritted my teeth but bit back on my angry rant so as not to taint the moment. "Well, now you have."

I looked anew, trying to remember the first time I saw a waterfall, and whether I appreciated the sight as much as the vampire beside me.

A few furtive glances confirmed at least four of the Indebted were seeing a waterfall for the first time. Laurel was one hundred and forty when her father committed his crime, so she didn't appear overly excited. Josie and Vie were appreciative, but not wondrous like the others.

I eyed the drop, taking note of where the boulders were. "Time for a bath."

Stepping back, I ran and leaped from the rockface.

I yelped as a body crashed into mine mid-air. Arms wrapped tight around me. The water came rapidly to meet us, and we plummeted through the surface.

The cold tightened my chest, and I struggled until the arms loosened.

Kicking for the surface, I scowled at a drenched Laurel, sucking in air. "What did you do that for?"

"You didn't check the bottom," she snarled an inch from my face. "You had no idea how deep that water was."

It was plenty deep. "I've been here before."

"Conditions can change."

I'd never seen her lose her cool. I'd worried her. A lot. "You're right, that was stupid."

She shook her head and swam for the small beach opposite the rockface.

Eek. Really upset.

Cannon splashes erupted around me, the squeals of the six Indebted filling the tree clearing as they joined me in the pool.

I snorted as they surfaced and began dunking each other.

Hands shoved me down and I sucked in a breath, batting at their hands and breaking the surface again.

Kelsea shoved Josie away. "You're not supposed to dunk our *client*."

Josie cast me a guilty look. "It's Miss Tetley."

Did she know my real name? Maybe Laurel hadn't told the others. I'd just assumed she would or that the others listened in at the time. Maybe Josie was just used to calling me that now. I coughed, my body tiring quickly. *Shoot.* Perhaps I should force myself to eat more. "Seriously, I don't mind. I'm just wondering if I'm fast or strong enough to get you back."

Kelsea displayed her teeth. "Want me to give you a freebie?"

"Where's the glory in that?"

Stretching my body flat, I swam to the beach to join Laurel.

Water poured from my stained clothing as I stood. The top was definitely a goner, but at least there weren't clumps of compost in my hair anymore.

"You like swimming?" Laurel grunted.

"Used to swim most days of the week." *At the estate. When the world was normal.*

She sat on a small rock, knees hugged in and chin propped on top. Her hair was a midnight black contrast to my butter-blonde, but to all other outward appearances, she could be my slightly older sibling.

"There's a pool on the 30th floor of Kyros Sky," she said.

There was? "I'll have to get a swimsuit." Or ideally just return to the estate and use my own pool.

How to get there though? Fred couldn't handle my business affairs forever. Maybe I could lie and say that a client from the estates had called expressing interest to sell. Kyros wouldn't know the exact property I was on, right? Or would he? Except *Live Right* would definitely want to know the name of the clients.

Dang.

Maybe I could go there for a fake social function as the date of a friend.

In that case, I'd just need friends. Which honestly seemed like the more impossible of the two.

Fuck my life.

"Thank you for giving them this," Laurel said in a low voice. "I apologise for snapping at you."

Everyone was apologising to me lately. Laurel, however, meant it.

I shrugged a shoulder. "I deserved a scolding. Sorry for upsetting you."

She hesitated. "If I act that way sometimes, it's because your actions, your ... *continued safety* has a direct effect on the lives of these women."

Finding a rock to perch on, I mimicked her posture, chewing on that tidbit. "If I'm injured on your shift, this crew will be punished?"

"Usually there aren't repercussions, but with how... tied Kyros is to you, I fear any injury to yourself could cost these women their lives."

That made me jumping into the water pretty selfish and stupid. I could understand her reaction.

"Noted and absorbed," I told her. "Thanks for explaining, and I'll be more careful in the future."

A small smile curved her lips.

"I'd love to help pay off everyone's debt one day. If I got the money," I added as an afterthought, aware that Laurel was the only vampire *in the know*.

I scanned the crew of female vampires, and my eyes widened. *Holy shit*, they were taking water fight to an entirely new level.

Was that blood?

"You'd do that for us?"

I tore my gaze from the water fight at her off tone. "Does that offend you?" She must know what my real name meant—that I was loaded.

"No, it's just... for you to offer is—" She broke off, her chest rising.

Stretching out, I punched her shoulder.

Ouch!

I shook out my hand.

"Though your intention touches my heart," Laurel said hoarsely, "our debt is not so simple. Our payment must be matched to a deed. Only a Vissimo can set the deed and pay the debt."

Crap. "There's no way around it?"

"They feared we would influence human benefactors to be free of our chains."

That made sense.

Her eyes glittered, and I pounced. "What aren't you telling me?"

Laurel shook her head.

"Whatever! You can't hesitate and then not tell me."

"If Laurel isn't telling you something, it's probably for your own good," Jillian said, joining us on the beach.

Laurel's lips quirked at my eye-roll as the others took seats around us.

"Fess up, Loz," I pressed, folding my arms.

"You expect me to speak because you're crossing your arms?" She arched a brow.

Kelsea cocked her head. "What about when she stomps her foot?"

"Or the hands on the hips," Josie added.

My jaw dropped. "I hardly ever do those things." *Anymore.*

Their silence didn't inspire confidence that I'd successfully kicked the habits.

Laurel sighed. "Humans who've exchanged blood with a Vissimo six times are no longer classified as human. They're well past the stage of being vulnerable to anyone's compulsion but their mate's. As such, they are able to hire Indebted of their own accord even though the mating bond is still incomplete until the seventh exchange."

I stared at her.

Exchange blood with Kyros three *more* times?

When he mentioned the ability to read each other's thoughts after the final swap, I'd assumed he meant the *fourth* exchange. There were *seven* of the fuckers?

Fuck me.

"Exactly," Laurel said, standing. "Which is why I wasn't going to tell you."

"Yeah." I drew out the word. "Sorry, ladies. I'd love to help out, but I can't get any deeper into that craziness or I'll never get out alive."

Kelsea's blue eyes didn't hold their usual glimmer. "We understand. We'd never ask that of you."

They'd never ask anything of anyone. That's what broke my heart. Their shackles were too tight, they couldn't remember a time when they hadn't worn them.

Josie peered through the trees. "Humans are running toward us. ETA: three minutes."

Ah, yes.

I cleared my throat, avoiding seven sets of blue eyes. "That would be Mr Lygon."

Grinning at their sudden tension, I bellowed, "Run!"

"Miss Tetley?"

I stepped off the elevator on to Level 44 and peered at Angelica. Behind the reception desk, her gaze widened at my dripping state.

I wiggled my toes, noting the wet puddle forming around me.

"What happened to you?" she demanded.

"This and that," I replied, waving my house files in the air.

"Secured a property in Pink. Laid some foundations for the suburb when your clan next lands there too. Did you need something else?"

The Vissimo blinked. "Which property?"

"9C Joker's End." I thumbed through the files as I approached, sliding the respective paperwork onto the desk.

Her mouth was slightly ajar. "The hippy activists?"

"Strongly opinionated bohos? Yes."

She shook her head, rifling through the papers.

I folded my arms, inadvertently squeezing a fresh torrent of water from my ruined bra. "We've established it's because I'm human. This isn't surprising."

Angelica glanced up from the file. "That's not all it is, and we both know it."

A compliment? I remained mute, not willing to accept it from her. She liked to act first and ask for forgiveness. I wasn't into that.

"He's not mad, Miss Tetley—that you said no the other night."

Uhm, subject change much? "Oh, goodie. The thought was keeping me up at night."

Her nostrils flared, and I kept my innocent expression locked in place.

In my answering smile, I made sure to show all my teeth. "He accepted my answer *awfully* quick when I asked what he was hiding, Angie. If you'd like to tell me *that*, I'll happily listen."

Amusement alighted her cool, blue gaze. "If you have a question for Kyros, perhaps you'll have most success asking him."

Yeah, you know I won't do that.

If Kyros had fucked up yet again, he could come to me. If he hadn't, that was still a win in my eyes.

"Could you join me for a moment?" she asked.

I gestured at my dripping clothing. "It can't wait?"

"We won't be more than a minute," the vampire purred.

My brows climbed higher as she led me to the hot water closet to the left of reception.

Angelica shut the door to the closet, pulling the cord above to turn on the weak bulb.

"Any particular reason you've brought me to one of two soundproof locations in this tower?" I folded my arms.

"Never forget the nooks and crannies, Basilia," she murmured.

And that means what? "You're up to no good. The last few days were almost normal. Don't screw that up if you can stand to keep your nose out of my business for three seconds strung together."

She cut me a small scowl. "I wanted to give you this." The blonde-haired, blue-eyed vampire pulled a grey device from her blazer pocket.

"...You wanted to give me a voice recorder?" *The fuck?*

She beamed, passing it over. "Exactly! I find them useful for taking notes. Right after client visits when everything is fresh. You've done so well, and with so much going in your life, I thought you deserved a gift."

I turned the recorder over in my hands. "Thanks?"

"Don't mention it," she snarled.

Yikes, okay.

Angelica recovered her polite smile with eerie speed. "Best put it in your pocket, Miss Tetley. You wouldn't want to lose it."

This conversation had achieved first percentile strangeness. Holding the recorder, I studied my sopping clothes and elected to hold the *gift*.

"You purchased new clothes?" Angelica murmured, eyes dropping to my compost-stained ensemble.

"New clothes," I grunted. "Sorry to put a kink in your matchmaking plans."

"Never be sorry for kinking, Miss Tetley."

Was that *don't apologise for doing what you have to* advice? Or *get yourself a harem stat* advice?

She pushed open the closet door. "After you."

"You're seriously odd, Angie."

The vampire's lips twitched. "How about you call it a day? Go up and change. I'll type up the notes on 9C Joker's End."

I groaned. "Mrs and Mrs Tilonia who *own* 9C Joker's End. They're women, *people*, not an address."

Not receiving a response, I stomped to the elevator and added to the wet patch in the lift as I rode to Level 61.

By the time I stepped into the shower, I was shivering up a storm. "Stupid blood exchange."

Since the last exchange, I was running cold. In Summer too. Maybe I should get some supplements or something. Iron? Usually, I drew from *Truth Ranges* for any medical situation, but funnily enough, they hadn't covered what to do when a fanged monster drank from a person three times in a row.

Hopefully it wasn't on tonight's episode because I had some sleuthing to do.

Dressed in a form-hugging black knit dress, black tights, and chunky heels, I threw on a half-thigh length grey cardigan to complete the look. Digging into my *Elegance* pack for a hair tie, I pulled out the binoculars I'd purchased two days before and the master key I took from Angelica during my second thrall.

Gathering my long curls into a messy bun, I pulled out a few wispy tendrils to frame my face and then slid my thick-rimmed black glasses on.

Feeling cute. Check.

Time to flush this spy fucker out.

Bouncing across the bed to the nightstand, I reached for Beast—making sure not to disconnect him from the charger. He didn't like when that happened.

Unfortunately, my mastermind plan necessitated some communication with Kyros.

I typed:

Flushing out spy tonight. Just go with what I say and don't interfere.

I sent the message to Tommy knowing she'd never receive it.

Sure enough, the security screening message came through a minute later.

Waiting another minute, I called Angelica.

"Miss Tetley?"

"Angie, darling. I need Kyros's number, please."

"... Certainly."

No questions asked. If there was a dedication award, Kyros's aunt would have won it five times over by now.

I jotted down the numbers she rattled off on the new notepad I purchased at the same time as the binoculars.

Hanging up, I dialled Kyros. Tuning into his emotional compass, I scowled at the delicious coiling that furled within me at the mere thought of him.

"*Basilia.*"

My heart pounded at the rumbling depth of his voice. I was happy to hear it. What was more, *he* was happy I called.

We were just *so* fucking screwed.

"Kyros," I breathed. Lust rolled through him as I said his name.

I'd have to feel this—*him*—for the rest of my existence. The thought made me want to crawl into a hole. One where he'd be waiting. Naked.

"Can I help you?" he asked.

"I'm going out tonight. Just across the road to a wine bar. I only want Laurel, Kelsea, and Josie to accompany me so the other patrons aren't weirded out. If the rest of my crew is on standby, is that good with you?"

It wasn't. I knew it before he spoke.

I gritted my teeth. *Damn vampire.* I just spent three days setting this gig up, and that wasn't easy. If he said no, I was going to find a baseball bat and end him.

"Just across the road?" he clarified.

Ha!

His need to find the spy was outweighing his assholery. "Yep. Yellow Otter."

"I know it."

That wasn't a yes. I focused on my frustration and shoved it at him—or the world. I had no idea how this emotional telepathy shit worked.

"This once. *Only* because the bar is in close proximity."

"Thanks so much," I said sarcastically.

"You're welcome."

The line disconnected. *Bastard.*

How could he go along with *my* plan and still manage to piss me off?

Shaking off the encounter, I dialled Laurel next.

"Hey, Loz. Did you hear that?"

"It's not polite to listen in to our master's conversations."

That's a yes. "Could you, Kelsea, and Josie take me across the road to Yellow Otter?"

"Of course. I'll put the rest of your team on standby."

Totally listened in.

I smirked. "Cool, I need to get ready, and I assume you guys will try to go as Jessica Alba during her *Dark Angel* days. So come up here to change, please."

"You don't want us to dress like Jessica Alba this time?" she asked.

Her innocent tone didn't fool me for a second.

"I dressed in leather *one time*," I huffed, hanging up.

I'd never live that down.

When they arrived, I was ready with my pen and notepad.

Was I sure that the trio weren't the ones who'd blabbed to Clan Fyrlia and triggered the attack on me? *Nope.* But I really hoped I wasn't mistaken in them. These three genuinely seemed to like my company.

I sighed at their Indebted uniforms as they huddled in the doorway.

I'd convince them against leather if it was the last thing I did. "Grab clothes off the rack suitable for a *wine bar*. Your objective is to fit in. Humans hate standing out."

Laurel watched me closely.

Winking, I jotted a note on the pad.

Don't respond to my notes out loud.

How far away can you hear my heartbeat in this building?

She scanned the message and nudged the other two, who were scouring my clothing racks.

Kelsea and Josie read the note, their eyes flicking to mine.

Laurel grabbed the pen from me.

Two levels average. Four levels at most.

Everyone I was interested in should either be on Lower Level 4, Level 44, or Level 66. I wrote:

I need your phones.

The part of the plan that didn't sit well with me. The bond between the Indebted was *for real*. If the trio was aware one of their sisters and brothers was the spy, they could try to warn them.

Laurel's mouth tightened, but she passed her phone over, the others following suit. I grimaced, hoping to convey that I appreciated their trust in me.

"*What's going on?*" Kelsea mouthed.

I pulled out a set of instructions I'd written earlier, handing it to Kelsea and Josie. Scribbling as quickly as possible, I passed a second message to Laurel.

Understanding dawned on the older vampire's face as she finished reading it.

Kelsea and Josie were yet to connect the dots.

I cast all three of them a stern look, holding up the final pre-prepared message.

From now on, we must be careful of every word we speak. The four of us are together and heading to the Yellow Otter. Don't mention any other details aloud.

I'd underlined the last sentence, and the other two finally seemed to grasp what was happening.

Now the fun could begin.

Expression serious, I said cheerfully, "Did you guys find something to wear?"

Laurel turned to the rack, wrinkling her nose.

I cracked a grin. "What? You don't like anything other than black leather?"

"Exactly," she answered, brows lifted at the selection before her.

"You wore that dress to the club one time."

She lifted a shoulder. "I pretended it was black. *You're* wearing black now. Is that all the black you've got?"

"My jeans are soaked with compost juice, so yeah." I perused the rack, drawing a slinky dark green dress from a hanger. "This one for you."

Laurel took the dress, sighing.

Holding back a snicker, I drew out a high-waisted sleeve skirt and crop top for Josie, and dress shorts and blazer with a spangled top for Kelsea.

"Change," I bellowed, clapping my hands. "We're drinking wine tonight."

"We're drinking with you?" Kelsea called from the bathroom.

"Probably should have mentioned that part. Well, can you guys drink on guard duty? If not, I'd still like your company as I drink myself into oblivion."

"It takes a lot of alcohol to get a Vissimo drunk," Josie said. "I drank a bottle of absinth one time and felt a pleasant warmth in my stomach."

"Right. That's... something else. I guess a few wines won't register."

My nerves ramped up as the vampires changed their outfits. All the pieces were in place, I was certain. This wasn't my first rodeo. I'd used this exact same ploy on my rich *friends* as a teen. That was about the time I came to understand the kind of people they were—or felt they had to be.

I wasn't nervous my plan would fail. I was nervous it would point the finger at someone I *liked*. But this spy had killed twelve Vissimo, put me in a situation where I killed another being and nearly died myself, *and* forced me closer to Kyros than either of us ever intended to be.

They had a lot to answer for.

I checked Beast.

"Happy hour will start soon," I said. "Shall we, ladies?"

Laurel was still standing. "Will this place have tequila shots like last time?"

I swept the trio with a shrewd look. If I had to guess, I'd say they were disappointed we weren't *really* heading out to drink. Guess they didn't get to party a lot.

Or at all.

"Yep, should do," I said as we walked toward the elevator. "Their main focus will be wine though."

"I like tequila," Laurel announced, pushing the call button.

I laughed. "I second that, girl."

Ding!

Kelsea and Josie stepped on, and I waved at them as the doors closed. *Go time.*

I held my finger to my lips for Laurel's sake, and she merely dipped her head and then bodily picked me up.

"Where to?" she mouthed.

"End of hall," I mouthed back.

On whisper-soft feet, Laurel snuck us down to the other end of the hall.

I opened the door as quietly as possible and she deposited me in front of the windows overlooking the street below.

More importantly, I had a view of *Yellow Otter.*

As silently as possible, I drew the binoculars out of my pack.

Laurel drew my notebook closer, crouching beside me.

She wrote:

Who do you suspect?

Pulling a face, I turned to the last page of the notebook and pointed at a list of fifteen names. On it were several vampires from

Level 44, as well as one of Kyros's seconds who didn't seem to like me much, Angelica's name, and a list of Indebted who'd been close to me before Clan Fyrlia's ambush. None of my personal crew's names were on there. There were others I'd considered. Since I was a human who'd exchanged blood with the crown prince of Sundulus, there could be jealous exes, friends of Kyros's who were trying to rid him of the human problem. Perhaps I'd pissed someone or other off by securing so many houses—though I'd be surprised to find that was the case. This clan was united in their goal. They'd only ever congratulated me and tried to hang damn pictures of the secured houses in my office.

There was a chance I had the wrong people entirely, which meant I'd need to widen my net if this failed.

Laurel frowned at my scrawlings next to each person on the list.

She traced the sentence next to Angelica's name. *Will be in white car, not SUV.*

Next, she traced the sentence next to Conrad's name—Kyros's disapproving second who constantly glowered at me in the cafeteria. *Will enter through east door.*

He'd been particularly annoyed when I'd followed him to *Sister Sushi* and mentioned I'd be going to *Yellow Otter* on Friday night with a few friends. I always liked to enter the side door because it led to a hidden section that was much more intimate.

Over the last several days, I'd told fifteen different people fifteen different variations on my trip to *Yellow Otter*.

Because I was certain of one thing.

The members of Clan Fyrlia's royal family wanted me dead. I'd killed their youngest brother in self-defence. The fight between us was ruled as closed by an impartial clan, but unofficially, the Tonyi triplets—who I'd gathered did most of the dirty work for the other clan—would come for me.

They'd intended to burn me alive in the basement.

Laurel finished reading my list and scribbled a single word on the notepad.

Smart

I lifted a shoulder to shrug off her comment before recalling Laurel knew who I really was.

I picked up the pen.

It's how I used to test which friends I could trust

She raised her brows in question, and I smiled wryly, jotting down a name.

Only Tommy passed

I set my attention to the street below, adjusting my binoculars. I swept my gaze over the various entrances I'd given to five of the suspects. *Yellow Otter's* many doors were part of the reason I'd picked it.

I couldn't see anyone lurking outside.

My usual black SUV rolled in, not stopping. I zoomed in on Kelsea in the driver's seat to make sure. Less than ten seconds later, the white car I used to practice driving pulled up to the front of the bar.

I couldn't see anyone loitering at the front entrance. No one approached the white car, and no one lurked outside the other four entrances. Heart thumping, I swept the binoculars to an alley directly opposite *Kyros Sky*.

I squinted through the lenses, and quickly adjusted the magnification.

Three figures stood half in the shadows.

Bingo.

One person on my list believed that two vehicles would be sent out as decoys and I'd go by foot instead, sneaking down Robbers Alley to circle the wine bar and enter from the back.

Adjusting my binoculars again, I focused on the three hulking figures. They were male from their outlines, but I couldn't make out their features. If I was going to accuse someone of spying, I needed to confirm the Tonyi triplets were below, waiting to attack.

The minutes ticked by, and one of the three men threw his hands in the air, finally stepping away from the wall. I tensed as the meagre city lights blanketed the Vissimo, highlighting his almond-shaped hazel eyes and cruel expression.

I lowered the binoculars and glanced at Laurel, who nodded.

It was them.

Wow. Suspecting there was a spy and *knowing* there was a spy were different things. Someone had endangered my life, Kyros's life, and killed twelve people. And they hadn't stopped reporting to the triplets since.

Kelsea stopped circling the bar in the black SUV. She'd be heading back to the tower. Moments later, Josie did the same in the white car.

The moment of truth.

I ran my finger down the list of suspects, stopping on the second to last name. One I'd only jotted down to dot my i's and cross my t's.

Fernando.

The male Indebted who I'd tucked into bed and given a fucking pinecone.

Raising my head, I stared at Laurel. Her throat was working, blue eyes riveted on the name and the note next to it.

Heart plummeting into my heeled boots, I picked up the notebook, flipping to an empty page.

I wrote:

We need to go to garage

If Fernando was keeping tabs on the cars, we had to complete the subterfuge or he'd know something was up. He was probably shitting bricks because I hadn't gone down the alley.

Packing my stuff, I let Laurel swing me into her arms.

She almost flew us down the stairs—though noticeably slower

than Kyros—and set me upright just inside the garage as the others parked.

I groaned loudly as they joined us at the lift. "I thought the ache would go away. The sushi I ate at lunch must've been bad."

"It's okay," Laurel said. "We can go another time when you're feeling better."

What was passing through her head now she knew one of her brethren was the culprit?

Beforehand, I'd envisioned taking the evidence to Kyros without delay. Mainly to smoosh my success in his one-hundred-and-fifty-year-old face. Then again, I'd really hoped the spy wasn't an Indebted, even though they had the biggest motives here.

Ding!

"A rain check for sure." I stepped onto the lift. "How about you guys keep the clothes in the meantime?"

Kelsea and Josie glanced at their leader. A tension rested upon their shoulders, and I was certain Laurel would fill them in if she felt they were worthy of the information.

"We'll do that," Laurel replied, her eyes glittering.

I pressed the button for Level 61, leaving them to take the rickety lift down to Lower Level 4, but Laurel whipped out a hand, stopping the lift doors just before they closed.

I didn't say a word as she beckoned for the notepad and pen, handing both over.

The Vissimo's blue eyes blazed, and she took an audible breath, her hand blurring as she wrote.

She handed the pad back and stepped clear without meeting my gaze.

The elevator slid closed, and I lowered my gaze to her message.

Look in his fridge

5

Beast blared to life as the doors opened on Level 61.

"Yello," I said.

"Miss Tetley," Kyros said.

I ignored the ugly emotion that accompanied the two words. "Yeah?"

"You're not feeling well. Please come to my quarters."

His quarters? Such a vampire prince thing to say.

"Uh, I'd prefer to be alone." I didn't want to see Kyros until I decided how to handle Fernando.

"I will care for you, true mate."

That was a crock of shit! Though his emotions didn't negate the comment… However, the rod of steel *beneath* the warmth made it clear he'd issued an order.

Fucknuts.

"That'd be nice," I said flatly, spinning on my heel to return to the elevator. *Damn it all*, part of me meant the words.

Kyros knowing my location forevermore may cramp my long-term style, but this emotional bullshit was twice as bad. Yes, I got to listen in on his feelings, but to have someone to have the means of deciphering what I meant *all* the time? Humans didn't do that. I spoke a quarter of what I thought—or less. I'd be more comfortable with my legs wide open, and Kyros in the front row sketching a likeness than this bullshit.

I jabbed Level 65 and waited for the inevitable *ding* that I love-hated.

My brain raced as I considered my next move.

Four floors were barely long enough to scrape a plan together.

Turning right out of the elevator, I dragged my feet to the very end of the hall, scowling at the double doors to Kyros's private office.

I barged in—he could both hear and feel me coming.

Shoot. Just knowing I'd be in his company made my fingers tingle. My breath came fast, my body betraying me, and betraying my *dignity* at the same time. I couldn't even remember all the times Kyros had lied or hurt me at this stage.

Saved and protected me.

Shouted.

Held me in his arms.

Intimidated.

Held himself back.

He sat in his office chair. "Basilia. How are you faring?"

"Mr Sundulus," I replied in a grave voice. "Thank you. I've been better."

Kyros cut off his focus on the three screens before him and shifted his gaze to me. "That's not my last name."

Oh. "It's not?"

"My last name is Smith."

My jaw dropped. "You're kidding—"

He flashed his teeth.

"—you *are* kidding." I couldn't stop the surprised laughter from breaking free. "That would be hilarious though."

"Atagio," Kyros said, switching off the monitors.

Kyros Atagio.

I hummed, unsure what to make of what sounded very like a *get to know each other* conversation.

He stretched to his full height, and my mouth dried as I took in his suit-clad specimen of a body. Someone needed to freeze that shit so the future could enjoy the view. I wanted his body hovering over me. Lying beneath me. Crushing me against a wall.

His voice jolted me to the present. "Congratulations on securing 9C Joker. That house has eluded us for a long time. Unsure why. It's barely remaining upright."

The house hadn't eluded them. The *people* owning the house had.

The vampire prince flipped back the password panel and jabbed in his long-ass code.

I ambled to the entrance of his lair, my thoughts on the avalanche of other issues between us. "Memories."

Kyros cut me a look. "What?"

"Memories are why people can't let go. Money can't buy everything."

He studied my face, pressing a warm hand against the small of my back to direct me up the stairs. I let it stay there, desperate for the contact and hating myself for it.

"Money can buy most things," he answered.

For a Vissimo, perhaps. Vampires existed on the brink of death. Their priorities—surviving, winning, protecting, and ensuring their bloodline grew, *those* things weren't always important to humans because we weren't constantly primed for a battle. Ours was a slower, less intense existence. Things that Vissimo accepted without batting an eyelash, I struggled to come to terms with or accept without a moral fight. I wouldn't have said their values were unethical or even immoral per se. Just that their values were streamlined and gave the appearance of ruthlessness. If humans were a tree branch teeming with leaves, Vissimo were that same branch whittled to a spear.

"Lower door," Kyros murmured.

As soon as the door clicked shut at our backs, he halted me on the stairs. "Who is it?"

Dang it.

"Inconclusive. I laid a pretty good trap, but the results were too vague to be sure. I won't give you a name without being certain."

His green eyes flared. "You're lying."

Yep.

I climbed the last few steps and pushed the top door open. "That's all I've got for you right now."

"You said you'd have the name for me in a week," he spoke at my back.

The hairs on my neck lifted. *Ugh*, I hated walking in front of him. Gave me the heebie-jeebies. "I still have a couple of days."

"One."

As soon as I passed the bed, I pivoted to face him. The extra tension dissipated.

Thank fuck. We didn't need any help in *that* department.

Kyros strode straight to the kitchenette and opened the fridge, and I jolted, staring.

Laurel's note in my pack was like a leaden weight. I thought she meant check *Fernando's* fridge. Which hadn't made any sense because he didn't have one—then I'd decided she was referring to a communal Indebted fridge.

She wasn't.

Laurel meant *Kyros's* fridge.

He poured blood into a glass and chucked the bag in the bin.

"This bothers you?" he asked, meeting my gaze.

Blinking, I diverted my attention to the sofa. "No. I just pretend it's shiraz and you enjoy wine out of bags."

"I see." His amusement tickled me through the bond.

I perched on his bed, pushing up my glasses. "Was there anything else you wanted to discuss?"

Meadow-green eyes riveted on my face as Kyros ran his tongue over his teeth. "We're still on the same subject. Tell me who the spy is. You were nearly killed."

"Forget me, Kyros, five Indebted died," I reprimanded him. "Twelve if you include those from Clan Fyrlia."

"This person needs to answer for their crimes, Basilia."

I set my jaw. "They will. Once I confirm their guilt."

"You're protecting the Indebted," he said over the rim of his glass. He took a sip, and I watched his throat work as he swallowed.

A man drinking blood shouldn't turn me on, but it did. To the point of pain. I clenched my thighs together, my voice breathless. "That's an assumption."

"A correct assumption. An educated assumption. Indebted are often the culprits being that their motive is strongest."

My brows slammed together. "No wonder with how they're treated."

"Or are they treated that way because they're often the spies?" he challenged.

He took another sip, savouring it like I savoured a strawberry mojito.

I needed a strawberry mojito to get through this. Or five.

"You're thirsty?" Kyros's eyes glinted. "What for?"

"Not your blood, I can tell you that."

A growl filled the space between us.

I sighed. "I didn't mean it as an insult, fang man. I'll just grab a wat—"

"I'll get it," he interrupted, at the fridge before I'd budged at all.

... Shit.

Laurel was onto something huge.

Kyros placed the water on the bedside table beside me and retreated to the circle sofa, kicking off his shoes and loosening his tie.

"I called you because we need to talk," he said. "No, not talk. You *deserve* an explanation for how things have been between us since the third thrall. I wasn't in a position to give it to you until now."

He was going to *what*?

My ears pricked up. "You're going to offer information to me out of the goodness of your heart?"

Is hell freezing over?

"You're my true mate. That is why I'm offering an explanation." He knocked back the rest of his liquid meal and set the glass on the armrest.

I scoffed. "You can't seriously believe that true mate garbage."

Sadness. Fear. Anger.

Look at me picking out his emotions like a pro.

His face hardened. "I do, Basilia. Absolutely."

... Unexpected.

The fierce burning in his green eyes was too intense. I shifted my gaze, rubbing my chest. He was drawn to me—but part of him had never wanted to accept that. It was the same for me. And that was true from the very first moment we met before the first blood exchange.

"My father heard of our third exchange after Fyrlia's attack. He'd approved the second—believing, like me, that my fascination with you would end after the second thrall. The third exchange was an accident, of course, but now it's clear we are true mates."

"You keep saying true mates instead of mates. What does it mean?"

His breath deepened. It was his turn to fidget. "Any pair who complete all of the blood exchanges are considered mates. When certain symptoms appear, there's a potential the couple are true mates. If these symptoms continue beyond the third exchange, their true compatibility is confirmed."

For starters, we weren't a couple.

"You gave me the extremely diluted version of what the exchanges meant," I said. Then shook my head wearily. *More omissions. Why am I surprised?*

Kyros's eyes narrowed. "Working off very old statistics, three in one thousand experience symptoms such as ours after the first exchange. In 76 percent of those cases, reports of singing blood disappeared completely after the second exchange. Of the remainder, 80 percent disappeared after the third. The odds were just over one in a thousand that we were true mates. I didn't expect it would come to this."

"Dare I ask what the symptoms of singing blood are?"

He arched a brow. "Mounting lust. A mindless thrall. Unexplainable calm and happiness in each other's presence. The appearance of mating gifts. The urge to fuck and reproduce."

Whoa, whoa, whoa. Who said anything about brats?

"A clan in the Middle East believes that Vissimo can have

multiple true mates, but it would be impossible to discover more than one. Once true mates find each other and complete the exchanges, they will never long for another."

This conversation was making me genuinely sick. Exhaling slowly, I grunted. "You've done your research."

"With my father, yes."

King Julius. "Right. You were saying he approved the second. I can assume that isn't the case for the third. But it's not like we intend to take it further, so he's okay with that"—*me*—"right?"

Kyros's expression was grave as he tapped a finger on the armrest. "My father wanted to compel you afterward. I spent the week after our third thrall convincing him not to place your mind in a cage."

My heart rate tripled. "He did?"

"You're afraid," he said in a low voice. "You should be. My father is the most powerful Vissimo in the world. Six hundred years old and from the most prestigious bloodline in the world."

The bloodline that Kyros was assumedly meant to propagate, even if he wasn't sure whether he belonged to it.

And now his supposed true mate was human. That must gripe extra hard. "This isn't just a shitshow for me."

"I have found my true mate," Kyros said softly. "Something I never anticipated, and something I haven't treated with the proper respect thus far. My absence after the thrall and after your grandmother's passing hurt you. My past lies have hurt you. I wish you to understand that I did want to see you and comfort you—it was my constant thought. I separated myself due to my father's surveillance over my actions after the third thrall. I had to convince him that my urges were under control to prevent him compelling you."

His disappearing act had hurt me.

Before the second blood exchange, things seemed to deepen between us, almost as though we'd come to a certain level of understanding despite everything.

This explanation was the closest thing to an apology that I'd get from the vampire—the word *sorry* probably wasn't in Kyros's vocabulary.

I thought of the needless fury I'd gone through, frustration filling me. "Why didn't you tell me sooner? I would have played along."

"If he compelled you, my father would have gleaned the truth from your mind."

I wrinkled my nose. "Is that what happens when you guys drink my blood? You just know everything in my head?"

He tensed, his gaze settling on my throat for a beat. "We have to actively search for what we want. The success of that depends on the age and power of the Vissimo."

Like reading a book? *Weird.*

"If I'm truthful, fear of what my father may do was not the only reason for distancing myself," Kyros said, capturing my gaze. "I was unsettled by the development between us too."

I leaned forward. "Unsettled how?"

He lifted a shoulder. "Furious that my enemies forced us into the third exchange and treated you like chattel. My true mate forced to crawl across the ground. I wasn't able to protect you from their wrath. For a male Vissimo, whether they have a mate or a harem, their duty is to protect. The force of that failure hit me harder than I cared to admit."

Lalitta had said as much—that Kyros couldn't figure out how to be free of his bindings. King Julius had placed bindings on him, too, but Kyros locked another set into position all by himself.

"It's not your job to protect me." I frowned. *Outdated.*

He blurred to kneel before me. "It *is* my job, Basilia. As surely as it is yours to protect me."

What was he saying? His emotions were all over the place. I held a hand to my head. "I don't understand what you mean."

Kyros took one of my hands in his. My hands were tiny in comparison. "It means that I have absolute belief in what our blood is showing us. Our blood *sings.* We are true mates."

I stared at our hands and then his face. *Shit just got real.* "W-What?"

"My beauty," he said, stroking my cheek with the back of his free hand. "None shall harm you again."

My breath came fast. "I'm not sure we're on the same page."

Kyros leaned in.

A whine slipped between my teeth at his proximity.

"Can you fight this agony for the rest of your life?" he asked simply.

Gasping for air, I shuffled back on the bed.

He followed me on to the mattress.

I rested a hand on his chest. "Kyros, please stop. I'm overwhelmed and can't think with you so close."

A slow grin spread across his face. "I know."

"You lied to trap me," I stammered, shuffling back farther.

Kyros stalked closer, running his fingers up the inside of my ankle. "I did. You would have never agreed to the second exchange otherwise."

"You bastard," I ground out, drawing my feet under me so I could stand in the middle of the bed. "That wasn't your choice to make."

He rose to his knees and ran his hands up the outside of my stockinged thighs. "The thought of you disappearing or being in danger while I had no ability to track you was driving me to insanity. I cannot apologise for it."

You don't apologise for anything.

Lifting the right hem of my knitted dress above my hip, he gently bit the hollow between the bone and stomach. My knees shook, and Kyros seized the advantage, guiding me back down to the bed.

We knelt facing each other, both of us panting. My eyes huge. His molten.

"Those glasses should be illegal." He growled, darting forward to nip at my bottom lip. "So fucking sexy."

I sucked in air. "*Kyros—*"

"I don't know who you're trying to fool with this outfit," he whispered in my ear. "But you missed the mark on cute. It just makes me want to tie you to this bed."

Gasping, I writhed on the spot. The ache between my thighs was agony. His smell or emotions or his *nearness* overrode all logic.

I lifted my other hand to his chest.

"I can't," I told him. There were so many reasons. Reasons that felt so small and insignificant. But weren't.

I was certain they weren't small.

Our gazes met and sealed. The space between us evaporated, sucked away in one fell swoop. I traced up his corded neck with shaking fingers, splaying them wide over his jaw before circling his lips with a fingertip.

He groaned low, pulling my hips against his.

My head fell back, and Kyros cupped the base, forcing it upright again. His gaze was hazy, half-filled with the dream-like quality I felt spreading through my body, but a question filled the rest.

He wouldn't close the gap this time.

Obeying my body, I pressed my lips against his.

Had I ever made the first move before?

I couldn't recall.

I don't care.

Kyros sank onto his haunches so I didn't have to strain upward, but otherwise didn't move. I felt his borderline-painful approval of my touch. He roared inside. *For me.*

My simple touch was bliss.

I lifted high on my knees, forcing him to angle his head as I parted his lips with my tongue.

We broke apart, and he panted, "I want to touch you, Basilia."

"Do it," I replied without a speck of hesitation.

He moved then.

Fire erupted over my skin as his hands ran up my thighs, pushing my dress to my waist. My breath quickened, loud and harsh. He worked my tights and panties to my knees, and I leaned down to get rid of them entirely.

Kyros lifted on his knees again and my hands latched onto the bottom of his waistcoat. His hands threaded through my hair as I undid the buttons frantically, shoving the garment off his shoulders before attacking the buttons on his shirt.

His hot mouth worked down my neck, and I moaned. *Bliss.*

"Hold on tight," he growled in my ear.

Mmm?

I yelped as Kyros picked me up, forearms under my thighs as he lifted me overhead.

Then his mouth was between my legs. I choked on a cry as his hot tongue roamed with abandon, my legs shaking with the inability to do anything but not upset the balance of our position. My hands gripped his hair tight, despite knowing he wouldn't let me fall.

I had no control.

And *fuck*. It was undoing me at the seams.

"*Kyros*," I pleaded as he moved faster and faster. "It's too much."

Yet my hips gyrated against his face, using his mouth. My hands left his hair to creep up my own body, kneading, and palming the parts left unattended.

Suspended, my lower body held motionless, I had no option but to follow the fire as it catapulted me higher and higher.

"*More*," I demanded hoarsely. My body jerked. Desperation filled me. *Anticipation.*

He sucked my clit into his mouth, circled hard and fast, pressing.

Too much. Not enough. Pain.

Utter ecstasy.

I pressed my hands against my mouth, screaming against them as heat obliterated me, rocking outward from my core to consume me.

I fell, tipped over the edge, *undone,* and my legs slackened as my mind blanked to numbing bliss.

I floated.

Floated with no intention of ever coming down.

Kyros sat back on his haunches and lowered me to straddle his lap. My legs curled around his back and tremors wracked me as I clung to him, breath catching.

"Beautiful," Kyros said into my hair, kissing my temple. "Passionate."

It wasn't often that I let loose in that way. And never with such a result. But I always felt halfway to the ultimate orgasm around Kyros. The blood bond between us was constant foreplay, even if I refused to heed it the majority of the time.

At least, I hadn't thus far.

"That was new," I said uncertainly, not sure I wanted to leave my position crushed against his chest. I was half-naked, and he'd just given me the most intense orgasm of my life. With his mouth. Holding me up as though I was a fucking feather.

I needed a second.

"I certainly hope so," he purred in my ear.

Growing a vagina, I peeked up.

His fangs were out, eyes blazing to the point of frenzy.

"Can I reciprocate?" I asked. Heat pulsed through me anew at the thought. Or were humans really bad at foreplay and sex compared to Vissimo?

Kyros inhaled sharply and turning my head, I latched onto his thumb, sucking hard on it. I smirked as his erection went from rock hard to bursting. He was under my spell.

I had nothing to fear.

"Not tonight," Kyros said as though the words were physically dragged from him. His eyes traced my neck. "Not unless you want to enter the fourth thrall right now."

The admission pulled me up short. "You want to bite me?"

He closed his eyes, taking a shuddering breath. "I want to put my cock inside you, bite you, and force my blood down your throat all at the same time. I nearly bit into your femoral artery when you orgasmed though I drank blood ten minutes ago."

A bolt of heat shot to my centre at the thought of drinking his blood. It had to be the blood bond talking. "Thanks for telling me, I guess. I feel bad that I came and you didn't."

His eyes snapped to mine and he drew me closer with a hand against the small of my back.

"Wrong thing to say?" I whispered as he moved up his favourite path, inhaling me from jaw to temple.

He stilled, hands bunching in my dress.

"Wrong thing to say," Kyros replied, pulling back. "For the record, the memory of you using my face to get off while wearing those glasses and palming your fucking perfect body will haunt me to the end of my days."

He lowered his voice, lips nearing my ear. "My reward was tasting you."

I flushed. It wasn't like I was a virgin. Far from it—I liked to have fun. But dirty talk fell from his mouth without a speck of embarrassment or shame.

Kyros lifted my chin with a finger. "My true mate is perfection."

I had to woman up.

Steeling myself, I met his gaze. "Your mouth felt like perfection."

His green eyes flared again, and I untangled myself from around him, bouncing to the edge of the bed.

Apparently I'd thrown my stockings and underwear across the room. Tugging my skirt down over my slick thighs, I plucked the garments off the pinecone ornament, staring at the thing.

"Don't break it," he grumbled, buttoning his shirt.

Yeah, yeah. I didn't feel like breaking it anymore. But it *was* kind of mortifying. I'd given a decorative pinecone to a one-hundred-and-fifty-year-old vampire prince.

I tugged up my panties—white and lacy with a cheeky cut.

Kyros swore as I tugged my dress back down.

"I need a shower," he muttered, reaching up to pull his shirt overhead. "*A long fucking shower.*"

I drank in the sight of him, body clenching in favour of a round two. "A shower, huh? I'll leave you to that then."

"No," he said, glancing at the white clock beside his bed. "We have time for dinner before I start work."

My brows climbed.

Blasted Vissimo didn't give me any time to think. We'd gone from strangling each other, to the bed and now to a *date*? I'd always maintained that Kyros was a one-night-stand kind of guy. Not a long-term partner. Our bodies wanted to force us into a long-term… thing. That didn't mean I had to agree to the second blood thing, whatever Kyros had already decided.

When he was open and honest like this, sure, I could

entertain the idea of more. But he behaved this way 5 percent of the time. What was more, I doubted Kyros was capable of casual sex.

"For me, this was a one-time thing..." I trailed off.

His face darkened, but the shadows were gone in the next instant. "Dinner isn't marriage, Miss Tetley."

I frowned at the ugly throbbing beneath the words. Well fuck, at least we both agreed marriage was out of the question.

"I need to eat before work, and I'd like company," Kyros continued.

I rolled up my stockings. "This wouldn't be you downplaying that it's a date so I don't refuse, would it?"

"It was me trying to save my dignity after you reduced what we shared to a *one-time thing*, actually."

His comment startled a laugh from me.

I groaned after, shoved aside my concerns. "I'll come to dinner. A *friendly* dinner."

"Do you fuck all your friends' faces?"

He ducked as I threw my stockings at his head.

The shower turned on a moment later, and I picked up the remote. Turning on the television, I flicked through the channels, not registering the content of a single one.

Whoa, that orgasm was *earth-shattering*.

When I first met Kyros, I told him that 25 percent compatibility, *physical compatibility*, wasn't enough to tempt me. He'd proved me wrong. I was willing to bet a whole heap of women would sign up to experience that.

The temptation was real. Part of me wanted to believe the brief connection we'd shared before the second exchange meant something—that it would morph to trust and respect in time. Except the urge to give in to such a massive commitment was the blood bond talking, *not me*. Kyros and I had always shared a certain tension, even before he first compelled me, so I could admit that part was real, but the rest wasn't.

We were still only 25 percent compatible in my mind.

I grinned as Kyros's shower extended. *Totally wanking.* I picked up my water from the bedside table and took a few gulps.

Swallowing, I lowered the bottle and glanced at the fridge.

Look in his fridge.

Laurel knew something I didn't.

I trusted the Indebted woman far more than I trusted Kyros. And I respected her. Really, we were far more compatible as life partners if either of us were that way inclined.

I gulped back my water and padded to the sink, filling the bottle.

He'd hear if I opened the fridge, but I'd seen inside of it already. There was only blood and water.

I drank more water—loudly. Filling the bottle a third time, I carefully opened the cupboard door beneath the sink. Easing up the lid of the rubbish bin, I reached inside, fingers fumbling for the empty blood bag I'd seen him throw inside.

I straightened, flipping it over.

Basilia Le Spyre

B-Negative

Blood rushed through my ears as I re-read the label.

Kyros knew my real name.

The bathroom door slammed open, Kyros ran out, a white towel fastened around his hips. "What's—"

His gaze landed on the bag in my shaking hands.

He knows my name.

I needed to pay attention to whatever he was feeling, but all I could do was think back through our encounters.

Every single one of them.

Right to the start when I'd stumbled out of this tower after my interview with Angelica and *happened* to nearly be run over by him.

Him waiting on the street to talk to me.

Coincidentally being present when I needed help with the *Monocle* login.

The blood compulsion.

The exchanges.

I covered my mouth, the trembling of my body strengthening. He knew my grandmother had died.

Kyros knew I'd just inherited billions.

"Right from the start," I whispered, my voice cracking.

He didn't move from the bathroom doorway.

"You've played me from day one. It was a setup."

I hadn't felt right after the interview with Angelica. "Did Angelica compel me to run out onto the street that day?"

His voice was soft. Flat. "She's the best there is at eye compulsion. You knew something was different after that moment, but you didn't seem to recall anything you'd told her under compulsion."

Not true. I'd had nightmares of blurting everything out. I just hadn't believed that was the real version.

None of what lay between Kyros and me was real.

From day one, he'd strung me along. I gasped, hurt spiking me in the chest so hard, I hunched forward.

We don't need a tax number.

We pay in cash.

"You followed me," I rushed to say. "You listened to my conversation with Tommy in the bar after the interview."

Kyros took a step forward.

"*Don't you dare,*" I shot at him, drawing myself up. "You've been seducing me for my money and position? Putting on a show to get a hold of my assets—my network." It was all a joke.

I felt sick. I tossed the blood bag in the rubbish, placing my bottle on the bench.

"What are you doing?"

"Leaving this shithole. The exact thing I would have done long ago if I'd realised you already knew my real name."

Kyros blocked me. "You're not leaving this tower."

"Get out of my way," I said in a dark voice I barely recognised.

"I can't let you—"

I screamed, "You made me drink your blood because I'm wealthy? You just—" I blanched, thinking of what we'd just done. My stomach roiled. "Oh my god, I can't believe I let you touch me like that."

Use me like that.

My chest seized and a burning slammed into the backs of my eyes like never before. I felt violated. Dirty.

Humiliated.

He blurred before my eyes and I pressed my nails into my shaking palms, swallowing hard. "You did this for *Ingenium*."

"I got close to you in the beginning because my father ordered it."

His father ordered him to. The words echoed in my head.

Voice hoarse, I summoned up every ounce of hatred in my system —a lot as it turned out. "*You're a fucking monster.*"

Darkness swelled between us, the connection between us twisting, decaying to shadows and loathing.

"Move." I would tear down this entire tower if he didn't.

Kyros stepped aside.

I strode past without looking at him, stopping only to pick up the décor pinecone to hurl it against the far wall.

It shattered, burlap and sequins flying everywhere.

I marched out of his lair down to his office and let the shock, abhorrence, and bitter, bitter regret wash over me. So many weeks feeling that I had to protect my grandmother and the estate. Time with her that I'd never get back.

Alone. Trapped.

I kept even steps down the hall and stepped into the elevator when the doors slid open.

I rode down to the ground floor.

And as Basilia Le Spyre, I walked out of *Kyros Sky* forever.

6

I saw the wooden stair a split second before my golf cart slammed into it.

My head whipped forward and the rear of the buggy lifted with impact. The cart bounced back on an angle, teetering on two wheels for a breath before toppling on its side and carrying me with it.

The air whooshed from my lungs. I thudded from the driver's seat to the wooden floor, landing heavily on my side.

"Ouch," I wheezed, untangling my legs from the wheel.

I blinked at my left hand and, smiling, lifted the intact tequila bottle in triumph. "Hey-oh!"

Didn't spill a drop.

Resting my head on the cool ground, I opened my mouth and tried to pour more of the alcohol into my mouth sideways.

The bottle was plucked from my grip. "Miss Le Spyre, are you hurt?"

I squinted up at Fred. "You're upside-down, Fred. Fuck, no wonder Grandmother hired you."

His eyes scanned my body for injury. "Driving the golf cart through the halls under the influence again."

"Sorry." I sighed, closing my eyes.

There was a *clink* as he set the bottle down. He gripped me under the arms and slid me free of the upturned cart.

"Where'd we get a golf buggy from?" I mumbled, trying to hook the tequila bottle with my foot.

"You ordered it online three days ago, Miss Le Spyre. Another decision made under the influence."

Arguably the best decisions were made with tequila.

Fred helped me to my feet, directing me away from the half-empty bottle when I glanced at it.

"Do you play golf?" I asked the butler, wobbling beside him.

"No, Miss Le Spyre. It's too uneventful for me."

He probably liked sports where he got to hit people. "I don't play golf."

"No, Miss Le Spyre. I'm aware."

The butler gripped my upper arm as I stumbled up the wide mahogany stairs.

"I'm going to order an elevator online," I told him as we reached the top. "Why don't we have one again?"

I burped. My stomach wasn't feeling so great.

A small smile graced his face. "Your grandmother said stairs built character. And that when she couldn't walk up and down them, she was ready to be put down."

Yep, that sounded like something Agatha Le Spyre would say.

I peered left to the mahogany panel doors at the far end of the long hall. Grandmother's suite. Those doors held so many memories for me—sneaking in to try on her jewellery and make-up, standing outside trying to work up the courage to confess after causing trouble somewhere, and barging in to drag her out for Sunday brunch or to snuggle on a Saturday morning.

Swallowing, I wavered on my feet. "Take me to her room, Fred."

Kind blue eyes on a weathered face looked out at me. "You're certain, Miss Le Spyre? Perhaps it would be better in the morning?"

Why did he think I'd made a small dent in the liquor bottles over the last week? It certainly wasn't for the fun of it, and it certainly wasn't because of *Kyros fucking Atagio.*

I pressed my hand against my mouth to smother another belch. I rubbed my aching stomach. "Nope, I'm ready."

"As you say."

He helped me navigate the never-ending hall. Ten bedrooms made up the second level, five either side of the staircase—with my grandmother's master suite at the end of the east wing. My suite down the end of the west wing was the same as hers, just slightly smaller.

I grasped the vertical iron handles of the mahogany doors, resting my thumbs on top of the levers. Taking a breath, I pushed the doors wide.

So familiar.

And so not.

The cleaning staff hadn't allowed a speck of dust to accumulate. Everything was immaculate—as during my grandmother's life. The only time to see the bed rumpled had been first thing in the morning. Even then, she always slept in the middle, hands resting on her stomach.

There was life in the room then.

Her suite felt lifeless now. Devoid of the person she was.

The sight of her in a white coffin surrounded by lavender flashed before my eyes, and I squeezed them shut.

"You don't need to do this," Fred said from just behind me.

I'd tiptoed around this suite, my grandmother's office, and her lavender tiers since slamming the door of the taxi from *Kyros Sky*. Agatha Le Spyre would have slapped me upside the head five times already for not tackling her death head-on.

I straightened. "Where did you find her, Fred?"

"She rang the bathroom bell. I found her collapsed by the sink."

My chest tightened. *The bathroom.* No one's grandmother belonged on the bathroom floor.

Fred stepped forward and glanced at me. "I called the ambulance and returned Mrs Le Spyre to bed. When she stopped breathing, I started CPR and continued until help arrived. The paramedics attempted to revive her for twenty minutes."

If I'd found myself in that position, I'd be a wreck.

"I'm sorry you had to go through that." I reached for his hand, squeezing it tight.

The butler blinked a few times, his gaze fixed on the bed. "I started working here after serving in the army. Mrs Le Spyre said she needed someone who had equal measure of brain and brawn to protect her family and that if I was stupid or weak to get the fuck off the estate before she set the dogs on me."

I choked on a laugh. We'd never owned dogs. Or any pet other than horses.

"Thirty-four years went by," he said, a soft smile on his lips. "Everyday part of me wondered if that would be the day she purchased dogs just so they could chase me to the gate."

I gave full throat to my husky laughter. "She was something else, wasn't she?"

Fred lowered his head. "That she was, Miss Le Spyre. And you'll be every bit the head of estate she was, in your own way."

"Like driving golf carts down the hall?"

His eyes twinkled. "Coping is to be expected."

Coping—so like him to spare my feelings and downplay my binge-drinking and online-shopping rampage. I sincerely hoped we hadn't taken on staff who were getting their first look at me. *Then* Grandmother would be truly disappointed in me.

I sobered, releasing his hand to wrap my arms around myself.

"Miss Le Spyre." He hesitated. "Have you considered calling Tommy?"

Everyday.

"She doesn't want to see me," I whispered.

"Forgive me for the intrusion, but did something happen?"

I managed to force the corners of my mouth. "You changed my diapers, Fred. Nothing you say is intrusive. And, yes. Something happened. I can't talk about it though."

His expression turned grim. "I see. Is there anyone else you can reach out to? A friend?"

I thought of Laurel—the only Vissimo to warn me about Kyros's fucking game. But she had to report to the very person who'd tricked the rich brat into thinking she was special.

I felt so stupid. I couldn't face Laurel.

The entire tower, his siblings, Kyros... they'd probably snickered over the farce from day one.

"No," I answered. "There's no one else."

He squeezed my shoulder. Or steadied me—that was always a possibility.

I scanned the room, my chest tightening. "I'd like to be alone."

"As you say," he replied softly.

Heart sinking to the floor, I watched the butler walk down the hall before reaching for the double doors to push them shut.

I woke in a cloud of lavender.

Drawing in an inhale filled with regret, I heaved onto my back and stared through bleary eyes at the maroon canopy.

Ugh, I didn't feel so good.

Crawling to the edge of the enormous bed, I tugged on the bell, then promptly collapsed.

The doors opened.

"Miss Le Spyre?"

"Rosie, thank god." I coughed. "I've awoken with a dire case of the dry mouth."

"... I see. Might I recommend a greasy breakfast, coffee, and a mango lassi?"

I waved a hand in the air. "You may."

"Very well, Miss Le Spyre. Will you take your breakfast here?"

Grandmother would arise as undead and stab me. "No, I'll take it in..." I steeled myself. "In the lavender tiers."

No answer.

I squinted at the doorway to see the plump head servant whose pallor was a direct contrast to her name. "Problemo?"

"Not at all, miss. Did you want me to wash your clothes?"

Crap. "Am I naked?"

The servant blanched. "You're in one of your grandmother's skirt suits."

Jesus.

Carefully rolling to placate the temple demons, I peered at the teal blazer and below-knee skirt that I'd pulled on—white blouse and mother-of-pearl brooch included. The skirt suit was about six sizes too big and I hadn't removed the lavender pouch from the breast pocket. That explained the lavender scent.

"No, Rosie. Don't worry about that. Just breakfast."

She curtseyed and backed out, closing the doors behind her.

Fuck me, I had to get rid of all the tequila in the house.

"Time to get up, fool," I whispered.

I stood without vomiting and swept up my discarded clothes before shuffling to my own suite in the opposite wing.

I stood on the threshold, eyeing my white canopied bed with longing. But I'd wallowed in self-pity long enough. It wasn't just me now. I had staff and an estate to manage. Poor Fred couldn't be landed with the job forever.

Plus, everything I currently felt could be felt by Kyros, too, unless he was working as hard as I was to ignore the foreign tendrils of emotion. I wouldn't give him the satisfaction of feeling my wallowing shame a day more. He'd played me for an idiot, and I had to suck it up and admit that head-on, no matter what my pride wanted to deny.

So many times in the last six weeks, I'd felt out of my depth or moronic. I'd had enough. This was it; the last time Vissimo would make a joke out of me. I wanted nothing to do with them—barring the Indebted.

They could visit. I'd shower them with gifts and kindness.

Kicking the doors to my suite closed, I shucked my grandmother's outfit, draping it over the heavy wooden seat in front of my dresser.

By the time I'd gone through my shave, wash, hydrate routine in the adjoining en suite, an aching stiffness had settled in my limbs, but I felt halfway human.

Returning to the bedroom, I skirted past the sliding lounge doors to the wardrobe. Striding past the handbags, shoes, and jewellery cases, I stopped in front of the activewear section, which I couldn't ever recall actually exercising in.

"No," I scolded myself. "Today is a conquering day."

I pivoted to the opposite wall and selected dark-blue jeans, light-grey stilettos, a belt with an obnoxiously large gold buckle. Then I snagged a loose linen white shirt equipped with a plunging neckline. The girls would free ball it today—with nipple pads of course. Didn't want to scare the staff any more than I had. Selecting a black G-banger, I pulled on the entire ensemble, tying a knot in the front of the shirt to highlight the dramatic curve where my narrow waist flared to my hips. *Thanks, Mom.*

My hair would dry into barrel curls, but I helped it along in the shine department with some oil blend my hairstylist supposedly invented. Returning to my dresser, I picked up a thin gold chain discarded there—a twenty-first present from my grandmother. One I'd flung here the night I argued with her and left. Heart weighing heavy, I clasped it around my neck.

I shifted my eyes to the other objects on the dresser. My phone—from this century, portable charger, headphones, and the voice recorder Angelica gifted me.

Beast would remain by my bed for Snake purposes, but otherwise...

I slipped my 21st-century phone into my back pocket, snagging the charger too. I snatched the recorder up. Today was a list-making day.

"Time to get shit done," I told the empty room.

Leaving the doors to my suite open for the cleaning staff, I strode to the central stairs, looking around the place for what felt like the first time in years.

All of this was *mine* now.

Mine to care for the next generations. Which would theoretically come from me.

Wow, I felt so ill-equipped.

I hadn't even wanted this. Yet my stint outside of the estate taught me there were worse things in life. To be out of that tower, I'd put up with a lot more than a net worth of one hundred and fourteen billion dollars.

Plus, the thought of someone else caring for the estate finances if I relinquished the position, made me feel... possessive. For centuries a Le Spyre had cared for our assets. Apparently that did mean something to me.

Like my grandmother, I'd make this life what I wanted, maybe even relocate to one of the estate's other properties if I could bear to leave the memories of this house behind. Kyros could find me, yes, but a ten-hour plane trip between us sounded fucking idyllic.

I passed through the ballroom and across the sweeping balcony, past the pool and outside entertainment pagodas, and wound between the towering hedge-way that extended to the west boundary of the estate. Turning left at the break in the hedges, I clicked down the paved path, stopping short when the path opened into the circular lavender tiers.

Rings of lavender bushes rose around a small glass table and wrought iron chairs in the centre.

I sat in one of the cold chairs, my bloodshot gaze trickling over the surrounding purple plants. Only the towering tips of the main house and the tops of the hedge-way were visible.

Did my grandmother sit here the day she died? Did she think of me or miss me in those moments?

Blinking several times, I inhaled, the lavender cutting through my self-inflicted headache.

"Miss Le Spyre?"

Glancing up, I smiled at the head maid.

She set the breakfast tray in front of me.

"Thank you, Rosie. Are the eggs soft but not too soft?"

"I hope everything is to your satisfaction, Miss Le Spyre."

Rosie had been around too long to fall for my mind fuckery. "I'm sure it will be. Thank you."

She bobbed and retreated.

I drew out the phone that could take pictures and stay awake longer than thirty minutes at a time, plugging it into the portable charger. I picked up the voice recorder next.

List time.

I was out of the tower, but that didn't mean I'd escaped *Ingenium* —not with the Tonyi triplets after me. They hadn't discovered my new location yet, which I assumed by the fact I wasn't dead, but I couldn't rely on that. I needed protection.

Shovelling eggs into my mouth, I pressed the buttons on the voice recorder at random.

"How the fuck does this work, Angie? I wasn't born in the damn 12th century." This thing was on par with a Walkman, aka did not compute.

I clicked the middle button, jolting when Angelica's voice blared out. Fumbling, I cradled the recorder in both hands, freezing.

"*... Vampires. Or Vissimo, as we call ourselves, are recorded to have existed from 4500BC.*"

Eyes widening, I clicked the button with a square on top.

The sound cut off.

This couldn't be what I thought it was.

Mouth bone dry, I clicked the play button again.

Her voice rang out. "*We exist in clans formed of one core clan and many sub-clans. Clans are led by a king and his queen, and often the sub-clans are headed by their children or other family members.*"

My heart thudded, cold shock coursing through me as Angelica detailed *Ingenium* and everything from my arrival at *Kyros Sky* to the blood compulsion and the attack by Clan Fyrlia.

I reached for the stop button as her voice trailed off, jolting when she spoke again.

"*I am trusting you with this recording, Miss Tetley, because I think you feel very alone right now. In return, all I ask is that you take care of whom you trust with this knowledge. You know what will happen if you err in this.*"

"Whoa," I hushed.

Whoa, whoa, whoa! Angelica gave me proof Vissimo existed—

while still upholding the Miss Tetley lie *and* neglecting to mention the first time she compelled me, but—

Fuck.

This was huge.

I didn't hesitate.

My phone took far too long to turn on, but she was on speed-dial at least.

The phone rang three times.

What was the time? And the *day*. Was she at work?

"Basi?"

I blew out a long breath, shoving away my barely touched breakfast. "Tommy."

"... Is everything alright?"

I cut her off. "Are you working today?"

"Yeah, I start in an hour."

Dammit. "Can you come by the estate after? I have something to tell you. Finally."

Her silence made my insides shrivel. What if things had gone too far to salvage? What if—

"I'll pull a sickie."

Hope swelled in my chest. "That'd be great. I can send Fred to pick you up."

She grunted. "Thanks."

"See you soon then?" I asked, beaming.

"I probably don't need to tell you this, but whatever you tell me, better be really fucking good."

Nerves twisted my gut. Revealing the truth to Tommy might be the most selfish thing I'd ever do.

I couldn't live without her in this cold, empty world.

My lips didn't so much as twitch. "Oh, it's good, Tom. Whether or not you believe it is another thing."

7

I clicked the stop button and looked at Tommy across the office. This room had the best soundproofing in the house because Grandmother had hated the slightest noise while poring over estate investments and accounts.

Tommy glanced up from her balled hands.

I remembered the feeling. Right now, she'd feel like Matt Damon in *Martian* when he was catapulting through space. "Tom..."

My friend stood, rubbing her mouth and nodding. "Vampires are real. Vissimo are real. You're under a blood compulsion." She stopped, shooting me a look. "You still can't talk about any of this—even if I know?"

Was it worth possibly alerting Kyros by testing the boundaries? I could talk openly around Sundulus vampires unless a human was near. And I'd wager if I tried to repeat anything from personal conversations with Kyros to a random one of his minions, I'd fail. I could work around the restrictions by being vague. If there was another way, I was yet to figure it out.

I pursed my lips. "I'm not going to try. Because of consequences." Now I'd let my friend in—and now my last family member was gone

—protecting Tommy took first priority. Just not, apparently, from myself.

Tommy hummed. “Okay, still a lot I don’t know.”

I watched her pace between the chaise and the ceiling-to-floor bookcase.

She pivoted. Paced. Turned again.

“Tom?”

“This is better than I could have hoped.” She burst out, a beaming grin pushing her cheeks high. “You only ended our friendship because vampires existed and you literally couldn’t tell me anything because of the compulsion. Then, you couldn’t live without me so you figured out a way around it.”

More like Angelica took pity. “You’re taking this really well.”

Strangely well.

Crossing to the chaise, I perched on the armrest.

She rushed me, gripping my hands. “Not knowing was so much worse, Basil. Thinking you were being abused by a powerful new boyfriend. That you’d gotten into drugs or some kind of organised crime ring so big even your grandmother couldn’t do anything about it.”

I grimaced. “Yeah, I can imagine.”

“So this is great.” Her smile stretched wider. “Perfect, really.”

Tommy walked to the row of decanters by my grandmother’s business awards. She filled a snifter with brandy and tossed it back in four gulps, thumping her chest after.

“Just *great.*” She coughed.

I shot to my feet as she burst into tears.

“Oh my god!” Tommy gasped, reaching for the brandy with shaking hands.

She didn’t bother with the snifter this time.

I wrested for possession of the decanter. “*Tom.* Shit, give it—”

The bottle slid free.

“—here.”

Tommy clutched her oval face with both hands as I set the decanter down.

"Vampires exist," she wheezed, hazel eyes huge. "Teeth. How is that possible? Wait, the lady said they don't know. But they've been around a while. *Fuck*. Fuck! Does this mean werewolves are real? They're like yin and yang, right? Corn cobs and butter. Teeth."

I let her babble wash over me and tugged her to the chaise.

She sank onto the cushions without prompt.

"Shh," I said, pulling her into my arms. "I've got you."

She shook in my embrace, and guilt swarmed me. Did I do right by telling her? I knew exactly how adrift she felt right now.

Knowing all that, I'd still told her.

"It'll be okay. I swear to you." I hushed into her chestnut hair.

"You went through this alone." Her voice cracked.

"Yeah, but I've got you now."

She hiccupped, arms clamped around my waist. "Damn straight you have. W-We'll get through it."

It wasn't a temporary thing, more like the rest of our lives. Tommy would have more freedom—not having a personal homing beacon in her blood or compulsion on her mind. Surely she'd be safer for knowing Vissimo existed in the long run.

I tightened my hold on her. "Yes. We will."

A knock sounded.

"Who disturbs my reverie?" I boomed.

"Fred, Miss Le Spyre."

I pulled away from Tom and fixed her with a look. "Did you hear the end of the recording?" It was crucial she understood the very real danger the vampire presented.

Her bottom lip trembled. "Yep. I heard."

"You can never, *ever* speak of what you know outside of this room? Not to your father, not to your future penis, not to brats you spawn. You never know when *they* might be listening."

She narrowed her gaze. "Was the woman speaking in fucking Icelandic? I understand."

Fuck me. Her emotions were bouncing faster than a rubber ball in a concrete room.

"Come in," I called.

He pulled the heavy doors open but lingered on the threshold. “I’ve come at a bad time.”

Tommy dropped her head into her hands, wailing and hiccupping.

I dragged my gaze from her to the butler. “Long overdue reunion.”

“I see.”

Tommy’s sobbing swelled, and I winced.

Fred kept his polite gaze trained on me. “Is there anything I can procure for Miss Tommy to make her feel better?”

“Tequila,” she choked out.

Couldn’t judge her for that.

The butler bowed, glancing my way. “I’m afraid we are fresh out of tequila, Miss Tommy. I will send someone to replenish our stocks, and in the meantime—”

Tommy wiped her nose on her sleeve. “Jägermeister?”

Ew.

“At once,” he replied.

He met my gaze again, hesitating.

I smiled. “Is there something else?”

He recovered, shaking his head. “Nothing that can’t wait, Miss Le Spyre. Do you require anything else?”

There was an entire list of things I required, top of that list being some way to sever the connection between Kyros and me. Could the butler do *that*?

Tommy slid onto the floor and began crawling to the decanters.

I cleared my throat. “Yes, Fred. Please set up the movie projector in my suite. We’ll need to watch musicals for the rest of the day.”

Across the room, Tommy pulled herself up, draping herself along the mantle as she reached for the brandy.

Shit.

“Better have some cheeseburger pizza and mint ice cream whipped up too,” I added, hurrying to intercept her.

He bowed. “As you say, Miss Le Spyre.”

This was going to be a long-ass day. I blew out a breath, knowing I should feel bad. *Terrible*, really. I'd completely undone my friend—for *life*.

But Tommy was back with me despite all odds. I had my best friend again, for better or worse. Call me soulless, call me the worst fucking friend in the world, but finally, something had gone my way.

And damned if I was going to let anybody take that away from me.

Sleeping was hard without tequila. Really fucking hard.

So the rap at my door didn't drag me from slumber whatsoever.

I froze, lifting my head, but Tommy didn't stir on the bed next to me. Thank the powers for small mercies.

I untangled myself from the duvet, the pleading voices of Sandy and Danny in *Grease* winding through my lounge from the projector.

Cracking open the entrance, I squinted at Fred in the dimly lit hall.

"Miss Le—"

I held a finger to my lips.

Sidling out, I drew the door closed. "She's asleep. I don't want to wake her."

"Forgive the intrusion. Is Miss Tommy well?"

Nope.

"She'll get there. Did you get the medical certificate to her boss?" I answered.

"Yes. I took the liberty of letting Mr Tetley know she was safe and cared for too."

I'd called the stable master to say Tommy and I were working through a few things and she was staying with me for a while. "Thank you. Does something else require my attention?"

Hesitation flickered on his lined face before his features hardened. "I had hoped to wait until Miss Tommy was better, but four days have passed."

Tell me about it.

Tommy was rocking this mental breakdown hard. I'd listened to back-to-back musicals for over one hundred hours. Around the thirty-six-hour mark, Tommy decided she really liked *My Fair Lady*. If I had to listen to "The Rain in Spain" one more time I'd lose the plot.

Again.

I pressed my ear against the door, listening. *Nothing.* Maybe she'd finally passed out instead of jolting awake every hour.

"We're good for a bit." I straightened.

He stepped back. "This way, please, Miss Le Spyre."

I frowned at his tone. "Something is *really* wrong?"

"The cameras picked up a group lurking close by. Daniel rerouted some of the cameras to the roads and properties surrounding the estate. It appears the lurkers retreat during the day, creeping closer at night, but there's no mistake they are surrounding the property."

Ah, fuck nuts.

"Do they come any closer?"

"They remain just inside the perimeter. I upped our security measures as a precaution, but for all intents and purposes, the group is either gathering intel or waiting for something. I am as yet unsure."

We entered the small office toward the front of the main house, tucked away down a smaller hall. Cameras lined one wall while the long desk was filled with screens.

"Hey, Daniel," I greeted the rake-thin man on the chair there who managed our online and our home security.

He smiled. "Miss Le Spyre. It's nice to see you again."

Sober? Or in general?

"And you. How are Marissa and the girls?"

"Better since the twins started school. Marissa feels halfway human again, I think."

I arched a brow. "I'm sure. Please send her my regards."

He beamed. "I will."

My grandmother's staid voice filled my head. *You do not ask, Basilia. You shall be the head of estate.* "Please bring up the footage of our guests, Daniel."

He swivelled in the chair, hands flying over the keys. "Take a look at the top-right screen. These people are good. They know where our main cameras are. But your grandmother asked me to hide cameras in the gargoyles last year. Our visitors haven't spotted them."

A tall, willowy shadow moved across the camera. Female visible by her silhouette. The night settings showed her as a green frame.

I relaxed somewhat.

"How many?" I asked. It wasn't the Tonyi triplets, or at least they weren't alone, and that didn't seem like their style. The female could be any of the Fyrlia princesses, I supposed. But I doubted they dressed in leather jackets. Still, the lurkers could be Fyrlia Indebted.

Daniel brought up more footage. I scanned the screens quickly. *All female. All in leather jackets.*

"Seven, we believe."

I'd say that was spot on. "All females, yes?"

"Correct, Miss Le Spyre. Any idea who it could be?"

Oh, I had an idea alright.

If Laurel and the rest of my crew were here, they were listening to this entire conversation. Which meant they'd intended estate security to notice them.

I pushed off the desk. "Where are they right now?"

"Spread out around the perimeter, miss. The last sighting was in the nut orchard."

"Okay, I'll go out there. Wait in the house, please."

Fred opened his mouth, and I held up a hand.

"I'll be alright," I informed him.

A smile trembled on his lips at my hand gesture before he bowed.

Yeah, okay. Agatha's hand raising thing had stuck around. *Only* because it was a time-saver.

Winding back to the lobby, I yanked on one of the monstrous front doors and padded out onto the gravel.

Dang, gravel was not foot-friendly.

Peering around, my gaze fell on the golf cart parked out front.

That'll do.

I whistled low at the damage to the front. Must've crashed into that wooden step pretty damn hard. *Oops.*

No more tequila-fuelled golf cart ventures for me.

Twisting the key, I sent gravel scattering as I blitzed down the driveway. Halfway to the southern gate, I yanked the wheel to the right to crash through the plants lining the driveway behind, wincing as the branches scratched the cart. Georgia, the estate's head gardener, hopefully wouldn't have too much fixing to do.

Where were the lights on this thing?

I couldn't see shit.

I zoomed past the stables where Tommy's father could be found during daylight hours, and reached the nut orchard, slowing when walnut shells popped and crunched under the tires.

Rolling to a stop next to my favourite pecan tree, I turned the engine off.

"Alright," I hollered, sliding out of the vehicle. "Come out. I know you're there. Stop lurking like creepy fucking stalkers."

A twig snapped behind me.

"Took you long enough," a voice purred.

I faced Laurel, grinning despite the fucked-up situation. "I was busy. Watching musicals."

She scowled. "We heard."

Snickering, I searched the trees behind the Vissimo. "Where are the others?"

"Spread out."

I folded my arms. "And why are you all here?"

I was happy to see her. Really happy considering I'd expected to be embarrassed. Certainly happy enough to know that not *all* my happiness was due to *her* being here. The presence of the Indebted was a tie to Kyros, and my stupid blood-bound body was delirious about the link.

"Kyros sent us. We've been here since you left."

"I don't suppose there's any chance he'll change his mind about posting you guys here?"

"You want him to?" She cut me a look before inspecting the scratches on my cart.

I mulled that over. "I don't. The Tonyi triplets are after me, and no matter how professional my staff are, they're human."

She crouched to peer at the front of the cart, whistling low.

"Yeah… I crashed."

"We heard."

Damn. Bet they'd heard a truckload I'd rather keep buried. During my tower stint, I'd gotten used to not saying stuff aloud that I didn't want overheard, but I was willing to bet tequila loosened my lips. Had I screamed abuse at Kyros at one point?

Before anything else happened, I had to get something off my chest. "Laurel, thank you so much." *For telling me when no one else did.*

Her blue eyes darkened. "I knew from the first time we went out with Tommy. You shouldn't thank me."

Why would anyone just blurt out the truth to a stranger when it could put their life and future at risk? That she'd told me at all reinstated my faith that not all vampires were fuckwits, even if she'd done it to save Fernando's life too.

I reached out and gripped her arm. "With the burdens you carry, I consider it an honour that you did. So don't be boring."

She looked at me quizzically.

"That is how I talk now I'm rich again," I informed her. "Now, please call the others to the house. No point in you all standing out here like weirdos."

Laurel snorted, clambering into the cart after me. "It's been nice, actually. Just me and the trees."

I slid a glance her way. "How many nuts have you eaten?"

"… A few."

Vissimo appetites were huge, so I didn't doubt that for a second. Though I did doubt what kind of nuts she was referring to. Pretty sure Indebted had harems too.

Firing up the cart, I gunned for the house, trying to stay in the same set of tracks on the grass because Georgia's mental state was linked to the smoothness of the lawn.

I screeched to a halt in front of the main house.

"It's big." Laurel took her time getting out.

I lifted a shoulder, spotting four of the other Indebted approaching. "Things usually get bigger when you get closer to them."

She threw me an exasperated look. "What I meant to say is that knowing you're filthy rich, and seeing just how rich, are different things."

Yep.

Which is why I'd never invited Tommy's school friends around. When people saw evidence of my wealth—and the estate didn't register as more than a sentimental blip on the Le Spyre overall wealth—they tended to become very, very uncomfortable. After that, they either smiled double as much or half as much.

Hardly anyone treated me the same after seeing where I lived.

"I guess," I mumbled. "I grew up in this house but don't really like anything else in the rich world apart from Grandmother's friends. I was trying to leave it behind when Live Right drew me in."

Laurel twisted to look at me. "It must be hard to be back here. Doubly so with your grandmother's passing."

Understatement.

Josie waved from the other side of the courtyard roundabout, and I waved back.

A throat cleared. "Miss Le Spyre?"

I whirled. "Fred! Hey. Come meet our stalkers."

"Laurel," the Vissimo next to me stepped forward, hand extended.

The butler took her hand without hesitation.

Laurel smiled, keeping her teeth out of sight. "I apologise if I caused you or the rest of the staff concern over the last week. We were assigned to Miss Le Spyre after an altercation with some high-profile criminals who attacked and killed the man she was with."

The jolt over her flawless switch from Miss Tetley to Miss Le Spyre was usurped by the casual mention of Rhys's passing. The loss of my grandmother had cast everything else in shadow.

Fred's eyes settled on me. "I see."

He saw too much.

I gestured at the incoming Vissimo. "Until the criminals are caught, Laurel's team will work with ours to heighten estate security."

"These criminals are organised and dangerous?" the butler asked.

I shifted my weight at the soft reprimand in his eyes.

He narrowed his gaze on Laurel next. "Do these criminals have anything to do with your presence outside this property a few days before Mrs Agatha Le Spyre passed?"

Whoa. I'd totally forgotten that he'd seen Laurel before.

The vampire tilted her head. "That's why we drove past, yes. We're not connected to the death of Miss Le Spyre's grandmother, if that's what you're insinuating."

The two stared off.

Uhm.

I glanced over my shoulder. Most of the others had joined us.

I clapped my hands to break their visual battle. "Let's reconvene inside for refreshments, shall we?"

Fred broke off first, recovering his polite smile. "Of course, Miss Le Spyre. Where would you like to take them?"

"The conservatory will do, thank you."

He bowed.

When the butler was out of earshot, I squared my shoulders. All seven of my crew were here.

I met each of their gazes. "I'm about to invite you into my home because you're my friends," I said. "As Vissimo currently in debt, I expect you to respect that what happens on this property is none of Kyros's nor King Julius's business. Aside from vague reports or attacks, what happens here on this estate remains *confidential*, always. That puts each of you in a tricky spot, I know, but that's the only way I'll accept Kyros's presence on my property, no matter how I feel for each of you personally."

Their smiles drooped.

Jillian glanced at Laurel, who surveyed me without emotion.

I held her regard without flinching. "If you can't accept my terms, stay outside. I *will* understand if you feel incapable of meeting my terms. For those who stay, I'll meet you in the conservatory presently." I scanned their ranks once more and turned to enter the house.

Fuck it all, I had to warn Tommy. If the Indebted were here for the foreseeable future, my friend would have some serious acting to do.

I hurried up the stairs to leave her a note on the bedside table.

"Miss Le Spyre."

My hand shot for my throat as I choked on a scream. "*Shit.*"

His face was stricken. "I apologise, miss."

My heart pounded in my chest. Freakin' butler standing in the pitch black. I just birthed kittens. "Are you okay?"

"I am well, thank you. I did have a separate matter I wished to discuss with you. Just regarding estate affairs. Is tomorrow morning convenient to meet?"

He wanted to speak about this right now?

I suppose it was past time I took the reins back. Running the estate wasn't even his job. "Of course. Thank you for being patient as I..."

He smiled. "No need to thank me, Miss Le Spyre. I'd do anything for your family. You know that."

"I appreciate that endlessly," I replied, my heart settling. "I'll meet you tomorrow morning at nine."

His gaze shadowed. "Tomorrow at nine, Basilia."

I jerked, staring at his retreating back.

Did Fred just call me *Basilia*?

My jaw bobbed. He did!

Never—not in nearly twenty-two years of being in this man's presence had he called me anything other than Miss or Miss Le Spyre. Even when I tried to trick him into it for a full month at fourteen years old.

I skimmed over our conversation again, wondering if I'd missed something—because there was no way in hell a butler trained by my grandmother just *slipped up*.

Fred had something big to tell me.

8

"Miss Le Spyre, how did you sleep?" Fred asked as he entered my grandmother's office.

Just fucking peachy after his *Basilia* bomb. I spent half the night furiously scribbling notes to Tommy who'd taken the news that seven vampires were sleeping on the first floor about as well as expected. That she'd already spent a night in Laurel's company, albeit in complete ignorance, helped not at all in calming her down.

"Good. And yourself?" I replied from behind the heavy mahogany desk.

The last person to sit here was my grandmother.

Fred closed the door. "As well as ever."

I gestured to the neatly stacked papers before me, setting my glasses down. "What's the go? I've flicked through our financial team's latest report—nothing seems amiss. Are there proposed investments that require attention? Staff matters? Issues with one of our major companies?" Fifty-five percent of the Le Spyre fortune originated from one of five companies. We were major shareholders in a further twenty-nine international companies.

When Grandmother insisted I learn how to run the estate, it was no skin off my back—even if my agreement to learn was really to better my understanding of how corporations ripped people off. What I found during that training only made me proud of my ancestors. The research Grandmother had done into the ethics and environmental impact on our investments was extensive. She—and those before her—had always upheld such a code—even in times when most of the world hadn't cared or *known* about such things.

"Not quite, miss," he said. Reaching up to the third shelf of the bookcase wall, he pressed a button.

My ears popped. "Whoa, what was that?"

"Noise-cancelling technology," he answered, turning back to me. "This is a conversation best conducted in a soundproofed room."

Soundproofed room.

With those two words, I knew.

My mouth dried as I contemplated the estate butler. Fred faced me as straight-backed and militant as he'd always been—impeccable manners beaten into an ex-army man. Now, I studied the awareness in his kind blue eyes with new understanding.

"*You know*," I whispered.

He held my gaze. "I do, Miss Le Spyre."

"How long?"

The butler lowered onto the seat opposite me, the massive desk separating us. "Just over one year."

Far longer than the six weeks since I'd left the estate. Which meant...

I rested my head in my hands. "Grandmother knew."

"She did. Long before confiding in me."

I could have come to her. She could have helped me get away from Kyros and his tower.

And no wonder she'd tried to push Tommy away. She'd known the entire time.

That was a bitter fucking pill to swallow.

I rested back in the upholstered seat, regarding Fred as I scrambled to collect my feelings and thoughts. A foreign focus invaded my own shock, and I honed in on Kyros's emotions for the first time since leaving his lair. His focus was intense. Pinpoint. Which was fine unless he was studying *my* emotions.

First things first. "This room is only soundproofed when you press that button?"

"Yes. Without the button, it's merely soundproofed against human ears. However, if you're concerned about outside ears listening to your conversation with Miss Tommy, I can assure you I set a high-pitched frequency through the speakers outside the room."

My brows climbed.

"Your grandmother believed Vissimo had trouble hearing through a specific frequency."

My grandmother didn't *believe* in things. She'd tested the frequency herself—or knew someone she implicitly trusted who'd done so.

I breathed fully as my chest loosened, the fear for Tommy dissipating. "Thank you, Fred."

"My pleasure, Miss Le Spyre."

Leaning forward, I clasped my hands together atop a stack of papers. Grandmother hadn't just known vampires existed, she'd learned about them. That was a whole other kettle of fish. "First off, you need to be aware my ability to talk freely on this subject is controlled. These are chains I cannot break."

His eyes widened. "I see. You've been compelled. Mrs Le Spyre suspected as much."

I swallowed. "Was Grandmother controlled, Fred?"

"No, miss."

My grandmother had somehow managed to discover vampires, elude them, *and* protect herself and her family against them. Meanwhile, I'd botched things right out the gate.

He added, "She wasn't sure if you'd been compelled the permanent way or not."

"Permanent," I replied.

He closed his eyes. "For that, I'm sorrier than you know. Can I ask if you're compelled to report to the beasts?"

"I am not." But he hadn't known that when broaching the subject, which had been a massive risk for him.

Fred took a breath. "Of course you could be forced to say that too. I have only a small idea how such things work. Your behaviour since returning gave me reassurance you weren't totally under their control."

"The tequila and golf cart?" I asked drily.

The butler's lips twitched before his solemnity reappeared. "Several of your grandmother's close acquaintances are also in their grip."

That was news—though Rory told me most of the city's rich were tied under the compulsion. I'd just assumed those I knew and loved would be free.

Hoped.

The thought of anyone from the front row of Grandmother's funeral being under the thumb of a Vissimo clan made me feel sick. "I'll need a list of their names later, but I'd like to know how my grandmother first made the discovery. Please tell me everything."

Fred tipped his head back. "She did confide in me on that point. I'll tell you what I know. She first discovered vampires when Sir Olythieu was placed under a blood compulsion nearly thirty years ago. She was on the phone to him when the beasts stormed his estate. The phone dropped but didn't disconnect. She overheard everything."

Nearly thirty years ago. So long ago.

"Oh my god." I'd been in her shoes. I'd felt that terror and disbelief and horrible loneliness. It was too late to show her that I understood her pain.

I'd regret that to the end of my days.

"I believe she was a great source of comfort to Sir Olythieu. For the others too. With her help, they could speak of the controls over them. In return, they protected your grandmother and yourself always. Before themselves even. She was their bridge to the human world and some modicum of independence and stability."

My grandmother hid this my entire life, maybe even from my parents.

"This is a lot to take in." I stood, striding around the desk, my head lost in that moment—all those years and decades—and how it must have felt. The threat of Vissimo discovering her involvement would have been constant.

How had she slept at night?

Though I knew the answer to that, really.

Her mind wasn't controlled. She wasn't tied to them.

Yet even then, she'd stayed here to help her friends.

Fred's gaze tracked me around the room. "I would imagine it's no small shock—though not as much as discovering the beasts exist in the first place."

They aren't all beasts.

I rubbed my forehead. "I hate that she had to bear that alone." Had I known, things could have been so different. I might have been here when she needed me.

"My knowledge on such matters is limited," the butler said softly. "But you can go through your grandmother's records."

I snapped my head up, lowering my arms. "What?"

He got to his feet. "Agatha Le Spyre had not a passive bone in her body."

True.

"Do you really think she'd let vampires take the city, her friends, and her beloved granddaughter without a fight?"

Not one fucking bit, but the glint in his eyes was almost frightening. Finally, I got a glimpse at what others saw when they looked at the butler.

Scary.

"How did she fight them?" I stated, lifting my chin.

Fred crossed to the bookshelf and pulled out the copy of Tom Hanks's autobiography. My grandmother had never read it but bought the book out of loyalty because *Sleepless in Seattle* was her favourite movie.

The butler pressed something in the gap and stepped away.

My mouth bobbed as the bookcase swung inward.

Well, shit.

Turns out I didn't know all the hidden nooks on the estate.

"Why don't you head down and find out for yourself?" he suggested.

I tore my gaze from the dark wooden hall visible through the bookcase door. "You aren't coming?"

He bowed. "This is a matter for the head of estate, Miss Le Spyre. And you can rest assured that once the bookshelf is sealed shut again, the area below is entirely soundproof."

"That's me," I said, my tongue thick in my mouth.

A small smile curved his lips before it faded into an expression as grave as I'd ever seen on him. "Time to find out what else that entails."

Two flights of stairs and low-ceilinged hall descended to a circular room that I guessed was somewhere beneath the vicinity of the kitchen.

The secret room was part of the original house if I had to guess. The other hidden passages were added during the second world war by Gloria Le Spyre and didn't use the same materials as the original structure, whereas the mahogany floors here matched the rest of the house.

I scanned the room—absorbing the huge bird's-eye map of Bluff City covering the walls. There were nine colour blocks surrounding me which correlated to the nine suburbs. The estates were in another section and the agricultural district in another. Eleven in total.

The map couldn't be coincidence.

"You knew the game existed," I whispered. "Not just them."

Turning in a full circle, I took in the filing cabinets lining the walls below the map wallpaper. Beneath the estates' section of the map was a desk identical to the one upstairs.

I perched on the upholstered chair and studied the contents of the heavy desk, swallowing hard at the picture of nine-year-old me with my parents a few months before they died.

A piece of paper stuck out from the silver frame. Working the paper free, I read the letters and numbers on it.

"Password," I murmured. It had to be.

Switching on the middle monitor, I clicked on the login box and drew the keyboard to me, typing:

LavEnDeR!@2274#

Not as impressive as the code for Kyros's lair.

Scowling, I tuned into the vampire prince again, relieved to find a vague peace floating through him. Was he sleeping? Colour me surprised he *could* sleep with so much on his conscience.

All three screens flickered to life, and I took a deep breath, pushing up my glasses to scan the contents. The left screen showed an open email browser with a stack of unopened messages in the inbox.

The right was a reporting system that looked similar to *Monocle.*

The middle desktop contained one file labelled *Basilia.*

"Fuck, okay. What have you got for me, Agatha?" I shook out my hands and touched the file on the screen, tapping twice.

My grandmother's face appeared on each of the three screens.

"*Basilia*," she said.

It was a video!

Fumbling, I rushed to tap the pause icon. The image froze and I stared at the video of my grandmother, breath harsh and quick.

Not even three weeks had passed since her death. I wasn't ready to see her.

To hear her voice.

My hands shook as I studied her direct topaz gaze, the colour an exact match for mine and my father's. Her shoulders were relaxed, and she was dressed in her token skirt suit, just like Queen Elizabeth —except her grey hair was long and thick and twisted into an elegant coil at the nape of her neck.

These would be the last words I'd ever hear from her lips.

It just wasn't an easy thing to come to grips with.

Closing my eyes, I dragged in a breath and slowly released it.

I tapped the play button, dread and determination filling me.

"*If you are watching this, I am likely dead,*" she announced, her statement sounding like an order. "*In fact, it is highly likely I was killed by vampires who call themselves Vissimo and will do anything to protect their race and their cause. At the time of recording this—*"

I glanced at the date in the bottom left of the recording.

Three months ago.

"*—you are yet unaware of the monsters in our world, and though I sincerely hope to keep it that way, my work against the Vissimo has recently entered a riskier stage than in past years. As such, I must plan for the worst in case I am disposed of.*"

She spoke so matter-of-factly about her own death. She'd forecasted her end.

My stomach threatened to revolt.

"*There are two vampire clans in Bluff City, granddaughter, totalling around fifteen thousand strong. One is named Clan Sundulus and the other Clan Fyrlia. For one hundred and forty-nine years they have been embroiled in a war, a game of sorts, called Ingenium. The clans will stop at nothing until one of them emerges the victor.*"

Her words were drops of water in the desert. I was deathly scared to miss a single one.

She rehashed information I'd already learned the hard way, explaining how the clans worked and how their game appeared to operate.

I leaned in, eyes riveted on her elegant, lined face.

"*Though I tried my best not to influence how you saw the world, I was prouder than you realise when you turned away from the ways of our neighbours. It was not an easy lesson for you, but that is when I saw what kind of woman you would one day be—strong like your mother and father. Kind. Aware. Passionate.*"

I blinked several times, digging my nails into my palms.

"*You deplore games as a result of your upbringing, so what I'm about to ask of you will demand a sacrifice—a left turn from the way I can see you wish to live life. Know that I do not make this request lightly. That I hope to live for many years to come to give you and whatever family you choose to have a full and blissfully ignorant life. I make this recording in case that goal is not realised.*"

Kids? A husband? I'd never thought much about having either except for errant fantasies about a runaway wedding.

But if I had children, they'd never meet their great-grandmother. Or their grandparents. That made me really fucking sad.

On the screen, my grandmother paused, clasping her hands atop the desk. She tilted her chin. "*I have watched these monsters place cages around the minds of my friends. I have seen them murder and torture and take what they want without care for human life. I will not let them claim Bluff City, Basilia.*"

Her furious conviction reeled me in until my nose almost touched the screen. I'd rarely seen her this impassioned.

"*What these beasts are not aware of,*" Agatha Le Spyre said, a small smile curving her lips, "*is that for nearly three decades, there has been a third player on the board.*"

I didn't dare make a sound as I stared into my grandmother's topaz eyes.

"*Do not belittle yourself by seeking revenge on my behalf. Instead, set your thoughts on a more honourable battle. Vampires have sunk their claws into this city, tearing through humans to do so. Now, they must pay that debt. My heart, my dearest granddaughter, it is your turn to play Ingenium. For the Le Spyres.*"

9

I sat in my grandmother's office—the official above-ground one—swirling my wine and staring at the deep red like the crystal ball it was.

Grandmother detailed everything.

The offshore accounts. The illegal aliases her staff bought houses under so the clans wouldn't come for us. Most of the mega-rich had teams for pretty much everything, and the Le Spyres were no different. Publicists, CEOs, financial advisors, brokers, property management, legal teams—*everything*. This was no different. Grandmother had a team in Churchill who handled conveyance, research, forecasting, and valuation of Bluff City real estate—including tracking the movements of *Live Right Realty* and *Foremost Realty*. They handled all of the leasing of rentals.

In twenty-seven years, Agatha Le Spyre had privately purchased and currently leased *thousands* of properties here. Only the estate was under our real name. Unlike Clan Sundulus, my grandmother ironically operated under a totally, *totally* illegal system. Fake identifications, banks, and tax accounts. Money laundering.

"Shit." I choked on a laugh, taking a sip and tipping back my head so the wine trickled past my taste buds.

In the hours I'd spent gazing at the copy of Tom Hanks's autobiography, aka the entrance to her mastermind cave, I'd ascertained several things.

One, I'd continue my grandmother's work without hesitation.

Two, my grandmother hadn't known the extent of my blood ties to Kyros.

Three, that the major weakness to her plan wasn't lack of money —not even close—but lack of intel.

She hadn't known what the clan's movements and plans were from day-to-day. She'd purchased an average of 325 properties each year for the better part of thirty years, starting slow and gradually accelerating her efforts to thwart the vampires. But she'd had to guess their strategy. Having personally seen how intricate their strategies were, I knew for a fact guessing would be near impossible.

Yet, to *win*, I wasn't sure a defensive strategy would work. Surely an *offense*, to hinder the other player's movements, was necessary too.

"We aren't restricted by rules," I murmured over the rim of my glass. We didn't need to purchase properties on a certain day or to sign contracts purely on our roll. That opened the board dramatically.

"*The number of properties not owned by either us or the clans are dwindling, Basilia. They will dig deeper into privately-owned properties, trying to figure out the puzzle. They cannot be allowed to discover the truth. Trust my inner circle of friends. Trust the butler. But trust few others unless you can be sure they will hold the lives of those around you with equal solemnity. Fight for our legacy, Basilia. Go forth with the courage I have seen in you since birth. Go with my forever love, Basilia, and my sincerest apologies.*"

I knocked back the rest of my wine and reached forward to fill it again.

"Pocketful of Sunshine" blared from my back pocket. I put Tommy on speaker. "Awake at last."

"Where are you?"

"In the office. Sorry I got caught up with business stuff. I'm drinking wine now. Wanna join?"

Her breath caught. “Like the office on the other end of the house?”

She’d have to leave the room sometime. Her behaviour was going to raise difficult questions if she didn’t suck it up. Harsh as that was.

“That’s the one. See you soon? We have some catching up to do.”

Remembering that I wasn’t speaking into Beast, I exited the call screen and tapped out a quick message:

The office is soundproof <3

None of the vampires here will hurt you. I swear it.
They’re the good ones <3 <3

There was a chime on her end. Then silence.

“I’ll see you in a bit,” she mumbled.

That’s my girl.

“Will do. And text your dad to tell him you’re okay.”

The line disconnected and I tossed the phone on the chaise next to me. *Shoot.*

I had a whole heap of decisions to make. Fast. There were fifty emails in the *Ingenium* inbox to catch up on. A team to introduce myself to. Modifications to the strategy to brainstorm and implement. And the legal face of the estate to manage on top of that.

My mind whirled… though not with dread. The challenge *excited* me. Not because of the game. For what I could get *back* by playing it. My dignity, for starters. And if one of the clans did kill my grandmother, then her plea for me to move on without seeking revenge would be ignored. I wasn’t as classy as Agatha Le Spyre and perfectly fine undertaking a trashy vendetta.

Did a part of me mourn the entire situation?

Absolutely.

My grandmother’s part in it. The strain that nearly three decades of this must have placed on her life. Yes, I’d left this estate because of rich games, and now was actively choosing to play a far worse game. That *did* feel like a sacrifice to who I’d been.

But it felt right. Good.

Tommy slid in, slamming the door shut behind her.

I crossed and pushed the button at the back of the third shelf. Each time the door was opened, the noise-proof seal broke.

My ears popped. “Alright. No one can hear us. Go wild.”

Her eyes flared as she sucked in a massive breath, shaking her hands. “*Oh my god, oh my god, oh my god.* That was the scariest fucking thing I’ve done in my life.”

She paced the room, shuddering at intervals.

Stepping around her, I grabbed a second wine glass and returned to the chaise.

“Fill it right up,” Tommy said. “If there’s not visible surface tension, it’s not enough.”

Okay then.

I emptied the rest of the Carignan into her glass. She bent down by the table and sucked the first sip without lifting it.

“How are you travelling, Tom?” I asked quietly.

She picked up the glass. “I feel like those people who are paranoid about every single person killing them. Except now I know they’re right.”

My stomach panged. “The only way you come to harm—unless it’s through sheer bad luck—is if your connection to me is discovered. There are bad guys from—” I gurgled and felt Kyros’s focus in response. *Shit.*

I tried a new approach. “Bad guys who are after me. Or if the… things… figure out you know about them.” *Ugh,* that didn’t make sense. Stupid blood compulsion.

She licked her lips. “What do you mean by the bad guys part?”

I sighed, guilt coating my insides. “I’m being hunted by triplets.” *Woohoo.* Apparently I could say that.

“That’s why the seven women are here,” I added. “For protection.”

“Triplets sound hot.”

I thought of them and shivered. “Believe me, kissing them would be the last thing on your mind. They’re fucking psychotic.”

She took a sip that was far more like a gulp. "Who sent the seven women?"

"Kyros." I still had no trouble saying his name. Made sense that his ego wouldn't allow it.

Her face dropped into a dark scowl. "I hate that d-bag."

My heart twisted. "Join the club."

Tommy's phone chimed and she drew it out, breaking into a smile.

"Anyone I know?" I asked, trying to steal a peek.

She shrugged a shoulder, typing out a reply. "Theodore. He's worried about me. We usually see each other every other day."

Hold the front door.

"Theodore, the same Theodore as before I started work for Live Right?"

Tommy smiled again. "Yeah. We're dating now. He ended things after we first started seeing each other but turned out he just had some shit to deal with. We reunited the week after in a big way. If you know what I mean."

"Oh." My shoulders drooped. "That's awesome."

"Awesome is generally said sincerely."

I wrinkled my nose. "I feel like I missed out on a huge milestone."

"FOMO is a disease, bitch. If it makes you feel better, he was my Basi rebound at first, but things haven't become boring or angry. I really like him."

My friend had some commitment issues and dating someone wouldn't have been an easy jump to take *whatsoever.*

I gripped her knee. "You sound happy, so I'm happy. Your first boyfriend, Tom. Cheers to that!"

We clinked glasses, guzzling the blessed nectar of our sacrificial grapes.

"What about you then? With *Kyros.*" Her face screwed up.

I copied her expression. "It's complicated."

Tommy's eyes widened. "Holy shit, really? Then stop right there. You should just change your status and not actually talk about it."

"Your sarcasm is appreciated, friend." I saluted her with my wine glass. "You know about my mind, uhm, chains?"

Ha! I could say mind chains.

"The blood exchanges. You've had three. He can feel where you are, and you can sense each other's emotions. That must be torture. As if being held captive in his tower wasn't enough. He got inside you."

Well... nearly.

I pursed my lips. "Yeah, it's weird. Foreign and invasive. I mean, I've lost privacy to my own feelings forever." I frowned as the words left my mouth. "That's really shitty."

Tommy set her half-emptied glass down. "What's he feeling right now?"

I frowned, concentrating. "He's relaxed, contemplative. He woke an hour ago."

Her eyes rounded. "Far out, girl. That is cray. *Bulk* cray. How is that possible?"

I borrowed Angelica's explanation. "A mouse looking at us would think we possessed magic."

"A mouse?" she said doubtfully.

I nodded sagely. "A mouse."

"You so didn't think of that yourself."

Laughter bubbled from my lips. "Tom, I am so glad you're here."

She sobered. "How do we free you from this blood thing then? Surround you with candles in the sewers or some shit? The personal GPS signal he has on you has to go. After that, we can get the fuck out of Bluff City. Except there are more of them—everywhere. *Crap.* Hey, can you afford an island?"

I closed my eyes. "We don't do anything."

She laughed. "You're not serious. Wait, you don't *want* the blood thing with him?"

"No," I spat. The utter rage I'd felt upon reading my real name on the blood donor bag struck me with full force. "He fucking lied to me."

Tommy stilled, lowering her voice. "I'd say that's about the least worrying thing he's done, really."

I shook my head. "You don't understand." I tried to tell her he'd known who I was from the get-go. Angelica probably alerted him after mind compelling me during the *interview*. He didn't coincidentally happen to nearly run me over. It was all fucking staged.

I gurgled and tried a different approach. "Surname."

Tommy was fluent in Basi.

She gasped. "He knew you were a Le Spyre the entire time?"

I stared at her.

"That *motherfucker*. I mean, it's a speck in comparison to the rest, but it just makes him even more cold and heartless."

A speck compared to the rest?

Hmm, I suppose she was right.

Then why did Kyros lying feel like the worst part? My chest tightened suddenly, and I took a half-hearted sip of wine as my breath quickened.

"I just can't believe he'd do that to me. After everything," I said into the silence.

"What do you mean by everything?"

Being together in the basement. Him waiting for me at the theme park. Losing his shit when the triplets attacked Rhys and me. His struggle over his alpha power was a constant thing, but somewhere along the line, I'd thought other feelings were pushing him toward me. Now, I knew otherwise. All that bullshit was plain possessiveness, nothing more and nothing less. He did those things for his family, to win *Ingenium*. I was just human collateral.

I forced down the lump in my throat.

It came back double force, and I dragged in a painful gasp of air.

Tommy's face dropped. "Basil, did he touch you?"

Did he ever.

"Yes, but it wasn't that. It's just." I didn't know. The bond between us made things so unclear—trying to gauge what I magically felt and *really* felt was nearly impossible.

"You don't *love* him, do you?" Tommy's hazel eyes were wide and fixed on me.

My horror echoed her own, but it was accompanied by a stinging burn behind my eyes. "God, no," I answered hoarsely. "It was just an extra low blow when I discovered the truth. He played his part well, girl."

The lump wasn't going away.

My heartbeat took off as my chest clamped.

My rasping voice faded to a whisper. "I've done a lot of stupid shit, Tom. Believe me. I've had to wake up real quick. When I found out the truth, he made me feel like I was waking up on the street again."

Powerless. Weak.

I tipped my head back and blinked rapidly as the crushing betrayal of what he'd done rolled over me. For the first time, I allowed myself to feel the sting without fury or shame overriding my hurt.

When all was said and done, I was upset because *he* betrayed me.

He'd taken off my clothes, telling me I was perfection while knowing he was stabbing me in the back.

My vision blurred as my eyes filled.

"I'd kill him if I could," she forced out. "With my bare hands."

I reached to set my glass down, searching blindly for the lip of the small table I'd dragged from the corner.

"Basi?"

"It's okay." The words didn't come out.

"Basil, if you're hurt. You can tell me."

A choked sound tore through my clamped lips.

Then another.

I was so hurt.

I clutched my chest, incapable of holding in the pitiful sobs and harsh, raking inhales between. Being terrorised, tortured, controlled, and *toyed* with. Rhys's death. The mass grave of the Indebted.

Lying to Tommy. Watching her walk away.

Losing my grandmother forever. Staring down at her corpse knowing I wasn't there. That she'd never speak again.

I'd never let the tears get so far. Not in so long.

There were too many to call back.

One slid down my cheek. Dashing it away, the tear was replaced by another. More came until they flowed freely.

“Holy fuck, Basi—” Tom whispered. “You’re *crying*.”

This is what crying felt like? I couldn’t breathe. I couldn’t think through the pain filling my chest.

Yep.

Turned out twelve years of practice couldn’t stop the tears now.

10

“Let me get this straight, Miss Tetley,” Angelica said from across the wrought iron table. “You wish to return to Live Right?”

I arched my brows. “It’s Miss Le Spyre.”

“Your real name is hard to get used to.”

Uh-huh. I bet.

“We both know that’s not the case.”

Angelica’s polite smile dropped. “It’s safer to go by Tetley outside of the tower. Especially if you mean to stay with Live Right. Clan Fyrlia is uninformed of your true identity. Kyros desires to keep it that way.”

With the spies in his tower, that desire would last about half a second.

We sat at one of my favourite brunch haunts in Green. One of those Instagram-worthy places with plants hanging everywhere and heaps of cute nooks.

I sipped at my hazelnut green tea. “If I return—”

“—Which is *why* exactly?”

My answer would be important in determining how closely they watched me for the next few weeks. “I’m not sure you deserve an answer, really. But I appreciate the voice recorder, so I'll be extremely honest with you this once. This *doesn't get back to Kyros*. I mean it, Angelica."

She'd tell him immediately. The vampire was a dark horse, but her matchmaking ways made her predictable.

Angelica took a dainty sip of her jasmine tea. "Of course."

Pfft.

"I left my estate for a reason. I hate the rich bastards I have for neighbours. I need to be onsite there now to manage estate affairs. A lot of people rely on me for income, but my loathing for the rich will not ever change. Added to that, my last family member just died. The house is empty without her. Despite my greatest efforts, I have become an idle rich woman."

Angelica hummed. "Why not take up pottery?"

"Do I look like the pottery type, Angelica?"

She smirked and made no answer. "The blood bond has nothing to do with this decision?"

No, but I wanted her to think so. I'd just waited for her to bring it up.

Pressing my lips together, I narrowed my gaze. "Nothing."

Her smirk widened. "You're one of our best realtors. I'm certain Kyros will accept your return."

Oh, goody.

"And," she added. "He'll stop moping around the tower. His temper has been shocking the last two weeks."

He'd stop moping, alright. In fact, Kyros would be freakin' ecstatic when he realised what I had in store for him.

Angelica finished her tea. "We'll see you tomorrow then?"

I finished my drink and set the porcelain cup down. "I have a few conditions."

She froze, already standing.

I waited patiently as she resumed her seat.

"I have the Le Spyre estate to manage." It was true. Even with the string of CEOs, CFOs, COOs, and other senior management titles between my presidential position and other employees, and even though my major companies were established and the teams well-oiled units, video calls and emails occupied several hours each day.

"I will work for Live Right twenty hours a week. Secondly, I will not live in the tower. Each day I will return to my home with my Vissimo guards."

Angelica shook her head. "If you return to the estate each day, Clan Fyrlia *will* find out."

I had to have access to the office and soundproof working conditions. "So be it."

"Kyros won't accept that."

"He can come to me with a counter-offer then," I informed her.

The vampire regarded me coolly. "Are those all your terms, Miss Tetley?"

I ignored the jab. "I'll need my bank account and tax numbers changed, of course. And there will be no 2:00 a.m. calls to drag me into the office."

Placing my empty cup down, I stood, grabbing my purse. "Get in touch if that works for Clan Sundulus."

Angelica's mouth bobbed.

I smiled down at her. "I'll get the bill."

Weaving to the counter, I dropped a hundred dollar bill there and winked at the pimply teen manning the register. "Keep the change."

She beamed back. "Thank you!"

"Don't do drugs, kiddo," I replied sagely.

After evading the many hanging plants, I waited as Laurel drew the SUV to the front. Josie got out and I clambered into my middle seat, rearranging my powder-blue shirt dress once situated.

Laurel sped off as soon as Josie shut the door, but no one spoke for five minutes.

"You're going back to the tower," Laurel said without inflection.

Her eyes glimmered, and as far as I could tell, they only did that when she disagreed or wanted to say something.

Meeting her gaze in the mirror, I replied in the same tone. "I am."

The glimmer intensified.

Hmm, what did she want to say? "Only if Kyros agrees to my terms. If he does, would you all like to stay at the estate? I just realised that I'd be dragging you guys out of the tower."

Laughter burst from Kelsea's lips. "You've seen where we live, right?"

I grimaced. "True."

Josie touched the back of my hand. "Thank you for checking. But I speak for everyone when I say that we're more than happy to stay in your massive fucking mansion. Our sisters and brothers are happy about our new situation."

"Okay, if that changes—let me know."

Laurel indicated, pulling out onto the freeway. "Kyros will assign you more Indebted. I'll recommend at least twenty of our best to contend with the Tonyi triplets."

Kyros always listened when Laurel spoke—which meant he respected her opinion.

Which meant...

Ah, I see.

"Noted," I said after a beat. "If you were to recommend thirty, that would mean twenty-three other Vissimo could live on the estate, no?"

Her lips twitched. "That would be the most logical position for us."

My own smile faded. "I'm happy to follow any recommendation you provide, Laurel. But to be clear, anyone who comes to my estate will follow my confidentiality rule. I must stress how important it is that I can trust each and every person who enters my property."

My comment hung heavy in the SUV.

Had I offended them?

Perhaps, but the words needed to be said. I wouldn't openly discuss my grandmother's secret agenda ever—not outside the hidden office, but the more vampires on my property, the greater the risk of discovery. My crew were loyal, but the Indebted were in a desperate situation. Issues like Fernando's spying stint couldn't arise.

This was a calculated risk, however. One I really had no choice but to take to protect the people in my care. To protect Tommy.

"I'll make the rules very clear to any who are selected," Laurel said fervently. "You are a friend to the Indebted. That hasn't changed even though you're no longer Miss Tetley."

"I appreciate that," I said with equal honesty. "In my experience, my name changes everything. People decide how they'll treat me before knowing me."

"Is that why you speak to us so much?" Jillian said from the back seats. "Because Vissimo see us as slaves and nothing more?"

"Could be." I lifted a shoulder. "I hate the way you suffer because of crimes you never committed. The seven of you saved my life not so long ago, and I consider myself in your debt, not the other way around. So with those words about confidentiality spoken, I won't bring up the subject of trust again. You have it unless you break it."

Laurel jerked her head. "Understood. Your faith in us will not be broken."

I stared past Kelsea as the estates whipped by.

There was another loose end. A loose end I planned to use to my advantage.

"Laurel?"

"Miss Le Spyre?"

I faced forward. "Make sure Fernando is one of the Vissimo who join us, would you?"

Her eyes flew to meet mine in the mirror. "Fernando?"

"Yes." I sat back, smiling. "It's time we had a little chat."

I'd avoided Level 66 at all costs while masquerading as Miss Tetley, but now it was the place I had to be. That was where Kyros delivered his verbal instructions to the team each day—where he spoke of the probabilities and forecasts and the team push and various long-term strategies. *There*, he met his siblings to discuss final plans before approval, and that's where the real strategies were hammered out. Where *Level Expert* bluffs were formed.

I had to wiggle my way into that room. The heart of Clan Sundulus' brainstorming for *Ingenium*.

Somehow. Without raising suspicions.

I'd spent three days formulating additions to my grandmother's established plans and re-establishing communication with her team. The new offensive side to the Le Spyre game would roll out immediately, fronted by the group in Churchill. Their first job was to double the size of my workforce.

But I had my own part to play.

Priority number one? Working my way back into *Kyros Sky*. I mentally ticked that off as I strode through the halls of Level 50 toward the cafeteria.

Priority number two?

Well. That would take a whole *other* level of commitment.

A visit to the salon and my hair was two shades lighter and silky to the touch. Barrel curls bounced gently with each of my high-heeled steps as I entered the cafeteria. Despite my ulterior motives for being here, I couldn't help feeling like a jilted girlfriend crawling back because I was desperate for Kyros's attention.

I'd dressed with that in mind.

Not by wearing less, by wearing *more*.

The dress was perfect for a cocktail party or romantic weekend getaway. The floating material was petal pink, knee-length, and the neckline drew together with a tie. I'd looped the ends into a floppy bow that rested off-centre at the base of my neck. With white buckle heels, a soft grey coat, and natural make-up to highlight my youth, my look screamed *I have my entire life ahead of me and I'm classy as fuck, you meaty bastard.*

Silence descended as I strode for the fruit buffet. The reaction of the Vissimo was the exact reason I'd come here for lunch—*their* breakfast—before my shift from 3:30 p.m. to 7:30 p.m.

That. And—

"Basilia." Kyros's voice slithered over my shoulders, eliciting a shiver I felt to my very core.

Damn him.

He stopped beside me, and I forced myself to take him in, to *feel* my raw reaction to his body and the desperate anticipation of a sweaty night tangled together.

Then I let the frantic need flitter away to the trash heap where it belonged.

"It's Miss Le Spyre. Use it."

His soft growl slipped between us, but I ignored the warning as I loaded strawberries and diced mango onto my plate.

"I didn't expect you to come," he said with a bite I knew was filtered excess from my order.

"To the tower or for lunch?"

When he didn't reply, I gathered the answer to my question was *both*. A yearning belonging to Kyros struck me full force, and my wide eyes flew to his before I remembered myself.

This fucker didn't get to yearn for me.

"There are things we must discuss," he said low, stepping closer. "Will you join me for breakfast?"

The warmth of his body seeped into mine. "You expect me to *sit* with you? After what you did?"

I popped half a strawberry in my mouth, insides clenching as his gaze dropped to my lips.

His meadow-green gaze flared. "I'm not deluded enough to expect that. We must arrange the finer details of your changed contract with Live Right. It's a business discussion, nothing more."

Yeah, sure. "Oh, then I'll figure things out with Angelica."

His jaw clenched, and I popped another strawberry in my mouth, humming with pleasure as the sweet juice flooded my mouth.

Kyros lifted a hand and wrapped a strand of my butter-blonde hair around his forefinger. He could surely feel my loathing, just as he could feel the white-hot lust spearing me at his touch.

"Four days ago," he said so softly I could barely hear. "Around this time. What happened?"

Four days ago, I'd cried hard enough and long enough to fill a lake. For a lot of reasons, but Kyros was definitely one of them.

His betrayal had pushed me over an edge I'd spent twelve years avoiding.

Tilting my chin, I closed the distance between us, resting my fingertips on his muscular chest. I let my gaze roam over his muscular frame, sliding my hands down to tug at the bottom of his charcoal waistcoat. Reaching up, I twitched the sleeves of his crisp white shirt into place and adjusted his perfect tie, my insides purring as his pure *want* rolled through me.

For a moment, just a calculated second, I allowed my yearning to rise too.

When his lips parted, I locked the longing away.

I patted his chest. "It could have been fun, Kyros. Such a shame you fucked it up."

I heard several gasps from the audience studiously pretending not to listen.

As I turned away, Kyros whipped out an arm, capturing my hand. He drew me back, eyes dipping and scanning as though searching for something only he could see.

"How do I un-fuck it all up?" he eventually asked.

More gasps.

Hushed murmurs.

Shit, even I was shocked at the show of humility in front of his minions. Except Kyros firmly believed in the *singing of our blood*. Or whatever the fuck it was. Despite what he did and did *not* feel for me, the alpha viewed me as his true mate. The humility wasn't for *me*—not because he loved me or was sorry. Kyros already believed I would be his and wished to know how most efficiently to get there.

Poor guy.

I wasn't going to *let* him lose me. Not really. But the chase had to be believable.

Checking my watch, I murmured, "You don't un-fuck anything, Kyros. We move on from here. It is *so* sweet of you to offer though."

He blinked, and I slid my hand free.

Waving at the staring vampires, I said, "Have a good day, everyone. Go knock 'em dead."

They redoubled their efforts not to openly eavesdrop.

That's right, fuckers. Listen away. You're playing my game now.

I'd returned as a spy in their midst—my grandmother's spy. They had no idea what was about to hit them.

Vissimo would rue the day they entered Bluff City when I was done with them.

11

“Mr Trenington,” I said as the door opened. “My name is Basilia Tetley. How are you today?”

The face of the early-thirties man didn’t even twitch in welcome. He had the appearance of a long-distance runner who forced himself into corporate clothing during the week. “Are you a Jehovah?”

I pulled up short. “What’s a Jehovah?”

“A Jehovah’s witness.”

Oh. “No, not a Jehovah.”

His gaze sharpened. “What electricity company are you from?”

Lucky I knocked back a coffee after seeing Kyros. This guy was a live one. “Not from an electricity company either. Would you like another guess?”

“You’re from Live Right.”

I pulled a face. “Is it that obvious?” And was that the ranking? Jehovah, electricity company, and realtor?

He started to close the door. “Not this time. Usually I can peg them straightaway.”

You’re one of the smart ones.

“Yeah,” I said. “Pretty easy to spot. Usually.”

The door widened a crack. “You notice it too? Their eyes?”

"Hard to miss, isn't it?" I dodged the question, scared I'd gurgle instead. "But you're right. I'm here to discuss the possibility of Live Right purchasing your home."

He seemed disappointed I wasn't eager to swap conspiracy theories.

"Right." Mr Trenington said. "I am looking to sell, but I won't sell to Live Right or Foremost. They're up to something. Aliens, perhaps. I won't give them more power."

I nearly whistled.

Wow, this guy had super good instincts. Shoving down the urge to pat him on the back, I instead answered, "Completely understandable, Mr Trenington. If you change your mind, here's my card. I assure you, I'm not an alien."

I'd had them printed myself, the number linking to my untapped phone that Daniel updated the firewall on yesterday. If Mr Trenington called this number, I wouldn't be buying the house on behalf of *Live Right*.

"That's what an alien would say." He still took the card, gaze boring into my back as I left.

I strode down the grass driveway of the small abode in Purple, rattling off a text to my Churchill team.

54 Page Street. Mr Trenington. Values local business and transparency. Two days.

The phone chimed a second later. I read the text.

Received. Forwarded to Head of Sales for acquisition.

The team of ten sent a report each day with proposed properties to purchase based on the recent purchases of *Foremost* and *Live Right*. In addition, I employed four real estate agents who travelled to Bluff City from surrounding cities. They had a 75 percent success rate for acquisition—25 percent higher than *Live Right*.

I planned to kill two birds with one stone during my *Live Right* shifts. I wouldn't lift a finger to acquire houses for Kyros. Maybe just one every so often to keep up the illusion. All other properties I visited were to gather intel for my team.

Doing it felt so fucking good.

But that wasn't enough.

Years of forecasting reports in the hidden office had told me that if I didn't expand my operations, then I'd never win this thing in my lifetime. Grandmother must have planned to accelerate acquisition—she'd mentioned finishing this before she passed, but there were no details of such plans. The Churchill team was on a need-to-know basis despite the confidentiality agreements—and the incriminating evidence I'd found for each of them in one of the filing cabinets in the secret office.

I'd looked over the books, studying how my grandmother had pushed growth. *Slowly*. Only every couple of years. She'd had me and my parents to worry about, no Indebted to protect her household, and the bigger operations got, the higher the risk of being caught.

My position was stronger.

My game had to be more aggressive.

This wouldn't occupy my entire life.

I opened the door and rolled over Josie to reach the middle seat.

She snorted, pushing my leg off her lap. "I was about to get out."

"Just saving time."

"Mrs Gaughton's, please," I told Laurel.

She peeled the SUV away from Mr Trenington's curb.

The vampire cleared her throat as we tore through Purple on the way to Orange via Pink. "I made the recommendation to Kyros last night, Miss Le Spyre."

"Thirty?" I quirked a brow.

She nodded. "He wants fifty stationed on your estate."

My brows shot up. "*Fifty?*"

Shit, this could work out *perfectly*.

Her grip on the wheel tightened.

"Typical guy trying to show off." I rolled my eyes, playing the part.

Laurel's eyes glimmered for a beat before she cleared her throat. "We know you won't want to house so many—"

"Oh, that's what you're worried about?" I blurted. "If fifty of you want to come to the estate, it's no problem. You'll have to double up on rooms, and some will need to sleep in the pool houses and old staff quarters at the back of the property, but if that's cool with you guys, I'd love to have you."

Quiet descended.

I tapped my lip. "I feel bad for the other fifty. Is there any way to rotate guard duty so everyone gets some time away from the tower? You guys will need to avoid my staff whenever possible—I don't want them terrified by your Vissimo-ness."

Jillian whispered to Evie, "*I told you she'd let us.*"

I pivoted on the seat. "You guys thought I'd shut you down?" Jaw dropping, I scanned all seven of them. "You totally did! *Ouch.* You know me better than that."

Kelsea hung her head.

"We apologise," Laurel said, her blue eyes burning. "It's hard for us to trust anyone who isn't in debt like us. Even then, it takes a while to let newcomers in. Our situation is tenuous—"

I held up a hand. "Truly, I'm not offended. But I want you to know, *all* of you, that no matter what's happening between Kyros and me, I would never do anything to bring harm to your sisters and brothers. Not willingly." *Because he can just compel the truth out of me.*

Josie sniffed, wiping her face.

The timing was right. "Laurel, when we get back to the estate, I need a word with you."

"Certainly, Miss Le Spyre."

"Just Basi, please. That goes for all of you."

Laurel shifted in her seat. "Basi. Only out here. Not in the tower."

I conceded the point as we pulled up outside Mrs Gaughton's.

I'd called her yesterday to explain why I'd ghosted our date, citing a breakup as the reason. "I'll be an hour at least. More if she turns this into an extended dinner."

"We'll be here," Kelsea said fiercely.

Laurel nodded. "We will. And Basi?"

"Yeah?"

"Fernando will be at the estate when you return. He's appropriately fearful of what you may say."

She'd totally laid into him.

"Good," I said grimly, climbing over Josie before she could hop out of the way.

"Stop it." She whacked my butt.

"Why would I when that's the reward?" I asked her, wiggling my behind.

Rolling her eyes, she gave me a gentle shove.

"Basilia!" Mrs Gaughton was already outside. "Do your friends want to come inside?"

Jesus, they'd fear her to death.

I straightened, marching up the driveway to meet the elderly woman. "Thank you for the offer. They already ate and they're listening to the *Harry Potter* audiobooks. It's at a good part."

"Stephen Fry's voice could melt my panties right off," Mrs Gaughton replied seriously.

Interesting. "How's the garden looking?"

We both surveyed the lavender bush.

"It looks great, Mrs Hannah." I wasn't lying either. "There's new growth. And the rest of the garden too. You planted fresh marigolds?"

She preened. "Sure did. Won't look right if the lavender is flourishing and nothing else."

"Got a hose? I'll give everything a water and weed."

The older woman protested. "Not in your nice clothes. You look like you've been to a high tea or something."

"Had to dress up to show the ex what he was missing." I sincerely hoped Laurel and the others didn't carry that tidbit back to Kyros. We were technically off the estate, so their reporting was fair game.

She sniffed. "His loss."

"My thoughts exactly." I kicked off my heels and shimmied out of my grey coat. "Where's that hose? This garden is going to look epic."

She pointed to a spot in the middle of the garden where a green hose was coiled. "It will look perfect for when my sister visits."

Her sister? "Didn't she visit a few weeks ago?"

Mrs Gaughton flushed. "She'll be here in a month."

I took in her flushed face. "That's okay. I must have misheard. I've had a bit on my plate."

She fluttered a hand my way. "Don't worry. She was coming but had to put off the trip because of health issues."

"I hope she's feeling better."

A shadow flickered across her face. "Right as rain."

I studied the clear blue sky. "Well, it doesn't look like rain. So how about I get to work and you offer me a cheese and onion toastie?"

The glint returned to her eye. "You enjoyed that, huh?"

"Understatement," I replied, picking through the new marigolds to the hose. She'd weeded recently, so this wouldn't take long. The irony of what I was doing when I had a team of gardeners in my employ wasn't lost on me.

When my parents died, I'd learned that matters of the heart didn't have to make sense at the time.

Such things always made sense in the end.

Want a new job? Triple your current pay. <3
I need to buy your house off you, plz. K thx <3 <3

I fired off the text to Tommy, sliding open the desk drawer to deposit the phone out of sight at a knock on the door.

"Come in."

Laurel slid in, shutting the door behind her. "Basi."

"Thanks for coming." I crossed the room, pressing the noise-cancelling button.

She blinked several times. "That's uncomfortable."

"The ear-popping? It's uncomfortable for humans too. What does it feel like for you?"

"As though I've lost one of my crucial senses and I'm more vulnerable to attack." The vampire moved her jaw around. "What is it?"

I smiled. "No one outside this room will hear our conversation."

She lowered her hands. "That explains your eight-hour silence four days ago."

Smirking, I returned to my chair and gestured to the empty seat on the opposite side of the desk.

As the Vissimo lowered into the cushioned seat, I released a pent-up breath, trying to shove down my nerves. "I have one personal question to ask. Is that okay?"

Her cloak descended, smoothing her features into an impassive Indebted mask. "Depends on the question."

"You're two hundred and forty years old. Are there any Vissimo in Bluff City who can compel you?"

She leaned back, kicking out her leather-clad legs. "King Julius can compel me with blood—if he should so choose."

Drat.

I tapped a finger on the desk, eyes darting over the papers covering the surface. "Not ideal."

"I assume there's something of great import you don't wish leaving this room?"

"Not until the right moment."

She didn't outwardly react to the statement.

"How often do you encounter King Julius?" I asked.

"Five times in one hundred and twenty years. It would take a great deal for him to tie himself to an Indebted with a blood exchange. For a king to exchange blood with a slave would cause huge loss of face in the community. He trusts my integrity. As does Kyros. I held a high position before my father went berserk."

High position, huh?

My ears pricked, but her expression closed off again.

I pondered her answer. "I'd planned to bring you into the fold later, closer to the time when I could free you. However, I need some reassurances before I make a choice that will affect the rest of my life."

She froze, blue eyes widening. "Free me?"

"Laurel." I struggled to find the right words. This was crucial to my strategy, but more than that, I'd be playing with peoples' lives. "How many Indebted are in Bluff City?"

"Two thousand. Sundulus keeps twelve hundred. Fyrlia, eight hundred."

"I don't know what the total debt owed is—"

"570 million dollars," she answered without hesitation.

Not as much as expected. "I'd like to free you all, pay off the debt of those in Clan Fyrlia and Sundulus."

I studied her sudden tension. Her expression hadn't altered but she'd stopped breathing.

Better keep going. "To do that demands an irreversible sacrifice on my behalf."

"You'd need to exchange blood with Kyros three more times," she whispered.

I had to exchange six times in total to be capable of *owning* Indebted. "Correct."

She burst to her feet in a blur. "Why would you make such an offer?"

This was the part I didn't feel 100 percent ethical about. "I'm glad you asked."

The tension drained from her body. "Oh."

Here goes.

"I'm working against Clan Fyrlia and Clan Sundulus in secret." My heartbeat quickened as the words left my lips.

Her eyes widened. "Working against *how*?"

I had to let Laurel in enough for her to gamble on me. Not so much that my grandmother's work would unravel if King Julius took a dip into her mind.

"By playing their game as a third, unknown player as my grandmother did before me," I replied calmly.

Laurel sat with a thud.

"They won't own Bluff City, Laurel. Not while I'm standing."

She looked at me like I'd sprouted a third eye.

"But," I said, sighing, "I'm human. My ability to defend myself against Vissimo is almost zero. In return for the freedom of those in debt, I ask for protection for the period of one year after I complete the sixth blood exchange with Kyros. All who join me will be paid a fair wage. All will have two days off each week, with twenty days of holiday leave annually. You will be provided house rentals at a discount while you get on your feet. When the one year is up, employment will be offered to any who wish to remain."

I couldn't tell how long *Ingenium* would go on. I dabbled with the idea of asking the Indebted to remain for three years, but I just couldn't do it—not when some had been enslaved their entire lives.

Laurel stared at me, the blaze of her eyes surging. I struggled to stay still as my body demanded I turn tail and run.

"You want to win so much?" she whispered. "I thought you hated games."

I inclined my head. "There's only one way out of *Ingenium* for me now, and that's to head further in. Innocent people are being hurt because of the pride of two kings. That needs to end."

"What you ask... if it failed, if the Indebted were caught, the repercussions to us would be catastrophic."

"I know. Which is why I don't want the others to know until I'm in a position to uphold my end of the bargain. I wanted to make the deal without involving you, but..."

She pressed her lips together. "We will attain our freedom and you will lose yours."

What remained of it.

"You know what your sisters and brothers need and want," I told her seriously. "If you believe they'll take my offer, then that's good enough for me to forge ahead. If you're unsure in any way, I need to know that too."

The vampire held my gaze. "They'll take it. Without second thought."

Okay. "Those from Clan Fyrlia as well?"

"Without a shadow of a doubt."

I relaxed and then tensed all over again.

I'm really going to do this.

Laurel fixed me with a level look. "Your relationship with Kyros. What you feel for him by the sixth exchange will be much stronger than what you currently feel."

If the first three were anything to go by, the change would be drastic—almost unbearable.

She leaned forward. "He'll be able to hear your thoughts at the sixth exchange."

I shivered, but I'd considered that possibility. "That's better than expected, actually. I'd feared it might happen at the fourth or fifth. Can he hear my thoughts always?"

"Only within a certain distance, or so I believe."

That was one silver lining. "Then that will be the period of highest risk. Though once I have the protection of your force after the sixth exchange, it won't matter what he learns from my head."

I hope.

The vampire didn't seem convinced. "What about what you might feel for him by the sixth exchange? Or even at the next?"

Over my dead body would I feel anything for Kyros ever again.

I spread my hands wide. "I loved my grandmother more than anything in this world, Laurel. I'll uphold her legacy until my dying breath. I swear to you that the bond with Kyros will not change our deal. I say that with certainty—because if I could free you all without any of this bullshit, I'd do it in a second. What the bond makes me feel for him may heighten, but who I am will not alter."

Her expression cleared. "When did you find out about your grandmother's hand in the game?"

"Four days ago."

She stretched out her hand. "You have a deal."

Uh.

"That was sudden."

"You offered to buy our freedom that day at the waterfall while still at the tower and ignorant of your grandmother's work. Your offer comes from the heart."

I scowled. "It annoys me that you lump me in with everyone who has shat on you."

Amusement flickered in her bright eyes. "One day I might not."

I rounded the desk. Having the Indebted at my back was the cornerstone of my midterm strategy. Her agreement on their behalf felt like a massive battle won.

"Would you like me to send Fernando in?" she asked, following me to the door.

"Is he nervous?"

"Extremely."

I smirked. "Another day to stew will help build character then. I've been meaning to ask what the penalty would be if Kyros got wind of Fernando's betrayal."

Her expression darkened. "Kyros lost face. His true mate nearly died. Five of his Indebted were killed. The penalty for that is death. The debt of Fernando's mother and his new debt would be passed on to his eldest child. Barring that, the closest family member. Which in his case, would be his only sister."

I whistled low. "Shit. That was a helluva risk to take."

"The desperate aren't known for 20/20 vision. His actions reflected poorly on all Indebted, however. He's being treated accordingly."

I wasn't surprised. I'd do the same. "If you see Fernando, please tell him to meet me here at 10:00 a.m. tomorrow."

Laurel bowed.

I couldn't stop myself fidgeting this time. "Please stop bowing to me. I'm not your superior in any way, shape, or form."

She straightened. "No."

"No, you agree?"

"No, I won't stop."

Alright then.

"You need to exchange blood with Kyros three more times," she said, searching my gaze. "Has he agreed to that?"

Less than two weeks ago, he'd been pretty fucking eager. If he suspected anything suspicious about my return, the password to his pants would be as impossible to crack as the code to his lair.

Priority number one was infiltrating *Kyros Sky.*

Priority number two?

Seducing the fuck out of a one hundred and forty-nine-year-old vampire.

12

The door to my suite cracked open.

Biting back a shriek, I bolted upright in bed.

Clutching my chest, I stared at the woman illuminated in the doorway.

"It's me. Josie."

"And the Pussy Cats," I answered.

"What?" she hushed, wrinkling her nose.

"Pinocchio," I croaked, then shook my head a few times until the haze of sleep receded. "What the hell are you doing here?"

Josie looked torn between horror and hilarity. "Sorry, Basi."

I narrowed my eyes, hissing, "You're not sorry one bit."

I twisted to check Tommy hadn't woken. A vampire in the room in the middle of the night was *just* what she needed, especially now she'd finally worked up the courage to walk around the house.

Josie sobered. "We have visitors."

Why didn't she say so?

I shoved back the bedspread, swinging my legs down. "Who?"

"Triplets."

Shit, shit, shit.

"That didn't take long," I murmured, knowing they could be

listening to this conversation. Clan Fyrlia officially knew who I was now. The psychos had to have more spies in *Kyros Sky*. Unless Fernando was still doing a bit on the side.

I slung a silk kimono over my nightwear and slid into matching slippers.

I padded out the room. "What's the situation? Have my staff detected their presence too?"

"No, they're yet unaware. The triplets are alone and scouting the perimeter. Laurel wants to speak to you regarding battle strategy."

Battle strategy. Was I a fucking army general?

Laurel was waiting in my office. In the dark. When I entered, she clicked the soundproof button and flicked on a lamp.

My ears popped. "Well?"

"They haven't entered the property, but a show of force is necessary. Not to reveal our full numbers, but to show the Fyrlia princes how many Indebted Kyros has provided for his true mate."

Right. A pissing contest.

"What do you need me to do?" I asked.

"Confront them head-on with twenty of us as backup."

Ah, fuck nuts. "I was hoping you wouldn't say that." I glanced down at my lace and silk purple nighty and kimono combo.

"Would you like to change?"

I blew out a breath. "Nothing says I don't care about your threat like showing up in your pyjamas."

Her teeth gleamed in the low light.

Pivoting, I paused in the threshold. "I'm not going to die, am I?"

Laurel's grin turned feral. "Not today, Basi."

Reassuring.

Attempting to crack my neck and failing, I swung the door open and strode through the attached lounge and the music room to reach the main hall. Heading for the lobby, I peered back as my crew of seven fell in behind me.

More I didn't know joined, a mixture of male and female. All of them dressed from head to toe in black leather.

"You guys know that only Jessica Alba in *Dark Angel* can wear that kind of getup, right?"

I didn't care what the second thrall made me do *once*. As long as they wore leather, they'd hear about it.

Laurel snorted. "So you've told us, Miss Le Spyre."

I gathered from her formality that the triplets were now within hearing distance.

Squaring my shoulders, I left the house, adjusting course for my golf cart by the roundabout. I'd parked it in the middle of the driveway, so someone had moved it.

A few snickers reached my ears as I slid onto the seat and twisted the keys in the ignition.

"It's a long driveway," I defended. And those fuckers weren't stepping a foot inside my fence line.

I gunned down the driveway, knowing the Vissimo would have no trouble keeping up. Parking by the front entrance, I hopped out and swung the gates wide.

"Here, Tonyi, Tonyi, Tonyi." I whistled for good measure.

This time my crew's snickers were louder.

"*You're brave with twenty Indebted at your back, Basilia Le Spyre.*" The cold voice slithered from the shadows and wrapped tight around me.

My heart sputtered and I worked to catalogue the fear. *I'm scared because a predator wants to hurt me. I won't underestimate him. For my mind to operate, fear needs to take a back seat.*

Which it did.

"Don't be shy," I said back after a beat. "It's not like I haven't seen your ugly mugs."

The first triplet left the shadows.

Where were the other two?

"Ugly? I think not. We could have you in our bed in a second." His eyes roamed over my thighs and breasts.

The brothers shared their bed partners? *Uhm*, gross.

I wrinkled my nose. "By all means, try and see how Kyros reacts."

"*You're his true mate*," a second voice came from the left of the gate.

Another triplet stepped from the shadows. "Yet you are not in his tower."

Fuck me, they were like Ursula's eels from *The Little Mermaid.*

"Well, no," I said, lifting a shoulder. "He stays here."

They froze, staring past me to the house.

I smiled. "Just kidding, boys. You should have seen your faces."

Their almond-shaped eyes blazed hazel, and my palms slickened with sweat.

"Our master has placed twenty-five of us here permanently," Laurel stepped forward, chin tilted high as she surveyed them. She peered straight ahead into the dark as well to where the third must be lurking.

"Twenty-four hours a day," she added.

"*Do not speak in our presence, Indebted*," the third hissed before slipping from the shadows to stand in the middle of his brothers.

My chest clamped at the sight of the three vampires who'd attacked me and Rhys. If not for the fourth Fyrlia prince down in the basement and the intervention of Kyros's siblings, I'd be ash right now. "That's some elitist complex you've got going there."

"Spoken by a fellow elite—though a mere human one," the third purred, stepping closer.

Indebted flanked me in a blink. Hands bunched in the back of my nighty, ready to yank me from danger.

Headlights blared bright, the roar of engines bearing down on us. Two black SUVs screeched to a stop and the back door of the front vehicle was flung open.

My eyes registered a grey blur before one of the Tonyi triplets doubled over.

I focused on the new arrival, drawing her name up from my time in the basement. *Gina*. The eldest royal child of Clan Fyrlia—though she considered herself the second, with Kyros as the real crown prince of their clan.

"Get in the car," she snarled at her brothers.

The triplet on the right sneered. "You—"

She snapped out a fist and he reeled away, clutching his nose. "Father has been informed of your little trip."

Their expressions smoothed.

Whoa. At least someone had these psychopaths in check. I did *not* want to meet the man who'd spawned them. Actually, make that either king. Their spawn were scary enough.

The triplets shot three matching smirks my way before stalking to the car.

Gina turned, scanning me from head to toe. I did the same right back as the car containing the triplets sped away.

"Gina." I greeted.

She arched a brow. "Miss Tetley. Or should I say Miss Le Spyre?"

The Vissimo peered past me to the estate. "Quite the secret you kept. Can't say I blame you—knowing who your true mate is."

Fresh hurt stabbed me, but I worked to keep my face and voice free of the emotion. "Why are your brothers visiting me in the middle of the night?"

"Because they're bitter and twisted inside," she answered.

Couldn't argue with that.

She pursed her lips. "I have the misfortune of being their sister. I don't have the fortune of being blind to their faults."

"They're seriously messed up," I told her. "An impartial clan ruled the matter between me and your family closed and done. Are they going to be an ongoing problem?"

Turned profile, she glanced at me. "I don't need to answer that, do I?"

I sighed. *Thought as much.* "Just so you know—because you seem to have some hold over them. My Vissimo will fuck them up if they step foot inside this property or go for me elsewhere."

"*Vissimo*," she murmured, eyes running over the ranks around me. "Interesting."

The same word applied to her.

Clan Sundulus painted their enemy clan as mindless savages. That wasn't to say that this woman wasn't part of what happened in the basement. She'd watched on. *She'd* held a blade to my throat to force Kyros to stop fighting. But Gina possessed reason and restraint. I saw her as no different to Kyros or any of his siblings.

I narrowed my gaze, forgetting for the moment that it was the middle of the night and I was surrounded by beings with fangs. "What do you think of *Ingenium*, Gina?"

The ghost of a smile floated on her lips. "What an unusual question, Miss Le Spyre. In apology for my brother's misdemeanour tonight, I'll answer it."

How nice.

She faced me. "*Ingenium.* I think that it's a great thing I'm immortal. The idea of wasting my entire life engaging in this bullshit farce would otherwise have driven me insane long ago."

I blinked. *Wow*. Really honest.

Weirdly, her answer did feel like a boon. "Thank you."

Gina dipped her head.

I smiled sweetly. "Now fuck off. I don't like being woken in the middle of the night."

She quickly recovered from her shock, laughing quietly. "I might like you."

"Mutual," I said before thinking of it. "Shame we're on different sides."

"*Are* you on their side, Miss Le Spyre?" Gina asked. "You and Kyros are separated. Tell me, is there trouble in paradise?"

Understatement of the year.

A lie hovered on the tip of my tongue, but I stopped myself from aligning firmly with Clan Sundulus, considering my reply. Should I look a potential gift horse in the mouth?

"I'm on no one's side but my own." Holding her gaze for a leaden moment, I spun on my heel. "Nighty night."

Her laughter followed me inside the gates. "Goodnight, Miss Le Spyre. Be a dear and say hello to my brother Kyros, won't you?"

I hummed. "Serious."

"Fucking serious."

"Fucking serious, Tom. You watched Grandmother's recording. I need you to work for me. And I need to buy your house."

Her throat worked. "The house is in my name. I had the mortgage transferred to me because Dad's credit history is bad and the interest rate was sky high."

"Things would be easier if your father doesn't have to be involved, obviously, *if* you decide to sell," I said carefully. "You'd receive the house back for free after I win—" I cut off, gurgling.

Ugh.

She shook her head. "*If* you win, I'll pay you every cent for the fucking house that you gave me. Tetleys don't accept handouts."

Boy, didn't I know it. Nothing made her angrier than charity—thus why I had to give her my hand-me-downs for Christmas.

"Just think about it," I said. "You know why I'm doing this. You know why Grandmother did it. If you work for me from the estate, it means I can better ensure your safety too."

Tommy shook her head, eyes fixed on the desk. "I just— My world was flipped a week ago and now there's this to add to the shit heap."

Guilt churned low in my gut. "I know."

"Lucky, bats are my spirit animal."

I frowned at her, then rolled my eyes. "Because bats sleep upside-down and your world was flipped?"

"That right there is why we're friends. You speak Tommy Tetley. Yes, lovely. I'll work for you—for *double* my current pay, not triple. I don't know jack shit about HR. When I'm earning you buttloads, we can talk again."

I studied her. "You have a way with words, friend."

"When do I start?"

"How long have you worked at that laundry place?"

"Eight years."

"How long have you hated it?"

"Eight years."

I stretched my hand out. "How's tomorrow?"

"You've got yourself a deal, Basil." She slid her hand up my wrist and we slapped each other's forearms in a salmon shake.

The telephone on the desk beeped. I swiped at it. "Yello?"

Fred's voice flooded the line. "Miss Le Spyre, your 10 o'clock appointment is here."

Fernando.

My lips curved. "Thanks, Fred. I'll be out soon."

Tommy's brows were nearly in her hairline as I replaced the phone in the cradle. "I've seen that smile before. That's your *I'm about to hand someone their ass on a plate* smile. Like that crazy bitch on *The Hunger Games* who files her teeth to points."

What? Like fangs? Tempting, but I wasn't a wannabe Vissimo.

"Fred will put you in touch with other members of my Churchill team who will mentor and guide you in your new role," I said. "Your job is to expand my acquisition team. To do this, you'll work under a fake name. I'll need you and your father to live here full time—in case of backlash."

Tommy pursed her lips. "That'll be a hard sell to Dad... You said that Daniel's under the impression a criminal chain is after us? I can just tell Dad that security measures are heightened until the criminals are caught and you want everyone on site until the risk passes."

And this was why I'd hired her. I trusted her brain.

"Not a bad idea for the short term." Most of my staff lived onsite anyway. "I'll get Fred to spread the word to reinforce it."

Tommy brushed off her ruby-red leggings and casual, mustard off-the-shoulder dress as she stood, looking effortlessly classy as always. "I'll leave you to open the can of whoop-ass on whoever's waiting outside. Just one more thing though."

I peered up from the email sent by the CEO of *MediKnow*, my medical supplies company. "What's that?"

She pointed at the three open jewellery cases by my elbow. They were delivered this morning. "We gonna talk about those massive fucking sapphires?"

The *Udytrite* sapphire set included a necklace, bracelet, and earrings inlaid in white gold. *Udytrite* was an invite-only custom jewellery designer. The set would have cost Kyros a small fortune.

I wrinkled my nose. “Want them?”

“Not my style. Maybe you could donate them to the op shop?” she said.

Huh? “What’s that?”

“A second-hand store. Y S I S, bitch.”

Your snob is showing. Dammit.

It was tempting, but donating the set wouldn’t have Kyros slamming down my door and demanding answers so I could seduce the suit pants off of him. “I don’t think so, but I’m not keeping them.”

She snarled. “Fucker thinks he can buy you back with bullshit trinkets?”

Sadness and amusement warred for first place. In the background of my mind, I could feel Kyros. Awake and frustrated. “Yeah. As a Le Spyre, I don’t have nearly enough trinkets.”

We exchanged a grin before she left.

Taking my time replying to the *MediKnow* CEO, I then tidied the strewn papers on my desk, and walked to the door.

I steeled myself at the sight of Fernando waiting on the piano bench.

“Fernando,” I said gravely.

The blood remaining in his face drained away and his blue eyes blazed—showing his loss of control. I had no idea how powerful this vampire was and knew very little about his mother’s debt or how much he owed. For what I had in mind, those details were insignificant.

He entered the office, and I closed the door, pushing the noise-cancelling button.

“Sit down,” I said.

He blurred to sit on the chaise, and I crossed my arms, studying him.

The vampire hung his head. “I’m a cowa—”

“I’ll make this quick, Fernando, because, honestly, your selfish actions nearly killed me, and they killed twelve people who you claim to uphold as brothers and sisters. I can barely stand to be in the same room as you."

Fernando flinched violently.

"All you need to know is that the lives of you and your sister are in my hands. Do you understand that one word to Kyros will end your life and throw your sister into slavery?"

He closed his eyes. "Yes."

Good. "We're on the same page. From this moment forward, Fernando, your ass is mine. You work for me until I say otherwise."

His eyes widened, in sync with my canary-eating smile.

He shifted on the chaise. "What kind of work?"

I ambled to my desk. "Nothing you're unfamiliar with. You'll spy on Clan Sundulus and Clan Fyrlia for me."

His silence was music to my ears. I looked up, allowing the memory of the Indebted's mass grave in Orange to fuel my hardness.

My voice was harsh. "I want their plans. I want their bluffs. I want their movements. Everything. You'll continue under the guise of spying for Clan Fyrlia to keep access to their inner workings."

Fernando hadn't blinked in the last minute. "I'll need to give them information to keep my cover intact."

I tilted my head. "I don't give a fuck what you tell them about Sundulus. If you must give them information about me or this estate, you're to discuss the details with me in advance. Is that clear?"

"Y-Yes, Miss Le Spyre."

"And Fernando?"

He waited, perhaps sensing the trap in my purring tone.

I perched on the desk. "If anything happens to make me suspect your allegiance has shifted again, know that I won't wait for confirmation of your guilt. I won't hesitate to alert Clan Sundulus of your betrayal. So you better ensure I'm *very* convinced of your innocence."

The remaining blood in his face drained away.

Bluffing Basi was out in full force, but Fernando had to believe I meant what I said. This was yet another risk that could go terribly wrong if he decided to blab to Kyros. Laurel had agreed to use eye compulsion on him at random to ensure his loyalty, but Fernando didn't need to know that.

"I understand, Miss Le Spyre," he said. "I won't let you down."

I fixed him with a quelling look. "Let me down again, you mean?"

He flushed.

Rounding the desk, I settled into my grandmother's chair, pulling out a notepad and pen. "Get comfortable. You're about to spend the next few hours recounting every single thing you know about the clans, the members of the royal families, their current movements, blood exchanges, past strategies, and the clans' positions in the game."

My past mishaps had arisen from ignorance.

No more.

13

The door to my *Live Right* office opened.

I'd felt his rage two minutes before and felt reasonably certain of the cause. In preparation for his arrival, I'd adjusted the low front of my skintight top so the swell of my breasts popped out to near nipple-displaying proportions. The bottom hem of the top was tucked into sailor-blue ankle-length pants, a thin brown belt accented my narrow waist, and a blazer with vertical stripes completed the look.

I'm too busy for small boys. That's what this outfit, equipped with a high ponytail, put across.

I liked to think.

"Basilia," he said.

I didn't look up from *Monocle*. "Kyros. Good afternoon."

His rage swelled in response to my amusement, but the control of his reaction was disappointing. He'd opened the door almost normally *and* maintained personal distance.

"You gave the jewellery I sent you to another woman," he said, stalking into the room.

That's more like it.

Heat smouldered deep within me as he drew closer, and I clenched my thighs together, trying to force the reactions of my body into a box as I did with vampire-induced fear. "Her name is Leila. She works for you. Doesn't the set look great on her?"

My amusement.

His rage.

"I take it you either didn't care for my gift or you're too angry to accept it." He reached the desk and didn't stop, continuing around with the same predatory grace to where I sat.

I tensed as he moved behind my chair. This must be what it was like to play dead while a grizzly sniffed at your neck.

Typing the next address on my list into *Monocle*, I said, "I take it you're either surprised I didn't accept your gift after you used me to get at my money or you're unhappy with the replacement woman I selected so you'd leave me the fuck alone."

His hands rested on the back of my chair. "I'm not interested in Leila. Nor any other. They don't have what I want."

Burn. Leila could probably hear him.

I jotted another few notes and snapped the file shut, shoving it in my oversized *Didi* purse.

Standing, I turned to Kyros and slowly removed my glasses. "What do you want in a woman again? A puppet, wasn't it?"

His green eyes blazed and he shoved aside the chair between us, clamping an arm around my waist to pull me flush against his hard body.

"You, Basilia," he said, drawing his nose from my jaw to temple. "I want you like none other."

My inhale hitched.

Allowing the thought of him to fill me, I lifted on tiptoes, ensuring my breasts brushed his chest. "How can you be certain of that? We don't know each other."

I trailed my lips up his neck in whisper-soft kisses, pausing at the corner of his mouth.

"You are my true mate."

Hmm. "I'm not so sure."

"You will be."

The white-hot flash under his words jolted through me, nearly eliciting a gasp. I tempered it, peeking up at him through my lashes. "You must have been with a lot of women in your time."

The question was out before I could stop it.

Not part of the plan.

Kyros's lips curved. "I was a teenager for thirty years. Does that answer your question?"

I refused to feel anything over his admission. There was nothing between us.

His green eyes glinted. "Female Vissimo don't find monogamy desirable, and I demand it. Most need a harem to have any chance at conceiving."

I stepped back, tucking my purse under my arm. "Pretty sure dating the crown prince would appeal plenty to those interested in furthering their social status."

He lifted a shoulder. "Perhaps. It is simple for me, Basilia. My true mate exists, and so no one else does."

Ugh, I hated that term. *True mate.*

I brought the conversation back to my initial script. "Did you really think I'd be swayed by meaningless jewellery?"

"You want me, I can feel it," he snarled as I walked to the office door.

I cast a look back, smiling inwardly as he tracked the swing of my ponytail. "You have nothing I want, Kyros, and I'm not something you can win. Let's keep it friendly and go our separate ways. After that thrall bullshit, I'm sure you have some pent-up frustration. Fuck knows I do. Turn your attention to one of your fellow Vissimo to scratch the itch, and I'll turn my attention elsewhere too. *That's* simple for both of us."

Black fury churned through our bond. He didn't move, but I could feel that simple restraint took every sliver of his control.

"You will enter another man's bed over my *dead fucking body*," he said in a voice of ice.

I shrugged. "Doesn't have to be in a bed. I've always wanted to have sex on a car bonnet. A wall. A swimming pool. I'm only twenty-one. Sounds like a good time to explore to me. Oh! But I did have something else to tell you."

His jaw clenched and he didn't answer.

I couldn't feel anything from him but intense focus.

Yep, he was one second from losing it.

"The Vissimo on my property. They're scaring my staff, dressed in black leather and lurking in freakin' corners. They either need to act normal or get the fuck off my property."

The churning possessiveness in him receded.

I'd play this to-and-fro seduction until he lost all control. *Fourth exchange, here we come.*

Kyros's eyes flashed. "The Indebted stay until the threat against you is cleared."

We both knew that was a lie. Unless I was in his *tower,* the Indebted would stay. His jerk ass couldn't handle anything less.

But that worked in with my plans.

I shook my head. "They'll have to act more like my friends and less like guards. People talk, I'm sure you can see how that's a bad thing."

The back of the chair cracked in his grip.

I continued. "Glad we could come to an agreement. I'll come by after my shift ends to pick up my stuff from Level 61."

Desperation curled around my heart, none of it mine. What was it that Laurel said? The desperate weren't known for their 20/20 vision?

Yeah, I was counting on that.

"I have no issue with you moving off Level 61," Kyros stated, slipping a hand into his trouser pocket as he approached me. "Reconsider taking your possessions from the tower."

My back pressed into the door frame as he leaned over me.

Lust. Anger. Hurt.

"Why's that?"

Kyros pressed a kiss to my forehead, so unexpectedly gentle that I felt it to my very core.

"You're angry because you're hurting," he spoke low, our eyes locked. "You wouldn't be hurt if you didn't care."

My chest heaved as we remained caught in the net of his making.

I turned my head away to break the contact. "What does that have to do with my things?"

"I'll fix what I broke, my beauty. Believe that. If you take your possessions away, you'll just have to bring them back. Save yourself the work."

His arrogance was fucking incredible, and my body loved every bit of it.

Shit. Was I seducing him or the other way around?

Finding my voice, I slipped out of the cage of his arms. "Do us both a favour, Kyros. Quit acting like the exchanges mean *or meant* anything."

Just come out, girl <3

I sent the message to Tommy and had barely blinked when her reply chimed.

There are too many of them.

Fifty Indebted hung around my pool and outside entertainment area in various states of undress.

I conceded the point with a text of heart emojis. Pretty sure I almost peed myself when I met a room filled with Vissimo for the first time.

It was Saturday, and I'd declared a pool party. A day lounging by the water under the hot sun served two purposes: a distraction from thinking of Kyros's body *all the damn time.* And gifting most of the Indebted with a new experience.

Plus, waking up to go through my shave, cleanse, and hydrate routine before donning my tiniest white bikini had felt good. Normal. My blonde hair gleamed under the hot sun. My skin was silken smooth. I looked and felt amazing.

"Is anyone getting in the water?" I called, scanning the Indebted strewn about the area over the tops of my sunglasses.

Not having swimsuits, they'd shucked their black leathers to lounge around in their underwear. Fifty *gorgeous* vampires surrounded me. Like, *shit*, they were unbelievably beautiful. In a scary *will I have the best night of my life or will I die* way. Which was probably why none of my staff had ventured out here—except my stoic butler.

"I thought we were sunbathing for this part of the day," Kelsea answered from next to me. "I'm just following your lead."

I scanned the Indebted. *Oh.*

"Sunbathing is one thing you do at a pool party," I said, knowing the others would listen in. "There's usually swimming and jumping in the pool and splashing and music." I cocked an ear. "Well there's our first problem."

Swiping up my phone, I opened my Sunday Session playlist and connected it to the outside speakers.

Josie sat up as the pool speakers blared to life. "I love George Ezra."

I threw her an approving nod. "Modern-day Johnny Cash, right?"

None of the Indebted budged toward the pool.

Cracking my knuckles, I tossed my sunglasses down and hauled my sexy ass off the sunchair and to the deep end of the pool. I lined up with where Laurel reclined in her red lacy underwear surrounded by male Indebted.

Was that her harem? I was totally asking later because while 49 percent of me was scared of knowing the gory details and being unable to forget, 51 percent wanted the logistics.

Without fanfare, I leaped out over the water surface, pulling my legs close to form a ball.

I shattered the pool's calm, carving an uncontrolled path through the water before kicking upward for air.

I grinned over the pool edge at the row of drenched Vissimo.

"Water looks good on you, Loz," I sang out, kicking onto my back to float.

All I heard was running feet.

Bait taken.

Splashes erupted as Indebted cannoned from all sides. I spluttered against a mouthful of water, treading as I tried to make sense of the chaos. Hands gripped my ankles and I managed a gulp of air before I was dragged *at speed* backward through the water.

Coughing, I clung to my attacker after surfacing.

"Got ya!" Jillian beamed.

"No fair," I spluttered, torn between spluttering and laughing. "I can't do that." Hopefully no one was looking out the second-floor windows. Because *shit*.

I pulled myself from the pool and studied the anarchy of my making. A job well done. Evie and Josie dunked Laurel, and I chuckled at the glee on their faces before grimacing. Hands were *definitely* roaming between a few small groups in the corners.

Spotting Kelsea, I let out a battle cry and cannon-balled into the pool right next to her. Grinning under the surface, I grabbed her waist, my head popping above the water.

"Don't drag me around like Jillian, please," I begged.

She wasn't laughing.

The silken baritones of George Ezra's singing aside, the entire pool area was deathly quiet—no splashing, no laughing, and no groping.

Kelsea shifted her eyes to my face, flicking them over my left shoulder.

Close to the edge already, I let go of her, flailing for the poolside as I blinked water out of my eyes.

Strong hands closed around my wrists, pulling me bodily upward. Torrents poured from me as I hovered over the water.

My insides clenched as I dragged my gaze up over black athletic shorts, a tight black tee, and a jawline that haunted my waking and sleeping dreams.

I glared up at Kyros. "What are you doing here?"

His anger thrummed through me, his green gaze riveted on the

Indebted in the pool and the surrounding pagodas, not on me. "Is that any way to greet your true mate?"

"Don't start with that crap." I tried to kick him, and he held me farther from his body. *Fuck*, the sight of him out of his usual suit was destroying me.

Kyros's attention finally left the Indebted to snap onto me.

He went predatorily still, body and mind as he took in my bikini-clad frame.

His Adam's apple bobbed.

Once.

Twice.

"You mind?" I snarled, my wrists starting to ache.

A growl slipped between his teeth, and I yelped as he let go of a wrist. His arm slipped around my waist before gravity noticed it could control me again. Kyros held me against his body. Water soaked his athletic clothes, but the vampire didn't seem to mind. Hell, most of *me* didn't mind.

"I meant that my feet would touch the ground," I said breathlessly.

He lowered me until my tiptoes were perched on the very edge of the pool. Without his help, I'd fall backward into the pool.

And that's what happened when I left things open for vampire alpha interpretation.

"Why are my Indebted in the pool?" Kyros asked, his menace unfurling overhead.

I clicked my fingers in his face. "Hey? Down here. We talked about this. I told you they were scaring the staff. This is them blending in—which you agreed to."

A rumble filled his chest as he returned his stare to the scantily clad Indebted. "I agreed to nothing of the kind. They're not guarding your property—therefore, they are not doing their job."

Wrath seeped through our bond.

Eek.

I gripped his chin. "They're not here to guard my property.

They're here to guard me. You think anyone is getting close with fifty Vissimo around?"

A snapping growl ripped from him. "I got close to you."

Screw it, I was choosing the pool, I tried to push out of his embrace to no avail.

"Dammit, Kyros. I told you: my house, my fucking rules! I bet my life that they know exactly what's happening on the estate right now. But this, pool parties and movie nights, is what they'll do while on *my* property."

His hands slipped lower, inching toward the high waistband of my thong bottoms.

I folded my arms across my chest, toes on the edge. "With that settled, why are you here? Haven't you got dice to roll or something?"

My brain finally caught up.

Oh my god, Kyros was at the estate. This was terrible for so many reasons, but I'd known there was a strong likelihood it would happen eventually. Consider me begrudgingly impressed he had the cahoonas to turn up so soon after betraying me.

"It's my weekend off," he said, gaze on my chest. "I'd like to spend it with you. At the beach."

He got two days off each month, and he wanted to spend them with me? "You spend your weekend off with your family."

"Usually, yes. If you aren't busy, it has been a long time since I visited Lyall Bay."

My favourite beach. I narrowed my gaze. Was he aware of that somehow? And why were normal words coming out of his mouth? I didn't like it.

I gripped his forearms and side-stepped him to gain a more secure footing. He let me anyway.

Licking my lips, I peeked glances at the eerily still Indebted. Laurel alone had moved to clamber out of the pool, ready to face execution.

"Or if you'd prefer that I stay here with your Vissimo, that's okay too. I just want to be in your company." Kyros purred his ultimatum.

My eyes flew to his. Did he just call the Indebted Vissimo? The vampires at my back didn't move or speak, but there was no way they'd missed that.

A smile widened my lips, and Kyros blinked, his face slackening. His mouth formed words I couldn't make out.

"I'll come to the beach with you." I decided. This suited my game and, more importantly, removed him from the estate. "For a few hours."

"Dinner as well."

I swiped up my loose white bikini cover-up, throwing it over my head. "Late lunch. Restaurant of my choice. Back by two."

Amusement. "Four."

I picked up my phone, floppy hat, and oversized sunnies. "Four, and I get to pick your meal."

"Why?"

"Why not? You scared?"

He smiled, and I frowned at the blatant admiration I was picking up through our bond.

I held out my hand. "Lyall Bay, late lunch, back by 4:00 p.m., and I pick your meal."

Kyros extended a massive hand to grip mine, surprising me when he all-but bent in half to press a lingering kiss to the back.

I swallowed my groan, my mind immediately placing his head between my legs. That really had been the most catastrophic orgasm of my life. Was he thinking about it too?

His nostrils flared. "We have a deal, vixen."

My beauty. Vixen. The words thrilled the blood-bound part of me and otherwise made me grossly uncomfortable. "Where's your ride?"

Kyros quirked a brow, turning. "Hop on my back."

"You snuck onto the estate like a rebellious teen?"

Taking a running leap, I wrapped my legs around his waist and looped my arms around his neck. "You only did this so I'd have to touch you more."

"When it comes to you, I take what I can get."

"Wait," I said loudly.

He glanced over his shoulder. "What?"

"You need to tell my guards they can do whatever they want while on my property."

"Why?"

"Because you ruined their buzz," I snapped. "Coming in here like a wet blanket and ruining my pool party."

Reluctance and humour rolled between us.

Kyros glanced at the frozen Indebted, fixing his gaze on Laurel. "When on this property, you may act like humans as long as your real purpose in being here is upheld *at all times*. I was able to reach her. Do not defend my true mate against Vissimo like the Tonyi triplets, plan to defend her against someone like me."

My gut churned at just how right his words were. He was the one I needed protection from. Kyros's grip behind my knees tightened.

Laurel peered up at the house before bowing low. "Of course, Master."

I scrunched my nose. *Ew*. The master thing was gross.

Kyros peered back at me. "Is there anything else you'd like me to say to your Vissimo?"

He said it again!

I beamed and caught his smile before he faced forward.

"That's all," I said grandly. "Onwards. Where are you parked?"

"Out front."

How the hell did he sneak in without my human staff and fifty Indebted noticing? I knew he was pretty powerful, but could I expect more visits from him? If so, that could get really problematic.

Kyros beelined for the house.

"Go around, please," I said. "Tommy's in there watching movies and I don't want her to see you." Or any of my staff, especially Fred.

"Your friendship with Tommy is re-established?"

Who even spoke like that?

I huffed. "We never stopped being friends, but she has forgiven me, yes. *Because* I moved back to the estate and you're in my past."

"You told another lie to get out of a lie?"

"Not a lie."

"You're wrapped around me right now."

Arms looped around his neck, I rested my head on his shoulder, inhaling his amazing man scent. I was soaking wet from the pool, and soaking him through, and yet all I could think about was how wet I was in other places.

I squeezed my eyes shut. "Lies, lies, everywhere. In my closet. In my hair."

His lust speared me. *Yeah*, he hadn't missed my ladyboner one single bit.

"Why are you taking me to the beach, Kyros? Are you still trying to get at my money? Because that ship sailed, well and truly. I'm not sure who had that bung idea in the first place, but you guys were never getting a whiff of my inheritance."

I waved at Georgia, the head gardener, who stared at Kyros open-mouthed. *Dang it*. Hoped to get away unseen but for Daniel.

"My father had the idea," Kyros said quietly as we left the gates behind.

"Angelica told you that Basilia Le Spyre walked into Live Right looking for a job, so you passed on the good news to Daddy?" I asked, bitterness creeping in.

Kyros lowered me onto the hood of his black car, and I sat, legs dangling. He rested on the bonnet next to me.

"I was with my father when Angelica called to report. I then orchestrated our first meeting and made the decision to hire you from there. After the roll that night, it was decided I would pursue an acquaintance with you."

I rolled my eyes. "For goodness' sake, don't tiptoe around it. You were ordered to seduce me to access my money, estate, and connections. That's where I'm confused though. Were we meant to marry so what's mine would become yours? Or was I just going to hand it all over on a silver platter when your magic dick bedazzled me?"

His lips twitched.

With my eyes, I dared him to laugh.

Kyros pushed off the car. "Would you believe me if I said I disagreed completely with the plan and was merely going through the motions to appease my father until it was clear seducing you wouldn't work?"

I hopped off the hood, walking to the passenger seat. "I believe you because I can feel your emotions. Not for any other reason."

Though that wasn't strictly true. Kyros had always given the impression he was forcing himself to be in my company—that he both did and didn't want to be around me.

Guess I knew why now.

Kyros held open the passenger door.

"So you didn't like the thought of lowering yourself to pursue a human?" I asked, sliding onto the pristine leather in my dripping swimsuit.

Kyros slipped into the driver's seat a moment later, gunning the engine. "Would it offend you if I said yes?"

I shrugged a shoulder. "No." I'd rather be disliked for being human than something intrinsic.

"That sentiment lasted up until you opened your mouth the first time. There are humans, then there are *humans*. After we had dinner, I was mostly irritated at being under my father's thumb."

We both knew he didn't take orders well. I guess most alphas didn't.

Kyros directed us past the estates at a sedate pace. I stared out the window until he interrupted the silence. "Just before the second blood exchange, I recognised the trap I was in."

I let him feel my curiosity rather than asking aloud.

"I wanted you," he replied. "Except if you'd found out the truth, you'd leave. That you might *not* discover the subterfuge didn't sit well with me either. Neither did the fact you wouldn't tell me who you really were of your own volition."

A knot of anger coiled in my stomach. "You had so many chances to tell me, Kyros."

"The thought has kept me up many a morning."

Good.

We turned onto the freeway, heading toward the theme park. Lyall Bay glistened beyond it.

"Thank you for explaining," I said, remembering my reason for being here.

"Thank you, but no thank you?" he murmured. No accusation filled his voice.

"Essentially. You had a shot. To say that you blew it is a gross understatement. I'll move on and you need to come to terms with that."

"No man can make you feel like I can."

Don't I know it.

I studied the ticking of his jaw muscle. "You assume sexual pleasure is vitally important to me. After what I've been through at the hands of Vissimo, I crave safety and security. You can't fulfil either."

A wall of shock descended upon me, none of it mine.

He pulled off the freeway, taking the ramp for Lyall Bay. Not a speck of his disbelief showed outwardly as we continued driving, but the emotion ran rampant through him.

That was news to him? I'd never been beaten up so much as during the last seven weeks.

Kyros was silent until we parked next to a beachside restaurant.

"You don't believe I can protect you?" he asked, killing the engine.

I observed him, inside *and* out. My answer mattered. I also wasn't willing to lie to spare his alpha ego—the work of over a century.

"No. Not with the game you play," I replied.

He reached across my hips and pulled the lever on the outside of my seat. The chair thudded back, taking me with it.

Kyros covered my body with his, braced on his elbows, his knee between my legs.

"You don't think I could fight off anyone who threatened to harm you?" He growled, dipping his head to the swell of my breasts.

He pushed my white cover-up down, baring a shoulder.

I gasped as he kissed between my breasts, moving across the hem of the tiny bikini triangles to kiss every inch of skin the swimsuit failed to contain.

I gasped as he bit the outside of my right breast gently, then lapped at the same spot with his tongue.

"You doubt my power?" His mouth moved to repeat the ministrations on my other breast. I arched up against his leg as he slid a hand up the outside of my thigh with grating slowness.

I'd mentioned car bonnets to him yesterday, but hell if I wasn't changing that fantasy to the passenger seat. My back arched higher, and I panted my reply, "Not your physical strength."

I'm going to combust.

"I'm already one of the most powerful alphas in the world," Kyros snarled. "In time, there will be few I cannot best. How is it you don't feel safe?"

Irritation crackled within me. "I feel safe from *them*."

His face blanked, and I turned my face away.

"This wasn't part of the deal," I mumbled. "I want to go to the beach."

"Tell me," the Vissimo above me demanded.

I shoved at his rock-hard stomach, glaring up at him. "I don't feel safe from *you*, Kyros. How can you possibly feel confused over that? Do I need to spell out that I don't trust you after everything you've done to me? Now get off me before I knee you in your damn vampire balls!"

His mouth covered mine.

Bliss.

A low moan left me. Or was it his?

Heat, want, desperation, relief, betrayal.

His feelings were my own. Mine his. Telling them apart when we both felt so strongly was impossible. A hissing sigh escaped my lips, and I opened my mouth to him, hands seeking purchase on his tight tee.

"That fucking bathing suit," he said hoarsely.

"More," I pleaded.

His tongue battled with mine as his hands roamed. My hands? *Fuck*, it wasn't just his emotion plus mine. The effect was exponential. I was at exploding point from sensory overload.

A knowing heat, a languidness built within me—the feeling of us meeting equivalent to multiple sets of hands roaming over me, stroking and nibbling.

"Kyros," I panted, eyes wide.

Fear coursed between us. Not all of it mine.

He dipped his head to my neck, cursing.

The vampire leaned forward, grinding his thigh into me, and my head thudded back onto the headrest. My knees clamped either side of his leg, hands reaching to yank him closer and position him exactly where I wanted. But there wasn't enough space. I was hovering on some kind of ecstasy. One I may never recover from. One that would consume me forever.

Breath catching, I circled my hips, pulling his toffee hair to force his face back to mine. With each passing second, it was harder to be afraid of coming undone.

"It's not enough," I said with a bite, a primal desperation filling me. I wanted to be consumed.

Kyros lifted his head.

Gleaming fangs.

I froze.

He dropped his head again, heaving with ragged breaths. "I want to drink from you," he said, pain screwing his expression. "We need to stop or I'll force the fourth exchange on you."

Right now, I needed almost zero convincing, but another second of clarity brought back our surroundings. "Uh, yeah. A restaurant filled with people probably isn't the best place for that."

Three giggling teens were staring at us from a park bench.

Oops.

"You'd let me?" Kyros moaned as his fangs retracted back into his gums.

I watched in fascination. "Not in my right mind, no. Now, absolutely."

"*Fuck,*" he hissed, hands curling to fists either side of my head. "That's not helping."

His phone vibrated in the console.

I glanced at him, but Kyros wasn't home right now. I fished for his phone.

"Yello?" I asked, pressing the cool device to my ear.

"*She's with him. She just answered.*"

I pulled the phone away to read the screen.

"Gerome? What do you want?"

Snickers trailed down the line, and I glanced at Kyros as he pried off my body and returned to the driver's seat.

"Are all of you there?" I sighed.

"*Shh, she can hear you.*"

Sometimes I found it hard to believe Kyros's siblings were older than seven. Except Safina. She was legit badass.

"Is my brother there?" Gerome asked.

I eyed the vampire next to me.

Nodding, Kyros extended his hand.

A ball of excitement formed in my gut. The fourth blood exchange would be easier than I'd thought. The same thing just had to happen in the right setting—his tower.

"What?" he snapped.

Couldn't blame him. I felt seriously unsatisfied too. I straightened on my seat and twitched my cover-up back into place over my boobs, fidgeting against the agonising ache between my legs.

Just what I needed.

I exhaled, fidgeting again. Ten seconds. That was all it'd take to get me there in this state.

"Please tell Father I'll attend him soon. I met up with Miss Le Spyre on a business matter," Kyros said.

Uh, what?

"To ask her to give the staff human lessons again, of course," he replied. "We were just finishing, tell him—"

Kyros's expression smoothed. "Father."

Shit.

"Yes. A business meeting." Kyros pressed his lips together. "Yes, Father. Of course. We'll be there in twenty minutes."

My eyes widened. *We?*

No.

No fucking way!

Kyros disconnected and looked at me.

I scowled bloody murder, folding my arms. "I'm not going."

His face hardened. "Fucking Neelan told them where I was."

"Your parents?"

Kyros turned on the car. "Correct."

I faced forward. "Drop me off before you go there."

"That's not how it works, Basilia. My father ordered us to attend him."

"He doesn't own me," I shot back, real fear spearing me. I had far too many secrets for a meeting with King Julius.

Kyros reversed, sending sand and gravel flying. "In our laws, he does. You're under my blood compulsion and I'm part of his clan. You are his. Until the fourth exchange when our laws officially recognise us as courting. Only then do I have more rights to what can and cannot be done to you."

I couldn't stop my suspicion at his words.

"It's the truth, Basilia," he snapped.

"Don't get snippy at me," I retorted. "I don't have to believe anything you say."

I'd extracted details from Fernando on what the next three blood exchanges entailed, but I should speak to Laurel in greater depth about Vissimo laws surrounding the exchange process. I wouldn't put it past Kyros to lie just so I'd run into the fourth exchange to be safe from his father.

Though that suited me, too, as long as there weren't any nasty surprises—which there had been so far at every turn.

Kyros ignored me as he navigated the car onto the highway leading farther away from Bluff City. "I'm going to kill Neelan."

Yeah, he could get in line.

I was yet to spend time with the brawny vampire, but Neelan seemed like he had a chip on his shoulder and a serious rebellious streak. Kyros's siblings were all alphas, but Neelan gave me the most unstable vibe of the lot.

I didn't envy him the malice in Kyros's voice though. That promised pain.

"You owe me big time at this point." I picked up the argument from a new angle. "Drop me at the estate and go yourself. I have zero desire to spend the day with your family or meet your parents. And I am so deadly fucking serious about that."

He clenched the wheel. "You think this is what I had in mind when I asked you to spend the day with me?"

My reply was calm. "I have no way of knowing, Kyros. Silly me for believing the beach gimmick, I suppose. Should've stayed at the damn estate."

Kyros didn't answer, but I listened in on his frustration and disappointment. And fear.

Which was totally reassuring.

I'd seen a live stream of King Julius rolling the dice, and he was one scary motherfucker.

"You must come, Basilia. As much as I wish it otherwise," he said, jaw clenching. "I can't defy a direct order from my king."

From his *father*.

I whacked the car door. "Why does he want me there? This is so messed up!"

I was in serious shit.

"Because he explicitly told me not to pursue you further after our third blood exchange."

"So you decided to take me to the beach and lunch on your day off that you usually spend with your family? Are you daft?"

He shot me an irritated look. "I have no idea how Neelan found out. But we met for business. You turned down my offer for human lessons again."

This was ridiculous. "Sure. What about if he decides to search my mind for the truth?"

Kyros's grip tightened on the wheel. "Then that would be very, very bad."

I nearly choked on the possessive rage unfurling from him.

"I won't react well," he added—as if I needed more explanation than the black violence coursing through him. "That, more than anything, will put us both at risk. Swear to me you'll do as he says. Be angry at me. Tell him I forced you to come here, but never, *never*, let him see the depth of our connection."

The depth of what connection?

I snorted. "Shouldn't be an issue."

I fixed my gaze out the window as I scrambled to think of a way to stay alive in the next few hours.

14

I was padding—barefoot—into a king's mansion. At least I wasn't intimidated by his riches, which included one hell of an art collection.

Was any of this stuff from the last three hundred years?

Kyros walked behind me, and I trailed before him like a good doggy.

Whatever. I'd act the part if it meant getting back to my estate with my secrets and life intact. *Shit.*

This was really bad.

"Miss Tetley!"

White teeth and pink material flashed a second before Lalitta barrelled into me.

She held me at arm's length. "Oh, it's Le Spyre now, isn't it? I'm so glad that's in the open. I felt really bad about lying."

I seized onto my anger at her with both hands, but it slipped between my fingers like sand. She was too guileless. I couldn't be mad at her. "Le Spyre. Yes."

A maid opened the heavy wrought iron door into the house—an Indebted? I smiled at her, but the woman's gaze was fixed on the floor.

I traipsed into the mansion beside Lalitta and realised the intense discomfort prickling my neck was gone.

Kyros had disappeared, so that was fucking great.

I stared at my damp cover-up. "Uh, should I take this off?"

Francesca appeared behind her sister. "I'll get you something dry."

That was uncharacteristically mature of the youngest royal. "Okay."

I tugged off my cover-up, passing it into the maid's outstretched hand. "Could you hurry?" I asked the youngest princess.

Meeting Kyros's parents in my G-banger bikini was pretty low on my priority list.

She displayed all her teeth. "Sure thing."

Fuck nuts. I was just played. Looked like I'd meet the king and queen wearing butt-floss.

"Miss Le Spyre," Safina said from the top of a small flight of wide steps embedded with flecks of quartz.

I climbed to join her, spotting Deirdre sitting at a table that appeared to have been carved out of a ginormous tree trunk. "Hey, how's it going?"

Safina paused in the act of arranging a vase of Singapore orchids. She pursed her lips, taking in my outfit. "Better now. It was boring without Kyros, but that's about to change."

Because the clown had arrived? Me being the clown.

Deirdre wrinkled her nose. "Do you dress in less to cover insecurities about your worth?"

What the hell?

"No, Deirdre," I answered calmly. "I was in the pool when Kyros came to discuss business. I don't like tan lines."

Her brow cleared. "He would have enjoyed that view."

Safina grinned.

"Can't say I give a shit if he did or not," I answered for all the royal parents who might be listening.

Oh my god, I was about to meet Kyros's olds.

My heartbeat took off anew at how many peoples' lives and livelihoods depended on me playing this right.

"You weren't aware of the business meeting then?" Safina asked, sticking in one last stem and cutting me a look.

Was this the pre-interrogation? "I'd hardly have agreed to meeting with a lying sonofabitch, would I? He jumped me."

Safina pressed her trembling lips together. "In what sense? It's obvious to anyone with a nose that the meeting wasn't just business."

Did that mean I stank? Or that Kyros's stank was on *me*. I sincerely hoped for the latter.

Gerome sauntered into the room. "Basil!"

I glowered at the vampire who headed the entertainment industry for Sundulus. *He* was the one who called Kyros and got me into this mess—even if it was Neelan's big mouth that did the real damage.

"Don't call me that," I said woodenly as he picked me up and squeezed.

He plonked me back down, tugging me through the mansion that rivalled the size of my own house. "Nonsense. I call you Basil, and you call me—"

"Germ."

"I was thinking more along the lines of Rome."

Slipping my hand free, I peered around—in vain—for Francesca. We were in a large interior courtyard that was open to the sky. Wide stairs ascended out of sight opposite where I stood.

"Hey, Germ? Can I borrow your shirt?"

"I don't like that nickname."

"But it suits you so much," I replied, hand out for his shirt. "What about Prince Germ?"

Rory and Neelan strode in through the west archway.

Neelan blurred to me. "You need a shirt? I'd be happy to lend you mine."

His hazel eyes gleamed with challenge, and *then* I was certain. He hadn't just opened his mouth to blab about me and Kyros. This whole thing was his *turn* to fuck with me. The siblings were playing a game with their eldest brother, and they'd decided to toy with me to get to Kyros.

Neelan had endangered my life.

I met his blue gaze. "You've gone too far, Neelan."

His almond-shaped eyes flickered.

"You knew that already," I added softly. "Give me your shirt."

His black brows snapped together, and I smiled sweetly at him.

Rory stepped around his brother, drawing me into his arms. "Darling, why cover up? You look absolutely ravishing. It drives the imagination wild. Why, I could just bend you over and slide back that little bit of white material. Imagine the view."

"Imagine my fist down your throat, Rory," I answered.

"I've thought of nothing but our clandestine night together. Our secret dance," he purred in my ear.

I dodged under his arm. "You mean in the brief moments you're not thinking about yourself?"

Gerome grinned.

"Darling, there's only you. Rory Senrite and Basilia Le Spyre. I can see the headlines now."

Oh, brother. He was fucking persistent. I couldn't help laughing.

Neelan's gym singlet smacked into my face.

I peeled it off, sniffing. "Yuck, did you work out in this thing?"

"It's my natural musk."

"Gross," I muttered.

Beggars couldn't be choosers. I shrugged it on and stared down. "Why do guys wear tops that show their nipples? I just don't understand it—do you think females enjoy the peep show? Because we don't. It's the burlesque show no one wanted tickets to. I mean, sure, show some lat and pec, but keep the nipples under wraps unless your entire top is off or you're capable of breastfeeding."

Neelan glowered.

"Does my criticism of your fashion choices hurt your little ol' feelings?"

"You talk too much. Too freely. My brother needs to take you in hand."

Wish he would.

Damn... Potentially still hot and bothered by our car frenzy.

"Miss Le Spyre, might I escort you to my father?"

I spotted Lionel halfway up the stairs on the opposite end of the courtyard. I couldn't see the top of the steps—which was pretty imposing. *Really* imposing. Was King Julius crushing a big-ass throne between his buttocks at the top?

"Lionel." I greeted the only sane brother. "Of course you can."

He smiled and held out an arm. I took it as though I wasn't dressed in two scraps of material and a stinking gym singlet.

"How are you today?" he inquired.

My heart rocketed higher with each upward step. I cut him a wry glance. "It started off great and has steadily worsened."

"I hope I'm not part of the problem?"

Oh, he was. And an absolute charmer. "I reserve judgement until you try to make my life a living hell as well."

"Who said I was planning anything?"

Uh-huh.

We reached the top, and I drew in a long breath, trying to settle my heartbeat. I peered back the way we came, jolting at the sight of the other siblings standing in a row across the top stair behind us.

Safina spoke, "You haven't judged Lionel yet. What's your judgement of me?"

I replied without thinking. "Badass bitch."

"Me?" Lalitta asked, cheeks pinkening.

"The sweetest person to ever live."

"What about me?" Rory asked.

I lifted a shoulder. "Bit bland."

The siblings broke into loud laughter.

"*Bland?* Take it back," he demanded.

"Nope."

Cocking an ear, Lionel directed me forward. I turned back to glimpse the rest of Kyros's siblings falling into two lines behind me in order from eldest to youngest. Had they seen *The Sound of Music* because they were emulating it to perfection? Which meant King Julius was the scary-as-fuck Mr Von Trapp.

My grip on Lionel's arm tightened, and he used his free hand to squeeze mine, thankfully not making an issue of my sweaty palms.

Heated voices rose from the closed room before us.

I cut Neelan a look over my shoulder. The worried crease of his brow cleared the moment he spotted my perusal. If his game screwed things for me and hurt the people I loved, I would end him.

The vampire's gaze hardened. He didn't look worried one bit.

Lionel took my hand as we stopped in front of black wood doors. Lalitta dodged forward to plant a kiss on my cheek.

Way to reassure me I'm not about to die, guys.

Just as I was about to ask if we should knock, the door swung inward.

I scanned the expanse of bare concrete floor for several seconds before finding Kyros at the base of huge steps. I didn't leave my focus on him—his warning ringing in my ears. I traced the huge stone steps up to the hulking giant sitting in the gilded throne at the top.

Shit on a stick.

My knees shook as the cold blue eyes of a predator alighted on me. What ancient looked like, I couldn't have said before that moment, but as King Julius watched me, I knew. Minds within minds, bodies within bodies, souls within souls. A thousand stories in one book that only he could read. He knew my past and future already.

Thank fuck for Lionel. The vampire supported nearly all my weight without visible effort as we walked to the base of the massive steps. Otherwise, I would have collapsed in a pathetic heap at the threshold.

Kyros was a lot to handle when he lost control, but his six-hundred-year-old father was completely muted right now—his eyes not shining in the least—and I had no thought but to lose control of my bowels and curl into the fetal position. This creature was so powerful, he couldn't hide it.

Breathe, Basi.

King Julius could be in no doubt about the effect he had on me, yet the Vissimo didn't relent in his stare. I was nothing to him. A pitiful human not worthy of empathy.

I'd have to conquer my reaction to him before *Ingenium* ended.

Lionel halted us beside Kyros.

I worked to straighten my spine, to ignore the weak sputtering of my heart as I met King Julius's gaze. For as long as I could anyhow—about two seconds at a time.

"This is it?" he spoke without removing his gaze from my face.

"I'm Basilia Le Spyre," I answered, locking my knees and releasing Lionel—for better or worse.

The king smiled, displayed his teeth.

I clamped my lips against rising bile.

"Did I speak to you, human?" he asked, a melodic lilt to his voice.

That was a rhetorical question. I was certain of it.

"Answer me."

Or not! My heart stalled and restarted. Blood pulsed in my ears. Recognising where one beat began and another ended was impossible.

"I'm unsure, King Julius. You looked at me, but I thought it strange you referred to me as it."

The fear wasn't mine this time. As though I needed to feel Kyros's as well.

"You're a modern-day woman," he said dismissively. "Predictable."

Oh, really? He wouldn't be saying that by the end.

There wasn't a speck of warmth in this being. Rigidity. Power. Steel. The Vissimo was a siege: an apocalypse.

I absolutely did not want to get on his bad side.

One blink. That's how long I'd survive if I decided to be a smartass. Thousands of people depended on the jobs the Le Spyre estate generated internationally. Then there were those on my property whose lives were more directly at risk.

Guess I was eating humble pie for lunch.

Bowing low, I said demurely, "My apologies, King Julius. I read the situation wrong."

"Spineless too," he stated, allowing me to see his disgust once more before shifting his gaze.

I nearly fell flat on my face, but I kept my shoulders back and my chin tilted, smiling inwardly at the thought of Grandmother's secret office.

Kyros stole a quick look my way.

The king arranged the folds of his coarse sarong. His attention had terrified me so much, I'd registered nothing but his cold eyes. Topless, with a goatee, he looked like a mix between a sexy pharaoh and rugged shepherd. "Heir, explain yourself."

Kyros was the outward picture of calm. Within, anything but.

He climbed two stairs and sank to his knees. "King Julius, Miss Le Spyre's acquisition rates are 25 percent higher than the best performing of my realty staff. I had previously asked her to hold a once-weekly class for my staff to improve their manner with humans in the hope of boosting the overall acquisition rate. I met her again today to renew my request."

King Julius's brows climbed. "*Requesting*, heir? Do you not share a blood bond with this human?"

Okay, the human thing was going to get old fast.

"Yes, Father. Three, as you know."

Was I alone in feeling the iron beneath Kyros's words? The glimmer in Julius's eyes made me think not.

Careful, Kyros.

The king growled. "Then it is your property. You do not ask a dog whether it wants to round up sheep. You do not *request* that those in your power complete a task. Have I raised you to be weak?"

Wow. Talk about old school douchebag. The temptation to woof was real, but his eyes flickered my way. This was as much a test for me as for Kyros.

"My mistake, Father. Thank you for your wisdom."

The iron was definitely noticeable in Kyros's voice this time. I sent him a tendril of caution, having no idea if the warning reached him or not.

"Human," the king said in bored tones, "do you think yourself above my heir's request?"

I forced myself to meet his gaze, managing one second. "I do not."

"Do you believe yourself to have some hold over my eldest son to deny his demands?" He leaned forward on his throne.

My chest clamped for a full three seconds before the fear from his tiny actions loosened. "I don't believe the lessons will have the effect he desires."

This was the perfect chance to get onto Level 66 on a permanent basis—if I didn't die.

I cut the king off. "The problem in your strategy is more deep-rooted than simple lessons can fix."

How many siblings gasped behind me? All eight?

The only sound in the low-ceilinged and gold-draped chamber was my ragged breathing.

"Problems in my strategy," the king said softly, his lips white.

Mentally, Kyros was waving his hands in the air and holding a sign that read *fucking stop.*

Too late.

King Julius's question was rhetorical this time, but I was already knee-deep in shit. "Yes, your... majesty. *Ingenium* is a game between two Vissimo clans, but the game board is a human city. I believe it a major weakness that you don't have more humans involved. I can understand the need to keep most at a distance—the CEOs and such, but the minds of Vissimo and humans work differently. Our desires and priorities aren't the same. *That* is a deficit that can be filled. My question to you is: Could the game plan of Clan Sundulus be further honed? Surely both clans are neck and neck. A tiny advantage could be the difference in winning."

Sweat trickled down my back. Would it look bad if I sat down for a rest? *Probably.*

"Indeed." The king sat back.

Was I meant to answer? Kyros sent a negative blast.

I remained mute.

"The game is so evenly balanced that a 2 percent difference would be enough to trigger the end cascade," he said, eyes flaring.

I gagged twice, slapping a hand over my mouth.

"Father," Kyros said sharply.

King Julius muted again, and I mentally walloped Kyros upside the head. *Good one, moron.* That was a freakin' test too.

"What are your recommendations, human?" the ancient vampire asked.

This guy had to have three brains working at once. His subject and mood changes were a six-way tug-of-war.

I paused. Somehow, leading in with *I can join your inner-circle meetings every night* seemed bound to raise suspicions.

"I hadn't thought that far," I told him, casting my eyes downward.

Kyros tensed.

His father scoffed. "Humans. So full of opinions, so lazy with solutions."

That was me. *Lazy Basi.* And hopefully alive Basi.

"Children?" The king addressed the vampires behind me.

Neelan stepped forward. "Form a focus group from those blood-compelled to our family. See what ideas they formulate after each roll, but leave them in the dark to those we take and implement."

King Julius didn't react other than a slight shifting of his gaze.

"Look for other sources of tutorship, human communication courses," Deirdre put in. "Though I don't agree that's a weakness in our strategy."

Rory cleared his throat. "We already have a marketing budget for research on human wants and needs. Increase that budget. We don't need to think like humans, merely know what they desire and pour more of our resources behind that."

"I disagree," I said, hands behind my back. "The game board is surely becoming smaller—especially in terms of realty, which is the largest industry. Your marketing tricks may fool the majority, but what about the trouble cases who have shown resistance to your current approach?"

Lalitta shuffled forward. "I think human lessons are a really good idea, if Miss Le Spyre would agree."

King Julius's gaze softened the veriest amount before firming again. It didn't surprise me that Lalitta had managed to touch whatever semblance of a heart he had left.

"Do we really want a group of humans aware of our clan strategy?" Gerome asked.

Lionel returned to my side at the base of the stairs. "All human liaisons barring Basilia are tied by a single blood exchange, Father. That is easily broken by Fyrlia royals. The risk is large for a mere theoretical gain."

My eyes shifted to Kyros, who still knelt in silence. When was the king going to let him stand? Humiliating him like this was a bit much for visiting the human, wasn't it?

Frowning, I glanced up at the king to find his attention riveted on me. *Crap.*

I forced my attention to the wall behind the king as Safina climbed to stand beside her eldest brother, resting a hand on his shoulder.

"A human liaison," she announced. "Someone already in our near-absolute control. Someone already aware of the workings of our game who can provide daily input on our proposals."

The siblings turned to me, and I was slammed by a wave of defeat from Kyros. He didn't want me further embroiled in the game?

I kind of appreciated that.

"Don't look at me," I shot at the siblings, playing my part. "I have my estate to run."

That really did take up several hours of my day.

Safina tilted her head. "You work for Live Right already. Your job role can be changed."

I blew out a breath. "Did I say I liked you?"

"No, you said I was a badass bitch."

I scrunched my nose. *I suppose that's still true.* "In all seriousness, your meetings are in the middle of the night. I like my current job—"

Fingers curled around my throat.

The king lifted me bodily off the ground, eyes flaring softly.

I hadn't even seen a blur when he moved!

My toes scrambled for purchase as I wheezed and gurgled through the burning grip constricting my breath. My eyes bulged and I pleaded with him silently to release me.

His blue eyes bored into mine, and like a stretched rubber band pinging back on itself, my mind and body were no longer my own.

"Why are you here?" King Julius demanded, his voice coated in icy daggers.

My feet settled on the ground as his grip on my throat relented so I could answer. My lips moved without my permission. "Because I have to be."

"Do you love my heir?" His eyes bore into every corner of me.

"No. The blood bond isn't real."

"Does he love you?"

"No. He's led by the blood bond."

King Julius regarded me. "How simple you are. Why did you return to his tower?"

"To win the game."

"By all reports you hate games," he replied.

It wasn't a matter of choosing words carefully or withholding the truth, I had to answer. "I do. This game has taken too much from me. I will win it."

His lips curved. "A human win *Ingenium* for Clan Sundulus? How ludicrous."

I awaited his command.

"Are you working for Clan Fyrlia?" he asked, his fingers tightening once more.

"I'd never work for those fuckers."

Tears squeezed from both eyes as spots filled my vision. My legs lost their strength, my arms fell away from where they'd gripped his wrist in some puny attempt to save my life.

The rubber band *pinged* again.

He released me from his mind compulsion, and I collapsed to the floor, sucking in great gulps of air through my bruised, raw throat.

"Rise, heir."

Kyros stood immediately, not sparing me a glance as I trembled on all fours, trying to force away lingering clouds from his father's mind rape. A vibrating wrath settled over me—Kyros's—and I realised just how much control he was being forced to exert. His need to kill and destroy was so strong, it made *me* want to attack the king.

Gerome had compelled me like that once before—after the first blood exchange—and Kyros lost it. His father just trampled the blood bond big time; even I knew that was a serious no-no.

I sent Kyros what I hoped were soothing vibes. He could *not* lose his shit right now.

"Son," King Julius spoke dispassionately. "You have disappointed and disobeyed me."

Kyros lowered his head, eyes fixed on his father's bare feet. I didn't mistake it as subservience. He was hiding the violence in his expression.

"I will do better, Father."

Managing to get my legs under me, I dragged myself upright again, mind furiously rehashing what I'd let slip to the king. I said I'd wanted to win. He'd assumed I meant on behalf of his clan. My hands shook.

His superiority complex had led him to grossly underestimate this particular human, and that's the only reason I was alive or not tied to him through a blood compulsion right now.

Fuck.

Julius resumed his throne. "You are expressly forbidden from exchanging blood with this human again. Do you understand?"

Kyros bowed low and remained that way. "With respect, Father. My control is no longer absolute around her."

"Was it ever, heir?"

Burn.

"My blood wishes to claim her without delay. In all ways. I have tried to seek physical gratification twice without losing control and met with failure."

That. Bastard. Was everything a fucking *experiment* to him?

Not that I wasn't at the beach for my own reasons, but just when I thought myself the ultimate seductress, he went and usurped my efforts.

"Then you best figure out how to control yourself," King Julius said in a silken voice. "Especially considering she is to be our new human liaison."

The king sneered down at me. "Present yourself for the dice roll each night. You will henceforth work from midnight to 3:30 a.m. on Level 66. Whether you spend the rest of your workday in house acquisition or in tutoring the other staff, I leave to the discretion of my heir."

This was perfect, but I had to put up some fight. "I don't believe I can keep up that kind of routine ongoing. It will take its toll on me physically and impede my decision making."

He ignored me. "Kyros, today I could have compelled this human through blood, and I did not. Do not do me the disservice of taking that mercy for granted."

I released a shaking breath.

"Thank you, Father."

Fuck you, Father.

"Thank me by not demeaning yourself with a mate bond to a human, no matter if she is smarter than the average cattle. Seducing her for her assets was acceptable when you maintained a dignified distance. My heir will not attach himself permanently to a baser race."

Hurt spliced me at his callous mention of using me like a dishcloth. Regret coursed through Kyros.

"Lover, are you telling a young male not to pursue a young woman?" A clear voice rang out.

An ethereal *goddess* of a woman appeared from between the curtains behind the throne. Kyros's mother. The queen of Clan Sundulus. I'd seen her on the live stream of the dice roll.

... Though not topless with only black garters and silken black underwear on.

Whatever floats your boat.

"Mom!" Neelan hissed, turning away.

I glanced back to see most of the siblings blurring from the room. Mirth bubbled up my throat as Rory covered his eyes while Safina merely looked amused.

"My queen," the king greeted, taking her hand as she approached him in some otherworldly gliding impression of a swaying walk.

I could barely take my gaze from her. No wonder both kings had wanted to harem her up. Milky skin seemed to glow and rich blonde tresses trailed to her lower back. Did vampire moms breastfeed? Because her boobs sat higher than mine. Her rosy nipples could have their own Twitter page.

Maybe I'd start one.

"Lover, do you think it wise to give our son an order he cannot possibly keep? To deny a blood bond with a true mate, is not that cruel? You know as well as I that being human is no real barrier."

Alarm coursed through the bond, every speck of it from Kyros. What the hell was that about?

The king's gaze trailed to his queen's breasts and then lower.

I glanced over my shoulder again, enjoying the sight of Safina turning faintly green. The only one left, she turned tail and marched from the chamber.

Kyros remained with his head down, but his discomfort and disgust were discernible through his continued rage. Turns out parent PDA was viewed the same by both species.

The king twirled the queen and she landed on his lap with a light laugh.

Were they about to get it on? Because even I'd have a problem watching that.

"Lover, our son and his true mate are still here," the queen said, shooting a curious glance my way.

The king growled.

"That is what she is, Julius," the queen said sternly.

His jaw clenched as he met her cool gaze. "My son is not meant to be with a human."

The queen said nothing, trailing her fingertips over his chest. And lower.

And lower.

I grinned as Kyros's wrath gave way to nausea.

"Leave," the king said without looking our way.

The queen jerked. "Oh, but stay for dinner, please, my first son."

"Yes, Mother. After I take Miss Le Spyre home," Kyros murmured, turning without lifting his head.

The king lowered his head to his queen's ample chest. "Neelan can do it."

He *totally* knew about his children's side game of tormenting me and Kyros.

"Yes, Father." Kyros bowed, looking at me for the first time. His expression was unfathomable, and I tried to make sense of the determination and resignation emanating from the massive vampire.

"Basilia," he said, striding to the door.

Woof woof!

But, really.

Like I needed any encouragement to get the fuck out of King Julius's sight.

15

"Miss Le Spyre," Angelica greeted as I exited the lift onto Level 66 on Sunday night. "Congratulations on your promotion."

I'd assumed my work week was Monday to Friday morning. No one had come to the estate to correct the assumption anyway.

"That's looking at it through rose-coloured glasses to the extreme, Angie," I replied, making my way to where the roll was held each night.

Tonight was Clan Fyrlia's turn.

"Perhaps. You might be interested to know that Queen Titania approves."

Fuck me, even the queen's name needed a Twitter page. I had a serious crush on Kyros's mother.

I picked up speed to lose the vampire whom I neither liked nor disliked. Actually.

I slowed. "You know what King Julius said to me and Kyros then?"

"My sister and I are close," she answered. "My sister is talking to him."

Chipping away at King Julius? Was that possible?

Hopefully.

Because if he didn't relent, my game plan was officially screwed.

I wasn't convinced my seduction strategy was working, but I'd have to up it somehow—except *that* was bound to raise Kyros's suspicions. What sane person would play with the fire that was King Julius?

"No need," I said. "I don't want to pursue the blood bond further."

Vissimo were already crowded around the glass tube, and I stopped behind them. *11:57 p.m.* Perfect timing. Not a minute more than needed. That surely sent the right message. And I'd try to leave early too. Anything to nullify any suspicion over my presence here—even though the king literally ordered me here.

The vampires in front of me parted like the two jagged columns of a zipper. I studied their expectant faces.

"No, no," I said, planting my heeled feet. "I'm watching from back here."

They continued to part, creating a path all the way to the glass tube.

For fuck's sake.

Angelica shoved me gently, and I stomped to the front, scowling through the huge glass cylinder to where Kyros stood on the other side.

My eyes drank him in, something settling within me just for being near him.

Stockholm syndrome.

His contentment thrummed through me as tangible as the rumbling in his chest on the few occasions my head had rested against it.

The screen lit up, displaying the two kings and their queens. Tonight, King Mikhail picked up the dice and rolled. *Huh,* Julius really did have a better roll. I thought that was blind admiration for the Sundulus leader from his adoring minions.

The screen disappeared and the large screen map of Bluff City descended with the glass tube just like I recalled.

Kyros clicked the tiny remote in his hand, and everyone watched the red dot zigzag around the board in a seemingly random order.

I memorised the order this time. *Grey, Estates, Orange, Red, Pink, Purple, Blue, Yellow, Green, Agriculture, and Black.*

The red dot settled on Agriculture, and a displeased murmur rippled through the surrounding Vissimo.

"Eleven," he announced. "Today Clan Fyrlia will work in the Agriculture district. While not an ideal roll, we are prepared for the worst-case situation. We will work closely with Prince Lionel's sub-clan tonight. Please include the relevant sister team in your strategy meetings. You all know that Fyrlia recently gained an advantageous development deal in this area. That advantage cannot be allowed to gain further momentum. Currently, Lots 72-94 are privately-owned farming lands. If Fyrlia secure just one of those, the probability of us securing the remaining twenty-one lots decreases by 8 percent. We know that humans are more likely to listen to word of mouth. Let's not allow Fyrlia to create that."

A begrudging respect rose within me as he continued. The dice could have landed anywhere. He had extensive knowledge of Bluff City. Far more than me. I had to constantly refer to my Churchill team's daily report for forecasting statistics.

"Live Right's agricultural successes must occupy the top of every realty search for Bluff City," Kyros continued. "Forecasting teams, SEO teams, you know what to do. Furthermore, today is a day to collect on favours garnered with our human liaisons. I don't need to explain this is a pivotal moment. We have never been in a tighter position. If Fyrlia win the rest of the available agriculture land, we will enter the end cascade."

I half listened as I processed that. Though I had no idea what an end cascade was.

The major bluff in Sundulus's play was only known to the siblings and select few others—that I was certain of. Mr Ringly's subdivision deal was meant to go south, but Kyros appeared deadly serious as he continued speaking of pulling in their council and finance contacts to inhibit development approval.

I guess that's where compelled humans—like my grandmother's friends—came in. The clans used them to facilitate and intercept deals. To influence the un-compelled human population against the opposition. Any free and uncoerced human could sign a contract, I assumed.

"Present your reports to the strategy teams by 1:00 a.m." Kyros finished.

He was flooded by a crowd of vampires.

This time I watched.

Some were his seconds. Others, I assumed, were the heads of the various teams, but I didn't know what those teams were.

"Time for your part," Angelica murmured in my ear. "This way, please, Miss Le Spyre."

I adjusted my lilac jumpsuit, pulling the large silver buckle of the belt cinching my waist back into the middle.

This was it.

Time to see how my masterplan worked in reality. Perhaps I hadn't completed the fourth blood exchange yet, but I *was* on Level 66. I'd expected that to take months, not days.

Thank you, King Julius—fucking douchebucket.

Following behind Angelica, I entered the glass chamber that I recalled Kyros exiting on my first visit to this level. There were twelve seats and twelve tablets.

"How do the meetings work?" I asked.

She gestured to a seat at one end of the rectangle table. I wasn't sitting opposite Kyros. That had to be a wife-mate thing. Whether Angelica was in the ongoing midst of her matchmaking game, or Kyros was playing a force-Basilia-to-be-my-wench game, I wasn't playing.

"Kyros and his seconds meet here. You've visited the other chamber where the princes and princesses meet. The rest of the rooms are for our various teams. My team is house acquisition—which is where I must go presently. Good luck, Basilia."

I saluted her and received the ghost of a smile before she swayed out of the room.

A quick peek through my lashes told me Kyros was still in the middle of the gradually thinning crowd.

Marching to my *wife* seat, I dragged it around to one of the long edges of the table and shoved the five seats already there down to fit mine in. I stretched across the table to grab the tablet.

The seat opposite Kyros was now bare.

Perfect.

I sat as men and women entered the room. I recognised a few from the cafeteria on Level 50 and my infrequent visits up here. Conrad was the sandy blond from the first night I discovered Vissimo. He called Kyros by name, so they had to be close.

Tonight, every one of them wore a scowl. Subtle, but present. And aimed at me.

Goodie. What was up their buttholes?

Kyros entered.

I tried—*fuck, I really tried*—to keep my libido under wraps. *Why* I still tried, I had no idea. My mouth bobbed at the sight of his perfectly tailored navy-blue suit, my rich man complex working at full power.

Seriously the greatest irony of my life.

At this point, part of me wanted to have sex with him to just *know* once and for all. Kyros was right; most of the allure had to be the suspense of not knowing how good—or terrible—sex between us would be.

The ache from the last two months was almost painful. I'd dismissed a one-night thing with him because he was possessive as hell. Now, that didn't deter me so much, maybe because I was already *in* this circus for life. There was no running away. Kyros had to learn to control his alpha tendencies—that was a certainty—but my choices had narrowed drastically with the three exchanges.

My body wanted him. The bond wanted him.

Acutely.

With increasing desperation.

Fuck. Tommy would legit disown me if I entered his pants.

Kyros crossed to where I sat, sweeping back one side of his form-hugging jacket to slip a hand in his trouser pocket.

He stopped next to me, and I met his hard eyes.

What are you pissy about?

He jerked my chair back and lifted me—seat and all—depositing me at the head of the table again.

"I'm not sitting here," I hissed at him. "It means something."

Kyros spun my chair around and leaned over me, one hand on the high back over my head. "It means you're my true mate. Sit here, Basilia. Or sit on my lap. Which would you prefer?"

His response shocked me. Was he taking his father's advice to heart? Or was this a *don't mess with me on Level 66* thing? I could tell from the satisfaction radiating from him through our bond that he enjoyed my startled response.

"In that case." I flipped open the case containing my reading glasses. Sliding the thick black frames on, I said huskily, "I choose your lap."

Dark lust spiked me.

Kyros was a sucker for my specs. I tilted my head, feeling my wing-woman hair slither over my shoulder. A shadow fell across his green gaze and his hands settled on my hips.

"Uh, sir?"

We both glanced at a dark brunette woman located two seats from Kyros's chair.

He replied, "Danielle."

"This is an important day in the game, sir, as you said yourself. I worry that having Miss Le Spyre on your lap will impair our ability to yield the best result."

The other seconds murmured their agreement.

I smirked at their interference.

"Noted." Kyros's hands slipped from my hips as he straightened. "Today, you'll remain here."

No one missed the slight emphasis he put on *today*. The air around me cooled as the vampire left to take his seat. Discontent thrummed through him hard and fast. More anger too. I hadn't seen him since meeting his father. I'd assumed things would carry on almost the same.

Apparently not. That put a major stick in my plans.

First things first.

I cleared my throat, scanning the ten occupants of the table—excluding myself and their boss. "Would someone like to explain why you're all scowling at me?"

Kyros's head snapped up as he sat. His gaze whipped to each of the seconds' faces in turn. Which, *of course*, were now smoothed of everything.

"Is there a problem?" Kyros asked them in a low voice.

Most shook their heads. Conrad answered.

"Old concerns rising again, Kyros," he said. "You admitted that focusing around Miss Le Spyre is harder. We're worried about the potential negative effect of having her in this room."

I really hoped there was a negative effect. Then I'd fuck Clan Sundulus simply by sitting here. After meeting Julius, I wanted him to lose nearly as bad as Fyrlia.

Before Kyros could reply, I shot in. "You're aware that King Julius requested I be here?"

Conrad nodded, lips pressed together.

Definitely not my biggest fan.

"Do you usually question King Julius's wisdom?"

He paled, as did several around the table. *Yeah*, the king gave me the willies too.

I leaned back and crossed my legs. "Don't worry your heads over the choices of your superiors. The main distraction so far to a solid strategy has been your unsought-after interference."

The words hung heavy, made heavier by Kyros's blatant admiration through our bond. It was all bravado. If his father was in the room, none of those words would have left my mouth.

"My true mate is right," Kyros stated.

Enough with the fucking true mate!

His lips twitched, and he pushed a red button on the table. "Begin, Ilion."

"Wait," I said, pointing at the button. "What's that?"

Kyros quirked a brow. "Vissimo have trouble hearing through a certain frequency. We use a frequency generator in this meeting and the meeting with my siblings and King Julius so Clan Fyrlia cannot hear our plans outside the tower."

My brows climbed. So they were aware of the frequency thing, too, huh? That made sense. "I see."

"Ilion," he said, shifting attention from me.

Everyone clicked on their tablets and I did the same. There was a file labelled *Seconds*. Glancing to check the tablet of the vampire on my right, I clicked on the file and tuned into the male on my left.

Ilion pressed his lips together. "Fyrlia knows our position. They'll throw everything they have at this. Absolutely everything. That means we must reciprocate. I suggest a higher budget for the day. 127 million."

There was a murmur of dissent.

Danielle was nodding though. "We can recover from an overspend. We can't recover if they're allowed to secure more agricultural land. That will start the end cascade."

I straightened. "What do you mean by end cascade?"

She cut a glance my way, her blue eyes a match for most around the table. "Have you played Monopoly before?"

Great, I was getting the stupid person explanation. "Yes," I said patiently. Until Tommy refused to play with me anymore.

"You know the point where one person is clearly going to win and the question changes from *will I win* to *how long before I lose*?"

"I do."

"That's what I mean by the end cascade. At a certain point, statistically, one clan cannot win. The scales tip and with increasing speed, someone will lose. That's how *Ingenium* will end for one side —just like in Monopoly or chess."

I dipped my head. "Thanks for explaining."

So Clan Sundulus wasn't in a good position—even *with* the bluff at play.

That was good to know. And really bad. The clans had to remain locked in an even battle for years to come for me to have any chance at winning.

If Sundulus was at risk of losing, it was in my interest to help them.

The conversation resumed, and I focused on it entirely, trying to ignore the fear-filled reactions of their bodies as the conversation heated and eyes blazed. I closed my eyes, blocking out the sight of their white teeth, and the discomfort eased somewhat, though it was annoying not to see their body language and expressions.

"We're owed a favour by a town planner. Julia Dinh," a male said. "If there are purchases today, Fyrlia will attempt to change the status of the secured land from agricultural to rural for development, of course."

"Bastards," another spat.

My brows climbed and remained there through what was essentially a roll call of every human they had in their control who could help them succeed and Fyrlia fail.

This was the real deal. And right now there were eight other conversations in eight other towers happening just like this one.

For a minute, I baulked at the sheer magnitude of their operations in comparison to mine. But my strategy possessed none of their restrictions, and they weren't actively working against me.

No. I had belief in the Le Spyre network. Being from here—and human—made my strategy *stronger* than anything they had.

The door opened, and I squinted at Angelica before checking my watch. *1:00 a.m.*

The head of each team was required to report back to the seconds and Kyros now.

I swivelled my chair so my back wasn't to her.

She stood, hands clasped, but her eyes darted to me and she smiled.

Angelica needed to get a life. If I didn't know she already had a harem, I'd say she should get laid.

Dang it. I was probably the only person in this room not getting any—aside from maybe Kyros.

"May I direct your attention to house acquisition," she said.

Ilion leaned over, tapping on my tablet. He exited the slideshow I was in, clicked on the file labelled *House Acquisition.*

"Thanks," I whispered.

The new document displayed a list of target properties for the day. Usually, I received a few properties from the *trouble* list to visit. Of course, I knew which suburbs the other realtors were working in, but not a comprehensive list of the exact properties.

This was exactly what I needed so my acquisition staff could work with confidence and ensured safety. If Sundulus was after these properties, I felt safe assuming Fyrlia would be after them too.

I worked to keep my glee under wraps, feeling Kyros's gaze heavy on me. Pretty sure glee wasn't the normal response to the house acquisition report.

The first page of Angelica's summary was a list of privately-owned agriculture properties. *Shoot*, there really weren't many left to secure. I read the first address and scanned the page anew.

I owned six of these. Well, I was reasonably certain.

Angelica continued talking, but I listened with half an ear, scrolling through the rest of the file. I'd already been briefed that no reports left this level. Taking pictures on my phone—even in a private corner or the bathroom—felt like a really bad idea.

Memory, it is.

I returned to the first page as Angelica detailed what was known about each property. Another head team member entered after her, and I opened the file *Internet Marketing* without Ilion's help.

I skimmed over what appeared to be an online marketing plan but soon went back to the first document.

How was I going to play this?

I needed the clans to keep fighting while I crept up in the wings.

Clan Sundulus kept Fyrlia weaker. Overall, two were easier to fight than one. I had my own forecasters for *Ingenium*. I knew what my position would be in two years or three decades based on my accelerated strategy.

Decades that, with enough expansion, I might have a chance to finish this thing.

Seven Vissimo came in and out to give their reports. By 1:30 a.m., in addition to the first two areas, we'd covered general marketing—television and street marketing, offensive marketing, council strategies, banking strategies, SEO, industry budget, human liaisons and the largest file—forecasting for what would happen in over one hundred different scenarios, arranged from most probable to least probable. Thankfully we'd only gone through the top five most likely situations.

Keeping track of the moving parts was nearly impossible, but I focused on the worst possible outcome. If Fyrlia acquired six of the remaining agricultural properties, the percentage of their Bluff City holdings would increase by 2 percent. The end cascade would be triggered.

If they acquired *one* agricultural property, it gave them 50.1 percent likelihood of winning *Ingenium* because of the power of word of mouth.

The report also detailed what the likeliest suburbs for their turn would be based on the most probable rolls: seven, six, eight, five, and nine. That only helped Sundulus so much. Anything could fucking happen—and the forecast covered fucking everything, extrapolating data over the next twenty years.

They had to have software to generate these crazy stats. Or, I supposed, several hundred vampires on the job.

The head of forecasting left the room. As soon as she did, the seconds launched into a furious debate that had my palms sweating in seconds. Eyes blazing and teeth flashing, growls cut through the air. Keeping track of the different reports and threads was near impossible as it was. With the reaction of my body around the Vissimo, I had no chance.

I watched Kyros who, for the most part, sat back observing his seconds. He chimed in every so often to realign the flow of ideas and criticism but otherwise sat much like his father had while listening to his children brainstorming.

When his father did it, I wanted him to trip on his sarong and fall down the stairs.

On Kyros…

My mouth dried at the way the massive vampire leaned back in his chair, at ease but attentive. If I *was* sitting on his lap, I knew what I'd be feeling under my ass at that moment.

I clamped my legs together, flushing as Kyros tore his green eyes from Conrad to look at me. Answering heat and no small amount of intrigue flooded my mind.

The seconds stood, and I blinked.

They turned to me, and I stared back in bewilderment.

"We stand before our prince, Miss Le Spyre," Ilion said, his keen eyes resting on the open housing report in my hand.

He isn't my prince.

I peered at Kyros. "If I sat here all day, you'd have to do the same?"

His eyes flashed at the challenge, and the vampires either side of me scattered away from the table.

I grinned, standing.

Kyros unfurled to his full height. I swallowed, and several vampires glanced my way.

"Stand by for the final strategy announcement at 03:45 a.m.," Kyros said grimly.

The seconds didn't just walk from the room—they blurred. *Thank fuck.* I took a full breath for the first time in two hours. I ignored Kyros as much as possible to power off my tablet.

It was no use. I *felt* him moving down the length of the table to watch me. Hugging the tablet to my chest, I straightened and returned his steady perusal.

His green eyes searched mine. What for? PTSD from his father's interrogation? Strangulation by King Julius was just one more shit on the poop heap.

Kyros gripped my upper arms and sadness pinged through our bond. "I'm sorry, Basilia."

Had he ever said sorry before? I hadn't thought the word was in his vocabulary. His apology did mean something—as unspecific as it had to be for listening ears. It just didn't mean enough.

I hummed. "I hear you."

"That's what you say when you don't forgive someone."

Totally true. I laughed despite myself. "I do not—"

"You say it to Angelica."

We moved slowly to the door, and I smirked. "Do you think she knows?"

"Now? Definitely."

Well, damn. "Where's the next meeting?"

"I'll show you, but one more thing before we join my siblings."

He stepped in front, blocking me from his minions' view. Kyros powered on my tablet, and opening the house acquisition file, he tapped a finger on the target properties in Agriculture.

"It will take a while to adjust to these meetings. I know the lack of control from my seconds was physically hard to withstand."

Yeah. I'd have to figure out a way around that.

Kyros lowered his head. "Between you and I, is there anything we need to pay attention to on this page?"

He flipped between possessive, insightful, overbearing, and kind faster than my head chef flipped pancakes. I'd take a room filled with debating vampires over this any day.

He'd phrased his words carefully, and I followed suit. "I need to make a call during human time."

To my team in Churchill. I needed to know which property was best to give up. And if I definitely owned the six I thought I did.

A smile graced his face before he exited the document and powered off the tablet. "Thank you, Basilia."

I wasn't imagining the tension within him one bit. Clan Sundulus really was on the ropes.

16

I entered the penthouse of *Dimtren Rise* armed with a floor-length deep-green gown, a set of my mother's earrings, and gold glitter six-inch *Shus* that they could bury me in.

The volume of the murmuring elite ebbed as I paused on the stairs to scan them impassively.

The top level of this skyscraper afforded 360-degree views of Bluff City and was decorated with the new-money opulence of most event venues I'd have to attend as *the* Le Spyre.

Last time I saw most of these people was at my grandmother's funeral.

"Miss Basilia Le Spyre," the herald announced as I descended the few steps.

I winked at him, watching the guy redden.

"Thank god someone worthwhile showed up," Lady Treena said loudly, approaching at a gallop with her token glass of champagne.

Those around us shared wide, amused looks—more fool them. I took her hands and kissed her weathered cheek warmly. "Aunt Treena, I'm glad to see you. I've been meaning to visit."

She eyed me, sipping at her champers.

The level didn't go down. Lady Treena always had her hand

wrapped around a chute, but I'd never seen her drunk. It was how she tricked the world into thinking she'd gone batty. Hardly anyone stopped to wonder how she'd become, *and stayed*, so rich.

Because 95 percent of people were idiots.

"I expect one soon," she replied. "After you've had time to adjust to your new position."

Her gaze sharpened on me.

I met it without disguise, allowing my sorrow to seep through. For the loss of her best friend, my grandmother, and the loss of her mind to Vissimo. I'd known this woman my entire life. Had she been under a blood compulsion that long?

She nodded curtly, taking another fake swig. "More champagne!"

Three waiters appeared out of thin air. She set down her full chute and took two fresh more. The staff didn't say a word.

Lady Treena passed one to me. "The others couldn't come tonight. Old people problems. Do you know what this gathering is for?"

I hummed into my chute. "New bank in town."

"Fuck me. Should have faked a broken leg."

If anyone could fake that, it would be Lady Treena.

I laughed, but it faded as a familiar face appeared through the crowd.

Rory Senrite bowed low. "Miss Le Spyre, we meet again."

He scrubbed up well in a white tux. He even managed to look dishevelled—probably took him hours.

"Rory." I sighed. "Should've known you'd be here."

"Maybe you hoped? *I'm* surprised to see you here. What with your *I'm better than other rich people* attitude."

My lips twitched. "I'm Miss Le Spyre now, Mr Senrite. That comes with ballgown burdens."

His eyes roamed my cinched waist and swelling breasts. "Darling, burden is not the word that comes to mind."

"Always the charmer," I said archly, glancing at Lady Treena.

She gaped at Rory, champagne forgotten.

Crap.

The Vissimo quirked a brow. I turned my back to him, holding out my arm. "Lady Treena, I'm getting boob sweat. Will you join me in a quieter spot?"

She blinked a few times. "Boob sweat won't get you laid."

Rory choked behind me.

"Depends how drunk both people are," I replied, leading her away.

She glanced up at me. "The caveman? Please tell me it wasn't that new-money trash you dated for too long."

Honestly, it probably happened with Ricky, too, but... "Caveman."

Kyros's brother didn't follow, but he'd definitely heard about my drunken conquest from six months ago. Which meant Kyros would hear about it.

Worked for me.

I nodded to a few people on the way. I'd screamed at them all a few weeks ago, yet here they were, simpering for my attention. I'd rather be in a tower of vampires.

After depositing Lady Treena on a soft chair near the jazz band, I went to procure a chute of water for her.

"*Miss Le Spyre, what a pleasure.*"

The jab of fear that accompanied the feminine voice was enough to pinpoint the race of the speaker.

I turned in a whisper of satin. "Gina."

The petite vampire looked like the devil's concubine in the hugging black mermaid gown with her auburn locks. Or maybe like the devil was *her* concubine.

Gina's back was to the wall as she scanned the crowd. They, in return, darted small peeks at her, half afraid and half turned on.

"I hate these things," she murmured.

The vampire couldn't do anything to me in this crowd, surely. And Rory was here.

I joined her against the wall. "Show up two hours late and leave two hours early. That's my motto. Does Bluff City need a new bank?"

"No. NJB will merge with a bigger bank within the year. The question is *which* bank."

Which explained the presence of Rory and Gina.

I sipped at my champagne. It wasn't terrible.

"It's a nice change not to engage in small talk," she said.

"You don't enjoy talking about the weather?" I lowered my voice. "Must be a Vissimo thing. I love it."

Hmm, I'd successfully said *Vissimo* in a crowd of humans. Not that any were close by.

Could I shout out restricted terms in a human crowd as long as a vampire was with me?

Somehow I strongly doubted it.

She cocked her head, sliding her dark gaze to me. "It's a shame we're on different sides. These parties would be far less dull."

Studying the almond shape of her hazel eyes, I answered. "I promise to attend these things if you do."

Gina smiled in a flash of teeth that transformed her face from maleficent to snow white. "I don't like the vagueness of that. Pass your phone. I'll put in my number."

Uhm, that was a whole new level of seriousness that could get my butt kicked by King Julius.

Her attention was elsewhere. Following her glance to Rory, I scanned his furious expression.

That was a resounding *don't fucking do it*, Basilia. Taking her number with Rory as a witness felt less secretive though.

I pulled out my phone from my dress pocket—a demand I made of my tailors so I didn't have to carry a clutch. "You're on."

She rattled in her number and passed it back. "I sent myself a message so I have your number."

I'd ask Daniel to do regular checks on my phone security.

"I need to speak to the boring humans now." Gina circled her shoulders a few times.

I watched her warm-up routine. "Talk to them or fight them?"

"Depends. I'm talking to Harriet Gregorian first."

Tossing back my champers, I set it on a passing tray. "I won't complain if you rearrange her face. She stole my favourite Barbie when I was seven."

Gina surveyed Harriet over the rim of her untouched drink. "Yes. She has a rampant petty theft problem. It makes her very easy to blackmail."

Clan Fyrlia didn't play by human law, but such a casual admission shocked me. Then again, with Harriet Gregorian, caring was hard.

"Go get 'em, tiger," I said lamely.

Gina didn't get far. She turned back to survey me in heavy silence.

I lifted my brows. "Something on my face?"

"Not a hair out of place," she said breezily. "But if I were you, I'd ride to the tower with Rory after the ball. You may avoid three problems."

Strong arms wrapped around me from behind.

A hand slipped into my pocket, drawing out my phone. I let Rory have it, not breaking in my conversation with the mid-fifties founder of NJB. She dragged her shocked gaze from the vampire and back to me.

Kyros's brother wouldn't find anything on there. Messages automatically scrubbed from the SIM and I had important contacts under bland names. I'd already changed Gina's name to Stanley Yelnats.

He slipped my phone back into my pocket a moment later.

"Darling, you have my number now." His breath was hot on my ear.

I extended my hand to Ms Cryt, a widow with a business mind. "A pleasure to meet you, Ms Cryt. I believe you're one of the few I'll actually like."

Amusement tinged her soft grey eyes. "Thank you, Miss Le Spyre. I look forward to bettering our acquaintance."

"My people will be in touch with your people." I looked over my shoulder. "Rory, what do you want?"

One hand slid across my cinched waist, the other trailed over my shoulder left bare by the off-the-shoulder design. "To take you home."

Ms Cryt's frowned.

Knew I liked her.

"*Darling*," I said in a low voice. "I hope your real pick-up lines are far better than that. But I could use a ride to your brother's."

His blue eyes danced.

"Now, my heart?" he murmured into my hair.

Laughter choked in my throat. "Yes, now." I had a few things to do before my shift at *Live Right*.

"Your wish. My command."

He was laying it on thick tonight.

I let him lead me through the crowd, waving at a pale Lady Treena. Gina had already left. Couldn't blame her really. I wanted to cry at how many of these evenings I'd have to attend. Probably one a fortnight if I only went to a quarter of events. At least I had a reason to take on Bluff City's elite bullshitery now. My efforts to buy more real estate weren't enough to win the game. I had to stay connected in other industries and push forward where I could. Finance and entertainment were two of the largest industries and big on their little social gatherings.

"Miss Le Spyre, good evening."

I looked around for the speaker, feeling Rory's hand clamp around my forearm.

Horror slammed into me as I came face-to-face with Rhys's aunt —the aunt who'd seen me leaving with her nephew the night he died.

"Ms Wannington," Rory said smoothly as my heart pounded.

The woman smiled at him, a wrinkle forming between her brows.

Wannington. I'd heard of the name—though I never knew Rhys growing up.

"Hello," I choked, the sickening crunch of Rhys's chest caving in, hitting me square between the eyes.

Rory dipped his head. "Not feeling well, I'm afraid. Must be off."

I tripped after the vampire, trying to school my features into a smooth mask for the crowd of leeches.

When we were on the stairs, I pulled free of his grip, moving to stand at the balustrade as I forced away memories of Rhys in the hospital. So many things had exploded in my life, I'd never stopped to ask about his funeral.

"She doesn't remember anything from that night," Rory said, leaning against the railing.

I lifted my head. "Tell me what happened, please."

He lifted a shoulder. "When the human—"

"*Rhys.*"

Rory arched a brow. "When Rhys died, the charge changed from assault to murder. His family has money and influence and they were making waves that could get back to you. Kyros had someone bring the aunt in."

Bring her in.

My eyes widened. "Someone put her under blood compulsion?"

"Correct. One of my Vissimo. I have enough humans to keep track of, and I couldn't be bothered dealing with her fear at these events. Her memories of you were removed from that night. We already had the CCTV footage erased."

They'd saved me from being dragged through the courts. I wouldn't have been able to answer any questions about Vissimo. Imagining how bad that could have turned out was all too easy. However, because of that, the Tonyi triplets were off the hook too. Rhys's murder hadn't been avenged.

My relief was bittersweet.

Rory gestured to the lift at the top of the stairs. "Are you going to yell at Kyros for protecting you?"

"I don't like yelling at him." I frowned at my hands. "And no. In this instance—no matter that it isn't right—I'm grateful for the interference."

Even though the mind of another occupant of Bluff City had to be put in chains to make it happen.

That seemed like a slippery moral slope.

"I've entered our numbers into your phone. All my brothers' and sisters'," Rory said as we entered the elevator.

I shot him a wry look. "Great."

"It will be if your three problems decide to show."

I had fifty Indebted. "I don't feel like the triplets are that smart. Their efforts are fumbling at best."

"And that's how Lady Treena disables her prey."

Contemplative, I looked at him anew, ignoring the elevator usher. "I see."

They made clunky moves until they really struck. "They're feeling me out."

He dipped his head. "Don't make the same mistake so many do."

My lack of criminal experience put me at greater risk than anything. I had no idea how depraved they could get nor what they were most likely to attempt.

"Thanks for the advice."

"Welcome."

I liked Rory when he forgot about appearances. Which was about as often as Gerome stopped joking around. By the time I'd rattled off a text to Laurel explaining the change of plans, vain Rory was back. He remained in charge on the short ride to *Kyros Sky*, schmoozing me with all manner of horrible pick-up lines. I played along to distract myself from thoughts of the triplets who could be following us at that very moment.

What would they have done if Gina hadn't warned me? Would I have ended up like Rhys? Chest caved in. Dead in ICU.

Rory didn't budge when we pulled up outside *Kyros Sky*. "Get out."

"Love you too," I said sarcastically. "You'll be back later?"

I guessed Rory had to go through his own meetings in his finance tower before the siblings met at 2:00 a.m.

"I'll try not to miss you too much, darling."

Chh.

I kept my steps even between the car and the lobby, certain the triplets were somewhere close by, but I didn't breathe easier until the elevator doors slid shut.

Clicking the button for Lower Level 1, I reached into my pocket to make sure the storage locker key was still there.

I dialled Laurel upon leaving the elevator, hoping Kyros had his listening ears on.

"Miss Le Spyre."

"Hey, Loz. Can you ask anyone on Lower Level 4 to meet me on Lower Level 1? I've got a whole bunch of house stuff in a locker here that they can have. I thought everyone could take a bit each? There should be enough to go around."

There was a pause. "I'm sure that would be appreciated, Miss Le Spyre. I'll call a few Indebted to spread the word."

"Thanks. I'll be in the tower until three thirty."

"Roger that."

Smiling at Kyros's fresh irritation, I flipped the phone and slid it back into my pocket. He'd already advised against me removing my possessions from the tower. This would push his buttons well and truly. I glanced at the number on my key and, heels clicking, strode down the concrete hall lined with storage lockers until I located mine.

I stared through the wide grates to the contents within. Reaching through the bars, I rolled the edge of my barely used duvet between my fingers. These things belonged to another Basi in what felt like another life. Trying to return things I'd brought so I could try to make rent. Clint taking my stuff. If I hadn't failed so miserably, I wouldn't have discovered Vissimo. I might still be living in that shithole. Or maybe Clint would've gone a step further. Kyros still wouldn't have tried to seduce money out of me.

Perhaps I would have ended up here either way.

The stairwell exit door opened.

I faced the male Indebted, fishing for his name. "Marcus, isn't it?"

"Yes, Miss Le Spyre."

Peering past him, I saw he'd brought ten others along. "I don't want to force this stuff on you guys, but I literally used the contents of this locker for four days and I don't want it to go to waste. Do you think anyone on Lower Level 4 will use it?"

He looked at me incredulously.

"Yes!" a woman at the back called. "My towel is barely holding together."

Anger swirled through me. They didn't even have fucking *towels*. "Is it Kristen?"

"Kirsten, Miss Le Spyre."

Oops. "I apologise. Kirsten, when you're next on a shift at my estate, can you come and speak to me? I'm certain my staff can find enough towels for everyone here."

She bowed low. "Thank you, miss. I will."

I tossed the key to Marcus. "Please make sure it's evenly distributed. I don't want anyone missing out."

He glanced at the key, then back at me. Edging closer to the grate, he inhaled deeply.

Amusement coloured my voice. "Does it pass the sniff test, Marcus?"

The vampire jerked away. "Of course, miss. I—"

I gripped his arm. "I'm just kidding. Is there a problem?"

Glancing back, he wet his lips. "It's just that, I'm not sure the master will like us taking everything. The blanket smells like you. I-If you were mine, I wouldn't want another male sleeping with it."

His face flushed red. *Adorbs.* I wanted to smoosh his handsome cheeks together.

"Thank you for telling me, Marcus. How about I take the blanket then? Is everything else okay to leave with you guys?"

The vampire ducked his head and inhaled again, moving along the locker. "Yes, miss. But we can take the blanket for you. Kirsten will pass it over to your estate guards."

I smiled. "I appreciate that. Walking in heels is dangerous enough without limited vision."

"Have you been at a party, Miss Le Spyre?" a petite brunette in the middle asked wistfully.

She sounded young. Older Vissimo had a steadiness to their tone. And the really old ones often sounded bored.

Holding out my dress, I swished to make the satin rustle. "Just another ball."

"I think any ball would be lovely to go to," she said, drinking in my earrings and dress and the point of my gold shoes.

There she went making me feel bad for taking things for granted. "It's nice to dress up," I said. "If the company was better, I'd have a great time. They're all rich fuckers with sticks up their butts."

Marcus threw Kirsten a grin.

I left them to distribute the contents of the locker. Whipping out my phone again, I dialled Angelica. *Time for the cherry on top.*

"Miss Le Spyre."

"Angie. I need to get into my old room to grab my stuff."

A pause. Murmuring voices. Kyros's anger.

"Certainly. I'll send someone down with the key."

"Air kisses, babe." I made a few kissing noises and hung up.

I leaned against the back of the elevator as it shot up to Level 61. A quick look in the shiny walls told me my hair was still in a flawless side-chignon courtesy of Rosie. Glowing skin was displayed from my neck to the large swell of my boobs—thank you, bodice. Loop sleeves hung loosely about my upper arms and the forest-green gown flared dramatically from my cinched waist, the material falling in folds to the floor. The piece wasn't the most original I'd worn, but Grandmother always said I wore classics well.

I agreed with her.

The doors opened and I took one step before clutching the base of my throat.

Leaning against the wall was a towering god of a man dressed to devastating effect in a cashmere suit that would bankrupt someone in Orange.

His green eyes were wide. His throat worked as he took me in.

In silence.

Not a peep.

Was Kyros struck speechless? I stepped off the elevator. "Kyros."

"I'll remember the sight of you in that dress to my dying day," he said quietly.

The fervent marvel behind his words took my breath away.

Not sure of my ability to talk, I closed the space between us, sliding the key to my old room from his grip.

Disappointment panged between us, and I couldn't be sure if it was all his.

I shook my head and began walking to my old room. "Your father was pretty clear. And I think he's right."

His heat was at my back. "No, you don't."

Dang. "No comment."

"If you *did* agree with him, arriving at my tower while looking like a goddess was a terrible choice."

I tensed as he twirled me back, pressing me against a random door. His warm hands slid down my arms, pinning them by my sides. A groan slipped from him as the action pushed my breasts higher.

"Your nipples are just below the edge," he whispered, gaze firmly on the low neckline of my dress.

His want was intoxicating. *Hypnotising.*

I turned my head away, eyes squeezed shut as I tried to control my response.

"Don't turn away, my beauty. That's for others. Never me."

Kyros drew my face back.

My breath hitched as I tipped my head back to meet his meadow-green gaze.

"Do you understand?" he asked.

I lifted a hand and traced his bottom lip. He sucked my forefinger into his mouth and I jerked violently.

With blurring speed, he took hold of my wrist, trailing his nose over my pulse. "I asked if you understood, Basilia."

His hooded gaze settled on my breasts again.

I clenched my jaw, trying to rein in the heaving of my breaths. "Sometimes you're too much to look at, Kyros. So no, I'm not agreeing to that."

He grinned, and the change was blinding. My heart squeezed and I just *forgot everything*.

Coming down to land was sobering. And frightening.

This isn't part of the plan. Or was it? I didn't know anymore.

"Move. I need to get my stuff before my shift."

His fangs lengthened, and his grip on my wrist tightened.

Seriously?

"Move, please?" I said impatiently.

Kyros flipped my hand and pressed a kiss to the back. My hand was scientifically attached to my vagina somehow. It had to be. I'd had foreplay that didn't feel half as good.

"Your possessions are in my quarters." Straightening, the vampire prince dropped my hand and strode back the way we'd come.

I stared after him, jaw dropping. "What do you mean they're in your lair?"

He didn't answer.

That fucker!

Maybe this suited my strategy just fine, but it was hard to recall that as I stomped after him. "Heels aren't meant for running, you jerk!"

Kyros was waiting in the elevator, face smoothed of the amusement I could *feel*.

I slammed both hands out to stop the doors closing, breath coming fast. Did I say I liked bodices? I lied.

"Why did you move my stuff?" I gasped.

He tilted his head, eyes on my bosom. "My tower. Don't need a reason."

"Has anyone ever drawn size comparisons between your ego and this building?"

Blurring forward, Kyros yanked me against him and retreated into the elevator once more. I struggled until that began to feel too good.

He crossed my arms over my body and my breasts popped up again.

Kyros growled, frustration filling him.

"Are you trying to force my nipples out?" I said, outrage swelling.

His face hardened and he set me down, striding to the far corner. “That dress is fucking lethal, vixen.”

That’s a yes.

Near boiling point, I pulled out my phone when it chimed, reading the text from Laurel.

Got your blanky

Grinning, I typed back:

Bitch <3 <3

Kyros jabbed the button for Level 65. “Who are you texting?”

“None of your business.” I slipped my phone away.

His gaze narrowed.

“It wouldn’t be the caveman that Rory mentioned in his text earlier this evening?”

I edged to stand in front of the doors. “So what if it is?”

The vampire pinned me with his stare, and suddenly the elevator was nowhere near big enough for the two of us.

Ding!

I almost ran to get off the lift, forgetting that Kyros at my back was the most uncomfortable feeling *ever*. He followed me to his office at a leisurely pace, footsteps echoing. *On purpose*. Because I damn well knew he could move silently as a shadow.

My flighty response was turning him on big time, and like some twisted positive feedback system, *his* reaction turned *me* on.

I threw open his office door and marched into the large, bland office space, beelining for the desk. I flung back the password panel for him, then continued to the far wall.

His amusement trickled through our bond as he punched in the long-ass code, and I sent him an extra-strong dose of ire, maintaining it as I climbed the stairs to his private rooms.

Ugh.

I hadn't been here since finding a bag of blood with my name on it in his fridge.

He was behind me, so I hurried to the fridge and ripped it open.

One bag left.

"The shelf was nearly full," I said, covering my discomfort. "How much blood do you need?"

Fisting my hands in my satin skirts, I whirled to stare at him. He closed the door to the lair. "The correct question would be how much blood do I need now that I've completed three exchanges with you. I'm happy to tell you if you let me know who the spy in the tower is."

I… What? "I never found the spy."

His eyes glinted. "I believe you wanted to ensure the spy was indeed the spy."

"Yes. And I didn't exactly get time after finding my blood in your fridge," I replied sarcastically. "I'll work on it when I next get time."

Kyros didn't accept that one bit. "I need to drink three times my usual at the moment."

His subject changes would give me whiplash one day. And the fucker did it entirely on purpose.

"What happens when you run out of my blood?" I asked after closing the fridge.

He crossed to the kitchen, filling two glasses with water. "I'm fairly certain that drinking your blood is the only thing giving me some shred of control around you."

Good. "My blood in particular?"

Kyros's nostrils flared. "Yes."

My hand crept to my throat. "Don't look at me like I'm a strawberry mojito, Kyros. I'm not giving you more. You'll need to sort out your control issues some other way. Your dad was crystal clear."

I spotted my *Elegance* pack on the dresser and ignored the glass of water he held out. Crossing, I riffled through the pack. *Razor, body wash, moisturiser, two sets of clothing, flats, sandals, bank cards, and cash.* Everything was here.

As I hoisted the bag, my eyes fell on what lay next to it. The broken pieces of the pinecone I'd gifted Kyros.

After I'd hurled it against the wall, he'd picked up the pieces and put them up here? I forced my eyes away. "Okay, thanks. I'll be going now."

I trailed off as Kyros crossed and gently took my bag, setting it on the bed.

Hooking an arm around my waist, he drew me to the round sofa where we'd completed our second blood exchange. He kept a firm grip on my hand as he shuffled back on the couch.

Pain suffused my chest.

This sofa was the only homey thing in the minimalist apartment. Kyros relaxed here after a hard day. We'd had a real moment on this couch in the past. Or one I *thought* was real at the time.

Being back up here hurt. Sitting on this couch with him would hurt more.

"Please let me hold you for a moment, Basilia."

I chewed on my bottom lip, a similar loneliness to what I'd felt the last several weeks hit me. A pain over our separation. Bitterness at how things had ended. Anger and hurt. *Regret.*

None of that stopped me crawling onto the massive chair—but my ball gown did. Kyros leaned forward and gripped my waist, lifting and depositing me on his lap in a puff of satin.

Heart in a vice, I slowly rested my cheek against his chest.

Our breathing synced, enough for the two chutes of champagne I'd consumed to lull me into calm. That's the explanation I'd stick to anyway. I'd conveniently ignore that I hadn't felt this tranquil and safe since Grandmother died.

Kyros dropped a kiss on the top of my head. "What if there wasn't a game?"

I inhaled where I remained tucked against him.

He continued. "You told me that you felt unsafe because of *Ingenium*. What if there wasn't a game? Where would you stand then?"

"Is that likely with the massive bluff you guys are playing?"

He didn't hesitate. "Yes."

Good to know. "I don't really understand how that works. Are you guys waiting for Mr Ringly's drug addiction to come to light or what?"

Kyros inhaled my scent, a dreamy feeling filling him. "For a decade, Mr Ringly has pushed for his land space to become residentially zoned, entering into steadily more debt with the council fees attached to that process. We've watched him since he submitted the DA—never expecting the development plan to be approved. Now, we're applying financial pressure to his drug dealer to repay her debt—that pressure then falls upon her clients to pay their tab. We control the bank where his loan is held—as soon as he fails payment, we'll seize his land. There's also the option of alerting the police to his stash, but Mr Ringly is close to breaking point, and we'll have use for him in the future."

I hummed. "I feel bad for him. He can't have any idea why all these crappy things are happening to him. Poor guy must feel vulnerable."

"Is that how you feel?"

Frowning, I turned my head away. With a growl, he drew it right back.

"Answer," he ordered.

Yes, your highness.

Shifting slightly, I gave his initial question my genuine attention, ignoring the second. "I don't believe there will cease to be a game with you, Kyros. Not ever."

"*Ingenium* is coming to a head," he retorted. "Things are approaching the end cascade. Either way, I survive. The game will end."

So he said.

I had a feeling Kyros wouldn't take the murder of his family too well if Clan Sundulus lost. "*Ingenium* could take years or decades to truly finish once the end cascade is triggered. If it does? What about the games between you and your siblings? Or if worse comes to worst, dangerous games between you and your new clan—the triplets, Gina, and King Mikhail. A game is what you *are*, Kyros. Every second of your life for one hundred and forty-nine years. You don't know how to be anything else. So no, I don't believe that the end of *Ingenium* will make me feel safer. What would make me feel safe is leaving this city with everyone I know to go to a place where no one could find us."

His arms had crept around me.

"I can't escape you, Kyros," I reminded him, sadness weighting my words.

Sorrow seeped through me. I hated being able to sense his emotions. I couldn't say anything mean without feeling bad.

"The end of the game doesn't make a difference," he said, settling back.

Why did that sound like a *may as well keep going as is* statement?

"Your father said no, Kyros. Please don't put my life in danger again. Thousands of people rely on me now."

"I'm a game, according to your words. Do you think I move without thinking first?"

"When it comes to me, because of the bond. Yes, I do." Though nowhere near as much as I thought. Even in the car at the beach, he'd been testing how handsy we could get before his fangs came out to play.

Jerk.

His hands slid down, sliding my legs apart so I straddled his thighs.

"This isn't *holding me*," I grumbled.

"That's all I want."

I choked on a bubble of mirth. "That's a lie. I know exactly what you want."

Kyros's eyes sparked. "And what's that?"

My smile faded. Was I really going to do this?

Yes.

I rested a hand against the side of his face, my other hand trailing over the base of my neck. "You want to sink your fangs into my neck. Right here. Then pin me down and force your blood into my mouth until I choke. You want me to *like* your blood."

He stilled, breath and all.

I rested both hands against his face. "You want the top of my nipples to show over the top of this bodice. You'll lick the parts you can see before disappearing under my skirts to taste me." The blazing of his eyes and the bulge growing beneath me elicited a shiver.

I braced myself against the back of the round seat and brought my lips to his ear, breasts in his face. "You want to claim me, don't you, Kyros?"

I smiled, licking his earlobe and relishing his pained hiss. "You want me to call you *true mate*." Every word and movement hypnotised him—every slither of satin and brush of skin.

He was my captive.

It was intoxicating.

Heady.

I felt like a queen. *Do it.*

Bite me.

"You want it," he groaned, letting his head tip back.

I followed him down, propping my elbows up so our chests were aligned. "Hard to remember what I should and shouldn't do when we're like this."

Sweeping my hands down his rock-solid torso, I glided back up his arms, shifting again on his lap, this time to align with his length.

We moaned at the contact.

"You don't know what happens with the fourth exchange," he said, hands clamping down on my hips.

"What makes you think I want anything more than sex," I answered, loosening his tie and first few buttons. I bent my lips to the exposed golden flesh.

He ground into me. "There is no such thing as sex without blood between us. Not until the mating process is complete. In the fourth exchange, you'll begin the change to Vissimo."

Whoa, what?

I yanked away. "I change into a vampire by the end?" Fernando did *not* fucking mention that. Talk about an ice bucket for my lady parts.

"It's a possibility," he said carefully. "And rarely done anymore. It's not your choice, nor is it mine. Even if that doesn't happen, you'll exist somewhere between human and Vissimo by the seventh and final swap. So far our exchanges haven't affected you physically, just mentally. After the fourth exchange, your senses will heighten. With my blood, I expect them to be as strong as those of the weakest of our kind."

I widened my eyes, though Fernando had told me that part. I just hadn't known the changes were due to me becoming some kind of human-vampire hybrid.

Kyros frowned.

Shoot, he wasn't buying my surprise.

"About time I got cool stuff in return," I said with difficulty. "But the fourth exchange isn't happening—your father will kill me, Kyros."

He studied me. "You think I'd let that happen?"

I lifted a shoulder, feeling my sleeve slip further. "He's strong. He's in charge."

Kyros watched my mouth. "Strength means nothing in this negotiation. Only what the clan stands to lose or gain."

What was he talking about? "You're confusing me. Why the hell are you telling me all this?"

"Because now I can find you anywhere," he replied.

His answer was at odds with what he felt. Kyros was lying?

I hugged my torso. "I really hate that you did that to me."

"I know, my beauty."

"At least pretend you don't know what I'm feeling."

Kyros closed his eyes briefly, grinding into me again. "Feeling what you feel is an incredible gift."

I leaned forward, kissing his cheek. Shuffling off his lap, I straightened my dress.

"Why did that feel like goodbye?" He stood, and I couldn't resist peeking at the front of his pants. I felt his amusement and cleared my throat.

Yep, that looked about as big as what I felt grinding against it. Aching stomach material—Kyros was proportional.

"Would you like to look again, true mate?" he asked.

I resisted the urge to stomp my foot. "Don't call me that. Or vixen or *my beauty*. And no. One look was enough for any future solo activities."

His initial look of bewilderment melted into burning lust.

"*Oops*, look at the time," I said, snagging my pack off the bed. "We best get up to Level 66 for *Ingenium*."

I ripped open the door, almost sorrowful at leaving the empty space despite *everything*. The bond was so messed up. Yet again, it had me believing there was something else between us.

But there wasn't.

His dark voice trailed down the stairs after me. "The games won't be here forever, Basilia. I promise you."

He promised? *Great*.

I didn't believe him.

17

"Lot 91 paperwork is finalized?" I asked the array of men and women on my middle screen—Grandmother's Churchill team.

The man's eyes darted from my face to the room around me, and I wondered how much of the underground office he could see.

"Yes, Miss Le Spyre. Everything is in order and the contract will be effective as soon as you add your signature."

"What's the name of the alias owner?" Probably best to know who I'd *secured the property off* when the inevitable questions arose tonight.

A woman flicked through a document. "Mr Barnaby Dwelt."

"Very well. Current acquisition numbers?"

A man tucked in the far corner shot to his feet. "Acquisition rate has increased by 6 percent in the last week."

Tommy was one of the differences. She'd thrown herself into her HR position and we had two new realtors from out of town doing the rounds in Bluff City. I was the other difference. Half of the trouble properties I'd approached in the last week had sold to private investors—or so the owners thought. In addition, Tommy's acquisition team was able to move with greater confidence with my knowledge of where Clan Sundulus planned to target each day.

I shifted my gaze to an open document on my right screen. "How many privately-owned properties remain in Bluff City?"

The tiniest woman I'd ever seen answered. "One thousand, two hundred, and seven."

So few. I needed most of those houses to be mine.

"Thank you for the update. Our next meeting will be Friday at 11:00 a.m."

The CEO smiled—an impersonal kind of smile that gave me more trust in his professional ability. "We look forward to it, Miss Le Spyre. The Lot 91 contract will arrive via private courier within the hour."

I disconnected the call and slipped off my glasses, my eyes scratchy. Shift sleeping didn't suit me. I always felt particularly crappy after my 3:30 a.m. to 8:30 a.m. sleep. I knew my second sleep before my measly hour or two of home visit appointments wasn't catching me up on Z's entirely. My hours for *Live Right* had crept up to the twenty-five-to-thirty hours a week, but the house visits were important for my plans, so I wasn't complaining too loudly.

I walked around the perimeter of the room, studying the bird's-eye maps covering the walls.

"We're getting there, Agatha," I said grimly.

My goal by the end of the year was to increase acquisition by at least 5 percent, and a further 10 percent the following year. If the rates for Sundulus and Fyrlia held steady—I expected a slight drop as trouble properties were targeted, all properties would be purchased within two years. Then my game would become more aggressive indeed. I'd hopefully have the Indebted in my employ by then. At that point, I'd focus on finance and manufacturing, already having easy access to the health industry here because of *MediKnow.*

The thought of that more aggressive game terrified me. But I had two years until it hit me. By then, I'd be ready.

Tommy pressed the noise-cancelling button as soon as I shut the bookshelf door and replaced Tom Hanks's autobiography. We met here each day at 10:00 a.m.

"Conquer some shit this morning, lovely?" she asked.

I smiled tiredly. "Getting there."

She hummed. "These weird hours are catching up on you. And the stress. When is our next spa day? I might actually be able to pay for a decent one now I have more money and zero mortgage."

Biatch wasn't fooling me. Tommy still paid the bill for her pop's retirement home. Though her circumstances were better now.

"A spa day would be nice. I can get Sansi and her girls around. Saturday?"

"I'd prefer to get off the estate. I think you need it. To go somewhere other than that fucked-up tower."

Maybe I did need some normalcy. "Deal. Don't tell Sansi if you see her. She'll never forgive me."

My restraints meant Tommy knew nothing about the meeting with Kyros's father. But she'd seen my lingering fear after and though I'd said her assumption was wrong—she'd put all the blame on Kyros.

I took my seat behind the desk. "How was your first week?"

She sat. "You laying the groundwork on those trouble properties really helped. Just that tiny bit of distrust for Live Right and Foremost has made the last few sales easy as pie. The new employees vetted by the Churchill team are showing promise, and tomorrow I'll put everyone through extra training based on what tips and tricks you've learned at Live Right."

Pride filled me. I knew Tommy would kick ass at this job. "How are you doing with scheduling?"

Her role was similar to Angelica's. Tommy arranged which workers went to which properties based on what I discovered the night before.

"It was a mindfuck the first few days, but I've got the hang of it. I'd like another week or two to get everyone in motion before adding more staff."

"Done."

We grinned at each other.

The phone on the desk rang. I picked it up. "Fernando is here?"

"Yes, Miss Le Spyre," Fred answered.

"I'll be with him presently."

Tommy waited until the phone was set in the cradle. "Fernando is hot. I pass him each morning on the way out of here."

My eyes narrowed. "He's bad news."

She held up her hands. "Jeez, put your best-friend daggers away. Just saying he's sex for my eyes and part of me wonders if he has ten abs like in *Fernando's Eighth Ab*. I'm happy with Theodore at the moment. He's taking me away to Furnley Gorge at the end of the month. To a winery."

I bounced on my chair. "No way! That seems serious. You've totally downplayed things."

"You know me, Basil. Quietly freaking out over here."

"I want to meet him." I winked.

She glanced away, not answering.

I blinked through the shock hammering my chest. "Oh my god, you don't want me to meet him."

Tommy stood. "*Ugh*, I do. And I don't. I'm part of this shit, Basi. If I had a choice, I'd pick to be by your side. I'd just never forgive myself if something happened to him. I want to keep Theodore away from it all."

Blood poured into my cheeks. Not anger at her, necessarily, anger and frustration at the situation. "I'm *it all*?"

She opened her mouth, and I held up a hand. "Seriously, I understand that more than you know. If that's the way you want it, I'll respect your decision. Just try to avoid lying to him. They catch up with you pretty quick."

Tommy rounded the table, taking my hand. "It's not you. Trust me, he's heard all about you. It's just this fucked-up situation."

That I'd be in for a long, long time. I should probably get used to being held at a distance. It hurt, but I really did understand. "I know, Tom. I wish it was different, but there's no beef between us."

She leaned back, her shoulders relaxing. "Good. Then... one more thing."

"Hmm?"

"Are we going to talk about these?"

I glanced around at the vases of white roses filling every available surface in my office. "What's there to talk about?"

"Well, was there a card?"

Opening my desk drawer, I passed over the note.

She snorted after reading it. "*Kyros.* That's all he wrote? His fucking name. Jesus, this guy is old as shit and still has no idea."

I had to agree. "Yep."

"You gonna give away the flowers? Seems a shame to just chuck them out."

I tipped my head back against the upholstered chair and smirked at her. "Oh, they'll be used."

Tommy grinned. "That's my girl. I'll leave you to the hottie then. Ask him how many abs he has, I dare you."

My smirk disappeared. My friend was hot-blooded to the extreme. Fernando had proved himself a coward and was therefore nowhere near good enough for her. It wasn't happening.

My personal spy strode in moments after my friend left.

Closing the door, he clicked on the noise-cancelling button.

"Fernando, report," I said, leaning back.

He placed a paper with a list of properties on my desk and I pushed up my glasses, scanning it.

"Fyrlia are yet to secure anything in the agricultural suburb. The divide between the triplets and the other siblings continues to grow. The triplets had three meetings with their father in the last week. I trailed them to an attack on Princess Safina and her daughter last night. It failed, but it seems Fyrlia are upping their illegal activities in an attempt to distract Sundulus. They believe a win is within their grasp."

Safina had a daughter? News to me.

"Are attacks like that common?"

"From Fyrlia? Yes, Miss Le Spyre. That is why Sundulus own more Indebted. Their vision to stick to human law leaves them vulnerable in many ways. Guarding their human liaisons and top workers takes up many of their resources."

"And the clans are still locked evenly." To me, that made it clear who possessed the greater business prowess.

Fernando bowed. "There was something else, miss. I heard your grandmother's name several times during the delivery of my report yesterday. And your name—though that's commonplace."

I froze. "My grandmother's name?"

He nodded. "I was too far away to hear the particulars of the conversation. But I picked up *Le Spyre* because I'm always tuned for conversations about you. Then I heard them say *Agatha Le Spyre* twice."

Who the fuck was talking about my dead grandmother? "Who is *them*?"

He grimaced. "The Tonyi triplets."

I smiled as fingers tickled my side.

"Elmo," I murmured against the desk.

"*What does that even mean? I just don't understand where the fuck her sleep mind is at*," a male said.

Kyros answered, "Tickle Me Elmo. Kid's toy."

"*Do it again, Lionel*," a female urged.

I snorted as the tickling fingers returned. I twisted and pushed away the multitude of hands attacking me. Some people had no manners. "Sit up straight."

"*Kyros?*" another man asked.

"That one's harder. I think she wants you to stop touching her. Have some manners. Sit up straight."

A female cooed. "*You talk sleeping human. That is so cute, big brother.*"

"Shut up, Safina," Kyros answered, not a trace of anger in his voice.

I cracked open an eyelid, peeling a paper off my cheek and straightened my skewed glasses. "I fell asleep? What time is it?"

"It's 3:10 a.m.," Kyros said, coming to stand behind me. He rested a hand on the back of my neck. "We thought you might like to be awake for the video call to my father."

Sleep wanted to drag me back under, but the siblings had assumed right. Or Kyros, more likely. I'd still be asleep if his brothers and sisters were in charge.

"Your human body can't keep up," Francesca said, wrinkling her nose.

I ignored her. "What were the final decisions?"

Sometimes the siblings veered wildly from the recommendations of the seconds and their individual sub-clans. Other times, the path forward was clear.

Deirdre spun in her chair to face me. "Your agriculture acquisition changes our position dramatically. We must press our marketing advantage now."

I'd had my own reasons for gifting them Lot 91 under the alias of Mr Barnaby Dwelt—an *old friend* of my grandmother's who'd since left Bluff City—but stunning Kyros's seconds to silence earlier had sweetened the transfer.

Because of me, Clan Sundulus was in the clear, and my game could continue.

Kyros kneaded my neck and shoulders, and I blinked sleepily, swaying forward and back in rhythm with his hands. That felt like heaven. I'd spent too much time at desks lately.

"You're tired, my beauty," Kyros said. "You should stay in the tower tonight."

It was tempting. The drive back to the estate only took twenty minutes, but when I was this tired, twenty minutes took forever.

Neelan piped up. "I'm not sure Father would like that."

"In a spare room," Kyros snapped back.

Neelan's jaw shut with an audible click. The room pulsed with tension, and I glanced between them.

"How long are you going to sulk, big brother?" Neelan asked the man at my back, who simply removed his hands from my neck in return.

Whoa, Kyros had cut Neelan out? That was kind of huge. Usually he beat the fuck out of them and it was done. I could only recall him giving Rory the cool treatment, nothing like this blatant animosity I could feel thrumming through Kyros.

What Rory did was a blip on Neelan's bullshit, really, and I was just as pissed—if not more.

"What you did went too far," I told Neelan as Kyros's vibrating wrath spilled into me. "I don't care if you have some kind of chip on your shoulder because you look more like you belong in Clan Fyrlia than Sundulus—"

His siblings froze. Safina shook her head rapidly, but I ploughed on.

"—You don't see Deirdre being a fucking dick because of it. I don't care if you're proving something to yourself or if you're coming to terms with who you are. When other people are hurt because of whatever imagined deficiencies you have, that's when I have a fucking problem with it."

Neelan was white-lipped.

I wasn't done. "Grow up. You've had enough time to do so three times over. No one's going to hold your fucking hand because your eyes have a different shape. Own it or *be* owned by it."

One moment the vampire was there, and the next he was gone. Papers flew in the wake of his blurring speed.

"Gerome," I said in the resulting lull.

He flinched. "Please don't make fun of my hair."

I arched a brow. "Does Sundulus own a nightclub?"

"Several. Don't you have one?"

Damn, that never occurred to me. Screwing up my face, I said, "Probably not. My grandmother would have left nightclubs to the new-money estates."

Gerome quirked a brow. "Your grandmother's not in charge now."

True. "There probably aren't any nightclubs left."

"Not buildings, no. But there are leases. There's one nightclub lease up at the minute, but the rich brat owner is being fucking greedy over rent. Unless he budges, I won't take it."

"What's the name of the brat?"

The vampire, the epitome of tall, dark, and handsome, scrolled through his phone. "It'll cost ya."

"What?"

"A favour."

I quirked a brow. "What *kind* of favour?"

He pursed his lips. "I can't think of anything on the spot, but the favour will be proportionate to what I'm offering."

Lie.

Kyros once told me that with Gerome, the third answer was the truth.

That sounded like a super bad idea. "It won't involve me being naked, right?"

Gerome held a hand to his chest. "I'm insulted."

Lie.

I stared at him until he abandoned the innocent act. "Answer the question."

He glared. "No."

Truth. I hoped. "Okay, a proportional favour. No nudity. Don't make me regret it."

Which was immediately as he grinned wide enough to display his teeth. "Owner's name is Ricky Pikar."

The world had a *great* sense of humour.

"I know him." *Intimately.*

"Hey, Kyros. What's happening out here?" Lionel said, peering out at the other workers.

Kyros joined his brother at the internal glass wall. I dismissed his slight confusion, focusing on the seven siblings before me.

"I might be able to talk Ricky down," I said. "For me though. Not for Sundulus. I want a nightclub."

Francesca narrowed her eyes. "What for?"

"To throw a party. What else?" And to edge into the nightclub scene. I owned a number of buildings in Grey, but there was a lot about the entertainment industries I had to learn in the next two years.

I'd call Ricky in the morning.

Though... why the fuck would I do that? He was my ex—and Kyros was right here. The Pikars were too rich to kill off—and plus, Sundulus operated within human laws. I extracted my phone and scrolled down to the contact named Live and Learn. I clicked it, listening to the phone ring.

Ricky never turned his phone off at night. Used to drive me nuts.

"I don't understand why all the women have a white rose," Lionel said, looking at his brother.

I may know something about that.

Kyros turned to me, clenching his jaw.

"Basi, baby?" Ricky's sleepy voice echoed down the line.

Could I have orchestrated this any better?

Trying not to laugh, I replied, "Pikar. Long time."

"Too long," he said, more alert. I listened to the shuffling in the background. "You around tonight?"

He *would* assume this was a booty call. I eyed the wide-eyed exchange between Francesca and Gerome.

"You're leasing a nightclub. I'm going to take it."

"2274?" he asked.

"What kind of name is that?"

Those were the numbers on the password into my grandmother's computers.

"Uh, well. It was back in the days we were together. I did it as a romantic thing, but you dumped my ass before I could tell you. Then the legal papers were finalized and I couldn't be bothered changing it."

"Cut to the chase."

"It's Basi in numbers."

I covered the phone as Gerome burst into laughter, concealing my own shudder. That right there was why Ricky Pikar was saved in my phone as Live and Learn.

"No need to change the name then." *The name will change first thing.* "I guess you knew that you'd lease the club to me for a reasonable price in the future."

"Sure, we could meet and—"

Even to make Kyros jealous, I wasn't doing that. "Time is money."

"Yeah, I heard about your grandmother. She never liked me so I didn't go to the funeral, but I'm really sorry, Basi. I know what she meant to you."

Dammit.

This is what appealed to sixteen-year-old Basilia. Ricky wasn't the smartest tool in the shed, but he was mostly genuine. That was hard to find in the estates.

I focused on the table. "Thanks, Pikar. I appreciate it. And you're right, she hated your guts."

We both laughed.

"Look, we have a history, so I'm willing to sell the lease to you for cheaper. Six hundred thousand."

My lips twitched at Gerome's outraged expression.

I lowered my voice, almost purring. "You can do better than that."

Ricky spluttered. "I've got to cover my own investment."

"Give it to me for a flat four seventy-five. I'll take an extendable and renewable option with that."

I didn't want to lose the asset at a crucial time.

"That's half what I asked from other interested parties!"

"Yes."

"You know? Then I'll need more incentive, I'm afraid. It's in *Black*, Basi."

"You'd be doing a Le Spyre a favour, *Pikar*. What other incentive do you need?"

I enjoyed the silence on the other end. Turned out I wasn't above reminding new money about their social position. *Oops.*

"Look, I'd rather deal with someone I know. Owning a nightclub turned into more work than I thought."

Work in general, he meant. "Deal."

He blew out a breath. "You always did bust my balls."

"I can't recall you complaining," I said sweetly.

The royal siblings quietened, each of them staring at Kyros.

Ricky snorted. "We never had an issue in that department. If you're ever interested in—"

"My people will be in touch." I disconnected, flipping my phone before sliding it in the pocket of my black woollen coat.

"Basilia," Kyros said.

His menace filled me.

"Mmm?"

"Do you care to explain how the roses I sent you ended up in the hands of every female Vissimo in my tower?"

I shrugged a shoulder. "Sure. I didn't appreciate the roses, so I asked a few of the men to hand the flowers out to the women after the seconds met."

The vampire was facing away from me. "You didn't appreciate them?"

"Nope."

He rested his hands on the glass wall, back tense. "What the fuck *do* you appreciate?"

He was pissed. *Big time.*

Served the idiot right for trying to buy me.

"I *appreciate* my friends," I answered, shaking my hair back.

The scream of shattering glass jolted through the room. I clapped my hands over my ears.

The interior glass wall was gone. Dissolved. Shards of glass littered the ground outside.

Kyros stood before it, shoulders heaving between ripping snarls.

The massive screen against the wall flickered to life.

King Julius surveyed the state of the room without a trace of emotion.

Fuck.

"Explain," he demanded in a silken voice.

18

My thumb hovered over the Send button. Because really, this wasn't a text I should send. As in, for my future survival, it was dumb. If my grandmother was here, she'd call me trashy. But the revenge I felt was strong. White-hot and ugly.

I sent the text to Gina.

We need to talk

I needed information on my grandmother. If Fernando was right about the rift between the Fyrlia siblings, then I might just be able to convince Gina to give some information up. Barring that, maybe her reaction would give me an idea.

My phone chimed. *That was quick.*

I read the message. It wasn't from Gina.

I need a favour.

Lionel needed a favour? I wasn't born yesterday. This was his turn. I rolled my eyes, typing back.

I suppose this has nothing to do with me or Kyros.
I thought you were the nice one

He replied:

I am.
What I do to you depends on how many times you say no before you say yes.

I groaned and opened a second text.

I won't bite :)

The damn vampire used emojis. How was I meant to resist that? I didn't know Lionel all that well—I didn't know any of the siblings that well, really. But Lionel was one of the brothers I thought might be trustworthy. I wasn't getting out of this, we both knew it. And was I going to turn down time with the head of the agricultural industry? Not one bit.

When and where? And WHAT?

I scanned his reply not even three seconds later.

Pick you up in ten.

Wait, what? I didn't agree to that. I fired back a round of texts, tapping my foot as I waited for the reply. Nothing.

That bastard! He wasn't a nice one at all.

"Fred," I called.

The butler materialised from wherever he stood to be at my beck and call. I had theories he could teleport. "Miss?"

"Please cancel my morning appointments." I paused. "Better cancel my afternoon appointments too."

Shit. I hated when emails backed up. My time was slim pickings lately.

"Right away, Miss Le Spyre." He held a finger to his ear. "A car is at the front gates."

"He said ten minutes," I seethed, glancing down at my pyjamas. Of course the one morning I decided not to get dressed for breakfast, Lionel decided to do his stupid sibling thing.

Argh.

"Let him in, Fred."

I wrapped my kimono tight around me and stomped to the front of the house, flinging back the doors to watch the nondescript black car rolling in.

Lionel slid out with unearthly grace. "Hey, Basilia."

"Don't you hey me, Lionel. I've changed my mind about you."

Kelsea approached, standing at a respectful distance.

Blowing out a breath, I said to her, "I'm going out with Lionel for a while."

She bowed. "We will follow close behind, Miss Le Spyre."

Lionel held open the door, and I hopped in, pulling my seat belt on.

I turned to him when he slid in. "You're not a secret psycho, are you?"

"Not at all," he said, displaying two dimples that offset his shaved head. "I just have a job to do that I've put off for a month or two. I thought you could share the misery with me. This really is a favour."

Sure. I folded my arms.

Pulling out of the driveway, he leaned forward and dangled a takeaway cup in front of me. I inhaled the rich aroma.

"I came bearing gifts," Lionel said.

Snatching the coffee, I inhaled it again. "Now I'm really worried about what you want."

Lionel dived into my kimono pocket and extracted my phone. "Need this for the day."

"Hey!"

He shoved the phone in the glovebox and locked it, popping the key in his breast pocket.

The vampire slid me a look. "What are you thinking about?"

"Whether I should drink this coffee or dump it on your penis and balls."

Lionel choked on a laugh. "You're vicious for a human. Openly vicious, I should say."

"Well, I did take a drill to a vampire," I replied before I thought better of it. Nausea found me.

"That was survival. And ingenious," he answered.

I scoffed. "A total fluke. I didn't like killing Callum, and I don't want to kill again."

Lionel was taking us out to Agriculture on the opposite side of Bluff City. The houses of Orange, Red, and Pink whipped by. I twisted on the seat, spotting my usual black SUV close behind.

"Are you okay about it?" he said.

I frowned. "You're the first person to ask me that."

His words were careful. "If Kyros didn't ask, it's because he saw you were okay."

Sometimes it was nice to be asked anyway. "The sound of the drill still bothers me. But I think going directly into a thrall helped. My mind didn't have time to latch onto what happened in the basement. I remember the wet crunch and the resistance of his heart against the drill bit."

A shudder worked up through me. "Have you killed before, Lionel?"

"Yes. Mostly Indebted who attacked us on Fyrlia's orders. Being the second youngest brother though, I have elder brothers and sisters to protect me. Overprotect me."

Fucking cowards sending Indebted in their stead. "I hate how they do that."

He lifted a shoulder. "You get used to it."

"Lionel, don't take this the wrong way, but you seem too nice for this. Not to say you aren't strong. Just too decent."

A shadow flittered across his face. "That's what Father thinks. From him, it's more of a deficit."

Yeah, I could imagine.

"What would you do if you could do anything in the world?" I asked.

He smiled, pointing at the farms either side of us as we entered Agriculture. "I want to feed the world. Healthy food and equal access. Right now, I'm interested in vertical farming and aquaponics."

We pulled down a driveway and stopped alongside an open barn. My eyes widened. "Uh, Lionel, why is there a camera crew here?"

I gasped. "And why is there a fucking photo shoot set up in there?"

"We're launching our vertical farming promotion next week—and sex sells. You and I are the eye candy."

My jaw dropped as he parked the car. "You're fucking kidding me. Where are these pictures going?"

"Just targeted spots in the city. I doubt you'll even see the pictures."

I lowered my voice. "Where, Lionel?"

"A few billboards. Pamphlets in every letterbox. That kind of thing."

Motherfucker.

Closing my eyes, I drew up the view from Level 66. Namely, the billboard that occupied the space immediately outside where I met the royal siblings at 2:00 a.m. each morning. "The billboard outside the Level 66 windows?"

The car door slammed shut, and I stared at the spot Lionel had been a second ago.

I changed my mind. He wasn't nice.

Not nice *at all*.

"I need my phone."

I waited as Lionel unlocked the glove box.

He slapped the phone back into my hand. "There you go. I hope it wasn't too arduous."

Actually, I had a good time today. A mostly normal day. "It wasn't so bad. Thanks for showing me all about vertical farming and aquaponics. And just a heads-up that no one says *arduous* anymore."

I was officially mind-blown by the plans for his vertical farming push. Consider me happy to help by doing the stupid photoshoot. Even if I'd felt like an idiot in jean shorts that were more like underwear, a checked shirt that showed underboob, and the token cowboy boots and hat. A half-naked Lionel had made the day easier on the eyes.

"Thanks. For some reason, the forties just really stuck with me."

Like... the 1940s?

"See you in the morning," Lionel called.

Which wasn't all that far away. It was already 9:00 p.m.

I checked my messages walking back into the house.

I groaned at the notification banner. Forty-five? Fifteen were from Ricky. Looked like the next two hours would be catch-up time. Maybe I could get a few emails answered.

My gaze landed on a message from Stanley Yelnats, aka Gina. *Crap*, I forgot all about that.

I stopped on the entrance stairs to read it.

Sure. 10:00 p.m. at Gingers

Gingers? Opening a browser tab, I googled the name.

A nightclub in Black.

Not surprising I hadn't been there. I avoided clubs in Black like the plague. Only social climbers and the elite went to them. I much preferred the rowdy places Tommy and her peasant friends frequented. Always made me feel like Rose from Titanic.

10:00 p.m. would allow plenty of time to reach *Kyros Sky* for my shift. And on a Wednesday night, the club wouldn't be too packed with leeches.

See you there

That didn't give me long to get ready.

I hustled upstairs, bellowing for Tommy.

"Miss Tetley is out with her boyfriend, miss," Rosie said, bobbing in a hasty curtsy as I barrelled past.

"How dare she have a life," I shouted at the maid.

Entering my suite, I kicked the doors shut and jumped into the shower to wash off the scent of hay and barn animals.

Hmm, tonight was a straight hair night. I hardly ever did it because my hair behaved, but I felt like going all out.

Drying off, I flipped my hair over and set to blow-drying the long strands. Then, while my straighteners were heating, I painted on my face, going heavy with the black eyeliner and mascara.

I was overdue for a clubbing night... I should drag Tommy out this weekend after our spa date and get some serious dancing in.

Crap! I had to leave in ten minutes.

I thumbed through my nightclubbing section. This was a night for something different. Something my grandmother wouldn't have let me off the estate in.

Something that, most of the time, I was hesitant to wear.

Something like... this. The tight skirt was shiny silver, as was the sloped panel across the breasts. Fine black mesh connected two panels and formed thick shoulder straps. The back was fine mesh, aside from the skirt that would theoretically cover my butt. Tommy had rated the dress ten out of ten swanky-skanky when I'd bought it.

Yanking out my most lethal black heels, I swiped a small white clutch, shoving in a few cards and my phone.

I hoofed it down the hall like a baby giraffe, hollering for Laurel.

She met me at the bottom of the stairs. "Going to a nightclub?"

"Yep, Gingers? How many need to come?"

Her expression smoothed. "Most."

"Okay, do you all need a minute to change because only Jessica Alba can wear black leather?"

I *would* convince them to change their ways.

Laurel didn't laugh. "For Gingers, we'll fit right in."

"What kind of place is this?"

"An establishment owned by Clan Fyrlia."

Fuck. "Oh."

Laurel eyed me. "I thought it an unusual choice. It's a Vissimo club."

An unusual choice? Loz was the queen of downplaying shit. I hadn't known vampire clubs were a thing. If Fyrlia owned it, I could expect most of the Vissimo there to be from their clan.

Dammit, Gina.

Laurel ventured closer, lowering her voice. "This is something Kyros will need to know. It will get back to him."

When it came to meeting with Clan Fyrlia, I'd rather keep it in the open. I had a legitimate reason for being there—this time. King Julius would 100 percent have a problem with the meeting though. "Do what you gotta do. I'll need at least ten minutes to speak with her. If you think he'll come charging down, then please time it right."

"He'll charge, Basi. I guarantee you. If there is any way to change the location of the meeting, I'd highly recommend it."

It was already 10:00 p.m. I pursed my lips. "No, it's too late now. But thank you for the advice."

Kyros charging was exactly what I was going for. He just needed to enter that possessive state of mind when he was powerless to resist the call of our blood bond. Me walking into the den of his enemies might achieve two things tonight.

Three SUVs left ahead of us to enter *Gingers* and scout. It was 10:25 p.m. by the time they'd given me the all-clear. In the midst of my crew, I was led to the front of the queue for the nightclub. The bouncer didn't hesitate to let us in. A quick glimpse confirmed he was Vissimo.

He smirked at me.

Whatever.

A steady bass took hold of me as I entered the club. Strobe lights flashed over my body, catching on the silver panels of my not-so-classy ensemble.

A Vissimo with an earpiece approached and ushered us to the VIP section. He frowned at my crew but didn't otherwise make a comment on my throng of bodyguards. This place was just a normal nightclub with a 100 percent vampire clientele. And they weren't muting one bit. Even with my muted guards as a buffer, my legs shook.

Next time, I'd meet Gina for brunch.

I gasped as white-hot rage slammed into me, staggering from the force of it.

The rage wasn't mine.

Laurel leaned down to put her lips close to my ear. "I've alerted Kyros. He's running here. At worst, you have twelve minutes from now."

No kidding.

Shit, he was not happy.

Doing my best to force his emotions away. I followed the male up to a room on the second floor with wrap-around windows on all sides. The sounds from the club cut off entirely as the door was shut behind us.

My crew fanned out to partner with the Fyrlia Indebted stationed around the room. Only Laurel walked with me to the eldest princess.

Gina sat behind a coffee table, draped on a red leather couch. The devil was her concubine. I'd said it once, I'd say it a million times.

Her dress was gold and glittery, and she'd paired it with white heels that I also owned.

"Gina, you picked a great meeting place," I said sarcastically.

"This room is private," she said, no flicker of apology on her face. "Sit down, Miss Le Spyre. I understand you have a question for me, and I assume our time will be limited."

I took the seat across from her, crossing my long legs. "Did the triplets have anything to do with my grandmother's death?"

Gina stared. "Now that I didn't expect. A plea for us to protect you from Kyros. A way to escape, perhaps." She laughed—a deep sultry sound that would act as a siren call for anyone vagina-inclined.

"Are you brave or stupid, Miss Le Spyre?" she asked.

I thought about it. "Depends how much I want to live." I'd act stupid any day of the week around Kyros's father.

A wrinkle appeared between her brows. "You expect me to tell you outright if my brothers paid a visit to Agatha Le Spyre before her death? Which leaves me to question whether you think *I'm* brave or stupid."

"Neither," I retorted. "You're smart and tired."

Her expression turned contemplative.

I leaned forward. "I'm certain I have something that would be of use to Clan Fyrlia. Or yourself, if you're more inclined to a private deal. All I want is a simple yes or no."

She perused me, one long finger tapping against her jaw. "The answers surrounding her death are worth a lot to you."

"I won't give you anything ridiculous, Gina. So be reasonable. There are other ways I can find out."

Her blue eyes flashed. "Yet you came to me."

I consulted my phone. "We have about six minutes before Kyros smashes down your doors. Best be quick about it."

Had I ever felt him this angry? I couldn't recall so. Nerves erupted in my stomach at the wall of wrath surrounding him. It was possible I'd severely underestimated how pissed he'd be.

She pursed her lips. "I know nothing about the events surrounding your grandmother's death, but I'm your safest chance of finding out. However, doing so poses a moderate risk to my life. If my brothers were involved, they were working under my father's orders. Asking questions could bring his attention and wrath on me."

"I'm guessing your father's wrath is not a good thing to have," I said quietly.

Her gaze darkened. "Never find yourself alone with my father, Miss Le Spyre. He's capable of acts that give centuries-old Vissimo nightmares."

King Julius gave me nightmares too. "Noted."

"In return, I ask that if Clan Sundulus wins *Ingenium*, you exert your power over the Sundulus royals to request my life be spared."

I rested back, knowing our time was short. "I have no influence over King Julius. And little over Kyros."

Especially in his current mood. I could only detect mindless fury.

"Untrue. I've heard that on occasion you deliver Kyros with direct orders."

More like every day.

I hummed. "To piss him off, yes."

"*No one* delivers Kyros with a direct order except a handful of clan kings. Doing so is tantamount to suicide. There are a lot of alphas in the world, Miss Le Spyre, then there's Kyros. He could rule all Vissimo one day, but he's a *growing* alpha. His control is still developing. Yet he allows you to command him. He listens. I saw him fight for you in the basement. Kyros should have been mindless with the thrall, but he was able to temper that enough to heed your warning, which shows that my eldest brother also cares deeply for you."

Man. Forget meeting King Mikhail. Her analysis of my interactions with Kyros made me want to stay on the estate for good.

Her words interested me too. I'd wondered why Kyros behaved and was treated differently to his siblings. I'd chalked the difference to him being the crown prince.

It was possible I'd really, *really* misunderstood the danger of delivering Kyros with an order.

Oops.

"I can't promise my request will help any," I told her. "In fact, I'm certain it won't help at all. Are you sure you wouldn't prefer something more concrete in exchange?"

Her eyes glittered. "No, true mate of my elder brother. That is my request in exchange for delivering you with an honest answer."

"Then you have a deal." I stretched out my hand and she stared at it for a moment before shaking it lightly.

I had about sixty seconds to get as far away from Gina as possible. "Thanks in advance."

"I'll be in touch," she purred.

Josie yanked the door open and I hightailed it out of there, hoping against hope I wouldn't break a damn ankle on the stairs to the dancing level.

I was nearly to the bar when the dancing Vissimo scattered back from the entrance.

Fuckity fuck.

Kyros stalked through the entrance, green eyes blazing, and fangs lowered. His hair was windswept, the veins in his forearms leaping from the tightness of his clenched fists.

Even I didn't want to approach him, but I squeezed between Laurel and Kelsea and hurried his way, keeping my gaze downcast because his eyes were too much to take in. "Kyros—"

He blurred, gripping my upper arms as he loomed over me. A terrible growl filled his chest, and I had no doubt every vampire within fifty metres heard it under the music though I could barely detect the sound.

He released one of my arms and towed me out of the club. I struggled to keep up in my six-inch heels.

"Slow down," I seethed as we made it to the street. He stared at the ground, his blazing eyes forming two green patches on the pavement.

He didn't respond, dragging me to an SUV where he all-but threw me into the passenger seat.

The door slammed shut.

Shit.

I'd officially pissed him off.

Glancing outside, I winced as he shouted in Laurel's face.

Nope. I wasn't having that.

I opened the door. "Kyros, Laurel didn't know where we were going until we got here. I told her we were going to Black." I focused on the décor of the club across the road, hoping that would distract him from my lie.

"*Get back in the fucking car,*" he said without looking my way.

"Don't speak to me like that," I replied, sliding out of the car.

He ignored me, shoulders heaving.

"Whatever," I muttered. "Count me out of work tonight. I'm going back to the estate."

I took one step in the direction of my usual black SUV.

Kyros slammed his hands either side of my head, and I choked on my scream, listening to the dull pop as the body of the car dented.

"*Get. In. The. Car*. I won't tell you again."

My insides quivered at the menace behind the words. My heart sputtered uselessly in my chest, my knees shaking in a way they hadn't in a long time around Kyros. I dragged in a breath, unable to meet his eyes when they were blazing like this. It was akin to staring at the sun.

I shouldered him as I yanked open the passenger door. "What a jackass."

He nearly ripped his own door off the hinges when he got into the driver's seat. The wheel cracked in his grip as he gunned the engine and took off. I gripped the *oh-shit* handle as he screeched around a corner.

"Slow down," I said, my voice shaking.

"But this is a *thrill*, Basilia," he snarled. "You wanted your life in danger. Or else you wouldn't have entered a club filled with my fucking enemies."

I'd never seen him like this.

We screeched through Grey, and I folded my arms. "How about when you regain control, we can talk?"

"Enough," he roared.

A scream tore from me as fear overwhelmed my senses.

Kyros didn't stop. He didn't leave the car. "Enough with pushing me away and wearing those glasses. Enough with living at the estate and calling your fucking past lovers. *I can't think straight, Basilia*. And I need to fucking think straight or my entire family dies. You think the terror of hearing you've walked into that place leaves me in a good mindset to do what I need to do to protect them? What if Fyrlia had hurt you? What if I was picking up your fucking pieces right now? Do you know what I would *become* if you were killed?"

I was locked in place.

"Of course not," he spat. "Humans have no fucking idea."

Black filled my vision and I slumped forward in my seat, my vision blurring.

"I can't even be angry with you because your human body can't handle it," he spat.

Reaching over, Kyros gripped my chin, forcing my eyes to his. "Breathe."

I dragged in a breath that hurt my oxygen-deprived brain. A few more cleared the spots in my vision.

The car nearly fish-tailed when he drove into the garage, and I pressed fingers to my spinning head.

Kyros ripped my door open and pulled me out and into his arms.

Then we were running. I squeezed my eyes closed until I landed on a soft bed.

I stared up at the vampire, tugging my short dress down.

He shook his head, expression twisted and cold. "Stay here until I'm back."

What? "You will not leave me locked in—"

Kyros left, slamming his door to his lair behind him. I was up on my heeled feet and at the entrance in an instant. Gripping the handle, I yanked.

My mouth dropped.

He'd locked me in here?

I kicked the door as hard as I could. "Possessive *motherfucker*!"

I was going to kill him.

19

The thing about being able to feel Kyros's emotions was that I knew his ire hadn't abated one single bit. That made it very hard for *mine* to fade.

Only in the last hour had I made any sort of dint in my anger.

Sure, I'd known Kyros wouldn't like it if I went into *Gingers*. I'd banked on him losing control—but not like *that*.

That was... terrifying. A long time had passed since I'd been scared of him to that degree. I got a glimpse at what other vampires and humans saw when they looked at him.

And I felt terrible that Laurel had borne the brunt of his anger.

Maybe if the entire club of Vissimo turned on me, my Indebted and Kyros wouldn't have been able to save me. And yes, Gina picked that particular time and venue knowing it would knock him off his game.

Yet I couldn't regret the move because I'd gone there about my grandmother.

Gina would dig into the triplets' movements on my behalf. That was a victory. I wanted to know that my grandmother had died of natural causes more than anything. If the triplets had visited her that night, then I needed to know too. Regardless, my grandmother's heart wouldn't have been anywhere near as stressed if she hadn't led the life she had against the clans.

Both were to blame. Just as much as my grandmother's revolutionary spirit that wouldn't allow her to roll over when she'd discovered the truth.

The door burst open and Kyros's siblings poured into the room. Leaning against the bench as I sipped my water, I closed my eyes and opened them again.

They didn't disappear.

Neelan shut the door, avoiding my gaze.

"What did you do to Kyros?" Lalitta hushed, her eyes rounded.

She thought I was the bad guy. *Yeah*, I pushed his buttons, but there was no excuse for how handsy and shouty and downright mean he got. I had bruises on my arms from his grip. Just like fucking Clint gave me. "None of your business."

Safina strode forward. "If it affects the game, then yes, it's our business."

I met her cool gaze. "Then ask your brother."

"He left the tower immediately after the video call with Father," Neelan murmured, glancing at me.

"Guess that means I can leave too." I gulped back my water and set the glass in the sink. Turning, I blinked at the wall of royals blocking me.

Deirdre's fangs descended. "If our brother put you here, only our brother can release you."

My anger was wearing off. I was tired. It had to be nearly 4:00 a.m.

"Looks like I'm staying the night," I said, unzipping my heels and kicking them off. I padded into the bathroom, looking around for supplies to remove my make-up. I was sure it looked a mess by now anyway.

Soaking a blue flannel in hot water, I scrubbed at the layers on my face, rinsing and repeating until my normal self was showing once more. I glared at her for looking so young and incapable. I steamed my face with a hot flannel and splashed cold water over my skin, patting dry with a fluffy white towel.

I eyed the shower and listened to the tense murmurs of Kyros's siblings. Shower it was. Locking the door, I started the shower, setting it to scalding.

I tied my hair in a knot, not having a hair tie, and stepped under the hot jets.

My shoulders relaxed as I sighed.

That felt fucking good.

In no hurry to rejoin the royals, I stood that way for several minutes before reaching for the soap. It wasn't as meditative as my usual routine, but I repeated the soaping twice to drag out the shower even longer.

Rinsing, I tuned into Kyros, blanching at what I felt.

Pain, fear, loneliness, regret, anger.

Felt like he was calming down at last, but I was still angry enough to be glad he felt like shit, so maybe it was a good thing Kyros had left the tower for a while.

I reluctantly turned off the shower and dried, slipping into the same clubbing clothes. My rabbit onesie would be ideal—or Kyros's loungewear drawer—but I didn't feel right about delving into his stuff after the shit between us.

And there was a lot of shit.

Where did it start and where did it end? Half the time I couldn't even remember what I was angry about. There was just *so damn much*. Him doing things to me. Me doing things to him. His family doing things to both of us. Fyrlia throwing obstacles into the mix.

I hadn't infiltrated *Kyros Sky* to get dragged into this again. I was here to fight my battle and do it right.

When Kyros returned, I'd apologise and get it over and done with. The more I fought him, the less likely he'd let me leave, and the less inclined he'd be to enter a fourth exchange.

Plan formed. Done.

I hung the towel over a drying rack and threw my make-up flannel in a hamper before joining the others. They'd turned on the TV and were watching female wrestling.

"Want to see how the photos today turned out," Lionel said from the middle of the bed. Only Neelan and Gerome hadn't managed to find a spot on the bed and shared the large round sofa.

As I passed Neelan, I touched his shoulder. "What you did was shitty, but I didn't have to get personal where others could hear. I can't imagine your family without you in the picture. You fit, Neelan—whatever you think to the otherwise."

Moving to the bed, I picked my way to the middle and huddled in a space by Lionel.

He shoved his phone under my nose, and I swore.

"Oh my god, that's not us." My eyes rounded.

"It is." He cackled.

Lionel cackling just wasn't right.

He scrolled through the images. We looked *hot*. Like one second away from ripping off each other's clothes *hot*. There was something carnal in my eyes and in his.

"These are being used for promotion of vertical farming and aquaponics?" I asked weakly.

"Nothing says *sustainable farming* like half-naked people," he replied. "Trust me, most vampires and humans are led entirely by their junk."

I didn't disagree for a second. It was a constant battle to disobey *my* junk. "How long until they go up?"

The timing was less than ideal. Hopefully a few days—

"Tomorrow," he announced with glee.

I chewed my bottom lip. "You're certain that's a good idea? I'm not sure Kyros is in the mood to be pushed."

"He never is."

Silently disagreeing, I conceded the point and stretched my legs out.

"You can't just force your way in," Francesca said as I popped my legs over hers.

I studied the youngest Sundulus royal. "Do you mean in this moment or in a more general way?"

She fell silent.

"I don't plan on replacing you or anyone, Francesca. I sure as hell didn't ask for any of this."

She sniffed and didn't answer.

I eased down between Lalitta and Safina. Mostly flat—success. I yawned loudly. "So tired." A thought occurred to me. "Don't you guys usually sleep now?"

Rory answered. "When our brother is unhappy, we're unhappy. Sleep hasn't come easy to you this night, and it won't come easy for us either."

Well, that made me feel terrible, not that I should take on their reactions. Kyros and I would undoubtedly argue again.

I sighed. "Then call him."

"You misunderstand me. Kyros told us that he lost control and you bore the brunt of that, nearly rendering you unconscious. We'll remain with you because it will reassure our brother as he works to regain control of his power. It's no small task."

From what Gina said, it was a constant effort for him.

Yawning again, I closed my eyes. "Wish I had siblings or cousins."

Though it would mean more people to look after. If I was in this game and had eight siblings, I'd be fucking terrified *daily* about their safety. Let alone having a vulnerable human mate who was careening around town like a cowboy.

I kind of felt really terrible now.

"You have no family left?" Safina asked.

A lump rose up my throat. My answer took too long.

"No," I said in a neutral voice. "No family. You're lucky to have each other."

"We are," she replied. "Family is a blessing in hard times. That's why we're so close. There are many working against us. And many spies. If we could not trust each other, we'd have no one."

I'd gathered that from the intense and almost desperate way they interacted. It was a sad way to live, and I could see why Kyros allowed them so much leeway in his life. They needed to test the strength of their sibling bonds—to be reassured of what that bond could withstand. And what it couldn't. These little games they planned were reaffirming for them in a city filled with creatures who wanted to tear them down.

I reached out and patted her leg. Or someone's. "Understand."

Arms I knew pulled me from a tangle of bodies that were too heavy and too warm. I'd been climbing up from the heavy tow of sleep for what felt like an age only to be dragged down again.

The last of their limbs fell from me, and eyes closed, I wrapped my legs around Kyros's waist, letting him otherwise hold me against his chest.

He sank down against a wall, holding me close.

I pushed away and met his tired gaze. He looked exhausted.

"Sorry I worried you," I rasped.

And I meant it.

Lowering my head, I closed my eyes again as his arms tightened around me. He smelt like cold sweat and his voice was just as weary as his expression.

"Why were you meeting with my enemy, Basilia?"

Not forgiven then.

I curled my hands together on his chest. "I need to know if the triplets caused my grandmother's heart attack. I went to Gina for information."

A spark of anger flared again. "You didn't come to me."

"No, I didn't." I may have fucked up, but our past was filled with lies and most of them were his. I may be able to rely on him, but I sure as fuck wasn't used to doing so *and* didn't want to.

He rested his head atop mine, inhaling deeply. "What are we doing, Miss Le Spyre?"

"No clue, Mr Atagio." I fidgeted on his lap, my tight dress digging in. Some things weren't meant to be slept in. I might have permanent imprints of the panels on my body after this.

We were silent for a time.

"Did Gina have information?" he asked.

"No." I hesitated. "But she's going to dig around."

A growl rumbled in his chest. "What was the deal?"

"The deal doesn't hurt your family in any way. It's all on me."

"I didn't ask if it hurt my family, I asked what it was."

I pushed away, irritation snapping through me. "I'm not telling you what the deal was. It won't harm me or any of you. That's all I'm saying."

Kyros looked and felt mutinous at that. His eyes blazed momentarily.

He could compel me easily. One second at any time and my secrets could be out.

I waited to see if he'd shit on me that way, too, holding his gaze with a stony one of my own. In this matter, I was more embarrassed than anything that he'd find out the details of the deal. Gina put a lot more stock in my ability to sway Kyros's opinion than I did.

"Your wellbeing won't be in danger in any way because of this deal with Gina?" he asked, attention riveted on me—and no doubt my emotions.

"No, Kyros. Not one bit. Or I wouldn't have agreed."

He paused. "Does it involve intimacy with another male?"

I let the exasperation of his question wash over me. "No men are involved."

The blaze in his eyes died down to the same bone-weariness of earlier. I fidgeted again, resisting the urge to peel the tight dress off to ease my discomfort.

I nuzzled into Kyros once more. The weirdness of this situation was like a temporary access card—a no man's land. "Where did you go?"

"Running. Hunting. Drinking."

Considering that, I said, "Hunting animals? And drinking blood?"

"Humans are animals. But I wasn't hunting humans, no. And yes, drinking blood."

"You've run out of my blood?"

He didn't answer, which was as much yes as I needed.

I yawned, pulling at the digging hem of my dress. "What's the time?"

"Midday."

Shit. Vampires were really messing with my sleep patterns. "What day?"

"Thursday."

At least I hadn't missed the meeting with my Churchill team. This fucking dress needed to go.

"Basilia."

I glanced up at him. His arms were looped around my lower back, his legs stretched out behind me. We were against the wall next to the door.

He watched me closely. "If I provide you with a list of the Fyrlia royals' personal properties and local businesses, will you promise me never to enter one without me again?"

That could prove doubly useful, and I could always meet Gina in other places. "Yes, I promise."

Kyros nodded. "Then you'll have it by tonight. Now..." His hands went to the bottom of my dress.

"What are you doing?" I blurted.

His eyes were shadowed. "You want the dress off. Let me help you."

His siblings were right behind us, probably *pretending* to be asleep. I glanced back, but they were—to my eyes—a tangled mess of deeply-asleep royal vampires.

Chewing on my lip, I faced Kyros again, sensing his need to look after me.

Feeling like I was doing something dark and forbidden, I nodded.

His hands were massive and so warm. He slid his hands under the hem on both sides, hooking the dress with his thumbs. I lifted onto my knees as he slid the dress up over my ass, taking his time. The removal was pain and pleasure as he worked the garment up over my stomach.

He stopped when the bottom of my breasts were exposed. This

was a no-bra kind of dress. Was he surprised? My boobs bounced as he freed them to push the dress over my head.

I steadied myself with a hand on his shoulder after. His eyes were as dark as I'd ever seen them, intent on me. A deep-rooted admiration twirled toward me, a fierce protective emotion. Combined, the feeling was almost like...

Reverence.

Drawing back, clad only in my panties, I covered my breasts and tucked my chin.

"Why are you covering yourself?" he said in a calm voice. "You're beautiful beyond compare."

I closed my eyes. I had zero issues with my body. "You've never looked at me that way."

"No," he admitted. "And that's overwhelming for you."

No kidding.

"Lower your arms, my beauty. Let me see you."

What did that mean though? This felt a whole heap more intimate than sex. So deeply erotic and invasive.

I opened my eyes first, just slightly, to peek at him through my lashes. He wasn't fooled, his meadow-green gaze latched on. Kyros tilted his head and reached for his loosened tie, discarding it before setting his attention to the buttons of his shirt. I watched as he worked down the line, exposing smooth, golden skin.

Hard.

I appreciated the reciprocation though.

Keeping my gaze lowered, I let my arms drop to my sides, resting my palms on the tops of my legs as I sat on his thighs again.

His hands slid up from my bent knees, up my forearms, and along my shoulders to follow the slopes of my neck upward. He forced my head upward until my eyes locked once more with his.

The vampire let go, leaning forward, and I tensed in readiness for a kiss that might end me forever.

My breath quickened as he reached an arm overhead and pulled his unbuttoned shirt off.

I drank in the sight of him, mouth drying at his unfathomable *beauty*.

Kyros drew my arms through his black shirt sleeves and set to buttoning the front. I sighed at the slither of warm material over the painful indents the dress had made.

"That feels better." Kyros tucked me back against his chest.

And I went.

Fuck it all, but I went; just to be pressed against him in the bubble where the world didn't seem to exist and we weren't at odds.

"I'm sorry for hurting and scaring you, true mate," he whispered in my ear. "So very sorry."

20

I studied my notes from the meeting with the siblings, snickering. I'd found a way to recall the various discussion threads despite the Vissimo-induced reactions of my body.

Now, I kept a separate document open on the tablet. I stared at my first hashtag.

#AgriWantAgriGet

Translation: The realty push in the agriculture suburb was at full tilt.

#ambanking

Rory's plans to merge the new bank, *NJB*, with *Bluff City Ban*k were underway.

#Grestival

Gerome had plans for a fashion festival to launch a new street of boutique shops in Green.

#Letsgetvertical

Lionel was set to launch the vertical farming to the public.

#Safinaforpresident

Safina, in charge of the second largest industry—local government—was having her politicians enter a bill to inhibit further categorising of agricultural land to housing land.

#IndustryLyf

There were no major current changes proposed for the health, manufacturing, retail, and education industries that belonged to Neelan, Deirdre, Francesca, and Lalitta respectively.

I sat back, pretty chuffed with my new method of keeping track. Really, being up on Level 66 was the perfect mentorship to learn how the industries in Bluff City worked together and how they affected each other. I was still scratching the surface, but in time, Sundulus would show me exactly how to strengthen my own game.

"They're taking off the cover," Lionel hissed at Neelan, dragging me from reverie.

Kyros had left to answer a question from a blushing minion after the call with King Julius, and Lionel was about to reveal his fucking billboard.

Oh brother.

He whirled to me. "Can you take a photo when he comes in?"

"Sure," I said drily, sliding my phone out as Kyros entered the room.

He was surrounded by his smirking brothers and sisters. Fingers racing, I clicked on my camera and took a few snaps of the nine royals.

Things with Kyros had been different over the last few days. Settled, yet more intense. Like a vibrating undercurrent existed between us at all times. Usually the bond made me feel burning attraction—and that wasn't diminished—but I was feeling an emotional clinginess that I'd never experienced before. And I could tell he was too.

We hadn't interacted much since our cuddling session in his lair. Perhaps he was studying the new development between us as well. I wasn't sure what to make of it—in that I sure as fuck didn't want to be emotionally dependent on anyone, including him.

Lionel slid a blindfold from his pocket, circling Kyros. "I have a surprise. You need to put this on, please."

Kyros arched a brow but did as bidden, an indulgent half smile on his lips. My heart squeezed as he allowed his brothers and sisters to shove him into place in front of the windows.

I snapped another few photos and stood aside to get into a better spot for the big reveal.

Lionel fired off a text, and the lights surrounding a billboard just below and opposite us flared to life. I groaned at the sight of Lionel and I tangled around each other between two towering haystacks.

Not everything has to be horizontal.
Vertical farming. A new position. A better ending.

A throaty chuckle slipped between my lips. That was actually pretty funny, the problem being that it was about me. Damn Lionel for being mostly likeable.

"What is it?" Kyros said, grinning at our quiet laughter.

Lionel winked at me and snatched the blindfold off his brother.

I wasn't alone in holding my breath as he looked.

And looked.

His siblings whooped after a few seconds, thumping Lionel on the back. Kyros smiled. But I didn't.

Not when I could feel he didn't find it amusing one bit. In fact, the vampire was unaccountably sad as he stood grinning at the billboard and shaking his head ruefully. He even snapped a few times at Lionel in false anger.

"Look how much she wants me," Lionel crowed.

The photographer had asked if I needed alcohol to loosen up.

"You know I was thinking of Kyros." I winced as the words left my mouth. That sounded pathetic. No matter how true it was.

Kyros's sadness didn't abate.

Okay, so it wasn't the nature of the photos that upset him.

"So you say," Lionel crowed. "Basilia and I spent the day getting to know each other."

The loneliness in his eldest brother surged.

I stared at the huge vampire. There was no way Kyros was upset because I'd spent time with Lionel and not him.

We rarely spent time together outside of this tower.

That surely couldn't be why he was sad. Whatever the reason behind his heartache, it was important to Kyros that his siblings didn't guess his real sentiment.

I glanced down at my phone, spotting a message from Tommy.

She sent it a while ago, but I'd been here since 11:00 p.m., catching up with Angelica on the sharp decline in my acquisition rate that was giving her cause for *concern*. I'd made a passable effort at reassuring her that it was fatigue affecting me, knowing the excuse would filter back to King Julius.

I opened the message.

YOU'RE IN FUCKING SHIT. YOU PAID OFF MY POP'S BILLS?

Wtf, Basi!!
I am SO angry at you.

Whoa, what?

I read the message again. Her pop's bill had been paid? That wasn't me! I wasn't stupid enough to mess with Tommy and money—that was a lesson learned the hard way at six years old.

I frantically typed back:

I swear it wasn't me, Tom
<3 <3 <3

My thumb hovered over the Send button, but I paused, realisation dawning on me. I lifted my head to study Kyros, where he still played the part of annoyed older brother in the midst of his siblings.

That. Fucker.

The timing was too coincidental after the episode with the white roses and him demanding to know what I appreciated. I almost groaned, remembering that I'd mentioned appreciating my friends.

That wasn't a hint to ply Tommy with money. I powered off my tablet and slipped my phone in my pocket.

He was already looking at me warily when I reached his end of the table.

"Kyros, could I have a word?"

Lionel and the others chorused a loud *ooooh*.

"Sorry if I got you in trouble, bro," Lionel said, leaving the room.

The others followed, smirking my way.

Yeah, whatever.

Kyros toyed with his tablet, not meeting my gaze. His sadness was still rampant, and yet a very clear line needed to be drawn in regards to Tommy.

"The list," he said as I opened my mouth.

What?

A list was slid across to me.

"Fyrlia's properties that you promised not to enter without me."

I stared at it, scanning the top few. "What do the nine addresses in red mean?"

"Those are the personal properties of Fyrlia royals. You must never enter them. If my family or I, or any of our people enter them, it's considered an act of war."

Interesting. "So Fyrlia can't enter any of the Sundulus royal homes either?"

Kyros nodded. "We can't always be playing a game. That was part of the original rules of *Ingenium*."

I set down my tablet and tucked the sheets of paper in my purse to study later.

"You have something to say," he said.

"This isn't a great time," I began, then tightened my resolve. "I need to know if you paid off a bill for my friend recently."

He glanced up, studying me more intently.

I sighed. "Kyros, you can't do that. Especially not to her. She just messaged me, blaming *me* for doing it."

Shoving the message under his nose, I watched as he read it.

"Undo it," I told him, slipping it in my pocket once more.

Answering anger rose in him, nowhere near the towering heights of mine. "I can't. I did it anonymously. To make you happy."

I threaded my hand through my hair and pulled it to distract myself from smashing the newly fixed glass wall. "She doesn't even accept money from *me* whom she loves. *Jesus*, Kyros. I understand what you're trying to do with these gifts, but just stop it, please. They're meaningless to me."

His frustration died and the loneliness within him swelled to greater heights. I gritted my teeth, holding onto my resolve. He *couldn't* involve Tommy in our shit. That was a hard no.

"Tell me, true mate. How do I reach you?" the vampire asked, leaning forward on the table. "You constantly draw away."

He slammed his hands down. "*How do I reach you*?"

I blinked at his sudden eruption, clutching the files against my chest.

What a farce this entire thing was. Kyros was trying to pull me closer emotionally and not bite me. I wanted to be bitten and nothing more. His *father* wanted me pushed away for good.

This was all so messed up.

Kyros had betrayed and lied to me so many times, and yet the blood bond was making me feel terrible for hurting his damn feelings.

I had to remember the blood bullshit wasn't real.

My voice shook. "You don't reach me. You *betrayed* me. Do you think jewellery and a few bunches of flowers will ever fix that? If you can't accept my decision on that front, then at the very least stay the fuck away from my humans."

I whirled from his hard gaze and rushed through Level 66, his heartache radiating through my chest.

Or was it mine?

Safina was waiting by the elevator. She grimaced. "I was waiting for you. I didn't mean to listen."

Part of working in a tower of vampires meant accepting that very few conversations were private. If Kyros had needed that private, he would have moved us to his lair.

"What do you want?" I muttered, stepping in and pressing the button, hoping Kyros would have the sense to not follow.

She hesitated as the elevator swept downward with a belly-dropping lurch. "It's Kyros's one hundred and fiftieth birthday tomorrow. It's late notice, but I've been waiting for the right time to ask because I know last time you met our family, things were uncomfortable."

I raised my brows, my incredulity speaking for itself.

The eldest princess sniffed. "Maybe that's an understatement."

Just a tiny one.

"It's just dinner with immediate family. You're important to Kyros, and I know he'd love for you to be there."

Ding!

We stepped off into the garage, and I glanced to where Laurel waited for me.

"Look, Safina. I appreciate that you're trying to make your brother happy. But what makes him happy doesn't always work for the longevity of my life. King Julius made it clear that he doesn't approve, and I have no protection against that disapproval."

She opened her mouth, and I held up a hand. "None of you would lift a finger against your father, so please don't offer empty promises. The answer is no. I won't willingly spend time with the people who used me. I hope you all have a lovely time together on his birthday."

Disappointment and guilt clouded her face, and I strode toward Laurel, weariness piled on my shoulders.

Guess the relative peace of the last few days was officially over.

"That dick actually thought he could buy you through me," Tommy seethed as we entered the Turkish steam room.

So far spa day had been listening to a steady stream of Kyros propaganda. "I genuinely think he has no idea. Like if something doesn't have a monetary value, he disregards it."

She snickered. "He must be floundering so hard."

I shoved down guilt at her words. "You said you were able to donate the amount to the retirement home?"

Tommy nodded. "I'm happily back in debt."

"Good. Then I'd like to stop talking about Kyros."

Kyros who was one hundred and fifty today. I hadn't texted him yet. Was it crazy that I felt so terrible for not going to his birthday dinner?

He was one hundred and *fifty*.

Tommy stripped off her robe and stretched out naked on the bench. I followed suit on the bench next to hers.

"I'll tell you about Mr Tommy then," she said, settling back.

There were ears on this conversation. I'd noticed that my friend was always very careful not to say Theodore's name outside of my soundproofed office. "He told me he loved me this morning before I left."

"Uhm, oh my god!" I sat up again. "What did you say? Please tell me you didn't freak out."

She grinned, eyes closed. "I said it back."

I beamed at her and jabbed her cheek. "Is that from the steam or are you blushing?" I jabbed her again.

Tommy batted me away. "I want to be grossed out with myself, but I'm totally blushing. I think this is serious. After two months. Is that crazy, Basil?"

Yes. But this was her first real crush. I was the same with Ricky at the start. "Feels pretty strong, huh?"

"So strong. I've never felt this way. *Ever.* He's literally a god. And in *bed*. Don't get me started."

Well, that wasn't going to happen. If I couldn't have all the Kyros sex I desired, then I'd live through my friend.

She caved with little resistance.

Jealousy swarmed in my chest as she recounted last night's sexcapades. Twenty-one, and I was as lonely as Mrs Gaughton. And Mr Trenington and Mr Triffz. Maybe my trouble list. They were like me—all of us some variation of the token cat lady.

"I'm so happy for you, Tom," I said, lying down again. "You're in love."

She fumbled blindly for me.

"That's my boob." I snorted.

"Whoops." Tommy located my hand and squeezed it. "The only thing making me unhappy is that he doesn't know you yet."

"Hopefully one day soon," I said lightly.

She didn't patronise me by agreeing to the statement.

"So massage, manicure, pedicure, hair, and make-up after this?" she asked.

"You know it." This was long overdue. Me and bestie time—healing time.

She grabbed us a water each, and I gulped mine back.

Tommy sighed. "It's been a month, lovely. How are you going without your grandmother? And running the estate and all that fancy stuff?"

How am I going?

"I'm going, I guess. It still doesn't feel real that she's gone. Every time I sit in her office chair, I expect her to stride into the room and order me out of it. You think I'd be used to grief after my parents, but at least I still had some family after that, you know?"

I took a breath. "I mean, she was always going to die when I was young. I just thought I had longer. It shouldn't bother me so much, but it just gets to me that she'll never meet the person I end up with or any children I may have. She won't see what I become. I hate that most of all."

"She knew you," Tommy replied softly. "She knew who you were and would be. And who's to say she isn't looking down on us right now."

My brows shot up as I scanned our naked bodies. "This exact moment?"

We both burst into hoots that echoed around the small tiled room.

"Shit," Tommy said, wiping her eyes. "Terrible timing. You know what I meant."

I did. "I haven't had grieving time, you know? Then again, life doesn't just stop. Does anyone really have time to mourn? It's more like thoughts of her hit me at random times—like when Nat King Cole comes on, or I see an advert for a new Tom Hanks movie, or when I see someone wearing brown shoes with a black outfit."

"*Who taught that unfortunate person how to dress*?" we chorused, falling into laughter again.

A few tears leaked from my eyes—not entirely from mirth. They felt a whole heap better than the last tears I'd shed. "I'm lucky to have a lot of good memories with her."

"Agatha was one of a kind." Tommy sipped at her water, wiping at her beading brow. "Did I ever tell you that she pulled me aside a few months after the last rich-bitch slumber party you ever held?"

It was the party that nearly broke my friend—and the reason I'd severed all communications with the rich girls my age. They'd cut her hair off and held her down to pull off her clothes and make fun of where she'd bought them. I'd nearly stabbed Harriet Gregorian with the scissors when I'd discovered them. She had Fred to thank for her life.

Tommy was a mess for months after. What teen girl wants to be naked in front of *anyone*? But it was more than that. Tommy never felt like she belonged in my world, and their actions had hammered on the cracks and left her so fragile.

"You didn't," I said. We rarely spoke about this. The memories of that night hurt her even now. Everyone carried a scar or two from childhood—kids could be fucking mean while figuring out who they were—but Tommy carried a larger scar than most.

My friend smiled. "She pulled me aside while you were trying to find out how to reunite Destiny's Child for a private concert on your fifteenth birthday—"

I'd settled for my second choice.

"—and said I better stop moping and toughen up because the world liked to beat everyone with bags of shit regardless of whether they were poor or rich." She tilted her chin. "*Everyone smells the same, Tommy. People like Harriet Gregorian may have enough money to cover their stench, but they never learn to accept who they are without disguise. You, my dear, have dignity. And so you are already rich in a way they can never replicate.*"

Only the slight hiss of steam filling the room disturbed the calm.

"I never knew," I murmured. "I wondered why you started smiling again."

"There you have it. She also said that if she caught my eyes on the floor one more time, she'd half my father's wages."

My lips twitched. "That sounds more like her." I took a full breath, exhaling loudly. "Agatha Le Spyre."

Tommy grinned at the ceiling, reaching out to take my hand. "Agatha Le Spyre."

21

"We look fucking good," I announced as we arrived back at the estate. Laurel and the others would be close behind, but I'd demanded that Fred drive Tommy and me to the spa and back tonight. "We need to do something. Maybe a nice dinner?"

I trailed off, noting Tommy's lack of enthusiasm.

"What's up?" I nudged her.

"Uh, well I kind of have plans. He texted this morning," she mumbled.

Oh.

"Right. Sorry, yes. I shouldn't have assumed you were free."

She searched my face. "Basil—"

"No, really. It's okay. Of course you want to hang with the guy you looove."

Tommy rolled her eyes. "Stop it."

I made kissing noises until she punched me on the shoulder.

"Go show him how fucking hot you look," I grumbled.

She *did* look hot with beach waves in her chin-length chestnut hair, and a subtle purple eyeshadow, which deepened the shade of her incredible eyes. She was a fun-sized man-killer, and with the lethal outfit I was going to force her into, Theodore better recognise how lucky he was.

"What will you do tonight?" she asked, chewing her red lip.

"Stop it, you'll rub off your lip colour. And don't ask hard questions." I whacked her leg and hustled out of the car so she couldn't get me back.

Rosie bobbed a curtsey at the entrance. "Miss Tommy, Miss Le Spyre, you both look beautiful. Will you take tea before dinner?"

"Did you not hear me declare a backward day, Rosie?" I answered. "Breakfast is to be dinner. Dessert is to be tea! Must I always repeat myself?"

"As you say, Miss Le Spyre." She bobbed again.

I grinned as she left.

"You're so mean," Tommy said.

Chuckling, I waved a hand as we traipsed up the stairs. "Rich people must have whims." Plus, Rosie fell for zero percent of my grand declarations these days. It only encouraged me.

Tommy snorted. "You're so full of shit."

"At least I'm full of something," I answered darkly.

She studied me. "Why don't you go get some then? Why are you waiting around for this guy who we've established is a total dickwad?"

We hadn't. She had. And he was.

But only when I said it.

My rebellion with Rhys had shown me *that* course of action was no longer open to me. I couldn't just go to a club and bring some guy home. Not as things currently stood.

I stared at Tommy but couldn't think of a way to convey my sentiments around the compulsion.

She searched my face and tapped her temple. I nodded, and she threw me a sad look.

"Need an outfit for tonight?" I said, forcing cheer.

Flinging open my clothing room, I dragged her in.

Indecision warred on her face. "I dunno..."

"Let me live through you," I whined. "I'd let you live through me."

Her lips curved.

Permission granted!

I dragged dresses off the racks, throwing them at her feet. Jewellery followed, then clutches and heels. Sucked to be Rosie later on. I hoped she had a maid minion to delegate the task to.

Tommy waded through the pile, selecting a few. I'd learned not to pick an exact dress for her because we had such different tastes. She always looked fantastic in the dresses she chose. I'd leave the decision to the master.

"*Whoa, whoa, whoasies*," she whispered. "What's this hunk of sexy?"

I hadn't worn most of my wardrobe, so I genuinely had no idea.

Squinting, I caught the white silk dress, holding it up. "It's classy. No wonder I never wore it."

Tommy didn't return my wolfish grin.

She dropped the dresses in her arms and held out the bottom of the dress. "It's like Marilyn Monroe, ballerina gorgeous."

"The silk is so thin." It was beautiful. Simple. The dress had thin straps and was form-fitting to the waist where the silk flared in soft, feminine waves. I wasn't fooled. The fabric would cling to every line of my body, hinting at but never confirming what lay beneath—which wouldn't be underwear because even seamless panties would show.

"I'll save it for a rainy day," I said, moving to hang the dress up myself. A masterpiece like this didn't deserve the floor.

My phone blared to life.

Sliding it free of my jeans pocket, I studied the name. Holding my finger to my lips, I warned Tommy with my eyes as well. She nodded, and I put the phone on speaker.

"Safina," I answered.

"Basilia. This is Kyros's mother, Queen Titania."

Oh, shit!

Tommy covered her mouth, and I shot her another warning look. "... Queen Titania, what an honour."

"Thank you. I understand you do not wish to join us for Kyros's birthday tonight."

Tommy's eyes narrowed to slits, and I turned away from her.

Busted.

How did you say no to a queen? I'd barely had any interaction with her. "I—"

"Do not make yourself uncomfortable," she interrupted. "I understand perfectly why you choose not to attend. If you would, I have someone here who wishes to talk with you."

My heart sank. I had a fair idea who—

"*Human.*"

My throat worked. "Hello, King Julius."

His voice was tight with anger. "My queen is upset. She tells me the only way to undo this is to assure you I will not kill you this night."

Uhm.

I rubbed my forehead. "Right."

I listened to their furiously whispering voices.

"Or hurt you in any way." He ground out after a beat. "You will come to Kyros's birthday dinner."

The phone disconnected, and we both stared at it.

"Fuck," Tommy hushed. "What kind of cosplay crazy parents does Kyros have?"

My friend was much smarter than me. I shouldn't have put the call on speakerphone. Tommy wasn't meant to know about Vissimo.

"Pretty crazy, right? That's why I didn't want to go," I hedged.

"Or tell me it was the douchebag's birthday," she accused.

We both jumped as a message appeared on the screen—an address.

Tommy slipped past me and returned with the white silk dress.

"Looks like you have a reason to wear this after all," she said sweetly.

I snatched it from her. "Sometimes I think about maybe disliking you for a small amount of time."

She scooped up her own pile of dresses. "Put it on, lovely. It may give you some enjoyment during the messed-up cosplay night you have ahead of you."

Truth.

This was a blank canvas dress that would suit pretty much any make-up and hair combination, but my nude lipstick and natural-palette smoky eye from today's spa day were perfect. Tommy emerged in a yellow dress with a green clutch and burnt-orange chunky heels.

"I seriously don't know how you do it," I said, kicking off my jeans. "If I wore that I'd look like a wearable arts version of a potted sunflower. Hot, girl. Seriously hot."

She curtsied. "Let's get that dress over your hair."

My long blonde tresses were gathered in a loose arrangement that gave the impression it could come undone at any time, but I'd seen and felt how many pins went in. That shit was there to stay. The stylist had pulled out lazy curls all around my face and at the back, reinforcing the sultry elegance of the updo.

I might go back to that spa one day. I'd booked under a fake name and they still did their best. Though Sansi would never forgive me.

Tommy's mouth formed an O as she looked me over. "Is it too late to switch teams?"

"Don't tempt me, Tommy Tetley. Come on. Let's go. The sooner you leave on your date, the sooner I can replace the memories of my night with yours."

She tapped the back of my hand as I slipped into pointy-toed white heels. I usually hated matching heels to a dress. But if I didn't rise to the unstated drama of this piece, it would crush me.

I looked at my friend, taking in her huge brown eyes.

She clutched my forearm, mouthing, "Will you be okay?"

King Julius said he wouldn't kill me tonight. So no, I probably wouldn't be okay. But I couldn't get out of this.

If I didn't live, Tommy was about to become a fucking rich woman. The condition of her inheritance hinged on her leaving Bluff City with her father without delay, however.

I winked. "Loves ya, babe. I'll see you later tonight—or

tomorrow." I thought about the incredible sex she'd described at the spa. "Or Monday morning."

We walked down to the lobby, and Tommy went off with Fred, and a carload of Indebted who left thirty seconds after. Tommy didn't know she was being followed, and that's how I wanted it to remain. They were under strict instructions to stay far enough away that she couldn't see them.

I slid into the SUV with Laurel and the others, a second car ahead of me, and one behind.

"What's in the bag?" Josie asked, gesturing to the black gift bag on my lap.

Something I'd planned to drop at the tower tonight while he was away at dinner. "Just a little gift for Kyros. It's his birthday."

Kelsea whistled. "Don't we know it. One hundred and fifty years is a huge deal in our world. Like, you know how eighteen is considered adulthood for humans, but then there's a bigger deal at twenty-one?"

I nodded, my gut twisting.

"*This* is Kyros's twenty-first birthday."

"So we're the same age?" I said weakly. "Yay."

My present was *not* a twenty-first level present. It was something I threw together on a whim. I clutched the top of the bag, wondering if I should ask Laurel to swing by *Vie* to get him something nicer.

Except that would give the wrong impression.

Shit.

Sighing, I passed Laurel my phone so she could read the address. Never knew if ears were lurking around.

She set off.

I was about to have dinner with Kyros's *entire family*. What was my status there? I wasn't his girlfriend, but apparently his mate. His father didn't want us any closer than we already were.

Then there was that lingering bitter taste in my mouth from last night's fight with Kyros.

Ugh.

Laurel pulled up to a set of black gates.

I lifted my head. "What? We're there already?" That wasn't nearly long enough to settle my nerves. For some reason, I assumed dinner was at the king's mansion again.

"Yes, Miss Le Spyre. I believe this is Princess Safina's family residence."

On the estate side of Black.

I'd assumed Kyros's siblings lived in towers too. But Fernando had said Safina had a child. "I see."

We were buzzed in, and Laurel directed the vehicle down the driveway.

I frowned. "I expected Indebted to be everywhere."

Fyrlia probably knew there was no point attacking all the royals at once. They were too powerful.

"This is a personal property, Miss Le Spyre," Laurel answered. "A no man's land. Fyrlia will not come here, but this evening does carry risk. Most of the Sundulus Indebted are guarding VIPs and other royal abodes during the celebration."

No wonder, this was prime time for Fyrlia to cause a ruckus.

Laurel stopped nowhere near the house. She pointed right. "That way, Miss Le Spyre. Across the grass."

Heels and grass. Perfect.

"Okay."

"We'll be close by," she said, smiling at me in the rear-view mirror.

Laurel didn't usually reassure me. I must look terrified. I took a deep breath and exhaled, trying to rearrange my face a bit so my topaz eyes weren't huge and my lips weren't parted. I circled my shoulders.

As ready as I'd ever be.

Josie helped me out, and Kelsea passed the gift bag to me.

I set off across the grass.

Rounding the corner, I spotted string lights in the middle of an otherwise open lawn. It looked like tables were set up. Spotting a bridge that spanned a small creek to get from this lawn to the other side, I adjusted course, trying not to fall on my face down the slope.

Lionel appeared suddenly, nearly losing the battle for me. I jolted, pressing a hand against my chest.

"Lionel, you brat," I said crossly.

Gerome appeared, shoving his brother out of the way. His grin lasted half a second before he was shoved away by Rory.

Lionel returned to the fold, and I stepped around the wrestling vampires to continue on, stopping short when I discovered Neelan behind them.

Face smoothed of any emotion, he offered his arm.

Walking to him, I studied the vampire closely.

He relaxed as I took his arm.

"Thank you, Neelan. Grass stains on white aren't ideal."

"No, and it would be a shame to ruin such a beautiful dress," he replied, clearing his throat.

Uhm, charming much?

I couldn't recall Neelan ever being nice to me, so I didn't respond in case it was a trick.

We crossed the small bridge, and I took in the bubbling creek lined with lilies on each bank.

Picturesque was a weak word for the romantic landscaping.

A long table occupied the apex of the curving lawn across the creek. Candles in tall holders and string lights surrounded the table, illuminating the space and lending a lilting glow. More candles were spaced out along the white tablecloth at random.

The occupants quietened as we neared, and my heart thumped faster. Neelan directed me to the middle of the table and gestured at his father.

"Miss Le Spyre has arrived, Father."

The king remained mute, and the queen hissed from the opposite end of the table.

"Welcome," he forced out. "Sit."

I curtsied, thanking my grandmother for forcing me to learn. "Thank you, King Julius. Good evening, Queen Titania," I said, curtsying to her afterward. Who the fuck knew if that was correct protocol?

She beamed back, and I sucked in a breath at her heart-stopping magnificence.

"Welcome, Basilia. Thank you for choosing to come."

Choosing? Sure.

"Where's the birthday boy?" I asked. Everyone else was present.

King Julius snarled. "My heir is no boy."

"*Father*, it's a human colloquialism, not an insult." Safina gestured to a seat on her left, and I squeezed Neelan's arm before untangling myself.

I did my best to ignore the king's unveiled dislike as I settled on the high-back seat. This was feeling more and more like the Mad Hatter's tea party.

"Kyros is inside getting more wine," Deirdre said to me. "But it doesn't take this long to get wine, so I'd say he's delaying because you arrived."

Francesca grinned into her glass of water.

Cocking my head toward the house—an enticing vision at the bottom of the hill—I tuned into Kyros.

Anticipation. Nerves. Dread. Frustration.

Weirdly, we both felt about the same tonight.

"My lady." Lionel snapped into existence on my left. "I apologise for not properly greeting you earlier."

Kyros's brothers were in *that* kind of mood tonight.

"Sir Lionel," I answered. "Fear not the mode of your greeting. Sir Neelan filled the position with sufficient aplomb."

I evaded his attempts to take my hand, whacking the vampire in the rock-hard stomach when he wouldn't let up.

"You wound me." He took the seat opposite Lalitta.

That'd be the day.

Gerome and Rory took their seats in the middle without teasing me.

"Any news on the nightclub?" Gerome asked.

I shoved the gift bag between my feet, feeling more and more uncomfortable about the present. "Settlement was a few days ago. The builders are in there. I'll reopen in a week."

"New theme, huh? What is it?"

I lifted a shoulder. "New name too. If you score an invite to the opening, you can see both for yourself. Or read about it the day after."

He scowled, and I smirked despite the relentless and heavy stare of the king boring into the side of my face.

"I'll get an invite, won't I, darling? Parties are our little thing." Rory winked across the table.

I frowned slightly. "The bar won't have any mirrors. Not sure it's your scene, Rory."

Francesca snorted and then glared at me.

Lalitta waved from the queen's end. "You look absolutely incredible, Basilia."

The entire table chose that moment to peruse my outfit with a critical eye. I steeled myself against fidgeting, inclining my head. "Thank you, Lalitta. You look beautiful too. Is that the dress from when we went shopping?"

She flushed. "Yes, it is. I wasn't sure you'd remember."

My nerves swelled and confusion filled me before I realised the emotions didn't belong to me.

Safina rose to her feet. "We may need to rearrange the seats, Miss Le Spyre."

I stood and eased around the back of my chair, lingering there, half my mind occupied with the slow hardening overcoming Kyros.

Crap, what did that mean? Was he still mad at me? Or was he about to be a jerk because his dad was here?

I shouldn't have come.

"Son," the queen exclaimed. "Look who has come."

Like he didn't already know.

"Yes, Mother. I felt her arrive."

My back tensed. Had Safina warned him I was coming? The dread within him intensified, but I hadn't sensed any shock yet.

"Basilia," he said quietly.

Foreboding twisted my gut, making me feel almost sick.

Withholding a sigh, I turned around.

His face slackened as he took me in, his grip on the open bottles of wine loosening. The hardness I'd felt him putting in place was obliterated—the dread, the frustration, the nerves, dissolved as he looked at me.

He closed his mouth most of the way, but his sharp inhale ruined the effort.

My eyes drank him in as if they hadn't seen him less than a day ago. He'd forgone a tie and the neck of his shirt was open—casual. His suit wasn't for business, it was for dinner, longer and with only one button.

The sight of him left me in denial he could exist.

"Wine," the king snapped.

Kyros didn't twitch. He was about five seconds away from pouring wine on his very expensive shoes.

I stepped forward and took the two wine bottles without resistance. My heart sputtered uselessly in my chest.

"Happy birthday," I said, my voice throatier than usual. "I'm told one hundred and fifty is an important milestone for Vissimo..." I trailed off awkwardly.

He inhaled deeply and stepped back to bow to me. "Thank you, my beauty."

Uhm, was that something he should say in front of his father?

His emotions were a jumbled mess. He was entirely off-balance.

Flushing, I pivoted to set one bottle of wine on the table and walked around the table to where the king sat glowering. I picked up his glass and filled it halfway with the ruby shiraz. I paused, glancing at him and then filled it to the top. Safina grinned as I set the wobbling glass in front of him.

The king's jaw clenched, but he merely stared at his queen in silent mutiny.

I wouldn't play up too much, King Julius. Not against someone with Twitter-worthy nipples.

"Would anyone else like some?" I asked.

"If there's any left," Rory grumbled over the general murmur of assent.

I went around the table pouring the wine, making sure to only put a mouthful in Rory's. When I got to my glass, Kyros placed a hand over the top.

He quirked a brow. "You may not want to drink this one."

"Oh. *Oh*." My eyes widened.

Not just red wine then.

Safina had moved across the table and Kyros sat in her vacated chair on the king's left. I picked up the second bottle and filled his glass, then sat.

As soon as I did, the tension with Kyros ratchetted to spectacular height. *Fuck*, it was at agony-levels tonight. I stole a peek at him only to find myself the bearer of his sole attention.

I did not want to die.

I kicked him under the table, and his lips twitched.

"You smell better than normal," Deirdre said, from two seats to my left.

"Thanks, Deirdre," I replied, my lips trembling. "I spent the day at a spa."

Her brow cleared.

Silence returned.

I jerked as a ball blurred at Safina's head. The woman twisted and caught the ball, beaming as she deposited the child on her lap.

Holy. Fucking. Cuteness.

The girl, two or three by the looks, launched into a string of words too fast for me to understand.

Angelica approached the table behind her. "Kearra, we speak slower in the presence of humans." She smiled at me. "Miss Le Spyre, how lovely that you could join us."

"Thanks, Angie," I said drily.

She took a seat beside Lalitta.

I glanced across the table to find two blue eyes on me set in a face as perfect as her mother's.

"You're human," the young girl demanded. She had to be older than three—unless vampires developed their language skills a whole heap faster.

"I am," I replied solemnly.

The toddler gasped and wiggled to be free.

"You may sit on your Uncle Kyros's lap," Safina said sternly. "Be gentle with her."

Maybe King Julius wasn't the most dangerous Vissimo here.

The child disappeared under the table and reappeared on Kyros's lap. He dragged his green eyes from me and wrapped the child in his arms. He leaned down to kiss her chubby cheeks and she squealed.

"Stop it, Uncle Kyros. I want to look at the human."

Ovaries. Bursting.

I'd thought Kyros couldn't get sexier. Oh how wrong I'd been. He loved kids—not that we were compatible like that—but hell, my womb was primed and ready.

Kyros snatched back her outstretched hand. "This is Basilia Le Spyre, Kearra. You must be very careful with her."

"I *heard*," the child said dramatically.

I bit back my grin. Kyros wasn't kidding when he said children were revered. She was spoiled rotten. The king had been rendered to a pile of goo since her arrival. The child dominated the attention of everyone at the table, including mine.

"Nice to meet you." I held out my hand. "You can call me Basi."

"You can call me Kearra. Nice to meet you too." She whacked her hand in mine and I grimaced at the sting.

"*Gentle,* Kearra," Safina reprimanded, looking at me. "This is a good opportunity for her to learn."

How weak humans are?

"Happy to help," I said half-heartedly.

Safina smirked and then—thank the powers that be—the occupants of the table began to converse.

I took a full breath and relaxed.

Kyros draped his arm over the back of my seat.

Brows rising, I glanced over at him, but someone else was watching me too.

"Are you really slow like a turtle?" Kearra asked, eyes narrowed.

I considered that. "More like the speed of an elephant or monkey."

"You don't look like an elephant," she said just as seriously. "A pretty monkey."

Safina gasped. "Kearra."

"It's okay." I struggled to contain my laughter. "At least she's honest about it." Leaning down, I said, "Humans are a lot like monkeys even if we like to think we're superior to them."

Without warning, the Vissimo child lunged for Kyros's wine. He grabbed her chubby hand, pulling her back without effort. "Not a chance, Kee. That's an adult drink."

"Let's do gifts before dinner," Francesca said as I battled with my womb again.

The queen smiled at her youngest child, adoration plain on her goddess-like face. "What a lovely idea."

If Francesca was spoiled like Kearra as a child, I had zero illusions about why she acted up so much in her thirties. Or however the fuck old she was.

A tiny finger poked my arm. "She's soft, Uncle Kyros."

He whispered back. "I know."

"She smells like I should eat her."

Oh my god. I choked on laughter and nearly lost it again at the slight possessive anger from Kyros.

"Yes, but you must never hurt Miss Le Spyre," he said in a grave voice.

"Do you like her, Uncle Kyros. You called her *my beauty* before." The young girl giggled.

His lips curved, and my heart threatened to implode. His reply to her was too rapid for me to make out.

Damn male.

Kearra squealed with laughter again and slipped off his lap, crawling up to join King Julius. She sat on his lap, looking in wide-eyed awe at her grandfather.

"Gifts," the king announced, curling his arm around his granddaughter.

Queen Titania stood, holding her wine glass high. "Kyros, my first son. You are one hundred and fifty. I so clearly recall holding you in my arms for the first time and feeling my heart expand to three times the size. I love you more than my own life, and that will not change in the next one hundred and fifty years of your life, nor the centuries after."

Warmth swept through the vampire next to me, and I stole a quick glance at him, tucking away the sight of his slight smile.

"Your father's seed was indeed strong that night," she continued. "I remember the union vividly—"

"*Mom*," Rory blurted, grimacing.

I covered my mouth, battling furiously to maintain my calm as Kyros's warmth turned to nausea. The queen glanced at them, a slight wrinkle between her brow.

I couldn't lose the plot. Not here. *Keep it together, Basi!* Heat filled my face as I shoved back the urge to laugh. *Just.*

The king stood, Kearra clinging to him like a, well, a monkey.

"I have rarely felt such love as when I looked upon your face for the first time," he said to Kyros without ceremony. "You have grown from babe to boy and from boy to man. Yet you are young. I look forward to many decades of watching you explore life and your power."

The king's eyes flickered to me, and I read the disgust in them before he returned his focus to Kyros and lifted his glass of blood wine. "To my heir, Prince Kyros."

There was a water in front of me. I picked it up and held it in the air.

"Prince Kyros," I murmured with everyone else.

His eyes were on me again. I swallowed the sip of water and did my best to walk the line of survival somewhere between vampire accessory and stupid human.

"We got you a group gift," Safina announced.

Lalitta reached into a bag.

"It's a house," Francesca rushed to say.

Everyone glared at her.

"What?" She pouted.

Lionel plucked a set of keys from Lalitta's hand. "You need a place away from the towers like the rest of us, bro."

"We found a cool house out by Lyall Bay and did a few renovations," Gerome said.

"And redecorated," Deirdre put in.

Lionel tossed the keys over my head, and Kyros caught them with ease.

"There's a new set of wheels in the garage," Neelan murmured.

Rory smirked. "We didn't let Gerome choose the car."

"Thank fuck for that," Kyros replied.

He smiled at the keys, and I studied his confusion. *Yeah*, Kyros out of his tower was a strange concept, even for me.

"Thank you. I look forward to seeing it," he said.

The queen beamed down the table. "Maybe during our next weekend off, we could meet there."

"That's next weekend," Lalitta said, bouncing. The two shared an excited glance.

Wow.

It was hard to remember how dangerous these people were when they were relaxed and joyful like this. A sadness entered my heart—none of it from me. I didn't need to peek at Kyros to know he was wondering how many days like this he had left with his family. His longing was intense.

I squeezed his hand under the table. He shouldn't be morose on his birthday—no matter how many of the fuckers he'd already had.

When I made to slide away, he tightened his grip.

"We filled your wardrobe with new suits," Safina announced, gesturing to her sisters.

I fixed my attention on her. "You didn't take the old ones away, did you?"

She cut off. "Yes, we do it each year—"

"Did you leave the air-force blue suit?" I said, frowning.

She blinked and peered at Deirdre.

"Chucked 'em all," she answered.

I pressed my lips together.

Not happy.

"Maybe it's best if you relocated it," the queen murmured to her daughter.

Deirdre stopped picking her teeth. "I'll try."

They were in the bad books until it was back. Kyros's amusement tightened around me, and I pinned him with a glare, daring him to laugh.

The king was watching.

Yikes.

Why couldn't we sit down the queen's end?

"The boys got you a little something for the house," Rory said, grinning widely as he glanced at me. "Probably best if you see it when you get there."

I ignored the bait, taking another sip of water as I contemplated my stupid present under the table. Turned out my gift idea was totally inappropriate for this occasion. Thank fuck I'd shoved it out of sight. Talk about mortifying.

"Shall I call for dinner then?" the queen asked.

Lionel glanced at me. "Didn't you have something when you walked in?"

I widened my eyes at him. "No. I didn't have time to—"

"There's a bag under the table by your feet," Francesca said, popping her head above the table.

Fucking. Francesca.

My cheeks heated and I pulled free of Kyros's hand to draw the gift bag out. *Great*, now I looked extra idiotic for trying to hide it.

"I already had a present for Kyros, but I didn't realise what a big deal this birthday was." Embarrassment poured through me in thick waves.

Kyros pried the rope handles from my grasp and placed the bag on the table. He studied my burning face for a second before drawing out the small and flat wrapped parcel.

Ugh, kill me now.

"It's stupid," I whispered at him.

They were going to laugh at me.

"Hush," he said. "I'll be the judge of that."

Sliding a massive finger under the wrapping, he worked the bindings free along one edge. Then he did the same on both ends.

Gerome grumbled loudly. "And now you know why we never give him wrapped presents." He jabbed an angry finger at me. "This is on you."

Sure, but he didn't have front row seats to how much his elder brother enjoyed unwrapping the gift.

Kyros pushed the paper off and turned the photo frame around.

I fidgeted in my seat as he stared at the picture of him and his siblings from earlier this morning. They were trying to pull him in different ways, smirks on their faces, and he grinned in the middle as though he hadn't carried a terrible burden on his shoulders.

"Well, show us," Francesca huffed.

Kyros ignored her, stroking a large finger down the side of the wooden frame. I tried to dissect what he was feeling, but whatever was going through his head, I'd never experienced before.

It was like he didn't know what to feel.

I flushed anew.

Was there any viable excuse to get me the fuck out of here? I glanced over my shoulder.

"Show me," the king ordered.

Kyros blinked and lifted his head. "What?"

The king held out a hand and—begrudgingly—Kyros passed it over. The queen blurred around the table to peer over her husband's shoulder. That apparently gave everyone else permission to do the same.

Their faces blanked one by one.

I got to my feet, pretty sure my entire body was red from utter mortification. I glanced back the way I came.

"It's *us*," Neelan whispered.

The queen sniffled. "Look how happy you all are. What were you about to do to your brother?"

"Lionel took sexy photos with Basilia and put them on a billboard for Kyros to see," Lalitta said.

The king roared with laughter, sending the fear of death through me as he displayed a few teeth.

Lionel grinned.

Gerome plucked the frame from his father's grip.

"*Careful*," Kyros snapped.

I hovered on the edge of their group, my discomfort mounting.

Gerome returned the picture frame to his eldest brother, who, after another good look, placed it back in the wrapping, face up.

"Basilia," Kyros murmured.

I folded my arms. "Yes?" My voice shook.

"Come here."

I resumed my seat and gasped as I was deposited on his lap, facing away from his avidly watching family.

He held my hand to his lips, closing his eyes as he pressed a lingering kiss there. Green eyes bore into mine.

"I will treasure it always."

The urge to smile was overwhelming, so I gave in to it.

"You're not allowed to smash this one," he murmured.

That would never happen. Not with this.

"Happy birthday, Kyros."

"It is," he agreed.

His family was less than a metre away and showing no sign of giving us privacy, so I made to slide off and return to my seat, but Kyros clamped an arm around my waist, touching his lips to mine in a kiss that awakened every part of me.

Kyros pulled back, capturing my chin. "I understand now."

"You understand?" I repeated in confusion.

His grin was blinding. "Yes."

22

I made my excuses at 10:00 p.m. last night to give them family time before they went their separate ways to play *Ingenium.* How did the game not wear on them as the years went by?

"Basilia? That you?"

"It's me," I replied to the flash of red lipstick through the twitching curtain. "The garden's looking great."

The front door swung open and Mrs Hannah rushed out.

I studied the ground and plants but couldn't see anything that needed doing. I'd expected to spend a good hour here on the way back from viewing the changes at my new club. "You're a green thumb."

She cackled and shooed me.

I wrapped an arm around her shoulders. "It looks just beautiful. The lavender and marigolds." She'd even trimmed the low hedge, which formed the semblance of a fence across the front of the property.

"The garden is perfect," she said. I peered down at her wet sniff.

She was crying.

"Shit, Mrs Hannah. What's wrong? Did I say something?"

"N-No, dear. Don't mind me."

We'd grown close over the last two months, bonding over the lavender problem. Maybe it was that old people reminded me of my grandmother and her friends, or maybe because I'd had an older guardian, me and the oldies just clicked.

"I certainly will mind," I told her crossly.

Leading her back into the house, I guided her to a kitchen chair and set about making peppermint tea—the only thing I knew how to do in a kitchen, let's be honest.

Her face was drawn when I placed a steaming mug before her and sat opposite, clutching my own.

"What's your beef with the garden?" I asked outright.

Her face screwed up and fresh tears leaked from her eyes. My chest squeezed and I shuffled my chair around so I could rub her back.

"Better out than in," I said quietly.

She shrugged a shoulder, leaning forward to grab a tissue from a box in the middle of the table. "Never really talked about it before."

I waited.

"Five years ago, I decided to re-do the front garden." She drew in a deep breath, and then words rushed out. "I asked my sister for some cuttings from her garden. Asked her to make a special trip down from Furnley Gorge to bring them because I don't drive. We grew up close, Basilia. Foster homes, in and out of bad situations, but we were lucky enough to stay with each other during those years. That kind of crap bonds people in a way those with normal upbringings could never imagine."

I could imagine.

"There was a storm the night she drove down. I waited up all night for her to arrive, sitting at the window, but I must've fallen asleep because her knock on the door woke me." Mrs Hannah drew in a shaking breath. "It wasn't her, it was the police. As soon as they said, '*Are you the sister of Ms Heath?*', I knew. They told me she'd gone over the cliffs, killed on impact."

Shock filled me as I thought back over our interactions. How she'd always said her sister was visiting and the garden had to be perfect for when she arrived. How she'd seemed to begrudge the garden the more it flourished. Had she been killing her plants on purpose?

"It wasn't your fault, Mrs Hannah."

She didn't agree, I could see it in her face.

"Plants everywhere at the crash scene," she said. "There were pictures in the paper and the stories all mentioned my name. *Driving to see her sister, Mrs Hannah Gaughton, in Bluff City.*"

When loved ones died tragically, the self-blame game was no small thing. "Have I ever told you my parents died when I was nine?"

She wiped her face again and stretched out a hand to take mine. "That's terrible."

"For years after, when I got old enough to process such things, I was certain their death was my fault. Maybe if I'd behaved better, they'd have taken me on holiday, and then they wouldn't be dead. Or maybe if I didn't play up all the time, maybe they wouldn't have needed a holiday and wouldn't be dead. Why did they need a holiday without me? Even now, when I'm feeling low, the self-destructive thoughts come back. With my grandmother's death, it's the same." *Just involving vampires.*

"She wouldn't have been out in the storm—"

I straightened. "Your sister was a grown woman and she had a choice to drive in those conditions or not."

Mrs Gaughton glared at me.

"You don't control the decisions of others," I told her. "You're not responsible for her death. What would she say if she could see you now, lying about her visits?"

Her eyes dropped to her lap. "She'd say I was a fucking moron."

I snorted. "Sounds like she was a hoot."

The older woman swallowed hard. "She was something alright."

I squeezed her hand. "Thank you for making your garden perfect for my grandmother. For me. Especially when it held such scars for you."

"I always said that when the garden was done, I'd pack up and leave. But I just couldn't do it. Not when I shared so many memories with my sister here."

"You don't ever have to leave."

A shadow fell across her vision. "I hate these halls. If I'd left straight away, the memories might have been preserved. Now, all that's left is pain. Still, I'm afraid of what's next. The garden is ready and I was meant to be ready too."

I studied the woman. I didn't see her as different from me—some wise elderly stranger. I could see my own struggles within this woman—a fellow soul who'd lost her way. She'd just misplaced her fire for the time being.

"The garden's ready," I told her. "And you are too. You just don't know it yet."

"What shit are you talking, dear?"

This was either an idiotic or ingenious move.

"Mrs Hannah," I said. "My real name is Basilia Le Spyre. Would you like to move in with me?"

"Foremost got 77 Bard Boulevard," Angelica hissed as we rode the elevator up to Level 66.

I pretended to think.

"Mrs Gaughton," she said.

I let my jaw drop. "I've been buttering her up for two *months*. She sold to them?"

"They landed on Orange yesterday and her property is registered as sold though the details are yet to be processed."

"Damn, I wonder how they got her. I tried everything." *Including inviting her to live with me. Which she accepted.* There had been the option to settle her in one of my many rentals in the city. But there was a greater chance the realtors at *Live Right* would recognise her when they went door knocking than for Kyros—who thought of humans as addresses anyway—to recognise her on the estate.

Angelica sighed. “Sometimes owners click better with another realtor. I’ll look into it to ensure she wasn’t coerced. Foremost do try upon occasion.”

Good to know.

She rubbed her temples. “Private sale rates are up by 0.5 percent.”

I shoved back my satisfaction. “Any idea why?”

“Kyros thinks the properties refusing to sell to Live Right and Foremost value local business and a social cause. He’s considering a rebranding of the business as we focus on the last available properties.”

I blew out a breath. “Drastic stuff. Surely half a percent can’t make too much difference? We can just approach the new buyers.”

“Not if they’re overseas investors. Which a growing number are. For starters, they’re not regular spenders in the city, and in addition, it makes them incredibly hard to track down to secure their homes.”

I looked at her. “I never thought about that. You’re right. That’s not good. Is there anything we can do about it?”

“Win *Ingenium* before the last of the real estate is gone,” she said, shooting me an amused look.

I smiled, smoothing my blood-red wrap-around dress. “Sounds good to me.”

My phone chimed as I stepped off the elevator.

“Go ahead.” I searched in my *Lili* handbag, pulling out my phone.

The message was from Gina.

My eyes narrowed. Tonight was King Julius’s roll. Her timing, yet again, was impeccable.

I clicked on the message.

Do you remember our deal?

Shit.

I typed back.

I remember.

She had an answer already?

I couldn't be on this level if the news about Grandmother was bad. Or good. Rushing back into the elevator, I pushed Level 65 and paced inside as the lift lurched down a level.

I ran to Kyros's office as fast as my heels would let me and burst through the doors, taking up my pacing there instead. *Shit, shit, shit.*

My phone rang.

"What's happening?" Kyros asked.

I released a pent-up breath. "Nothing. I'm okay. I just got a message from her. I think she has something."

"... I see. I'll be right down."

"No." I glanced at my watch. *11:56 p.m.* "She'll message back just before the roll. I'll wait to look until you give your debrief."

I could feel his frustration. Oddly, that meant something.

"Truly," I told him. "I'll wait."

There were things I wanted to handle by myself—most things. There were others I knew I couldn't without Tommy. Clearly, I didn't want to do *this* without Kyros.

"I'll be there as soon as I can," he said.

I nodded—because that made sense on a phone call—and disconnected.

I set the phone on his desk and resumed pacing, trying to keep calm, both for myself and for him.

My phone chimed, and I glanced at my watch.

11:58 p.m.

Yep. I'd called it.

If Gina wasn't using information about my grandmother's death to affect Kyros through me, I might've admired the tactic.

The phone chimed again.

11:59 p.m.

And again.

00:00 a.m.

I squeezed my eyes closed, perching on the seat in the middle of the room. *Fuck me*, it was the torture chair.

Oh well. There were worse things in the world. My phone chimed again, and I gripped either side of my head, focusing on my breathing.

Was it good?

Did Grandmother die a natural death? Was there an undiagnosed problem with her heart? Or did the Tonyi triplets visit her that day? Maybe someone else from Clan Fyrlia. Or ... I lifted my head, from Clan Sundulus? This clan knew who I really was—most of them anyway. What if someone I *liked* had gone to see her? What if I'd joked and laughed with them for the last month? What if it was Lionel? Or Angelica... one of my Indebted.

The door hit the wall as Kyros arrived. He strode to the desk and flipped back the panel, entering his code. I crossed the room and grabbed my phone, heading up to his lair.

"I'll be quick," I said.

"My seconds have their orders for the night," he said. "I'll join my siblings at 2:00 a.m."

"You don't have to—"

He leaned down. "Basilia. I'm staying with you."

I stared into his eyes, my last attempt at bravado melting away before him. "Thank you."

Kyros took my hand in his and drew me up the stairs to his lair. I drew in a breath that did absolutely nothing to calm me.

"Check it," he said, giving me space. "Delaying won't help."

He was right, but I was so scared to reopen the grief I held over my grandmother. I'd lost my parents to traumatic deaths. But *murder*. How did a person get over that? How could you ever be okay again?

I was afraid of what knowing would do to me.

"I'm with you," Kyros said, placing his hands on my shoulders.

Latching onto his steady strength, I slid open the first text from Gina.

I broke into their trophy room
Are any of these your grandmother's?

The next two texts were images.

Despite the wording of the text, I mentally prepared myself to see my grandmother dying on the bathroom floor. She was out of pain now. I had to remember that.

I opened the first image and my legs buckled with relief. Kyros led me to the couch and I sank down upon it.

"It's some kind of cat pin," I whispered even though Kyros was looking over my shoulder. "My grandmother said cats were the devil's toenails given life. That's not hers."

Emboldened, I opened the second.

Blood drained from my face and the phone toppled from my shaking hands. Kyros grabbed the phone, looking at the picture.

"You recognise that?"

Grandmother always smelled like lavender because she kept pouches of dried leaves in her wardrobe. Pouches identical to the one in the picture.

Bile surged, and I shoved Kyros aside, racing for the bathroom. I threw myself down by the toilet and emptied the contents of my stomach into the bowl, tears squeezing from my eyes.

I vomited again and again, the yellow pouch of lavender leaves flashing behind my eyelids.

They'd killed her. Why else would they have it?

A *trophy room*, Gina had said. The triplets kept mementos of the people they killed?

My stomach cramped as I gagged again, but nothing came up.

Fumbling, I flushed the toilet and sat back on my heeled feet. Kyros passed me a glass of water and stepped around me to run a flannel under cold water. I swilled the water in my mouth on autopilot, spitting it into the toilet.

Scooping me up, Kyros returned us to the couch and held me tight with one arm, dabbing at my forehead with the flannel.

He didn't say anything.

The shock began to ebb, but the shaking worsened. My teeth were going to rattle right out of my head. "Grandmother kept lavender pouches in all her clothes."

Kyros picked up the phone, looking at the picture again. "You're sure it's hers?"

I gleaned nothing from his tone. Through my numbness, I couldn't feel anything.

"There's another message." He glanced at me.

"Read it," I said hoarsely.

Kyros scanned the contents. "*I'm sorry if the news is not what you hoped for. Gina.*"

His fingers curled around the phone, and I eased it free, worried he'd crush my evidence of the triplets' guilt.

"Basilia," he said.

I rubbed at the phone's surface.

"Basilia."

The taste of bile still filled my mouth. "What?" I croaked.

"Tell me what you're thinking."

I dragged in a painful breath. "What is there to say? They must have visited her that night. They intended to kill her—why else would they take a trophy?"

I pressed a shaking hand against my mouth. "She must have been so afraid, Kyros."

My grandmother killed by those monsters. My eyes filled and hot tears spilled over my cheeks.

Kyros stared at me. "You're *crying*."

"It happens," I stammered as my shoulders shook.

"That was a stupid thing to say. I mean, I've never seen you cry." He was horrified.

I wiped at my face to little avail. "I hoped so badly she'd just died naturally." I hiccupped. "They scared her to death, Kyros. My grandmother. What do I do about that?" My stomach threatened to empty again.

"You're in shock. We deal with that first."

"First?" I hiccupped again, looking at him through blurring eyes.

Darkness spread through my chest, a hatred and a promise that didn't belong to me.

"The vermin will pay for what they did," Kyros stated calmly.

I wasn't fooled, not with the front row seats to his emotions.

His meadow-green eyes met mine. "They'll pay for what they did."

23

Kyros tried to give me the week off, but when I turned the offer down, he didn't push the issue. Perhaps he knew that sometimes distraction was the only way to keep swimming.

I was drowning in hatred. In thoughts of revenge. In horror of what ifs. Had Grandmother pleaded with them? How many times had they let their powers flare before her heart gave out? I'd been sick too many times to count in the last four days.

Those around me were worried—Tommy, Fred, Laurel, and the girls.

Talking about it was impossible—literally, but I couldn't bear to show anyone the messages from Gina, which I'd saved to an external drive so they wouldn't be lost.

Kyros knew the truth. And his siblings—who I'd told the same night.

"My beauty, everyone has left."

I blinked at him, then around the empty room. "They have? Sorry. I zoned out."

He perched on the desk by my chair and circled his thumb beneath my eyes. "You're not sleeping."

"No." The nightmares wouldn't stay away.

Kyros studied me. "I have something I need to talk with you about. Two things."

Nothing could surprise me at this point. "Go ahead."

"I know driving lessons are important to you. With the tightening in security, your lessons have stopped. I wondered if you'd like to resume lessons. With me."

What?

"You'd teach me?" I repeated dumbly, straightening in my chair.

His stare was intense. "I'd like to. If you still wish to learn."

A blush tinged my cheeks. I couldn't keep the small smile at bay. Darting a look up, I said shyly, "I'd like that."

I could finally get my licence!

Triumph rocketed through the vampire.

I cocked my head, trying to quell the butterflies in my stomach. "The second thing?"

"This is in no way related to my first question."

Truth.

I was glad because it hadn't occurred to me that Kyros was buttering me up for something.

He perched on the edge of the table, studying me. "I want to exchange blood with you again."

My eyes flew to his and I peered out of the glass meeting room. We were alone, but not really. "Is this a conversation for here?"

"Considering I plan to call my father for permission if you say yes, I see no problem with the location."

I had no objections against the fourth exchange. It's what I'd wanted when I came back to *Kyros Sky*. In fact, I had more reason than ever to run *toward* it. I wanted to be lost—oblivious—for three days.

"An exchange will put you out of action for three days. Is the timing right?" I asked him.

My decision making would be impaired, but I could put things in order for seventy-two hours.

"Waiting until later could prove more disadvantageous for the clan," he said. "That risk is not why I want to exchange blood with you again, but it is why I feel the need to do so without delay. You're vulnerable to compulsion by others until we do."

I whispered. "I can't be compelled once we exchange blood again?"

That was extra appealing considering what nearly happened with his father.

The vampire inclined his head. "Only by me. Therefore you appeal less to those who may wish you harm. Though I have some stipulations. And one question."

"Go on," I said warily.

He studied me, one hand in his trouser pocket. "You'll need to remain in the tower for the duration of the thrall."

That was a given. "I'll have my Vissimo crew for protection again."

Kyros nodded. "It's hard to gauge with the circumstances of the last exchanges, but I believe having you in my space where only my siblings can enter helped. Would you consider remaining in my quarters for the thrall?"

I considered that. "Yes, but I want to take some of my things up to your lair. Three days might drive me batty." *Battier than the thrall usually makes me.*

"My sisters can visit, but no one else. Your Vissimo can guard you from the office below."

Fine by me. The fewer people to witness my thrall, the better. "Anything else?"

"I'd like to call you during the thrall. Or at least try. I don't know if it will make things better or worse, but not knowing how you are—if you're safe—is the worst part."

I tipped my head back. "What does the thrall feel like for you?"

"Like if I don't get to you, lesser males will take you away and hurt you or convince you they're a stronger mate. The need to see you and fuck you is nearly undeniable, but I feel capable of anything necessary to protect you. Invincible. Furious. And insatiable."

Which is about what he looked like. "You get the raw end of the deal," I admitted. "What was the question?"

Kyros hesitated. "Do you have any requests?"

"That's your question?"

"No."

I thought about it. "I don't want your siblings to play any pranks while I'm under the thrall. I'm vulnerable in that time, and so are you. I want them to respect that."

"I'll see it is done. Anything else?"

I knew the details of the exchange, but maybe I should ask more so his suspicions weren't raised. "When you say my senses will change, what do you mean?"

Kyros leaned forward. I offered no resistance as he pulled me to my feet. Turning, he sat me on the glass desk. When my tight dress wouldn't allow him to stand between my legs, I shimmied it high on my thighs to make space.

He didn't hesitate to occupy it.

"Now we're more comfortable, go on," I said drily.

Amusement flickered within him. "Your sense of smell, vision, touch, taste, and hearing will improve. Multiple blood exchanges between Vissimo are rare these days. Between a human and Vissimo even less so. From what I've researched, you will feel off-balance for the first couple of weeks."

I considered that. "How easy will the changes be to hide from my staff?"

"I'm unsure. There's a chance you may have to remain here until you adjust."

Mmm-hmm, and he didn't hope for that at all.

"I'm sure I can fake vertigo," I said sweetly.

A spark entered his gaze. "Do you agree to the exchange? If so, I'd like to enter the fourth thrall tomorrow after meetings."

"One more exchange makes sense," I answered. "But I won't accept further compulsions on my mind."

He searched my expression. "I'll never do so without your permission. And that's something I can uphold once we exchange blood again as the risk you pose to the clan will be obsolete."

This time, I'd known the consequences in advance. Part of me was left uncertain by the fact Kyros's explanation matched Laurel and

Fernando's information, and then some more. He was telling the truth. All the truth.

But if Kyros talked to his father, there was a huge chance King Julius would interfere again—perhaps permanently.

I couldn't take that risk. This had to happen now. No matter what the king did in retaliation, at least I'd be safe from his compulsion after the fourth exchange.

Tapping my lip, I dragged my eyes from his hips, which were just shy of pressing into my core, all the way to his chest. "We should have sex too."

Kyros froze.

I traced a line between his pecs and up his throat, stretching my arm up to splay my hand over his jaw. "I'm down for being less appealing to your enemies and having better senses, but I'd like a more immediate reward. Maybe several of them. What do you say?"

Kyros's eyes blazed. "In the past, you've requested physical separation. I assumed that would remain true." He leaned forward, and I leaned back onto my hands.

The unsatisfied urges of my body were driving me insane. It wasn't desire at this point. It was an acute need. "I'm in a state of constant ache for you," I whispered.

His breath came fast.

"I need you inside me soon."

He hooked my lower back with his arm. Bright green eyes, furious with lust, latched onto mine.

I cocked my head. "Don't you want to be inside me, Kyros? If you want physical separation, just say the word."

He began to shake. "Yes."

I smiled at his pained hiss. "Yes, what?"

I hovered my mouth over his, my smile widening as he closed his eyes. The desperation pouring out of him swelled to unbearable heights.

"I want to be inside you," he answered in a rumble that reverberated through me.

Drawing away, I picked up his free hand and captured his opened eyes as I lifted his hand to my mouth and pressed a kiss to the palm.

"Show me then," I breathed, lowering to lay across the glass, back arching over his arm. As though tied together, he moved forward with me, aligning his face with the top of my thighs.

Agony swept through me, a twin for his torment.

His growl filled the office space, shaking the glass walls. He inhaled deeply against the apex of my thighs, and *fuck*, I should have been embarrassed. It was the kinkiest thing anyone had ever done to me, but the action was so deeply erotic my insides clenched to snapping point.

Sliding his arm free, he inched his hands to my knees and used a burst of speed to spread them.

He lowered his face.

"I won't be able to get through this without entering the fourth exchange," Kyros rasped against my thigh.

Counting on it. But perhaps some effort on our part would help with King Julius damage control afterward. In a haze, I slid my phone free.

"What?" Deirdre snapped down the line three rings later. "I don't like technology."

"Kyros and I are about to bite each other. You all better come back. No promises on what you'll see." I squirmed, trying to push closer to Kyros's face, but he held me still.

I hung up on his sister.

The air left me in a rush as Kyros flipped me, pressing me into the glass table.

"We can't have kids, right?" I blurted.

"No," he snarled. He drew down my dress zipper to the top of my ass.

"I'm clean," I added, seeing as he didn't seem too worried about the tiny details.

"I can smell that you're clean, and Vissimo can't contract sexual diseases."

Okay, then.

I gasped as he whirled me back, setting me on my feet to slide the dress from my shoulders, like I was nothing more than a doll in his hands.

The low-cut dress fell away to reveal my lacy half-cup bra and matching thong.

Kyros gazed upon me like I held all the answers, like I alone could decide his fate. When he looked at me like that, I was tricked into believing I could. His hands squeezed my sides, caressing upward until his thumbs rested on the underside of my bra. He pushed my breasts up, lowering his head to drag his extended fangs over the swell.

I was wetter than I'd ever been in my life. "Kyros..."

He met my gaze.

"I'm so fucking angry at you," I admitted.

His eyes glittered. "I know, my beauty. And I'm sorry."

My hands fumbled for his shirt, yanking. Buttons popped off, and I shoved it off his shoulders. Usually, I liked to joke in the bedroom and that would have had me snorting.

Neither of us were laughing.

His hand swept over the curves of my stomach and he ripped my panties off.

Finally.

His finger lodged inside me without warning, and I screamed at the contact. He paused for the bare second it probably took to feel that my scream wasn't the pained kind.

Then he moved.

At Vissimo speed. I think he added another finger. A thumb on my clit? So much was happening. *So fast.* My senses were overwhelmed with slippery ecstasy. It felt like three sets of hands were on me, but that was impossible.

It was impossible.

I—

The doors opened on an inferno, and I had no time to process the fire about to consume me. My eyes were wide on his face, and I inhaled my scream, my entire body *tightening* around his fingers.

He watched me, fangs lengthened, rage etched over his face.

Not at me.

He was about to claim me.

"Come, *mate*," Kyros rumbled.

I choked on a pitiful sound as a heavy languidness filled me from head to toe. Flames rolled through me, eviscerating awareness of myself.

He picked me up, laying me on the table. I shuddered at the cold glass, merely adding to the shaking of my limbs as aftershock after aftershock hit me.

"Inside," I rasped.

His clothes were gone.

Kyros whirled away, giving me a glorious view of his ass. His shoulders heaved and he covered his mouth, snarls ripping from him.

"Bite me," I said dreamily. "I don't care. But you better fuck me without delay. And that's an order."

He approached the table, and I shimmied my ass down to the edge.

Kyros positioned himself at my entrance.

Gripping both of my hips, he pulled me onto his erection. My eyes rounded and my insides clenched in warning at the size of him.

The vampire didn't stop sliding me toward him until I was situated all the way on his cock.

"Fucking perfect," he said, nearly too rapidly to make out the words.

I'd never been filled so completely. I wanted so much all at once. Gathering the feeling, I shoved it at him as he drew his hips back.

His answering growl was terrible. He slammed into me and I saw fucking stars.

Holy fu—

Again.

I had no chance of matching his strength and speed, but my body knew I needed this more than breathing right now. My hips strained to meet his.

We found our rhythm.

I clutched onto his shoulders as he lifted me, his hips pumping below. My cries intertwined with his pained moans.

He couldn't hold on much longer. And I had no illusion about just what he was holding onto.

Swallowing a scream as he adjusted to piston deeper, I kissed him gently and let my head fall to one side, my hair slithering across my back.

Snap.

I felt the restraint detonate within him. His fangs cut into my neck. This time, the uncomfortable sensation of blood being drawn only spurred me to greater heights, the small hurt catapulting me to animalistic.

He spun, shoving my back against a wall. I shoved at him, raking my nails down his arms as he drank.

Kyros yanked away and roared, my blood dripping from his mouth.

The wall behind me cracked and shattered and he ripped me away, lowering me to the carpeted floor. He tore at his wrist.

All I could focus on was him inside me. I needed more.

More.

He clamped his bleeding wrist over my mouth, and I swallowed the thick blood without thought, occupied entirely with chasing the hot bliss low in my stomach. Kyros tilted my hips forward so my back arched and slowly slid until his erection hovered at my entrance.

Kyros locked onto my gaze as he slammed all the way home.

My mouth rounded as I catapulted down a narrow tunnel, my being imploding to an impossible, tiny point. His roar echoed around me, *through me*. His blood dripped from my mouth. I rose higher.

Higher.

As the desperate fire of the thrall slammed into me, I came undone.

Undone.

24

I stretched in the bed and was stopped by a blanket cocoon of my own making. "Butterfly."

Kicking, I managed to find a loose edge and throw the prison open. Cool air washed over me, and I sighed, stretching my arms above my head and eliciting a delicious shudder.

I sat bolt upright. "Fuck."

"We did."

Clutching my throat, I blew out an annoyed breath when I spotted Kyros on the round sofa. I inhaled, blinking as his man scent filled my senses. *An earthy musk—patchouli?* The warm aroma was punctuated by citrus, maybe lime.

"Did you just shower?" I asked, inhaling again.

His face was shadowed. "No. Your senses changed with the fourth exchange."

Wait. "Is the thrall over?"

"It is."

What the fuck? I had no memory of it. I searched my mind. *None.* "I blacked out? What happened? Was the sex that good?"

He shifted. "You were unconscious for the first day of our thrall."

Really? "*Was* it the sex then?" For all I knew, it could be.

Kyros's lips crooked. "Safina wondered if your state was due to the huge changes your body was undergoing. Regardless, my siblings thought it best to keep us separated again once you woke." He paused. "You don't remember the rest?"

"Nothing." That freaked me out. *Big time.* What did I divulge?

I inhaled again, and this time screwed my face. "Yuck. What's that smell—"

Half turning, I stared at the wall behind me.

No.

No!

Kyros's amusement speared me, and I clambered off the bed. My head spun and I wobbled before sitting on the edge of the bed.

"The changes to your ears will take the most to get used to," the vampire murmured. "That's where your balance system is contained."

The dizziness died away, and I stood carefully, inching to view what could only be my artwork.

I'd painted the wall behind his bed fucking purple.

Not a soft hue that might have suited the grey and white tones of the room—a garish, primary-school purple. I hadn't stopped there. Two stick figures were holding hands in the middle. There were little stick figures around them. And what could be a dog or cat.

There was a house in the background.

A sun.

Grass.

Flowers.

My cheeks burned. "I'll fix it. I'm so sorry. Your sisters should have stopped me."

Kyros approached me from behind. "No one tells a woman in thrall what to do. As long as she's safe, she is allowed whatever her heart desires."

"My heart currently desires that they'd stopped me."

"They did stop you from cutting your hair."

My jaw dropped as I spun to face him. I kept going sideways, the floor slanted.

Kyros gripped my arms, steadying me.

I didn't wait for the dizziness to fade. "No way. Why was I doing that?"

"You'd just announced you were vegan."

What— "You're kidding."

But he wasn't.

Groaning, I let my head drop into my hands. Maybe I'd curl into a ball and die. "I can't remember anything."

Kyros forced my hands down. "You did my sister's hair and make-up. Tried your best to start a charity. Safina was able to stop you from depositing over a billion dollars in the venture. She hid your phone after that. Which was a shame because I was enjoying the naked pictures."

Heat flooded my face. I placed a hand on his chest. "Enough. No more."

A lump rose up through my throat as I glanced down and saw I was dressed in one of his suits. The air-force blue one that Deirdre chucked out. Clearly she had the incentive to find it during the last three days.

"You're upset," Kyros said, sounding mystified.

I ignored that statement. "I don't suppose any of my clothes are here?"

"Your Vissimo brought some. You put them in my bottom drawer." His eyes tracked my careful movements across the room.

Of course I fucking did.

I moved right on in and detailed my plans for a house, family, and miscellaneous animal in a painting on the fucking wall.

Yanking open the bottom drawer and ignoring Kyros's rampant bafflement, I pulled out black leggings and a loose off-the-shoulder long tee.

I wobbled to the bathroom like Bambi on skates. My toiletries were in the shower.

I love you, Laurel.

Turning the water to scalding, I grimaced at the thundering pour of the water as it hit the graphite. Reaching in, I pushed down the handle until the streaming water was halved, and my ears could handle the volume.

Shit. I really, really hoped that I didn't blab anything to his sisters. If they knew something about my grandmother's work, they would have already told their eldest brother though. I couldn't sense anything but confusion and lingering amusement from his emotions. Not a trace of the oily throbbing associated with concealment lurked within him.

Relaxing somewhat, I shucked Kyros's suit, draping it over a towel rack before inching my way under the jets. I yelped at the boiling contact, leaping back.

The floor slanted again and I fell heavily on my ass.

"Ouch," I wheezed as the door crashed open.

Pulling my knees into my chest, I held my sopping hair away as I glared up at him.

"Why are you glaring at me?" he asked. "I didn't make you fall."

The vampire was playing with fire.

Crouching just outside the shower, he made no effort to touch me. *Clever man.*

"You weren't kidding about the off-balance thing," I grumbled, a definite bite in my voice.

Adoration. Amusement.

"Don't laugh at me." It might have sounded ferocious if my voice hadn't caught.

"Let me help you," he said softly, inching closer.

I hiccupped. "I'm n-not a monkey."

The thrall was over, right?

Why did I feel so out of sorts?

"The sensitivity of your skin is heightened. Most vampires take cold showers. I didn't think to warn you. This is new to me as well. I apologise."

I stared at him. "I like hot showers though."

Fully suited up, Kyros entered the shower and grabbed my body wash. I eyed him warily, knees still hugged to my chest.

He grabbed my arm and lathered the lemon myrtle blend onto

my arms. I tensed at the current bouncing between us everywhere he touched. *That's new.* The current was a step up from the itch of the third exchange. Not unpleasant. Warm. Almost vibrating. Focusing on anything else when he touched me was difficult.

Shaking my head in a failed attempt to shake my brains back into gear, I fixed my gaze on him. The vampire ignored me, foaming the wash and working up over my shoulders.

"In our culture," Kyros started in a quiet voice, "the actions of females and males in thrall is not an embarrassment. It is looked upon with great fondness by Vissimo—more so because it is rare for two people to enter such an agreement in this age."

My body rocked in rhythm to his ministrations and the deep melody of his words. His voice had levels I hadn't noticed before, a velvety layer over the gravel that soothed and reassured.

My chest tightened. Kyros's voice was *beautiful*. The vibrating current between us made me squirm and tense, but the timbre of his voice eased and relaxed.

He continued. "The thrall takes a male to his base animalistic nature. It takes a woman to the root of her character. Why are you embarrassed for my sisters to see that you are caring, assertive, and inventive?"

I didn't answer immediately. "That's not what it looks like to me. Those were the actions of someone who decided to dabble in ecstasy followed by cocaine."

The conversation was becoming too personal. My scars were as rampant as the next person. Talking about the dislike I held for myself in moments like this wasn't high on my to-do list.

I felt his intense focus.

"You have a glorious heart," Kyros said, water dripping from strands of his toffee hair, "sharp intelligence, courage, and a husky laugh that echoes in my dreams. Your body drives me to insanity."

The thing about feeling his emotions? I knew that he meant every word.

I fidgeted, not liking the new territory he was pushing us into. "What happened after we had sex?"

Sex didn't seem an adequate term to describe the heights he'd taken me to.

"That wasn't sex," Kyros said, a growl beneath his voice. "That was perfection."

Glad to know I met Vissimo standards. Seriously. I was nowhere near as strong or fast. Who knew what those women could do?

"Thank you..." I trailed off awkwardly and instead sent him my emotions of awe and remembered pleasure.

He dropped a kiss on my forehead. "We broke the office. Again."

"I didn't break it first time," I murmured.

"Your phone call with the human triggered it."

Ricky Pikar had been demoted to *the human*. "What kind of damage are we talking?"

"The table, inner and outer walls."

I stopped his hands. "*The outer wall*?"

The wall protecting us from thin air and a sixty-six-storey high tumble to death? I remembered a cracking sound and moving to the carpet.

Fuck.

Kyros frowned. "Outer walls are inconvenient to fix."

Me and my petty human death concerns. "Your siblings interrupted us, right?"

His throat worked. "Uh, yes."

I didn't want to know. "They separated us?"

I felt his affirmation.

Why was I worried about his *siblings*? Gasping, I rose to my knees, gripping his shoulders. "Your father."

The warm water washed away the suds and he circled my hips, hands settling half on my back, half on my ass. "I've spoken to my father."

"And?"

"I was able to convince him of the wisdom of the fourth exchange."

"He was okay with it?" I wasn't buying that.

His hands slipped lower and the current between us radiated outward from my belly. My toes curled.

Kyros eyed my closest nipple like a cat eyeing a mouse. “Not even close. He particularly disliked the part where I intended to call for permission but forgot because of the calling of my *phallus*.”

Phallus. Gross.

I had a feeling that was the least offensive thing King Julius said. “You’re downplaying things. A lot.”

A quick study of his emotions confirmed it.

“Tell me straight, are things okay? I don’t want any nasty surprises. He was pretty deathly adamant that the fourth exchange wasn’t happening.”

“There’s always room for negotiation, vixen. Last time he was angry at me, so I had to wait before showing my hand,” Kyros said. “He was calmer at the dinner last weekend, and I decided to make my move. However, though he agreed to the fourth exchange for security reasons, he does not anticipate further exchanges will occur.”

Right. Damn. “That’s a relief.”

Water pounded down on us, and my chest began to rise and fall as Kyros’s hands roamed. How was it possible that I wanted him more? I’d known this feeling was coming, but how did the want keep expanding? When he touched me, I felt so settled. Instantly calm. And then my body just wanted to fit itself around him—on him—and never leave. It was beginning to feel like—

“Possessiveness,” I whispered.

My nipple still held Kyros hypnotised. “Hmm?” he murmured.

The fourth exchange hadn’t been anywhere near the mercurial impersonal swap I’d imagined when forming my plan to secure the Indebted. I had feelings for Kyros that I suspected were no longer mindless infatuation.

Yet I’d known my feelings—natural or not—were going to deepen as a result of the exchanges. So which were they? Natural or unnatural?

“Never mind,” I whispered.

“Okay,” he answered.

Kyros wasn't home right now.

I pushed away. "What's the time?"

"Four in the morning."

Fuck. My sleep pattern was messed up these days. I felt wide awake. "I need to go."

Recalling my messed-up balance, I stood with the help of the graphite wall. "I'll pay for the wall to be repainted."

"I'm keeping it."

I set my jaw. "It's going."

Kyros growled.

"I mean it," I snapped back, backing out of the shower slowly so I didn't fall on my ass again.

He didn't answer. "I'll give you privacy to dress."

Yeah, I saw right through that answer. The painting was *going*. He'd lose that battle, guaranteed.

Towelling dry was excruciatingly slow—as was dressing. I managed without being rendered to helpless maiden a second time.

"How long until I get used to this again?" I asked, blinking several times to adjust my vision upon entering the main room.

"Anywhere from a few days to two weeks. When Vissimo exchange blood, their senses heighten, but they're more used to exerting control, so I believe your adjustment will be closer to two weeks."

Huh. "Did your senses change?"

"A little. You're human, so the effect of your blood on my power level wasn't as dramatic."

He'd felt a tiny blip of difference, I took that to mean. I felt kind of bad that the big bad alpha was pairing with a comparative weakling.

He stared out the windows. "You should consider staying here so I can show you how to handle the influx."

I wanted to go home to remember who I was in isolation from Kyros. Because right now we were so tangled, I couldn't tell where I started and ended. "Will the influx be bad?"

"This room is soundproof. I'm speaking very softly right now."

He was? I thought back to how loud the shower was. "That's a yes then." *Dammit.*

"You're still leaving?"

I nodded.

Jaw clenching, Kyros sighed. "Then come here."

I teetered over.

"Look outside. As far as you can see." He steadied me in a cage of his arms, his voice centering me.

Doing as bade, I gasped as dizziness slapped without warning. His arms tightened around me.

"What can you see?"

See? What about feel?

His voice. The current between us. His scent. His heat.

Focus, Basi.

The dizziness receded somewhat. What could I see? Shit, I could see the theme park. Not just the Ferris wheel. I could make out the blurred outlines of the people *on* the Ferris wheel.

Freak out time!

I wasn't entirely human anymore.

How had I accepted this with cool calm before?

"Hush," Kyros rumbled. "You're not in danger, true mate. You are the same. Just a different model."

My body trembled in his arms. "Do *not* compare me to a fucking car."

His chuckle rolled through me.

"I think I'm really overwhelmed, Kyros." My voice was thick and the urge to cry fell upon me like a heavy blanket. *Really* overwhelmed.

"Then here's how you will sort through each sense," he said, his lips next to my ear. "Look as far as you can, my beauty."

Latching onto his voice, I obeyed, staring at the blurring forms on the Ferris wheel again.

"Draw your vision back. Just a little. Say, to the freeway."

I adjusted and found myself staring instead at the houses in

Green. Frowning, I tried to find the middle and ended up back at the theme park.

Pressing my nose to the glass, I shifted my gaze backward by a whisker. "Ha! Got you, fucker." I watched the cars zip over the freeway.

His pride swirled through me. *Adoration. Humour*. "Now to Blue."

I managed after three tries. It was somewhere between short and long vision.

"Grey," Kyros whispered.

Following his prompts, I tried with varying success to move my eyes. It was as though I was driving a car with touchy brakes compared to a car where I had to shove the pedal in all the way.

Blinking to return my gaze to the room, I carefully turned in his arms.

"Thank you," I told him, tipping my head back. "I should do that with each sense?"

Kyros's pride made me uncomfortable. Like he was a doting parent.

"Yes," he said, smoothing the grin from his face. "Hearing will be hardest because it's also your balance. You'll need to practice locating where sounds are coming from and how far away they are. You must learn how to block out noise so you're not overwhelmed constantly. This is something all Vissimo have to go through. That's why we tend to raise our young in isolation—like Safina."

Phew. I was nowhere near ready for this. "I guess our driving lessons are on hold for a while."

He placed a finger under my chin. "Yes. But they will happen."

A tiny bit of normalcy.

Right now, it was nowhere near enough to latch onto.

25

He wasn't kidding about the overwhelming part.

I'd taken the last three days off work, barely able to manage my own agenda and estate with my exhaustion from trying to isolate and sort through *everything*.

For a segment of each waking hour, I forced myself to practice honing my new senses. Turned out there were a lot of waking hours when you could hear really fucking well. I'd taken to sneaking down to the noise-cancelling office to sleep on the chaise.

Touch and vision exercises done for the hour, I closed my eyes and tuned into my ears.

I could hear just past the edges of my property to the front, left, and right. My hearing pattered out about one hundred metres from the back of the estate. I'd had Kelsea walk out and stop every twenty-five metres to test it.

Focusing, I stretched my hearing as far as possible. Recognising a passing car was easy. Muted thuds—*hmm*, Indebted around the perimeter? I drew my hearing in and picked out Georgia and her team of gardeners spread through the lavender tiers and hedge-way. *Splash*. Pool. Squeals and shouts. Seven or eight vampires in the pool.

I listened a while longer and then checked the pool houses. I backed the fuck away at a rhythmic grunting. My head chef was apparently partial to an afternoon delight. With Rosie—that sly ol' thing.

Drawing in again, I studied the area immediately surrounding the main house. Pretty quiet. A maid was cleaning windows in the west wing. I shuddered at the squeaking of cloth on glass. Daniel typed frantically in the security room. Fred was whistling.

Three people in the kitchen.

Oh my god, who was watching *Truth Ranges?* I was nowhere near up to date! Spoiler alert!

I latched onto Tommy's voice in my suite upstairs.

"Tonight?" she said breathlessly. "I thought we weren't leaving until morning. Where are you taking me?"

A man answered, and I strained to hear—eavesdropping without shame. I was yet to figure out some way to alert Tommy to the changes in me. She'd been absent every other night and exhausted on the nights she stayed in.

I wasn't so jealous now that I'd gotten *some*. Though sex with Kyros hadn't solved my problems one bit. I'd sampled the goods and couldn't stop thinking about taking a bigger bite.

"Well, what should I wear, handsome?" Tommy pressed. "Or is this an activity that doesn't require clothing?"

That's my girl.

I backed out before she said anything more. Phone sex was only fun if I was involved. Though tuning *out* sounds was much harder. I could focus on another sound to block out another noise but blocking out *everything* was nearly impossible.

After the first day spent trying to block out one sound by focusing on another, I'd tried visualization—first, squishing the sound to nothing, then by placing an imaginary glass over the sound. In the end, stuffing my ears with figurative cotton worked the best. I'd shoved in more and more cotton until only whispers in the bordering rooms remained. The problem being it took me twenty minutes to achieve and I needed total focus.

Today, I'd try something harder.

I focused until my ears were adequately *stuffed*. Holding on to the muting feeling in my ear tube things, I opened my eyes a crack. The sounds around me flared to life again, and I paused to stuff in more cotton until I regained control. I opened my eyes wider, repeating the process until they were totally open.

I fixed my gaze on Tom Hanks's autobiography, my mind entirely on my ears. I stood and walked around the room until my head began to hurt from the concentration of managing two senses at once.

Phew. That wasn't comfortable at all.

Fatigue rocked me, and I sat again. Morning practices were the easiest. Pretty sure I'd fainted last night while practicing.

Time for smell.

This was the easiest. Maybe I didn't use my nose very much or maybe it was that smell was the weakest sense—it only extended a couple of rooms at the most. I wasn't constantly assaulted with information as with my eyes and ears. Touch, I could control by avoiding contact—and by turning down the water temperature in the shower. The worst thing with my heightened skin sensitivity was clothing. At the beginning of the day, I could don tight clothes, but inevitably by lunch, I'd switch into something flowing and loose.

Nakedness would be preferable.

Settling in, I catalogued the smells around me, picking up Fred's spicy cologne, the maid's window cleaner, my body wash and hair products, and Grandmother's lavender.

Adding another sense, I sniffed while shifting my gaze around the room.

Whoa, dizzy, dizzy.

That was enough for now. I crossed the room and switched on the noise-cancelling, sighing as my ears popped and normalcy returned. Throwing myself on the chaise, I slipped out my phone. My *Live Right* shifts only took up about five hours each weekday, but I had some serious downtime without them. The Le Spyre teams were so efficient, I literally listened to their reports and redirected them as needed, researching when I didn't understand something.

I had a whole three messages. "Miss popular."

My heart raced as I saw one belonged to Kyros. We hadn't spoken since he, well, washed me and gave me a baby Vissimo lesson. I'd made myself look like a fool being a wuss over all the thrall stuff.

Dammit, I didn't like that Kyros saw me acting all insecure and vulnerable.

Practicing?

His question was accompanied by a GIF of Magneto, arms out either side of him and metal flying everywhere.

A laugh burst from me. *What?* He knew how to send GIFs? And I couldn't believe he'd watched *X-Men* but not the television phenomena known as *Truth Ranges*. Though I seemed to recall him mentioning one of his sisters liked the movies.

Humour filtered through our bond, and a small smile graced my face. Was he amused because I'd laughed? He couldn't possibly know that it was at his joke.

Perhaps I'd tell him.

Using a heart emoji was okay, right? I used them all the time. It didn't mean anything.

Get a grip!

I clicked Send and tossed the phone aside.

Tommy burst into the room. "I'm going on a secret date tonight."

I feigned surprise as I rapidly tried to stuff cotton in my ears. "I thought you were heading to Furnley Gorge tomorrow?"

"We are. But he said he couldn't wait to see me."

Uhm, cute. "What kind of secret date? Like *fun* secret or *I'm going to propose* secret?

"It's only been two months," she said, rolling her eyes.

My jaw dropped and I abandoned my efforts. "Oh my god. You're totally hoping he asks you."

"I'm not. I'm twenty-one."

"Are."

"Basi."

"*Tom.*"

She plonked down next to me. "Don't be silly."

I nudged her with my foot. "If he did ask?"

Her eyes widened, and my heart squeezed—not in a good way. I hadn't even met this guy yet. No photos or details. I had to put him through the best friend grinder and make him nervous to the extreme. I had to threaten him with a show of power and money and ask what TV shows he liked.

"It'd be a maybe," she said. "As in, let's reassess in a year. He wants to take things slow, too, so I guarantee you it's nothing like that."

Better not be. "Any guesses then? What are you wearing?"

We settled into a gossip session, and I kept half my mind on curbing my powers in her company. I was already so relaxed with Tommy—in that I could look as strange as needed—that I succeeded in toning her voice down to levels that wouldn't deafen me by age twenty-two.

"Hey, Tom?" I asked, yawning. My watch beeped, and I groaned.

Practice time.

"Basil?"

I smiled at her flushed face. "Can you take a picture of you and the man? And maybe call me while you're with him one time so our voices can meet."

She snorted. "That's gross."

"So our voices can meet."

"Stop it."

I hollered the words after her as she all-but floated from the room in her happy bubble. It made my heart lighter to see her so in love.

My phone vibrated—because allowing it to ring was no longer an option. The sound was like nails on a chalkboard.

Huh, what did he want?

"Neelan," I answered.

"Basilia. Are you coming to work tonight?"

I contemplated that. "Not sure I can handle that many people yet. Should be okay by Monday though."

Their whispers were 100 percent audible to me now.

"—we'll have to ask her now then—"

"—it's too easy for her to say no—"

"—I can't wait until she sees the pictures of her all over the walls—"

My brows climbed. I wouldn't be revealing *this* advantage anytime soon. Kyros's siblings gave me the shits even if I also liked most of them now.

Neelan cleared his throat. "What are you doing this weekend?"

"Not coming to Kyros's new house to hang with your family," I said, hanging up.

Snickering, I flipped my phone in my hand, grinning at the ceiling. Kyros's amusement flared again. What was he so happy about?

A knock sounded at the door, the booms battering my brain.

I sat up in case it was someone I had to scare. "Come in."

Mrs Gaughton poked her head in.

"Mrs Hannah! Have a seat, please."

The mid-sixties woman shuffled in, glancing around with wide eyes.

"Have you settled in okay?" I'd placed her on the first level right at the back of the west wing. I'd moved the Vissimo out, letting Laurel, Josie, and Kelsea share my grandmother's suite after making it clear that harem activities wouldn't occur outside of the room.

I'd have to pack up Grandmother's stuff soon to make more room for them. Not something I looked forward to.

The older woman sat, perching stiffly. "Yes, dear. I'm just wondering how on earth I ended up here. It's so fucking fancy."

I relaxed, glad she wasn't going to be one of the weird ones.

"Basilia Le Spyre pulled my weeds and watered my garden." She cackled. "Wait until I tell my bingo friends."

"Let me know what they say." I lay down again, crossing my feet.

"The gardens are beautiful. Makes me ashamed of my old one."

"You're welcome to get in the garden, too, if you like," I told her. "If you want your own patch, just talk to Georgia, the head gardener. She'll set you up."

"I do want to make myself useful somehow," she said darkly. "You're sure you won't take any money?"

I shrugged a shoulder. "Don't need it."

"Why do you work then?"

Pondering my answer, I replied, "Regular penis and world domination."

"Better reasons than most, I suppose. Got a picture?"

Twisting, I fixed her with a look.

"Of the *man*, Basilia. What do you take me for?"

She didn't fool me for a second.

Opening my phone, I clicked on the picture of Kyros and his family—having deleted all my naked thrall pictures—and held it over my head for her to look at. "He's the one in the middle."

"You sure you ain't got a penis picture?" she whispered.

Snorting, I yanked the phone back.

Mrs Hannah hummed. "He the one that messed with you?"

"Yeah. He pretended he didn't know who I was, then I found out he was interested in my money."

God, that felt good to say to someone other than Tommy.

She swore long and hard, then added, "Still. Great body."

Tipping back my head, I laughed. "*Excellent* body."

"Back to me being useful," she said abruptly. "I've been hiding in a closet for five years and I need to catch up on life. I want a challenge. Maybe some new friends. My bingo crowd is too wild. I want to find a quieter circle."

I considered her.

This was the perfect entry point for what I had in mind for her. It would require a bending of the truth with how my operations worked, but if I was right about the remaining properties in Bluff City, Mrs Gaughton would boost my acquisition rate *big time*.

"You know who you should talk to, Mrs Hannah? My friend, Tommy."

"The pretty brunette who's disgustingly in love?"

"That's the one. She set me up when I was looking for work.

Maybe she could help you find something interesting. I only have one friend, so I'm not the best person to talk to."

Mrs Hannah stood, touching my shoulder. "We both know that's a lie. You must have forty friends or more here at the moment. The sexiest friends I've ever seen."

"Yeah, I met them through Live Right. They're here for security, but I'm also helping them out of a jam."

The older woman smiled. "Yes, I guessed. You're good at that."

I watched her leave, happiness thrumming through me. Her house belonged to me now, but things weren't just business when it came to Mrs Gaughton. I wanted her to be content because she'd looked after me when it felt no one else was.

I owed her.

My phone vibrated again. Fishing for it to delay the inevitable honing practice, I smirked at the missed calls from Neelan. And Safina. And texts from six other fanged pains in my ass.

You're coming whether you like it or not.

Kyros would really love if you were there :) :)

There's something you need to see at his house before I leak it to the paparazzi.

The more times you say no, the worse it will get.

Don't come

Deirdre's was the best.

Do you constantly say no because you crave attention?

"I'm falling in love with her," I announced to the room. Because that's what I did on Friday nights now—spoke to empty rooms.

Kyros had texted again.

Was this a thing now? Was he sliding into my messages like we were something? Was he my blood friend? Were we fang buddies?

Actually, there *was* a term for what we were. I just refused to acknowledge the phrase *true mate.*

I lowered my voice. “True mate.”

Yuck.

Not happening.

I skipped Kyros’s message and bolted upright at the last text.

Gina.

I hadn’t messaged her back after receiving proof of the triplets’ murder.

What did she want? It wasn’t near midnight, so it couldn’t be too dire.

I opened the message.

My brothers are up to something. Watch yourself.

Whoa, she was my warning system now? I’d be a fool to disregard the message. Just as I’d be a fool to disregard she could be part of said trouble. Hesitating, I slowly stood to switch on the noise-cancelling again.

Taking a deep breath, I called her.

The ringing cut off immediately, but a text came through a second later.

Give me a minute

Listening ears? I paced the room.

My phone vibrated and I exhaled before answering, “Gina.”

“What is it?’

“Interesting message.”

She was silent. “Like most people who enjoy killing and inflicting pain, my brothers have behaviours they exhibit before striking. You’re their only target right now. They’re showing those tells. You need to be very careful.”

Fear landed heavy in my gut. *Fuck.* "Why can't they just handle your brother's death like the rest of you? I didn't mean to kill your brother even if he was attacking me. If I could take it back, I would."

Gina didn't answer straight away. "Thank you for saying that. My youngest brother was too decent for this life. But I wouldn't say my other siblings are content doing nothing. What they are is content to let our most vindictive brothers handle you."

Good to know. "What kind of shit are we talking then? Are they killing critters?"

She sighed. "Trenit likes to listen to a particular death metal band before he strikes. For Tynan, he sharpens his blades. Theodore likes to get laid."

My heart stopped. "What did you just say?"

"To get laid."

I sucked in a ragged breath. "*The name.*"

"Theodore."

No.

The floor tilted and my legs crumpled.

"What's wrong?" she demanded.

My heart hammered in my chest. "Does Theodore have a girlfriend?"

Gina snorted. "When doesn't he have someone in his bed."

"A petite brunette?" I whispered.

"I'm uncertain. Fuck. Is she seeing a Theodore?"

Fuck didn't sum up my horror of this moment. "Yes."

"She's part of their plan then," Gina rushed to say. "They're going to lure you out. Do *not* do what they say. If you set foot—"

I hung up, vacant eyes landing on the office door. "Tommy."

I burst to my feet and collected the table with my shin.

Ignoring the pain, I flung open the door. *Tommy.*

Please tell me she hadn't left. *Please.*

Sprinting for the stairs, I took them two at a time. "Tom?"

"Miss Le Spyre?" Fred was at the bottom of the stairs. "I drove Miss Tetley to meet her boyfriend half an hour ago."

My face crumpled and Fred rushed up the stairs to take my arm.

He led me straight back to the office, clicking on the noise-cancelling once more.

I ignored my vibrating phone.

The triplets had Tommy. They had my only fucking friend. My family. The only person I loved in this world.

This couldn't be right. It wasn't happening.

"Miss Le Spyre, is Tommy in danger?" Fred gripped my arms.

A sob left my mouth. I nodded, my hands shaking as I gripped him for dear life.

His expression was grim. "Then I'm afraid you need to snap out of it for her sake, miss."

He was right. She needed me.

By now, boxing up my fear was almost habit. *Tommy is with the Tonyi triplets. I have to get her back. I'm afraid because they're stronger than me. They'll try to separate me from everyone, but terror will get in my way.*

I straightened. "Where did you take her, Fred?"

My phone vibrated again.

"To a restaurant named *Finale* on the waterfront."

Finale. They'd picked a restaurant that fit with the theme of their game. It was the triplets. I should check there first.

I met his gaze. "We need to go there."

The butler bowed. "I recommend calling the restaurant first."

Genius.

He moved to the landline on the desk.

I watched as he dialled.

"Yes, hello," Fred spoke into the headset. "I was wondering if you could do me a favour? My granddaughter is at your restaurant for a birthday dinner with her boyfriend, but we're setting up her surprise party at home. He's meant to message when they're having dessert, but I haven't heard from him. She's petite and has chestnut hair to her chin. She's wearing a sparkling black dress. Is it too much trouble for you to—" He paused. "—thank you."

A black dress? Tommy *never* wore black.

I paced and wrenched to a halt. Five Indebted were tailing

Tommy at all times. Laurel hadn't been in touch, so they can't have sensed anything wrong.

Maybe things weren't beyond control.

"*Sorry, sir. There's no one here by that description. Do you know if they went on our sunset cruise?*"

His face fell.

I closed my eyes, dread curling around my heart. Tommy's guards would be waiting on land.

"They must have," he said smoothly. "I don't suppose you could put a call through to your staff there?"

"*I can try, sir. But they may be out of reception already.*"

When Fred hung up a few minutes later, he didn't need to tell me the verdict.

I covered my face.

"They're after me," I whispered. I could say that much. "Triplets."

Fred crossed the room with a speed belying his age. "If they're after you, then Tommy is bait. If that's the case, they'll want you to go alone."

I'd come to the same conclusion.

"You need people you can trust not to charge in," he said.

Which meant him and the Indebted. Except Kyros would never forgive them for failing to report this. It could mean their deaths.

Fred glanced at my cell phone. "The person on the other end knows something has happened."

I stared at Kyros's name flashing on the screen.

"If he's the charging kind, you need to get rid of him."

Not so easy when he'd literally felt what I'd felt for the last ten minutes, but Fred was right, when it came to me, because of the bond we shared, Kyros would charge.

I couldn't let him in until I knew what was going on. One wrong move could mean Tommy's life.

The call ended.

Should I call Gina back to work with her?

No, I couldn't risk that if she was on their side. Without information of any kind, I'd have no idea how to interpret her answers.

I whirled, stumbling slightly before recovering my balance.

Where would the triplets have taken Tommy? There wasn't any alarm from the Indebted, so they must still be waiting for the cruise to come back in.

"Think, Basi." I tapped my forehead.

Fuck it, maybe I'd have to let Laurel into my confidence. Out of everyone I knew, I trusted her nearly as much as Fred. I didn't want to endanger her, but to save Tommy, I was capable of almost anything, including shitting on other friendships.

My phone rang again. *Private number.*

The timing was too coincidental. It was them.

Fear filled me, but somewhere, I managed to locate a sliver of resolve. Channelling Agatha Le Spyre, I snapped my back straight.

Lifting the phone to my ear, I answered, "This is a private number. Do not call again."

And hung up.

Fred watched on in grim-faced silence.

The phone rang again a bare second later, and I held a finger against my lips, warning the butler to stay quiet.

Accepting the call, I opened my mouth for a second round. A voice that chilled me to my core cut in.

"I'd suggest you stay on the line, Basilia Le Spyre. Or should I say Basil?"

"Who the fuck is this?" I demanded.

Laughter echoed down the line. "Don't act coy. My brothers heard you running up the stairs shouting for your little friend ten minutes ago. And I heard the waitress answering questions about a petite brunette in a black dress back on shore. *Smart.* We expected you to rush down to the restaurant."

"Is this Theodore?" I asked softly.

He hissed. "So nice to be on first-name basis at last. I feel closer to you already."

I bit back on a sob.

"Would you like to see your friend?" he asked next. "Crap lay, your bestie. One more day with her looking at me with that pathetic expression and I might've slit her throat. Maybe I'll do you a favour and kill her anyway."

My throat worked. "Kill her and you'll never get to me. Stop the shit talk and show her to me. Then get on with whatever psychotic plan you have in place."

Savage growls abruptly cut off.

"Careful, careful," Theodore breathed down the line. "Let's not forget who's in charge. You may have a cunt dipped in gold, but from now on, you're our whore. And because you're a stupid whore, I'm going to spell the rules out clearly for you."

"My Indebted would love to hear what you have to say," I snapped back.

"So many lies, Basil. My brothers are on your property and can't hear this conversation. That soundproof room of yours has come in handy. All Indebted, but the useless five I left on shore, are accounted for."

I remained silent, listening in on the background. They were in an echoing room—maybe like a garage. I couldn't hear Tommy or any sounds of struggle. Was she knocked out?

"Here's what's going to happen. After this call, you'll go outside and inform your chauffeur that Tommy doesn't need to be picked up tonight. Her boyfriend hired the entire boat and she is staying there overnight. Do you understand?"

My mind worked frantically. There had to be some way out of this.

"Last chance before she loses a hand."

I clutched the base of my throat. "I understand."

"Good," he purred. "Now, you will meet us alone. In return, your friend lives. If you bring backup, inform Kyros, or if we're ambushed at *any* time... well, you can guess the rest."

"What's my guarantee she lives? I'm supposed to trust that you'll let her go? I'm not stupid."

"Oh, but you are. Didn't you hear me? You're a stupid whore. Tell me what a stupid whore you are or I'll carve my name in your friend's pretty face."

My chest seized, and the words flowed from my mouth. "I'm a stupid whore."

Fred jerked beside me as though slapped.

Theodore's laughter rang in my ears, and I just couldn't give a fuck what he forced me to say. If they hurt Tommy, I wouldn't make it in this life. That realisation made what might happen next almost insignificant.

The thought calmed me more than anything else had so far.

"Good girl. Want a look at her as a reward?" His cold laughter faded away as he turned the video on.

Pulling the phone away from my ear, I scanned the concrete room on the screen. A garage. I was right. At least five cars. Not a tower—too small. Private house, perhaps?

"Hey, Tommy?" Theodore sang, his voice echoing through the room now. "Say hello to your rich friend?"

They hadn't bothered to tie her up. She'd thrown up at some point and lay in her vomit. In response to his question, she mumbled, a small frown between her brows.

"What did you do to her?" I said, fury shaking my voice.

"Whores don't ask questions," Theodore replied. "But I'll answer this once. I know how stupid you are. We gave her a little mix of a few pills we had lying around. Doesn't look like she's reacted too well."

A smirk that chilled me to my core spread across his face. He couldn't see me or Fred, but I had to doublecheck because his almond-shaped hazel eyes seemed to bore into my own.

"Listen very closely," he said, eyes gleaming with a twisted fever. "Because we don't hand out second chances. You'll meet us out the front of your property in thirty minutes. If Kyros is there, your friend will die. And it won't be clean."

I couldn't fuck this up. Kyros couldn't be part of this. Or anyone, barring Fred.

"That won't work," I told him. "I'm surrounded by Indebted, and

Kyros can feel what I'm feeling. He could already be on the phone to them as we speak. They won't let me out of this house."

The smirk in his voice was evident. "Not our problem. If you aren't there, don't expect to see your friend again."

If they could get to me, they would have by now. Instead, they were relying on me to get out. My Indebted's defence was too good.

And now it was a near-impossible obstacle for me.

I closed my eyes, struggling to keep it together for Tommy. "What happens when I get to the front gate?"

The call disconnected.

I stared at Fred in mute horror.

"Did you get that?" I whispered.

His lips pressed together. "Enough. We don't have much time before the rendezvous."

Kyros's name appeared on the screen again. If he was frantic, I was unable to focus enough to feel it through my own frenzy.

"He'll come over," I said softly. *Or could already be on his way.*

That couldn't happen.

I glanced up at the butler. "You need to tell Rosie not to wait up. Tommy just called and said she won't be home tonight. She's staying overnight on the cruise with her boyfriend."

Fred nodded, his gaze dropping to my phone. "I'll do so immediately. Remember to switch the noise-cancelling back on."

I did as bade when he left, thinking rapidly as I answered the phone.

"What do you want?" I snapped. "Jesus, Kyros. I'm busy."

Silence.

"Busy doing what?" The menace in his voice shook me.

I steeled myself. "Catching up on *Truth Ranges.* So if you don't mind—"

He snarled. "You're lying. Something just happened. You're terrified. Panicked. I'm coming over."

I let real anger fill me, all of it aimed at the Tonyi triplets. "Don't you dare."

"Non-negotiable," he said coolly, his voice echoing.

"Like all our interactions then," I seethed. "You want to know why I'm terrified? Because three fucking psychos are after me. I have Vissimo all over my fucking property. And I made the worst decision of my life."

I gripped my hair, pacing.

"What decision are you talking about?" he said in a low voice.

I sobbed, thinking of Tommy. What the fuck were they doing to her? "I'm not human anymore, Kyros." My breath was harsh. "*I'm not human anymore.*"

"Basilia—"

Would they kill her? How would I know she was alive. *Oh fuck.* I couldn't breathe. "I thought I could handle it," I whispered. "I thought a few days would clear up my doubts, but it all just hit me. I don't want to be a fucking monster like—"

"Like who?" Kyros said tersely.

His voice was echoing. Was he in the tower garage?

Shit.

Metal crunched on his end. Probably an innocent car. "Like *who*, Basilia?"

I swallowed, focusing on the moment I first heard Theodore's name from Gina's lips. I focused on the triplets and the disgust I felt for them. My utter loathing and abhorrence.

"Like you," I forced out. "I'm finally doing something about it."

A tinge of desperation wove through his fury, but otherwise, he wasn't swallowing enough of my academy award performance.

Time to switch tactics.

Gritting my teeth, I said, "I won't be returning to the tower or to work, Kyros. I'm leaving Bluff City. I won't be back."

That hit him. Hard.

I wouldn't have otherwise known it from his calm tone though.

"You're not leaving this city before I see you and we discuss this matter further," he replied. "I'm in the car and on my way."

I latched on to every speck of black rage—a lot right now—attempting to push aside my mounting panic. "I don't want you in my house. Not after everything you've done."

Hurt. Regret. Suspicion.

"So the sensory changes take more of an adjustment than we thought," he rushed to say. "It will get better. I'll *make it* better, Basilia. If that's all this is about—which I don't believe is the case. Hate me for coming, but I will see you."

I needed to get to the gate. Kyros couldn't be there! He also couldn't ambush the triplets on the way.

Fuck, fuck, fuck.

Maybe telling him was the only option. Yet Tommy's *life* was on the line. I didn't trust anyone with her—not now my grandmother was gone.

I stared at the bookshelf lining the wall, eyes lingering on Tom Hanks's autobiography.

... Maybe I was overcomplicating this.

"I don't want you here. I want space," I whispered, letting my very real hopelessness creep in.

His hurt vibrated through me. "I know, my beauty. And I wish I could give you what you want, but I must give you what you need."

I sighed down the line. "Please then. I mean what I said, I don't want you on the estate. Laurel can bring me to the tower after I shower and change."

He wouldn't take it.

His voice regained its menacing edge. "Is there a reason you don't want me there?"

"Besides the list I've already given you?" I snapped. "Let me rephrase that for you. You're not stepping foot inside my house. If you can't control yourself enough for me to come to the tower, then drive over. I'll meet you outside. If that's what it takes to convince you that I'm leaving this vampire-infested city, then whatever. I won't change my mind."

Kyros was holding onto his control by a thread, but he managed to hold it together. "I'll be there in fifteen minutes."

"Make it thirty. I'm tired and need to shower. So I don't try to kill you." I disconnected, holding fast to my furious and panicked cocktail of emotions. That mask couldn't crack. Regret and sadness couldn't slip through my fingertips.

Not until the triplets had me in their possession.

Ten minutes had passed since Theodore's call.

Twenty minutes remained.

By the time Kyros got here, I'd be long gone.

26

"The master called and told Laurel you'd meet him outside the house," Evie said as I stepped outside into the night.

Four minutes to go.

Her eyes widened at my apparel.

"Do I look like Jessica Alba in *Dark Angel*?" I asked the Indebted, forcing a bright grin.

Dressing head to toe in leather made sense considering I was likely walking to my death. Last time, it turned out pretty handy in keeping my organs inside my body.

She smiled back. "No idea. I've never seen it."

"Today's youth." I tutted.

"I'm fifty-nine."

Of course she was. I started walking down the driveway, crossing my fingers inside the pockets of my leather jacket. "I'm meeting Kyros at the gates."

"Okay," she said pleasantly, falling into step beside me. "How are you going with your new senses?"

I groaned. "Not great. Apparently things will improve over the first few weeks. It seems like a long wait when everything is so off-kilter."

She grimaced in sympathy. "I bet."

The gravel crunched underfoot. I focused on keeping my breathing even, grateful beyond measure that Evie was here instead of Laurel. She'd know something was up immediately.

My hands were slippery on the metal of the front gate when we slipped through a few minutes later.

"Hey, Evie?" I asked in a low voice.

She bowed. "Yes, Basi?"

Guilt panged, and I swallowed it back. Tommy needed medical attention without delay. That was *if* I could keep the triplets from killing her before then. Despite this, I didn't want any of my Indebted friends hurt in the coming minute.

I glanced at her, wrinkling my nose. "Do you mind giving me some space for a few minutes? I've got bad news for Kyros and want to get everything straight in my head before he arrives."

On time, I hoped.

If Kyros arrived early, I was fucking screwed.

"Of course," she replied, concern etched on her beautiful face. "I can't go too far though."

The moment Evie put a few metres between us, a body slammed into me.

Snarls and shouts erupted, but they were lost to the whoosh of wind and blur of trees in the warped mess of my new senses. I fought against dizziness, staring up into one of the triplet's face.

He didn't sneer down at me, entirely focused on putting distance between us and the estate.

Knowing Kyros was fast on our heels, I couldn't blame him.

"How far away is he?" the triplet spat.

I breathed through nausea. "Ten minutes. He'll be running now. Don't count on more than a few minutes."

"If he catches up, you know what happens" was the cold reply.

A blurred glimpse of a huge house told me that we were on the estate opposite mine—the Gregorians'.

A car waited on the far side of the property.

I stared at it, blood pounding in my ears, my body otherwise numb.

This is it.

"Get in and shut up," the triplet hissed as he shoved me in the back seat.

"Stop talking and drive," I hurled back, glaring at him.

The back of his hand met my face with a sickening thud of flesh. I crashed against the seat, landing behind the driver's seat.

The door closed.

With a screech of tires, we were moving.

I blinked through the pain, testing the movement in my jaw. My senses were more sensitive now, and I would have expected pain to have heightened. The sensations on the skin surrounding my throbbing cheek were stronger though, overriding the pain somewhat.

"Which triplet are you?" I asked the vampire as I pulled myself up onto the seat.

His lips twisted in a smirk. "I'll give you one guess."

Theodore. Hatred filled me as I stared at him in the rear-view mirror. "There are a few things you should know if you want this plan to work."

His fangs lowered and his fingers curled around the wheel. "Is that so?"

I didn't waste time. Tommy's life was riding on this. "Kyros can feel where I am at all times."

From Gina's cut-off sentence, I'd pieced together our destination. "I know you think that Kyros won't enter your private territory, but—"

Theodore's hazel eyes glinted. "He won't interrupt us. Not for you. I guarantee it."

Hesitating, I relented to curiosity. "Why is that?"

He barked a laugh. "You think he'd forfeit *Ingenium* for you? His family will die."

Oh, shit.

I'd known the penalty would be steep. Not *that* steep.

Even then, Kyros would come. I knew that categorically. Our bond would drive him past the point of control.

"He will," I replied on a breath. "I can feel his emotions, and he isn't in control right now. You don't have to believe me, but if you want this plan to work, you should consider the risk he'll do the unexpected. I can prevent him entering your territory with a single call, but I need to make that call immediately."

I expected more laughter, but really, out of the two of us, the vampire probably had a far better understanding of who he was messing with.

He ripped the wheel to the right, and I scrambled for purchase as the car skidded onto an on-ramp. "Who?"

"His siblings." They could stop him. If they could get there in time.

"Do it then," he snarled.

It gave me perverse satisfaction that Theodore was so scared of Kyros. With the solid black rage currently filling the vampire, he should be deathly afraid.

I dialled Safina without delay, not needing the triplet's warning look to remind me what hung in the balance.

"Basilia," she said in her usual clipped voice.

She didn't know yet.

"Safina, listen. The triplets took Tommy hostage. I'm with them now and on the way to their private territory. Kyros is coming after me and he's out of control. He will enter their territory. You know what that means. I need you to gather everyone and stop him."

Credit to her, she took three seconds to process that. "Which of their private territories?"

Theodore rattled off an address at vampire speed, and my new hearing managed to catch that it was in Red—as far from the tower as possible.

Cowards.

"You all need to get there before he does," I told her. *And I'm sorry.*

"We will" was the reply before she disconnected the call.

I put down my phone, surreptitiously making sure the GPS tracker app Fred insisted upon was still open.

"Well done, Basil," Theodore purred, not slowing our murderous speed.

"You said Tommy would be freed if I came." I crossed my arms.

"I said we wouldn't kill her."

"That's a shame," I said. "Because I just texted the address of your territory in Red to one of my staff. Before I left, I instructed her to call the media and law enforcement if she didn't hear from me in thirty minutes. Your territory will be crawling with humans if Tommy isn't alive and receiving medical care at a human hospital in the next twenty minutes." Hopefully changing Fred to a woman protected him somewhat if this went pear-shaped.

Theodore smirked. "That's a good try. For a stupid whore."

I stilled as our gazes met in the rear-view mirror. My heart stalled at the unhinged light in his hazel eyes.

He licked his lips. "Do you have any idea what my brothers and I can do to you and your little friend in thirty minutes?"

"Tommy!" I gasped.

Theodore let me go.

I staggered through the heavy iron doors to where she lay in a heap, black dress barely covering her ass.

"Oh my god, Tom," I whispered frantically, dropping to my knees beside her. Her pulse was steady. Maybe slow? I had no idea what was good and not, but she wasn't conscious and her skin was cold.

Ripping off my leather jacket, I rolled her onto the warm fabric to get her off the freezing concrete and placed her on her side. I'd wanted to bring some kind of antidote with me, but Fred said the cures for drug overdoses had to be given intravenously.

"I like her better when she's unconscious," Theodore called, ambling into the room.

I ignored him, gripping her chin. "Come on, girl. It's Basi."

"*Basil*," he corrected.

She wrinkled her brow.

It was enough. I could get her out of this somehow.

I had to.

Spinning in my crouch, I reached out a hand to steady myself. "Our deal stands. Get her to the hospital. I'm here. She goes."

Bravado was worth a try.

A second voice carried from behind Theodore. "*Our deal, brother?*"

"*Or a bluff?*" a third voice added.

The remaining triplets slipped out of the shadows like the fucking eels they were.

I looked around.

This wasn't where Theodore called from.

Though there weren't stairs leading up to a throne, the long concrete room was just like King Julius's chamber. His gave the impression of an ancient trial chamber in Egypt. *This* one gave the feel that a train could run overhead at any moment. As though blood was hosed off the concretes into drains each morning.

The ceilings were high and dripping, and the lights weak and dim. There was a wide stage along the opposite wall. Another set of heavy iron doors sat there.

Two exits.

We'd walked through a garage, multiple halls and levels to get down here. My chances of getting Tommy out by escaping somehow were nil.

I've fucked us both.

There was no Plan B. There wasn't enough time to make one after figuring out they had Tommy. I'd spent all my time ensuring their trap was Kyros-proof.

The triplets regarded me, the tilts of their heads so eerily similar that I couldn't help the shiver working through my body.

Slowly, I stood next to Tommy, inhaling. The dizzy sting of ammonia and sweet decay hit me. Bumps erupted over my arms left bare in my black tank.

"She's scenting us," the one on the left said. A long machete hung from his belt. "The rumours are correct. They've completed the fourth exchange."

Theodore answered, "Yes, brother. Her balance is impaired."

The vampire on the right was dressed in a death metal T-shirt. He grinned. "Her ears must be very sensitive. Tynan, do we still have those metal barrels from last year?"

Tynan wheeled away from the other two, leaving the dingy chamber.

All I heard was barrel.

What were they going to do? My heart sputtered and thumped in turn.

Trenit circled me, machete swinging with each step. "Four exchanges with a *human*. Kyros is no brother of ours."

"Take care," Theodore said, his gaze flashing to the ceiling.

There were others around? I assumed King Mikhail might take issue with Trenit's statement.

"No matter. We will take care of the problem for him," the other continued. "Perhaps he *hopes* we will kill her."

They were trying to get in my head.

Whatever. I hadn't come into this expecting to be saved. I just needed to get Tommy the fuck out of here somehow.

Tynan re-entered the chamber at a run, a large barrel between his arms. I staggered forward as my eyes and ears battled for control. *Shit*, I could make out running vampires. Not that seeing them running would help me if I couldn't stay standing.

He set the barrel down and strong arms circled my body. I kicked out, connecting with flesh.

My head was dragged back via a ruthless grip in my hair. I gasped against the stinging pain, staring into hazel eyes. Theodore forced my head to look at where Tommy lay. The third brother held a knife just below her ribs.

"*No*," I wheezed, stilling.

Theodore ran his nose up my neck. "You struggle, and we cut. Now tell me, what are you again?"

"Stupid whore," I blurted, tears squeezing from my eyes at the pain erupting across my scalp. If he thought the words bothered me, he could think again. I'd call myself that any day to keep Tommy and myself from harm.

His brothers smirked as he dropped me into the rusty barrel.

My throat constricted as they sealed the top and I was left in pitch darkness. A tiny hole was opened and I felt around, shifting to a crouch in the tight confines.

Water poured in through the tiny hole.

Oh my god.

I stared at the water gathering at the bottom. They were going to drown me? Surely not. They hadn't been anywhere near manic enough when Theodore put me in here.

This had to be the warm-up.

I managed to stay quiet until the water climbed to my chest. Panting, I called, "I'm disappointed. I expected a beating at least."

Dying before Tommy was out wasn't an option. My voice echoed in the barrel and I winced, covering my ears.

The water stopped.

Thank fuck.

I strained to hear as the cap was replaced, cutting out all light once more. Why were they so quiet? I lowered my hands.

Bang.

I screamed as the clash of wood on the barrel exploded in my sensitive ears. Their laughter followed, and my hands inched to cover my ears again, my mind and senses in numb shock.

Shell shock.

They began.

Boom!

Boom!

Boom!

The barrel echoed and rang without pause, and my screams joined into one endless cry.

I couldn't fathom anything through the agony.

I had to force away the sound, but I couldn't remember how.

I thrashed in the barrel, breaking from my crouch as I tried to force the lid off. My nails scratched at the inside, and I threw my body against the walls in a bid to push the barrel over.

No more!

I shoved my fingers in my ears and submerged under the water to no effect. Knives were stabbing into my ears over and over. It had to end.

Breaking the surface for air, my vision began to blacken.

So much pain.

"Enough," a voice said.

The lid was removed. I couldn't have lifted a finger to resist as two of the triplets hauled me out. They threw me to the ground and I rolled, drawing my legs underneath me. My hands shook either side of my ears. They felt blistered and raw—a pulpy mess.

"Father," the triplet behind me said.

"Theodore, Gina has informed me that you have Kyros's human embarrassment down here."

Gina was here.

I lowered my hands, raising my head gradually so I didn't pass out.

A hazel gaze, not Gina's, slammed into me and I immediately lowered mine.

Gina stood next to her father, along with five other Vissimo who I assumed were the other royal siblings. I recognised one of the sisters and one of the brothers from the basement.

The king's eyes were heavy on me, and I sagged as his gaze shifted. "Who is the other human?"

"Her best friend, Father," Tynan replied. "It's how we lured her here."

King Mikhail ambled closer. "Why is it that you *lured her here*?"

I glanced at Trenit, catching the flicker in his eyes before he dropped his head in a small bow.

"Because she killed our beloved youngest brother, my king."

Gina's gaze flicked to me and away.

My head hurt like shit, but I couldn't afford to stand here. Gina had brought her father to this chamber. Assuming she was trying to help, I had to figure out how to work his presence to my advantage. The stone-cold truth was that she couldn't and wouldn't protect me against her family.

Whatever hand Gina was playing, it didn't include championing me.

The king was able to keep the triplets in check. I knew that he wanted to win the game.

Think, Basi.

"What is your name?" the king demanded. My body seized, but I was already on the ground.

I craned my head. "Basilia Le Spyre." Like he didn't already know.

"The richest woman in Bluff City, Father," the triplet answered.

Why was the king pretending he knew nothing about me? It was as though he and the triplets were playing some kind of game—the wink-wink-nudge-nudge kind of conversations adults had when kids were in the room.

Theodore stepped forward. "We began collecting information on this human several months ago. The staff lives onsite, making them hard to approach, but we discovered the daughter and heiress of the Le Spyre fortune only had one friend. I took the liberty of getting to know her."

I tensed, rage splicing me.

He'd had *sex* with Tommy. He'd utterly played her and used her body while digging for information on *me*. I felt fucking sick at the thought of her happy face and our conversation the night before.

"There's no online information about Miss Le Spyre," he continued.

Daniel was fucking amazing at his job and he'd been around since my parents died. There weren't pictures or records of me online whatsoever. People knew my name, but I was a mystery to anyone who hadn't met me in person.

"When we had enough information from her human friend, we went to pay her grandmother a visit."

A quick peek told me that news surprised the king not one bit. My jaw clenched. The king already knew *all* of this. Which meant he was playing dumb. He had some kind of deal with the triplets. They did his dirty work, and in turn, they took the rap when it came to light?

Gina exchanged a dark look with another of her siblings.

Yep, I was on to something.

Which meant the king ordered the triplets to kill me. How the fuck was I meant to work around that?

"Unfortunately, the grandmother's old heart couldn't hack our interrogation. If we'd known that, we would have compelled her at the start and saved time," Theodore said, smirking at me.

I'd said I didn't want to kill again.

How wrong I was.

I might not even be above torture.

Trenit took over, hand on his machete. "Agatha Le Spyre told us her granddaughter was away at finishing school, but we knew she'd be back for the funeral of her last relation. We'd get close to her via her friend upon her return."

They were saying this like they hadn't known Basilia Tetley and Basilia Le Spyre were one and the same. There were pictures all over the estate house. Surely they'd seen one of those and connected the dots.

Except that wasn't true. Most of the pictures in Grandmother's room were of me as a child with my parents.

"That was about the time this pathetic human reminded me of her full name," Theodore said, sneering down at Tommy. "*Tetley.* Not only did we know of another Tetley, but her name was *Basilia*. The heiress was under our noses the entire time, already aligned with Clan Sundulus."

They'd approached Tommy before I knew Vissimo existed.

"Enough," the king ordered, his voice battering my damaged ears. "Your underhanded actions reflect poorly on this clan."

I licked my lips.

The king had to maintain a certain image. I wasn't sure exactly what, but clearly he had ties or boundaries that his lapdogs didn't.

The king wanted to win *Ingenium*—to gain possession of Kyros? To protect his family? For pride?

I didn't know. But that may not matter.

He wanted to win the game.

"I have information," I croaked, lifting my head. "About *Ingenium*."

Their focus snapped to me.

Amusement flickered over the king's cold face. "You? The filthy human my eldest son is consorting with. What could you possibly know that I don't?"

Probably not much more than one thing. But it was a big thing.

"If I tell you, and you use it right, the likelihood of you winning increases by two percent," I said.

Everyone stilled, including the three psychos around me.

I pushed to my hands and knees, staggering twice before I managed to waver before him. My hands were covered in blood, and I had no idea where it was from. "My friend will be dropped at the closest hospital without delay."

The king's eyes bore into mine. "You wish to strike a deal, human? What is to stop me from merely *taking* the information?"

He was before me. Though my sight had improved, I barely tracked the blur of him.

I sat heavily on the ground, my legs folding, and he held me captive in his blazing vision.

My body seized.

The king stilled. "What's this?"

"The fourth exchange, Father," Gina murmured. "Only Kyros can compel her now."

Air returned to my lungs as Mikhail muted the flare of his almond-shaped eyes.

Disgust twisted his features. "Julius has no pride in his bloodline. How has he allowed this to go so far? I would have killed her before the second exchange."

No, he would have killed me after taking every cent to my name.

I never thought I'd be glad that Kyros got to me first, but *fuck*, I was.

“I could allow my children to torture the information from you,” Mikhail told me. “I’m not convinced you know anything.”

This was my shot. If the compulsion would let me tell him anything.

I drew my legs beneath me again but stayed kneeling. “You recently entered into a large development deal with Mr Ringly.” Okay, I could say that much.

The king’s face smoothed.

Gotcha.

I lowered my gaze and voice. “All I ask is that my friend is dropped at the hospital without delay. In return, you win *Ingenium* after one hundred and fifty years, your family lives, and you get Kyros.” I covered all the bases and then added, “The filthy human was weak and divulged information. You didn’t even need to torture her. She just blurted it right out. All the easier to work on Kyros afterward when he’s by your side.”

The king’s expression hardened.

I didn’t dare breathe.

“Hector,” he said aside, “take the heap on the floor to the nearest hospital, leave her in the emergency room. Remove any trace of your brothers from her before you do.”

Anger filled me at what his words implied.

“She’ll be left there alive?” I pressed.

The king snarled, and my limbs locked.

“Alive,” Hector said, descending the single step to pick Tommy up. He looked at Trenit, and I wasn’t imagining the dislike in his eyes.

Hopefully that meant he’d keep his word. If this was some kind of trick, I was officially out of ideas.

I watched Tommy disappear, swallowing hard as I said my silent goodbyes to her. She’d wake in hospital minus a boyfriend and a best friend. Fred would be there for her. Maybe Laurel if she could forgive me for tricking them.

“When Hector rings from the hospital showing me she’s there, I’ll talk,” I said, my eyes fluttering closed.

27

"*Wake up*," someone said roughly, jostling me.

The pain in my head cut through my sluggishness.

I was on the ground.

Shit, did I pass out?

Dragging myself to my knees again, I swayed, staring at the phone in front of my face. It was a video of Tommy on a stretcher bed being wheeled into a hospital. She disappeared through a set of double doors.

She's safe. I choked on a sob. *She's safe.*

"I grow impatient," the king said. He lingered a few metres away, the triplets on his left, Gina on his right.

I was about to throw Kyros's family—his entire *clan*—under the bus. Regret filled me. But for Tommy, I'd do it three times over. It occurred to me to renege on the deal, but Hector could surely still hurt Tommy if the king demanded it. And if I told them, maybe there was a way to still make it out of here alive.

But...

I could say words like *blood* and *fang* out of context, but this entire conversation was in the context of me selling Kyros out—the exact thing I was compelled *against* doing.

"I don't know what I can say around the compulsion," I told the king.

His lips pressed together, showing white. His hazel eyes flashed. "You try me, human."

Gina stepped forward. "I believe she tells truth, Father. My elder brother would have ensured she could not share confidential information. He clearly does not trust her."

The king's brow cleared somewhat, and he surveyed me in thinly veiled disgust. "Sundulus compulsions are usually centred around intention. Think of something else as you speak."

If I wasn't in so much pain, my jaw would have dropped to the floor. *That's it?* All this time and I'd just needed to focus my thoughts elsewhere to speak freely?

Closing my eyes, I thought of Tommy in the hospital. "Mr Ringly has a—" I cut off, gurgling.

Fuck. Not as easy as it sounded.

"You have thirty seconds to give me something substantial before I behead you," King Mikael said in bored tones.

My stomach swooped, churning in the wake.

Okay, okay, focus.

Maybe thinking of Tommy was too *close* to the current situation. Mr Ringly had a drug addiction—just like Licky Lips who I met in the alley so long ago.

I drew forth the image of the tall homeless man in my mind, holding tight to memory of me handing him a one-hundred-dollar bill.

"He has a heroin addiction," I announced, eyes popping open at my success.

Oh my god. It worked.

My compulsion *was* centred around my intention while speaking.

The next words left my lips freely—common knowledge to their kind. "Vissimo can't smell pure heroine."

I read their shock and disbelief.

What else could I say?

I forced my mind back to Twister games with Tommy—to all the times I let her win because I was taller and could reach more colourful spots on the plastic sheet than she could. "Allowed you to win."

The Vissimo went entirely still. They knew what that meant.

Was that enough though? Kyros expected Mr Ringly's finances to crumble any day now, and for *Ingenium* to end in short duration, but I had no idea how to convey any of that.

The king smiled.

I tensed, awaiting execution.

"My son," he said, pride filling his voice. "I'm not surprised he could execute such a manoeuvre. His mistake was to put trust in a human."

Yes, it was.

I tuned into Kyros for the first time and jerked at the panic and rage consuming him.

"You have fulfilled your side of our bargain," Mikhail said, sliding a glance to the triplets before returning his cruel gaze to mine. "For your *friend's* life."

Sweeping his robes aside with a practiced gesture, he clasped Gina's shoulder. "There's no honour in slaughter. Make sure this human has a fighting chance, eldest daughter."

The king left through the iron doors, and the triplets exchanged a fevered look.

Gina's mouth set, and I knew that she understood as well as I did.

I wasn't leaving here alive.

It became clear the other siblings would stay as witnesses when the king disappeared through the iron doors alone.

Gina stood in their midst, arms folded, impassive expression in place.

A fighting chance, King Mikhail had said.

What did that mean?

I'd watched as the triplets set up. A large red circle was drawn around where I crouched in a daze. Trenit strapped a collar to my neck. A matching collar was strapped around Theodore's neck.

Hector, the brother who took Tommy to the hospital, reappeared and strode to stand with his siblings. My eyes narrowed on him until he nodded. The Fyrlia vampire didn't owe me shit, so I appreciated the reassurance Tommy was safe.

"I'm sorry for killing Callum," I told the sane siblings.

Tynan carried in a small table and got to work setting up a camera. I guess a lock of my hair wasn't enough of a trophy this time.

"The begging has already begun," he murmured, fiddling with cables at the back of the camera.

I smiled. "Does it sound like begging, you stupid whore? Let me explain in a way you'll understand. I'm sorry Callum was the one to attack me and not you. Because I would have loved to drive a drill into your rotten heart."

The triplet lifted his head, fangs lengthening.

"You're not killing me to avenge your brother," I told them, hoping for a tidier death than whatever torture they were setting up so elaborately. "It's an excuse so you can hunt Kyros's mate. It's a thrill for you. Fucking psychos."

The other two paused in their preparations.

I continued. "What I can't figure out is whether you have an elder brother complex because Kyros doesn't accept you. Or if it's a jealousy thing. Maybe the fact you're triplets fucked you up in the womb somehow. Or were you dropped on your heads a few times?"

My head snapped back from a blow, and I choked on blood.

As the ringing in my head subsided, I laughed. "What part got to you? Really. I'm curious."

"You heard Father," Gina boomed. "Get on with it. I haven't got all morning."

I squinted through the pain, catching the dark looks the triplets shot their eldest sister.

Closing my eyes, I focused on Kyros, drawing on his rage to strengthen me for what lay ahead. Through no intention of his own, I was overwhelmingly grateful to have his company in my mind and heart—or wherever his emotions resided within me.

His fear and anguish left a bitter tinge on my lips.

"Turn the camera on and put the call through," Theodore said.

The call?

"A fighting chance," Gina hissed. "Make sure of it, or I won't hesitate to humiliate you in front of Sundulus."

"Ah, *that's* it then," I murmured, forcing myself to stand. Staying on my knees wasn't an option. They weren't just recording my death. This was a live streaming event.

Looked like I was fighting after all. I owed it to those watching and my grandmother.

Theodore unzipped his leather jacket halfway down his chest, circling his arms a couple of times.

"What?" he snarled.

I smiled at him. *He had a complex because Kyros didn't accept him.*

"Your blood will fill my mouth." He pointed at my neck. "You'll bleed out on this concrete floor. Without family. Without friends."

The triplet circled me. "Little Tommy told me all about how lonely you are in your big castle. *Rich girl, rich girl, sitting all alone. Rich girl, rich girl, sad in her home.*"

Didn't he understand I'd come here knowing the end result?

"Your poems are shit," I said.

"Tommy didn't mind them. Neither did your grandmother."

I was human, but fuck me if I wasn't going to attempt to take a chunk out of him before the end.

I owed it to both of them and myself.

"Call's going through," Tynan announced.

Theodore retreated to the far side of the red circle. They'd made it look like a wrestling area.

Great, my specialty.

"King Julius, I hope this call finds you well," the triplet spoke into the camera. "Now, my brothers and sisters and I have hooked up a live stream because we thought you might want to watch what's ahead. But we can't hear you. That might steal away the ambience of the moment."

He'd implicated the entire Fyrlia family. Gina and the others didn't seem surprised.

I just couldn't believe anyone would dare to speak to Kyros's father like that.

"This human, Kyros's true mate, was found sneaking into our territory early this morning. Now that she's tied to Kyros via the fourth exchange, we consider this an act of war and are seeking our rightful retribution."

Kyros answering fury made me physically stagger.

Shit, he was watching this? Which meant he was with his father. I'd envisioned him fighting with his siblings just outside, so it was reassuring to know they got him away from here.

In some ways, that made it easier to face what lay ahead. The only thing I had to accept was my path.

Trenit approached me with the camera.

I had to look terrible. While they set up, I'd discovered blood dripping from my ears, nose, and after the blow from Theodore, my mouth was swollen and cut.

"We warmed her up a bit," he said, shoving the camera in my face. "Such sensitive ears. I wish you'd heard her screams, big brother."

I fixed him with a flat look. "Get on with it, little boy. Kyros isn't going to love you any more for the narration."

Behind the camera, his hazel eyes flashed, but he forced a laugh. "That's not what you were saying before when you were calling yourself a stupid whore."

I let his words wash over me, glancing at Theodore, who'd pulled out a small blade from his boot.

Gina stepped forward. "The magnanimous King Mikhail decrees that despite the declaration of war from our eldest brother's true mate, she shall be given a fighting chance. Prince Theodore, if you fight with a blade, she does too."

I blinked as my vision adjusted and blurred, lifting the bottom of my top to wipe at the blood on my face.

He'd cut me to ribbons.

Unless I pissed one of them off enough for them to end it quick.

"*Kyros* hating you could be blamed on the game, I suppose," I spoke to the triplets. "Which is stupid, by the way, everyone can see he's King Julius's child. But your *actual* brothers and sisters hate the three of you. It must feel shit to be unwanted and detested by your entire family."

Talk was all I had, and they knew it, but the words were still getting to them, and the insults made me feel like I wasn't going down without a fight.

"You will scream as you die," Theodore said coolly.

I shrugged. "I'll probably cry and vomit too."

His eyes darkened, the muscles in his neck cording.

Tynan spoke. "Calm, brother. She'll be dead by your hand soon." He turned to me. "Each of you has a bomb around your neck."

Well, fuck.

Not a dog collar then.

I resisted the urge to tear at it, fear pulsing through me.

His lips curved and he held up two clickers. "Leave the red circle and you'll die."

I grimaced. Not for my fate. For what Kyros was about to see.

Look away, please.

I didn't want this to be his last memory of me.

Holding the camera steady with one hand, Trenit freed his machete and threw it at my feet. "A fighting chance," he sneered.

Bending, I swiped up the blade. *Jesus*, I'd kill myself by landing on this thing. Or Theodore would take it and slice me.

I'd rather be sliced with a small dagger.

"Piece of junk." I chucked the blade from the circle.

Trenit snarled.

"A present from Daddy?" My voice wobbled.

Yep, I had a bomb strapped to my neck, and I was about to die.

The camera hadn't left my face, but it was shoved closer. "Any last words to your true mate?" Tynan said with glee.

Anger found me. "If I knew you all talked this much, I would have just drowned myself in that fucking barrel."

The death metal fan of the trio smirked. "Some talk like this before the end. But everyone wants to live."

Oh, I wanted to live. That wasn't in question.

Trenit set the camera on the table and strode to stand beside Tynan, who held up the two bomb controls.

Nausea churned in my gut.

I heard my grandmother's friends talk about dignity and death all the time, but now I understood why the elderly feared dying in their own shit. That's why the triplets were streaming this. It was the worst part of the situation—worse even than the end result.

I strode to the middle of the circle, a mere three metres from Theodore. Perhaps standing on the edge would give me more time to react, but the thought of reacting in time was laughable, really. I'd start farthest from the edge.

Theodore entered the circle and his growl surrounded me.

I focused on him, blinking several times. My ears were shot, and maybe that was ideal. There wasn't any competition between my two main senses anymore.

I just needed one good punch for Grandmother, then I was happy to go.

"Begin," Gina called.

Theodore didn't budge.

He sang, "*Rich girl, rich girl, sitting all alone. Rich girl, rich girl, sad in her home. Rich girl, rich girl, dead behind her smile. Rich girl, rich girl, dead in just a while.*"

Any number of poetic replies occurred to me. I shoved them down.

He moved.

I saw him.

And what could my human body do about it?

Absolutely fucking nothing.

Theodore kissed me hard, hands pressing against my damaged ears.

I couldn't scream. Black filled my vision and I fell to my knees, rolling in agony. Fresh blood dripped from them.

But I hadn't got my shot in yet.

Head squeezing to the point of unconsciousness, I slowly sat, then crouched.

His knee was coming for my face. I threw myself to the side.

Fuck. I dodged him!

"That's really embarrassing," I slurred. "*Vissimo, Vissimo, all the speed in the world. Vissimo, Vissimo, couldn't catch the human girl.* Write that on my headstone, you motherfucker."

I spat out blood—

Then doubled over at the brutal blow to my stomach. A slash across the back of my thighs sent me sprawling. On my front, I blinked at the red line one inch from my face.

I was dragged away from it, the concrete scratching at my skin and jolting the aching wound in my gut.

My head was forced upward, my back arching to accommodate the movement. I tried to prop myself up, hands slipping on the concrete.

"Nothing to say to the people watching, whore?"

I stared at the camera, gasping.

He flicked my ear again, and I choked on a scream, tears squeezing from my eyes to drip down my face.

"Do you want to tell Kyros what you are?" he whispered in my other ear.

I sucked in a painful breath. "*He knows what I am.*"

All I wanted was to curve around my stomach. Arching my back like this was agony. *Acute pain, thudding pain, so much pain.*

Theodore licked my cheek. "*Mmm*, you taste delicious. Fear makes blood taste *divine.*"

He flipped my body and straddled me, leaning down.

Got ya.

I went to knee him in the junk, and when he jerked back and looked down, I punched him in the throat as hard as I could.

Even Vissimo needed air.

That's for you, Agatha.

He gasped, and I kicked him—to no effect.

Pulling me up, he lashed the back of his hand across my face.

I *flew.*

Landing in a heavy heap, I struggled to maintain consciousness.

The camera was in front of me, just beyond the red line. I smiled at it, knowing this was the end.

Tommy was safe. Kyros was safe.

I was happy for that.

If he'd come, his family would be dead. No one deserved to carry guilt like that.

Theodore grabbed the back of my neck and lifted me, turning me to face him. His eyes were blazing, his lips curved.

I screamed as his fangs sliced into my neck, *ripping.*

Blood had dripped from me in multiple places, but now it gushed and spurted in thick waves.

He dropped me, and I lifted a hand to staunch the wound.

This is it.

Eyes wide, I rolled onto my back, just shy of the red line. As I did, the strap around my neck slipped.

I tightened my grip on my throat, holding the bomb in place.

Theodore bit through the strap?

His growls reached my ears, and in a daze, I rolled to my side and managed to crouch again. My right arm was slippery with bright blood, and I didn't need the sight to reinforce what my body already knew.

I didn't have long.

Theodore gripped my upper arms this time when he bodily picked me up, turning so our profiles were to the camera.

Gurgling, I brought my free hand up to grip his leather jacket. It was still unzipped at the top.

I blinked at Gina over his shoulder. They couldn't see me from here. There'd be no shouted warnings.

"You're going to kill me," I said softly. "Like you killed my grandmother."

His hazel eyes weren't muted at all. My body was too near death to feel any effect.

"You can beg harder than that," he roared.

I brought my second hand to his leather jacket. "I choose when I die."

He hadn't seen me bring the bomb collar to his chest.

He *did* feel me drop it inside his jacket. Theodore's eyes widened and he glanced down.

Heaving up both legs, I kicked at his chest with all my strength. I didn't fly from his hands as intended, but my right arm was slippery with blood. His grip failed, and I tumbled over the red line.

Time slowed as I glanced at Tynan on the stage. Theodore turned to him, fear in his hazel eyes.

Tynan's triumphant, fanatical gaze was fixed on me. He smiled, holding the remote aloft.

Click.

The explosion catapulted me back, rocking the entire building. Head ringing, I stared vacantly at a hazel eyeball by my head, trying to process the chunk of tissue attached to it.

More body pieces surrounded me—pieces of Theodore.

I couldn't hear the other siblings, but I could feel my life essence slipping away. Reaching a hand up, I pressed into my gushing neck wound weakly.

Death.

How funny.

Shivering, I laughed, but only a gurgle came out. Head lolling, I frowned at the camera. It had fallen from the table and lay on its side covered in dust.

I fumbled for it. Was it still on?

If so, Kyros could be watching.

He'd seen me kill his enemy, and pride pulsed through me.

Acceptance. Warmth.

"Do you feel that?" I slurred at the camera, spluttering as blood trickled from my mouth.

My lips twitched, but as I stared into the camera, my smile faded to nothing. "Don't blame yourself, Kyros. Family is everything."

I gripped the cables at the back and gave up the battle to keep my eyes open. "Thank you for being with me at the end."

I wrenched the cables from the camera.

28

I whimpered at an incessant beeping trying to worm its way into my brain.

Beep, beep, beep.

My body hurt. My head...

Why did they hurt?

"Someone turn off the machine," Kyros snarled.

"Atagio," I tried to say.

Pain ripped through my throat and my eyes flew open, heart thundering as I was catapulted from delirium.

I struggled, kicking at the restraint around my legs.

Kyros pinned my shoulders. "Basilia, you're okay." He released one of my shoulders to loosen the tight blanket across my legs.

Cool air swept over my hot skin. I stared at him as blood pounded in my aching ears.

"The Tonyi triplets took you. You're in my home," he said quietly. "You have some injuries and that's why you can't move."

I relaxed as his explanation sunk in. My gaze shifted to the tubes coming in and out of my body. *Machines. Bags of fluid. White blankets.* I fumbled for my neck but my fingers encountered hard plastic.

I was in a neck brace.

"She's in pain," Kyros spoke to someone behind my bed. "Where does it hurt?"

My ears. Tears stung my eyes. *Christ*, they hurt so much.

"Perhaps some water, Kyros?"

Safina.

His growl filled the space as he snatched a bottle from her, unscrewing the lid and holding it to my mouth. It took three attempts to swallow, but I got a mouthful down.

I licked my lips and rested back. "Ears hurt. Neck broken?"

Kyros squeezed my hand, glaring at someone over my head.

The ache in my head subsided, and I sighed.

"Not broken," he said. "The brace is to keep you from tearing the stitches from your surgery."

"Off."

"No," he snapped.

His fear and rage blasted me.

Tears slipped from my eyes. I had no fight left in me. Every part of me hurt, including my soul. The part of my mind not hurt was absolutely confused by the fact I was alive.

He whirled from the bed, shoulders heaving for a full minute.

Turning back, he snapped, "Lalitta. Help me."

Lalitta edged in, wary eyes on her brother. She skirted back to the wall as soon as the neck brace was removed.

Feeling the thick bandages around my neck first, I felt my mouth and nose, then gingerly probed around each ear. *Ouch.*

I touched Kyros's forearm. "Am I. Alive?"

As soon as the question left my mouth, I regretted it. His despair was terrible to behold. Far worse than mine.

"You're alive," he said tersely, turning from me again.

A leaden silence filled the room.

Turning my eyes more than my head, I blinked at Kyros's sisters and his mother lined up against the wall.

I had so many questions. "How?"

Safina answered when he didn't. "You killed Prince Theodore Tonyi. When you won, by King Mikhail's own rule, you had to be released. Especially as we had a recording of the proceedings. We'd gathered in our territory in Red close by, but when you won the contest, we ran to claim you back. The other Fyrlia siblings brought you outside and delivered you to us."

Guilt. Rage. Hate. Shame.

I was assuming Kyros's current turmoil had everything to do with me, rendering him useless in the situation. I made my bed in full knowledge and acceptance of the cost of saving Tommy's life. So had I expected to live and face him afterward?

Not one bit.

Swallowing again, I stared at his back. "Kyros, I knew you couldn't enter their territory before I left the estate." *Or at least before Theodore's fangs ripped into my neck.*

I rasped. "I had to save Tommy, and that had nothing to do with—"

"If you say it had nothing to do with me, I'll tear this fucking house down." He roared. "It wasn't your choice to make."

It felt like the inside of my ears split all over again.

"Son! Her ears," the queen gasped, striding forward.

"*Stay away,*" he snarled, sinking into a predatory crouch.

She bared her teeth at him. "If you cannot control yourself, you cannot be here. Your true mate has been beaten within an inch of her life. She doesn't need another round."

The fight drained from Kyros.

He lowered his head.

"You have nothing to feel guilty about," I whispered. "I had to make sure you stayed away."

My forgiveness wasn't enough.

He strode from the room, and the queen gazed after him, a dullness in her blue eyes. With veiled looks cast my way, his four sisters trailed out after him.

"If Kyros had entered their territory, all of us would be dead right now," the queen said to me.

I met her impassive gaze. "I know. I'm incredibly grateful that Safina and the others were able to get there in time to prevent that."

She walked past the foot of my bed and stared out of the window. "His siblings had to prevent him storming the territory twice before Julius got there."

Oh fuck.

"He lost control, putting us all at risk."

The queen was a mother who'd nearly lost her children because of my actions.

"Kyros didn't put you at risk," I said. "I did. He can't help what the bond makes him do."

Her tone hardened. "You dishonour him by believing he wouldn't come of his own volition. You are his true mate. He could feel—and later *see*—you dying at the hands of his enemy."

All this talk of honour. What did it even mean? "I don't think of myself as part of a pair, Queen Titania. I don't assume that Kyros will protect me because of this thing with our blood. That's not intended to disrespect him. It's because I don't believe in the mate bond."

"Yet you disrespected him grievously. Protecting you is his role as your true mate. Just as it is yours to protect him."

Frustration bubbled within me. "My going there had nothing to do with him or the exchanges."

She smiled, a hint of iron showing beneath. "You went willingly into the triplets' hands to protect your dear friend whom you consider family, yes?"

I nodded.

"My king and I watched as you absolved Kyros of guilt at the end. With what you considered your dying breath, you protected your true mate, having successfully protected your family, and having taken steps to ensure my son could not endanger *his* family. Kyros was unable to do any of those things. On top of that, you don't give any credit to the connection you both share. Do you understand why he feels inadequate to be in your presence right now?"

That's what this was about? He felt unworthy as well as disrespected?

I wanted to sleep.

Scrap that. I wanted Kyros's arms around me. Fear tinged my every thought an ugly green. I'd been tortured and beaten and had no idea how the fuck I was here. Right now, I wanted him so badly.

But I'd gone into this alone.

I'd suffer the ramifications alone.

"Queen Titania," I said wearily, "this is one of those times when being a Vissimo and being human are very different things. I'm too tired to argue and too tired to see your point of view."

The queen dipped her head, unscrewing the water bottle.

I drank and rested back.

She leaned forward to kiss my forehead. "Your friend is alive and well, Miss Le Spyre, and guarded by Indebted on your estate. My first son cared for her personally, knowing you would wish it. He tells me she doesn't remember a thing from the dinner to waking in hospital."

My lips trembled. "She's okay?"

The urge to cry was agony on my neck wound.

"Kyros made sure she was," she whispered. "Just as he made sure to attend to your wound until you got to our surgeon and doctors. If not for him, you would not be alive."

The last thing I recalled was the camera. "His saliva?"

She nodded. "Do you know how hard it was for him to do that without forcing the fifth exchange on you?"

Some idea, yes.

"Kyros could have killed you himself if his control had slipped for even a second," she said.

The strength of her son's disagreement battered my mind. He was listening to every word of this conversation. I got the feeling the queen's words were more for Kyros than me.

"I owe him my life then. Trenit and Tynan, are they...?"

Her eyes clouded. "Alive. King Julius and King Mikhail negotiated a deal to prevent involvement of an impartial clan. Neither clan was willing to risk losing all."

That amazed me—that an impartial clan may not have ruled Fyrlia in the wrong.

Kyros re-entered the room behind a doctor. Patting my hand, Queen Titania left the room with a long glance at her eldest son.

The Vissimo doctor grabbed a chart at the end of my hospital bed. The room was filled with medical apparatus.

"Severe abdominal bruising without internal bleeding," the doctor read aloud with a nervous peek at Kyros.

I didn't blame her; he looked—and felt—murderous.

"Repaired laceration of the jugular. Laceration to the lip. Severe inner ear damage with—"

"Is the damage permanent?" I asked.

She flicked to another page. "Likely, yes. Once the canal is fully healed, we'll run tests. There didn't seem to be entry wounds and yet your canals were obliterated. How were they damaged?"

"I was put inside a metal barrel. They beat against the outside," I replied.

Kyros turned away at my words.

She paled. "I see."

"What is the prognosis of her neck?" Kyros asked, menace filling his voice.

The doctor jolted. "Her n-neck? Scarring will certainly occur. The vascular trauma will result in weakness there for life. Our immediate concern is to prevent potential blood clots as we care for the wound. My recommendation, sir, is that you don't drink from the right side of her neck again in the future."

Why was that making me flush? He'd literally done it four times already. Except I'd never seen him behave like this. So uncertain. Inside, Kyros was a stormy sea.

That made *me* uncertain.

I recalled drawing on his rage to get me through the fight with Theodore, wondering if our emotions were starting to mix more than I'd realised.

"Thank you, Doctor...?"

"Olive."

The Vissimo was terrified. "Thank you, Doctor Olive."

She inclined her head and backed out of the room, eyes downcast.

"Kyros," I said.

He didn't respond. *Outwardly.*

"Guess I'll come to you."

His hand pressed down on my shoulder, and I rested back. When he made to pull away, I snatched at his hand.

"You want to ask me something," I said. "So ask while I'm still awake." I had a feeling I'd be dead to the world again soon.

Kyros freed his hand, leaning forward on the bed, head bowed.

I waited.

Eventually he spoke. "I need you to tell me, very clearly, why you felt you couldn't tell me the Tonyi triplets had Tommy in their possession. I need to know why you pushed me away instead of trusting me to handle the situation. And I need you not to lie."

Why couldn't he understand this wasn't about his ability to protect me? It was about me doing everything in my power to keep Tommy safe while terrified that one wrong move could kill her.

That *I'd* be responsible for the death of my last family member.

My throat constricted, and I winced at the pull on something deep within my throat.

"Look at me when you answer," he growled.

I obeyed. "The triplets were explicit in their instructions. If an ambush occurred at any time. If you interfered in any way. Tommy would be killed immediately."

"You walked to your execution," he said, closing his eyes. "You forced me into a fucking corner."

I didn't disagree.

"I'm so fucking angry at you," Kyros said, looking at me.

We locked gazes, and I knew he was recalling the same words leaving my mouth before the fourth exchange.

I inhaled. "Betrayal is a sour pill to swallow. You betrayed me when you thought it would save your family."

"Under my father's orders."

"I did so under the triplets' orders."

He pushed away. "It's not the same thing."

"No," I agreed, my ire rising. "One was calculated and one was desperation. I didn't go to the triplets *seeking* to make you feel this way. I didn't plan to use you for your position and wealth. I was saving the person I love most in this world, not trying to win a stupid game."

He was trying to contain the thick waves of black rage within him. Half dead I may be, but it felt fucking good to finally say some of that aloud.

"You're saying we're even?" he said sarcastically.

"I nearly *died*, Kyros," I rasped. "Honestly? I'm wondering why the fuck we're having this conversation when I should feel thankful to be alive. But if you want to act as though I've betrayed you, there's my answer. My choice to save Tommy had absolutely nothing to do with you because *involving* you risked her life. If involving you was possible, I would have done so. That's it. Clean cut. Accept it or don't."

He'd turned away again during my whispered lecture. Sadness swelled within him. *Uncertainty. Loathing. Betrayal. Guilt. Wrath.*

"We both feel like shit," I said, deflating. "If it's okay with you, I could do with your arms around me for the next three days instead of arguing."

I had trouble accepting his Vissimo point of view but hated that Kyros felt so torn apart by my actions. Some of the guilt bouncing around was definitely mine. If I didn't feel like twice-cooked death, the guilt might be *all* mine.

Because many things happened in that dark chamber.

I doubted Kyros would have saved me if he knew I handed his family's heads to Fyrlia on a platter.

Walking to my execution was my smallest betrayal.

"No," Kyros whispered, still turned away.

I blinked at his back, covered in a charcoal shirt, wondering if I'd heard right.

He didn't budge.

I croaked. "I know you're angry at me, Kyros. But I need you."

The vampire turned to me, hard gaze snapping to me. "You need me *now*?"

My breath hitched as hurt filled me. In this state, I had no resistance to cruelty. "Yes."

Kyros scanned me, and as his expression smoothed so did his

emotions. Wrath was drawn in. Loathing and betrayal swept aside. Uncertainty and sadness were locked in a box.

The vampire loomed over me, meadow-green eyes muted and impersonal as though regarding a stranger. “Basilia Le Spyre doesn’t need anyone.”

I turned my head away, closing my eyes against the awful sight of what he was doing, wishing I could close them to what was happening inside. His comment wasn’t directed at me. Not really. But it shattered the few undamaged parts I had left.

I listened to his fading footsteps as he left.

Basilia Le Spyre doesn’t need anyone.

I curled into a ball around my bruised stomach, sorrow surging through me.

But as weariness piled heavy on me, the sorrow dissipated, replaced by a cold determination I’d lost sight of in recent weeks.

It snapped back into place now. For good.

Kyros Atagio was right.

I didn’t need a fucking thing from anyone.

DEATH GAME

Basil's story continues in Death Game!

WHILE YOU WAIT

COMPLETE SERIES
~ Dragon Shifter Romance ~
Start Book One Today

BOOKS BY KELLY ST. CLARE

Supernatural Battle

Vampire Towers (Paranormal urban romance)

Blood Trial

Vampire Debt

Death Game

The Darkest Drae (Dragon shifter romance)

with Raye Wagner

Blood Oath

Shadow Wings

Black Crown

The Tainted Accords (Royal fantasy romance):

Fantasy of Frost

Fantasy of Flight

Fantasy of Fire

Fantasy of Freedom

Novellas:

Sin

Olandon

Rhone

Shard

Pirates of Felicity (Pirate fantasy romance):

Immortal Plunder

Stolen Princess

Pillars of Six

Dynami's Wrath

Veritas

Eternal Gambit

Mortal Trinity

The After Trilogy (Dystopian romance):

The Retreat

The Return

The Reprisal

www.ingramcontent.com/pod-product-compliance
Lightning Source LLC
Chambersburg PA
CBHW020932310726
48980CB00007B/739/J

* 9 7 8 0 6 4 8 3 3 4 4 9 1 *